京市社会科学基金青年项目“对立与补充：巴特勒与达尔文作品中进化论思想范式构建”
项目编号：16WXC015）阶段性成果

国语言文学与文化研究文库
IGUO YUYAN WENXUE YU
NHUA YANJIU WENKU

U0888444

A Companion to the Studies of Samuel Butler's *The Way of All Flesh* (1903)

塞缪尔·巴特勒《众生之路》的研究

◎ 苏明鸣/著

首都经济贸易大学出版社
Capital University of Economics and Business Press
·北 京·

图书在版编目(CIP)数据

塞缪尔·巴特勒《众生之路》的研究/苏明鸣著. --北京:首都经济贸易大学出版社,2018.12

ISBN 978-7-5638-2897-5

Ⅰ.①塞… Ⅱ.①苏… Ⅲ.①塞缪尔·巴特勒—小说研究 Ⅳ.①I561.074

中国版本图书馆CIP数据核字(2018)第275489号

塞缪尔·巴特勒《众生之路》的研究

苏明鸣 著

责任编辑 浩 南
封面设计 小 尘
出版发行 首都经济贸易大学出版社
地 址 北京市朝阳区红庙(邮编100026)
电 话 (010)65976483 65065761 65071505(传真)
网 址 http://www.sjmcb.com
E-mail publish@cueb.edu.cn
经 销 全国新华书店
照 排 北京砚祥志远激光照排技术有限公司
印 刷 人民日报印刷厂
开 本 710毫米×1000 毫米 1/16
字 数 299千字
印 张 17
版 次 2018年12月第1版 2018年12月第1次印刷
书 号 ISBN 978-7-5638-2897-5
定 价 52.00元

图书印装若有质量问题,本社负责调换
版权所有 侵权必究

作 者 简 介

About the author

苏明鸣(1980—),女,黑龙江省哈尔滨人,博士(法国巴黎第七大学),首都经济贸易大学外国语学院讲师。主要研究方向:19 世纪英国文学、历史与文化。电子邮箱:sumingming1980@ hotmail. com

Mingming Su, PhD (Paris Diderot University Paris 7), lecturer at School of Foreign Studies, Capital University of Economics and Business in Beijing, her research interests include English literature, British history and civilisation. E-mail:sumingming1980@ hotmail. com

作品简介
About the book

塞缪尔·巴特勒的代表作《众生之路》(*The Way of All Flesh* 1903)于1873年开始写作,到1885年完成,前后共经历十多年。该书是一部半自传体小说,也是一部成长小说(Bildungsroman)。巴特勒将自己的进化论思想完美地融入了这部小说的构思创作中,这实际上是一场他对自己的进化论思想的全面演绎。这部作品是巴特勒为探索科学真知耗尽毕生精力,最后结合自己的人生经历书写的进化论的绝唱。虽然对达尔文自然选择理论抱有误解,但是巴特勒在其发表的小说与专著中表达了自己的一套进化论思想,开创了进化论成长小说中独特的一派。遗憾的是,巴特勒的作品在他生前没有得到足够的重视,后人也没能全面系统地理解其著作与思想。本书意在对巴特勒《众生之路》这部小说中进化论思想展开全面、系统的研究与解读。

Samuel Butler (1835 – 1902) stood out among his contemporaries for engaging into a famous controversy with Charles Darwin. The unconscious memory analogy is the key element in Butler's concept of evolution. In order to illustrate his views on this issue, he published four books on evolution as his scientific responses to Darwin's theory outlined in *The Origin of Species* (1859). This thus offers us a unique and valuable case of an interlocking presentation of the author's scientific and philosophical ideas about evolution. Although Butler has been ignored for more than a century, except for his novel *The Way of All Flesh* (1903), the visionary power of his ideas is still extremely fascinating to contemporary readers and scholars.

Contents

Introduction ······ 1

Chapter One ***The Way of All Flesh* (1903): a summary** ······ 21

Chapter Two ***The Way of All Flesh* as a Lamarckian novel of inheritance** ······ 28

2.1 Lamarckian essence in the novel: change, will and environment ······ 28

2.2 Heredity: the oneness of personality between parents and offspring ······ 38

2.2.1 Heredity in *The Way of All Flesh* ······ 38

2.2.2 Ernest's parents—Theobald and Christina ······ 56

2.2.3 Ernest's childhood in a God-fearing family ······ 61

2.2.4 Alethea and Overton ······ 70

Chapter Three **Ainsi va toute evolution—Butler's utilitarian taste** ··· 75

3.1 Butler and God ······ 75

3.2 Vice and virtue ······ 92

3.3 Butler and utilitarianism ······ 101

3.4 Butler and money ······ 108

Chapter Four **Self-help and free-will: the reconstruction of personal identity** ······ 120

4.1 Unconscious Memory and Cunning as two limbs of man—Ernest's growth ······ 120

4.2 Luck or cunning? Butler's ideal gentleman ······ 146

4.3 "Sensible teaching" in *The Way of All Flesh* …… 164

4.3.1 On childhood …… 165

4.3.2 About Dr. Skinner's school at Roughborough …… 171

4.3.3 Ernest's Cambridge years …… 178

4.4 Samuel Butler on education …… 189

Conclusion …… 210

Bibliography …… 219

Selected index and glossary of names …… 237

Appendix …… 240

Acknowledgements …… 261

Introduction

Heaven forbid that I should compare myself to the author of *Hudibras*, but still, if my books succeed after my death—which they may or may not, I know nothing about it—any way, if they do succeed, let it be understood that they failed during my life for a few very obvious reasons of which I was quite aware, for the effect of which I was prepared before I wrote my books, and which on consideration I found insufficient to deter me. I attacked people who were at once unscrupulous and powerful, and I made no alliances. I did this because I did not want to be bored and have my time wasted and my pleasures curtailed. I had money enough to live on, and preferred addressing myself to posterity rather than to any except a very few of my own contemporaries. Those few I have always kept well in mind. I think of them continually when in doubt about any passage, but beyond those few I will not go. Posterity will give a man a fair hearing; his own times will not do so if he is attacking vested interests, and I have attacked two powerful sets of vested interests at once [The Church and Science]. What is the good of addressing people who will not listen? I have addressed the next generation and have therefore said many things which want time before they become palatable. Any man who wishes his work to stand will sacrifice a good deal of his immediate audience for the sake of being attractive to a much larger number of people later on. He cannot gain this later audience unless he has been fearless and thorough-going, and if he is this he is sure to have to tread on the corns of a great many of those who live at the same time with him, however little he may wish to do so. He must not expect these people to help him on, nor wonder if, for a time, they succeed in snuffing him out...[①]

---

① Samuel Butler. *The Note-Books of Samuel Butler*. Edited with a preface and biographical statement by Henry Festing Jones. London: A. C. Fifield, 1912. IndyPublish Edition, 2007, p. 130.

The above text was written by Samuel Butler (1835 – 1902) under the title of "Myself and My Books" in his *Note-Books*. From this passage, we get a sense of the author's obstinacy and clear-headedness but also the loneliness and desolation he must have experienced as he remained ignored by the world and unappreciated by his contemporaries. With the exception of his last book *Erewhon Revisited* (1901) published in his lifetime, Butler was obliged to pay for the publication of his own works because—aside from *Erewhon* (1872)—they were very few editions which were sold out. The printing and publishing cost him nearly 100 pounds, which was a considerable sum of money considering his limited financial resources. It is interesting to observe the reception of this strangely stubborn writer who published 16 books in his lifetime, of which only slightly over 7 000 copies had been sold up to 1899. We could imagine that such indifference he suffered would trigger what kind of reaction in Butler's mind.

Butler's most important novel and what is considered his representative work, *The Way of All Flesh*, was published in the second year after his death, in 1903; however, its publication also had not attracted any attention. Until 1916, John F. Harris, a prominent researcher on Butler, lauded its publication as "a literary event of the last thirteen years". ① Today when we read this landmark work in the history of English literature, with its sharp satire hitting right upon social ills in the Victorian times, we cannot help but feel that its impact would have been comparable to a crack of thunder above the heads of his contemporaries! Alas, this crack of thunder seemed to fall on deaf ears in his time! Such ignorance drove George Bernard Shaw to lament his desperation with the English literature. ②

---

① John. F. Harris. *Samuel Butler, Author of "Erewhon", the Man and His Work.* New York, Dodd, Mead and C., 1916, p. 18.

② Bernard Shaw. The preface of *Major Barbara. Selected Plays, with Prefaces.* New York: Dood Mead Company, 1898, p. 313.

Today Samuel Butler's reputation rests almost entirely on his three fictional works—the posthumously published novel *The Way of All Flesh* (1903), together with the philosophical tales *Erewhon* (1872) and *Erewhon Revisited* (1901). Although he also authored a few poems, a brief portrait of the fictional author of his 1873 work *The Fair Haven*, and two *oratorio libretti* (in collaboration with his friend Henry Festing Jones), he was not essentially what today is called a creative writer, a creator of fictions. Almost 17 of the 20 volumes comprising the Shrewsbury Edition of his collected works fall into the category of nonfiction prose. In these works, Butler reveals himself as a polemicist on religious and scientific issues, and as a philosopher, moralist, logician, classical scholar, art historian, editor and translator.

Being a freethinker, he was a didactic writer with a strong urge to engage in controversy and criticism. Indeed he preferred to be identified in the British Museum catalogue as "philosophic writer"—justly so, for even in his fiction he was concerned with hammering out his views as much as he was with developing character and narrative. From the moment of its publication *The Way of All Flesh* (1903) was regarded as an intellectual autobiography, and commentators have treated it as a compendium of Butler's most characteristic and influential convictions ever since.[①] What remains most striking about Butler's prose works are not so much the theories and arguments as the moral observations, witticisms, paradoxes and self-indulgent musings of the sort that are scattered throughout *The Way of All Flesh*—nuggets that came to be called "Butlerisms":

> Dog-fanciers tell us that performing dogs never carry their tails; such dogs have eaten of the tree of knowledge, and are convinced of sin accordingly—they know that they know things, in respect of which, therefore, they are no longer under grace, but under the law, and they have yet so much grace left

---

① This fact would be confirmed by Henry Festing Jones's voluminous biography published in 1919.

> as to be ashamed. So with the human clever dog; he may speak with the tongues of men and angels, but so long as he knows that he knows, his tail will droop... We must all feel that a rich young nobleman with a taste for science and principles is rarely a pleasant object... Principles are like logic, which never yet made a good reasoner of a bad one, but might still be occasionally useful if they did not invariably contradict each other whenever there is any temptation to appeal to them. They are like fire, good servants but bad masters. ①

The passage, written half in fun and more than half in earnest, is a characteristic "Butlerism". It appears in the midst of a serious Lamarckian (and essentially anti-Darwinian) interpretation of the effects of inherited characteristics on the evolution of species, but its charm and significance are quite independent of the validity of Butler's theoretical position. Although he had limited direct influence on the scientific community, Butler was in fact a representative of neo-Lamarackians,② sharing their belief that living things possessed the freedom to shape their own evolution. ③ Butler helped to define certain key implications of

---

① Samuel Butler. *Life and Habit*. London: Trübner, 1878. Revised edition, with author's addenda and a preface by R. A. Streatfeild, London: A. C. Fifield, 1910. The Echo Library edition, 2007, Ch. II, pp. 22-23.

② "The term Neo-Lamarckism was invented in 1885... A dominant element in neo-Lamarckism was the idea that adaptation could occur through the inherited effects of use and disuse. In addition, however, many neo-Lamarckians believed that there were internal forces that made evolution progressive and goal-directed". See Eva Jablonka and Marion J. Lamb. *Evolution in four dimensions: Genetic, Epigenetic, Behavioral, and Symbolic Variation in the History of Life*. Cambridge: The MIT Press, 2005, p. 21. Moreover, "prominent figures such as Herbert Spencer, Samuel Butler, and later even George Bernard Shaw, ensured that Lamarckian aspects of evolution were given the widest publicity".

③ Peter J. Bowler. *The Eclipse of Darwinism: Anti-Darwin Evolution Theories in the Decades Around 1900*. London: The Johns Hopkins University Press, 1983, p. 72.

Lamarckism, and his views on evolution also seemed more independent.[①]

Butler was once acknowledged by his contemporaries for treading into the Darwinian controversy. As he consented himself, he had "attacked two powerful sets of vested interests at once [The Church and Science]", becoming an Ishmaelite among his generation of writers for having had the presumption to attack respected opinions in religious, artistic and scientific matters, especially those of Darwin and his defenders. Indeed, Butler was the most independent of the late-Victorian thinkers and reigning intellectual fashions. He shrank instinctively from influential circles after enjoying the brief lionhood *Erewhon* earned him, consoling him with the hope that he would be vindicated posthumously. He followed his intellectual curiosity and interests instead, and these led him to out-of-the-way subjects of little general appeal then as now. His contribution to the theories of evolution did gain him the discipleship of George Bernard Shaw, who retailored Butler's neo-Lamarckism into his own "Life Force" philosophy; nevertheless, Butler's books on evolution and other longer prose works, except insofar as they serve as commentary on the outlook presented in his still-popular fiction, have remained of interest only to scholars and specialists.

When *On the Origin of Species* was published in the autumn of 1859, Butler had just arrived in New Zealand. At that time, he was, as he recounted, living "eighteen miles from the nearest human habitation", and he spent "three days' journey on horseback" to get hold of Darwin's book from a bookseller's shop. Soon afterwards, he became "one of Mr. Darwin's many enthusiastic

① Peter J. Bowler argues: "Butler symbolized the emergence of a new Lamarckism dedicated to ideals that were derived from his way of thinking rather than from the more mechanistic approach of Haeckel and Spencer." *Ibid.*, p. 72.

admirers". ① But later, he found himself disagreeing with Darwin. The first discord occurred with Darwin's claim that *On the Origin of Species* was a Melchisedec document, that is to say, it was unprecedented. ② Butler refuted this claim, believing that denying the traditional studies on evolution by their predecessors was equal to burying their previous achievements. Furthermore, he recognized that, on the subject of biological evolution, Darwin's theory of natural selection did not go as far as Lamarck's theory on acquired characteristics. Butler's second point of contention was Darwin's use of natural selection as the main means of modification. He called Darwin the apostle of luck, and Darwin's grandfather, Erasmus Darwin, and Lamarck apostles of cunning. ③ Butler claimed that Darwin's natural selection is in itself insufficient to account for organic evolution, for the causes of variations are indefinite and unintelligent. ④ Basically, Butler's views were inherited from Jean-Baptiste Lamarck (1744 – 1829) who, insisted that organic evolution should not avoid involving the elements of need, faith, intelligence and memory. He appreciated Lamarck's theory for it asserted that the origin of variations is due to the need of the individuals. For Butler, life itself is intimately linked with memory: "Life is the property of matter whereby it can remember. Matter which can remember is living; matter which cannot remember is dead", therefore, "life, then, is memory". ⑤

① Firstly found in *Unconscious Memory* (1880) chapter one, later see Samuel Butler. *The Note-Books of Samuel Butler*. Edited with a preface and biographical statement by Henry Festing Jones. London: A. C. Fifield, 1912. IndyPublish edition, 2007, p. 27.

② In the predecessors' works cannot find its paternal or maternal blood, which is never accepted by Butler.

③ Samuel Butler. *Luck, or Cunning as the Main Means of Organic Modification?* London: Trübner, 1887. The Echo Library edition, 2007, pp. 49-50.

④ Samuel Butler. *Life and Habit*. London: Trübner, 1878. Revised edition, with author's addenda and a preface by R. A. Streatfeild, London: A. C. Fifield, 1910. The Echo Library edition, 2007, pp. 126-127.

⑤ *Ibid.*, p. 152.

The memory analogy is the key element in Butler's concept on evolution. In order to illustrate his views on this issue, he published *Life and Habit* (1878), his first pseudo-scientific response to Darwin's theory of evolution outlined in *The Origin of Species* (1859). It was also the most important of Butler's studies on evolution. With this book, one of the first to make extensive use of the concept of the unconscious, contemporaneous with his exploration of unconscious motives in *The Way of All Flesh*, Butler explains heredity as identical to memory—memory of practices so often repeated as to be unconscious. In *Life and Habit* (1878), Butler had expounded his theory of hereditary memory as the basis of the evolution of men, with the hope that it should be an adjunct to Darwin's theory. Memory, for Butler, was the accumulated experience of all the past generations of man's ancestors. Personality or personal identity transmitted through ancestors is built up through the contributions of the further development of each individual's own experiences; thus the instinctive actions of men, as well as the unconscious activates of their bodies, are memories from the lives of their ancestors awakened by the association of ideas. It is this inherited memory that equips men to deal with most of the problems that they are confronted with during their lives.①

Such a theory on memory and the relativity of human knowledge and action led Butler into an essentially Lamarckian position.② Much of *Life and Habit*, however, was written before his breakaway from Darwin's camp. The catalyst was St. George Mivart's *Genesis of Species* that he received from Edward Clodd after

① Frank Miller Turner. "Samuel Butler: The Man of Temper." In *Between Science and Religion: The Reaction to Scientific Naturalism in Late Victorian England.* New Haven: Yale University Press, 1974, p. 182.

② Peter J. Bowler. *The Eclipse of Darwinism: Anti-Darwin Evolution Theories in the Decades Around 1900*. London: The Johns Hopkins University Press, 1983, p. 73.

finishing *Life and Habit*. ① Reading Mivart, he became aware of the inadequacy of the theory of natural selection, which was not, as he had believed, synonymous with the theory of evolution. Moreover, he immediately rejected natural selection in favour of a more purposeful mechanism—without, nonetheless, accepting Mivart's theism. ② Butler's rejection of natural selection did not, however, mark his break with Darwin. ③ The famous Samuel Butler-Darwin quarrel arose in 1879 and revolved about Darwin's historical sketch of the development of evolutionary theory rather than about natural selection. ④ After reading Buffon, Erasmus Darwin and Lamarck, Butler felt that Darwin took too much credit for the discovery of evolution and did not sufficiently acknowledge those earlier writers. ⑤

Three increasingly critical responses to Darwin ensued: *Evolution, Old and New* (1879), *Unconscious Memory* (1880), *Luck, or Cunning as the Main Means of Organic Modification*? (1887). In *Evolution, Old and New* (1879), he sharpened his criticism of Darwin. This book was a scholarly review and

① Henry Festing Jones. *Samuel Butler: Author of Erewhon (1835 – 1902), A Memoir*. London: Macmillan and Co., Limited. 1919. Vol. II, pp. 433-434. For Mivart's theory, consult Jacod W. Gruber, *A Conscience in Conflict: the Life of St. George Jackson Mivart*. New York: Temple University Publications by Columbia University Press, 1960, pp. 52-70.

② Frank Miller Turner. "Samuel Butler: The Man of Temper." In *Between Science and Religion: The Reaction to Scientific Naturalism in Late Victorian England*. New Haven: Yale University Press, 1974, p. 175.

③ Samuel Butler to Francis Darwin, 25 November 1877, and Francis Darwin to Samuel Butler, 28 December 1877. See Henry Festing Jones. *Samuel Butler: Author of Erewhon (1835 – 1902), A Memoir*. London: Macmillan and Co., Limited. 1919, vol. I., pp. 257-261, 263-264.

④ Samuel Butler-Darwin quarrel has been generously recorded for posterity. Samuel Butler presented his case in *Evolution, Old and New* (1879). H. F. Jones and Francis Darwin published all the relevant letters in *Charles Darwin and Samuel Butler: A Step Towards Reconciliation*. London: A. C. Fifield, 1911. Nora Barlow published other materials in Charles Darwin, *Autobiography* (1809 – 1882). London: Harcourt, 1959, pp. 167-219. The best discussion of the quarrel is found in Basil Willey. *Darwin and Butler: Two Versions of Evolution*. London: Chatto and Windus, 1960.

⑤ Frank Miller Turner. "Samuel Butler: The Man of Temper." In *Between Science and Religion: The Reaction to Scientific Naturalism in Late Victorian England*. New Haven: Yale University Press, 1974, p. 175.

explanation of the work of Darwin's predecessors—Dr. Erasmus Darwin, Buffon and Lamarck. It was filled with extensive quotations from the principal works of theses seminal authors, and was designed to show that they had individually and collectively constructed a complete theory of descent with modification almost entirely harmonious with Butler's own *Life and Habit* theory, and superior to Darwin's natural selection. These writers had succeeded in identifying, as Butler put it, "principles which shall give a definite purpose and direction to the variations whose accumulation results in specific, and ultimately generic differences."① Butler wished to show that while they might have been cavalierly waved aside by Darwin, Darwin had actually learned much more from them than he was prepared to admit in the preface to *The Origin of Species*.

To get a sense of Butler's own inflated sense of his achievement in these writings, we might glance at a summary statement from his *Note-Books*:

> To me it seems that my contributions to the theory of evolution have been mainly these:
>
> 1. The identification of heredity and memory and the corollaries relating to sports, the reversion to remote ancestors, the phenomena of old age, the causes of the sterility of hybrids and the principles underlying longevity—all of which follow as a matter of course. This was *Life and Habit* [1877].
>
> 2. The re-introduction of teleology into organic life which, to me, seems hardly (if at all) less important than the *Life and Habit* theory. This was *Evolution Old and New* [1879].
>
> 3. An attempt to suggest an explanation of the physics of memory. I was alarmed by the suggestion and fathered it upon Professor Hering who never, that I can see, meant to say anything of the kind, but I forced my view on

① Samuel Butler. *Evolution Old and New*. London: Hardwicke and Bogue, 1879, beginning of the chapter VI.

> him, as it were, by taking hold of a sentence or two in his lecture, on *Memory as a Universal Function of Organised Matter* and thus connected memory with vibrations. This was *Unconscious Memory* [1880].①

Since Butler was known by his readers as more of a writer of novels than science, it is not surprising that Butler's writings on evolution were at first either ignored or treated as a joke.② However, most critics have either bypassed the evolutionary aspects in *The Way of All Flesh* or read *Life and Habit* and the novel as mirror images of one another. A closer, more nuanced reading would more appropriately situate them in the development of the era's psychological theories and literature.③ By now, the similarities and coincidences between Butler's four evolution treatises and *The Way of All Flesh* have not been fully explored and analyzed. In view of his isolation and ignorance by the scientific community, it is reasonable to assume that Butler wished to illustrate his theory by using his own life experience. When R A. Streatfeild, Butler's friend and literary executor, wrote the preface for *The Way of All Flesh* (1903), he tried to emphasize the connection between the evolutionary scheme of Butler's theories and the self-portrait in the novel. He suggests that the novel "may be taken as a practical illustration of the theory of heredity embodied in that book [*Life and Habit*]."④ As with *Life and Habit*, the novel challenges Darwin's popular theory:

---

① Samuel Butler. *The Note-Books of Samuel Butler*. Edited with a preface and biographical statement by Henry Festing Jones. London: A. C. Fifield, 1912. IndyPublish edition, 2007, p. 51.

② Peter J. Bowler. *The Eclipse of Darwinism: Anti-Darwin Evolution Theories in the Decades Around 1900* . London: The Johns Hopkins University Press, 1983, p. 72.

③ Danielle Nielsen. "Samuel Butler's *Life and Habit* and *The Way of All Flesh*: Traumatic Evolution." In *English Literature in Transition, 1880 – 1920* , vol. 54 No. 1, 2011, p. 79.

④ "Samuel Butler began to write *The Way of All Flesh* about the year 1872 [actually 1873], and was engaged upon it intermittently until 1884 [actually 1883]. It is, therefore, to a great extent contemporaneous with *Life and Habit*, and may be taken as a practical illusion of the theory of heredity embodied in that book." See preface by R. A. Streatfeild, in Samuel Butler. *The Way of all Flesh*. First published in 1903. London: A. C. Fifield, 1908.

> The novel serves as a literary laboratory where Butler conducts new philosophical and psychological experiments about heredity, memory, and instinct; he uses himself, through the characters of George Overton (the narrator) and Ernest Pontifex (the protagonist) as case studies. ①

It is unusual to find so many clashing flavours—scientific observations, philosophy, history, fiction and autobiography—within one novel. Any assessment of *The Way of All Flesh* as a novel of ideas must take account of the fact that it was written over a period of 11 years (1873 – 1884), during which time Butler also wrote and published *Life and Habit* (1878), *Evolution, Old and New* (1879) and *Unconscious Memory* (1880),② in which he elaborated upon his evolutionary theory. This thus offers us a unique and valuable case of an interlocking presentation of the author's scientific and literary ideas. ③

After publishing *Erewhon*, Butler considered to compose a novel as his next literary project in April 1873. ④ He began *The Way of All Flesh* in the summer of 1873, working at it until he left for Canada in the following summer. The first five chapters of the novel were completed by September 1873. *Life and Habit* (1878), the first of his scientific books, was written in Montreal from June 1874. ⑤ By way of illustration, in a passage in *Life and Habit*, Butler asserts that "it is one against legion when a creature tries to differ from his own past selves...

① Danielle Nielsen. "Samuel Butler's *Life and Habit* and *The Way of All Flesh*: Traumatic Evolution." In *English Literature in Transition, 1880 – 1920*, vol. 54 No. 1, 2011, p. 88.

② Peter Morton. "Butler on Heredity." In *The Vital Science: Biology and the Literary Imagination: 1860 – 1900*. London: Allen and Unwin, 1984, p. 180.

③ *Ibid.*, p. 180.

④ This is clear from the extant correspondence with Charles Darwin and Eliza Mary Ann Savage.

⑤ Here, Peter Morton argues that from this account it is plain that "both the novel and the speculative investigation which in due course became *Life and Habit* had exactly the same starting-point; that is to say, a reconsideration of the problem of heredity". See Peter Morton. "Butler on Heredity." In *The Vital Science: Biology and the Literary Imagination: 1860 – 1900*. London: Allen and Unwin, 1984, p. 180.

our former selves fight within us and wrangle for our possession."① This assertion implicates that Butler already prepared "some sort of intellectual structure to act as truss to the imaginative presentation of Ernest's ancestry" at the beginning of *The Way of All Flesh*.② When he returned to England he turned not to the novel again but to the matter of *Life and Habit*, since Butler's "very dry but exceedingly interesting subject...the force of habit" took a firm grip on him and he laid aside the novel for several years.③ The second stage of the composition of *The Way of All Flesh*, starting from February 1878, emerged from his work on evolution. Butler had reached the climax scene of Ernest's arrest by July 1878 where he once again took up his scientific studies.④ Many revisions were made, very probably in the light of his adoption of Lamarckian thought. From the analysis of the novel, it can be deduced that the evolutionary schema underlying the first chapters of *The Way of All Flesh* was far less defined initially than in its finished state.

Butler's pattern of creative bouleversement after a period on the front line of biological debate was repeated and in even more dramatic fashion after the second and third interludes imposed by the writing of *Evolution, Old and New* (published in early 1879) and *Unconscious Memory* (published in 1880).⑤ Thus the composition of the final sections of the novel and the revisions of its early sections (May 1882 – February 1883) were influenced by these two evolutionary treatises; In turn, they also reflected *The Way of All Flesh* in its emphasis on

① Samuel Butler. *Life and Habit*. London: Trübner, 1878. Revised edition, with author's addenda and a preface by R. A. Streatfeild, London: A. C. Fifield, 1910. The Echo Library edition, 2007, Ch. III, p. 30.

② Peter Morton. "Butler on Heredity." In *The Vital Science, Biology and the Literary Imagination: 1860 – 1900*. London: G. Allen and Unwin, 1984, p. 180.

③ Letter to E. M. A. Savage, dated by Jones about 15 January 1876. See Henry Festing Jones. *Samuel Butler: Author of Erewhon (1835 – 1902), A Memoir*. London: Macmillan and Co., Limited. 1919, vol. I, p. 233.

④ Peter Morton. "Butler on Heredity." In *The Vital Science: Biology and the Literary Imagination: 1860 – 1900*. London: Allen and Unwin, 1984, p. 180.

⑤ *Ibid.*, p. 180.

cunning and conduct. [①] Concerning Butler's departure on composition of *The Way of All Flesh* in 1882, Claude Bissell recorded, "all of the early material was rewritten, and what was intended to be merely the first draft of the concluding section was finished by the end of 1883."[②] We know that it was in November that Miss Savage, Butler's confidante and critic, read the complete manuscript in one night. [③] The novel was written intermittently, as Butler's chief preoccupations during the intervening years were evolution-related issues, and his answers to them influenced his novel inevitably. Besides the chronological overlap, critics have argued that there is a tangled relationship between Butler's scientific works and the story of Ernest Pontifex, the protagonist of the novel, whose "priestly" functions "bridge" in a sense science and autobiography, polemics and fiction. [④] Butler's evolutionary theories are fully embodied in the development of Ernest Pontifex in *The Way of all Flesh*. Peter Morton argues that Butler trimmed all the

---

① For biographical information, see Philip Henderson, *Samuel Butler: The Incarnate Bachelor*. London: Cohen and West, 1953. Chapter V. Eliza Mary Ann Savage. For Miss Savage was closely response to Butler's composition of *The Way of All Flesh*.

② Claude Thomas Bissell, "A study of *The Way of All Flesh*." In Herbert Davis, William C. DeVane and Robert Cecil Bald (eds), *Nineteenth Century Studies*. First published in 1940. Greenwood Press, 1968, p. 288.

③ Philip Henderson. *Samuel Butler: The Incarnate Bachelor*. London: Cohen and West, 1953, pp. 131-132. However, Butler was not satisfied with the ending and according to his own evaluation: "My own idea is that the first vol. is the best of the three, the second the next best, and the third the worst...I must begin again with the third volume." Letter to E. M. A Savage of 3 December 1883. See Samuel Butler. *Letters Between Samuel Butler and Miss Savage*. 1919, P. 245. From 1884 onwards, he worked on restructuring the final chapters, adding much material before Miss Savage's death on 22 February 1885. For Miss Savage was "his sole confidante and so effective a critic that the composition at times seems almost to have been a joint enterprise. For eighteen years after her death the manuscript gathered dust." See Peter Morton. "Butler on Heredity." In *The Vital Science, Biology and the Literary Imagination: 1860 – 1900*. London: G. Allen and Unwin, 1984, p. 181.

④ Carl Dawson. "Strange Metamorphoses: Samuel Butler's 'Unconscious Memory' and *The Way of All Flesh*." In *Prophets of Past Time: Seven British Autobiographers, 1880 – 1914*. London: The Johns Hopkins University Press, 1988, p. 74.

"excess fat" from his theory into the novel; thus there are four key ideas carrying the flow of events in *The Way of All Flesh*:

> First, there is the oneness of personality between the four generations of parents and their offspring. We are required to accept, in strict literality, that Ernest is the same person as his father no less than his great-grandfather, and that their personalities are full, through latently, part of his own. Heredity is memory: "this feature of memory is manifested in heredity by the way in which offspring (e.g. Ernest) commonly resembles most its nearer ancestors (Theobald), but sometimes reverts to earlier ones (John Pontifex)."
>
> Second, if heredity is memory there must be a somatic equivalent to forgetfulness. The cumulative experience of past generations is available to the child only until he reaches the age when his parents conceived him; after that point he is thrown back on to his own resources.
>
> The third and fourth core biological principles may be summarily sated here since their artistic significance emerges only under closer analysis. One is that habit-memories are normally latent in each individual, and can be roused from dormancy only by environmental shock or (Butler's own idiosyncratic term for it) "crossing". Providing these shocks are not violent enough to damage or destroy the organism altogether, their effect can be beneficial... The other principle is that the highest evolutionary ideal is not an intensification of consciousness but, rather, its replacement by "grace"—a manifold virtue which encapsulates all of Butler's Hellenism, his antipathy to Pauline Christianity and his admiration for instinctive physical excellence and social poise in young men. ①

---

① Peter Morton. "Butler on Heredity." In *The Vital Science, Biology and the Literary Imagination: 1860 – 1900*. London: G. Allen and Unwin, 1984, pp. 181-182. Peter's quotation in the first paragraph is chosen from Butler's essay "The Deadlock in Darwinism". Here, he says: "The interpolations have been added to make the connection between novel and theory clearer, but it is reasonable to suppose that Butler had his complete but unpublished novel in mind when he wrote this."

I agree with Peter Morton that the analysis of the connection between Butler's novel and theory is of great interest and merits scholarly attention. However, in his book he dedicates only three pages to such an exploration. This seems grossly insufficient and it leaves an unfinished project, therefore, I propose in my thesis a more thorough and coherent analysis.

By way of introduction, I shall start with some proof on the relationship between theory and novel. From R. A. Streafeild to Claude Bissell, critics have demonstrated the close relationship between the four treatises on evolution and *The Way of All Flesh*. Bissell especially sees intimate and fruitful links between Butler's evolutionary and philosophical stand and his choice of the novel, arguing that Butler's "scientific ideas were ... inseparable from a moral philosophy that could find its fullest expression [only] ... in the literary form that deals most directly with problems of human conduct."① This is a just observation and shrewd remark since one of Butler's key emphasis was the purposive life, and he rejected what he saw as Darwinist mechanism or all forms of determinism.② Thus one worthy approach to the novel is to see it in terms of the growth of an individual (Butler-Ernest). As critics have asserted, "Butler admitted to substantial parallels between himself and Ernest, wanting at the same time the detachment of a narrator who, if an alter ego, could assess his life with unsentimental regard."③ Butler's vision of life as slow "accumulation or accommodation" is an individual's response to his changing environment, which

---

① Claude Thomas Bissell. "A study of *The Way of All Flesh*." In Herbert Davis, William C. DeVane and Robert Cecil Bald (eds), *Nineteenth Century Studies*. First published in 1940. Greenwood Press, 1968, p. 278.

② Frank Miller Turner. "Samuel Butler: The Man of Temper." In *Between Science and Religion: The Reaction to Scientific Naturalism in Late Victorian England*. New Haven: Yale University Press, 1974, p. 169.

③ Carl Dawson. "Strange Metamorphoses: Samuel Butler's '*Unconscious Memory*' and *The Way of All Flesh*." In *Prophets of Past Time: Seven British Auto-biographers, 1880 – 1914*. London: The Johns Hopkins University Press, 1988, p. 89.

thus "can fit the generic framework of a book about education and development".① Ernest's story lent itself perfectly to the *Bildungsroman* that Butler hoped to make of *The Way of All Flesh*.②

In 1888, Butler's sisters presented him with the papers of their grandfather, Dr. Samuel Butler, the headmaster of Shrewsbury (1798 – 1836) and bishop of Lichfield until his death in 1839. Contrary to what might be expected from his disparagement of education and educators in the two *Erewhon* books and in *The Way of All Flesh*, Butler held his ancestor in great esteem. The editing of these papers occupied him intermittently for the next seven years and culminated in *The Life and Letters of Dr. Samuel Butler* (1896), a two-volume annotated selection of Dr. Butler's correspondence intended to illuminate the subject's personality as well as public school and church affairs during the early nineteenth century.③ Butler found much to admire in his grandfather's personality and outlook.④

① *Ibid.*, p. 89.

② Peter Morton. "Butler on Heredity." In *The Vital Science, Biology and the Literary Imagination: 1860 – 1900*. London: G. Allen and Unwin, 1984, p. 183.

③ Butler lets the letters speak for themselves; nonetheless, his polemical purpose is apparent. Much credit for the reform of the rough public schools of the early nineteenth century had been given to Dr. Thomas Arnold, headmaster of Rugby from 1828 – 1841. Butler suggests that this reputation is undeserved: Arnold's record, in fact, can not match that of Dr. Butler, who, starting with but three or four pupils, expanded his school to a pupil population of 300, initiated scholarly competitions and examinations, and so improved the teaching of the classics that the two great universities had to change examination rules to prevent Shrewsbury boys from defeating the resident alumni.

④ Dr. Butler disliked the gloom of evangelical Methodism and sectarian self-righteousness; unlike Dr. Arnold, he possessed a robust sense of enjoyment, and he disliked the morbid "sentimentality" of his time. He was a tolerant, practical divine with a manly common sense, firm but kind, eager to promote his boys' interests, restrained in the common practice of flogging. Though he revered the classics, he objected to teaching them by gerund-grinding and accent-counting. In 1822 he had criticized (in an anonymous pamphlet) the university curriculum for promoting speculative knowledge by an excessive emphasis on mathematics: the "practical clown," Dr. Butler observed, is after all superior to the "speculative academic"—a sentiment not unlike those his grandson later expressed.

Butler's admiration for Dr. Butler softened the bitter memories of his former school and of its headmaster, Dr. Benjamin Kennedy, Dr. Butler's successor whom he had ruthlessly satirized as Dr. Skinner in *The Way of All Flesh*. In fact Butler concludes the work on his grandfather by confessing that Dr. Kennedy "treated me with great forbearance far more than I deserved." Under him he learned the Shrewsbury virtues: "Sincerity, downrightness, hatred of sham, love of work, and a strong sense of duty. What little of these noble qualities I dare pretend to, I owe hardly more to my parents than to the school at which they placed me, nor do I believe Shrewsbury would have possessed them in the measure in which they certainly existed among my own school-fellows but for the deep impress of Dr. Butler's masculine and sagacious character."① With memories of his admired grandfather, Butler transformed *The Way of All Flesh* into "an epic of domestic felicity, with old Pontifex as the kindly patriarch, anxious for the welfare of his children and grandchildren."② In contrast, Butler felt he owed hardly more to his father, Cannon Butler, who left his son with only a memory of bitterness.③ It has been suggested that Butler's earlier unhappy family life had left scars, insofar as it created the oppressive home environment chronicled in *The Way of All Flesh* (1903) and which later formed his approach to the world.④ Butler obviously deflects onto his favorite heroine his bachelor suspicions of Victorian familie—the fiercely independent Aunt Alethea in *The Way of All Flesh*could well have been created by Butler as a foil to this paterfamilias.

Being highly appreciated and praised in the novel, Alethea Pontifex embodied

---

① Malcolm Muggeridge. *The Earnest Atheist: A Study of Samuel Butler*. London: Eyre and Spottiswoode, 1936, p, 238.

② *Ibid.*, p. 238.

③ R. S. Garnett. *Samuel Butler and his Family Relations*. London: J. M. Dent and Sons, 1926, pp. 223-224.

④ Online Source: http://en.wikipedia.org/wiki/Samuel_Butler_(novelist)

for Butler an ideal of the right education of children. He has another ideal—the "gentlemen", mentioned frequently in his *Note-Books*, whose essential characteristics were "gentleness, to absence of such things as brow-beating, overbearing manners and fuss, and generally to consideration for other people". ① In *The Way of All Flesh* Butler exalts a dominant figure of gentlemen portrayed by the character of Towneley, who is a perfect combination of good breeding and knowledge. For Butler, the growth and development of individuals are attuned to the mechanics of evolution by virtue of their good breeding. He expounds:

> If people require us to construct...we set good breeding as the corner-stone of our edifice. We would have it ever present consciously or unconsciously in the minds of all as the central faith in which they should live and move and have their being, as the touchstone of all things whereby they may be known as good or evil according as they make for good breeding or against it. That a man should have been bred well and breed others well; that his figure, head, hands, feet, voice, manner and clothes should carry conviction upon this point, so that no one can look at him without seeing that he has come of good stock and is likely to throw good stock himself, this is the desiderandum. And the same with a woman. The greatest number of these well-bred men and women, and the greatest happiness of these well-bred men and women, this is the highest good; towards this all government, all social conventions, all art, literature and science should directly or indirectly tend. Holy men and holy women are those who keep this unconsciously in view at all times whether of work or pastime. ②

① Samuel Butler. *Note-Books of Samuel Butler*. Edited with a preface and biographical statement by Henry Festing Jones. London: A. C. Fifield, 1912. Edition in use: IndyPublish edition, 2007, p. 24.

② Samuel Butler. *The Way of All Flesh*. London: Grant Richards, 1903, published posthumously. Edited with an introduction by V. S. Pritchett, London: Penguin English Library, 2012, Ch. 85, p. 459.

During the last decade of his life Butler began editing his notebooks he had been keeping since 1874. There were notes Butler had been writing for himself throughout his life, selections from which were later published posthumously by Butler's biographer Henry Festing Jones as *The Note-Books of Samuel Butler* in 1912. Butler used his notebooks to record stray thoughts that he often developed in his books or essays. They therefore contain his most characteristic observations in the attractive epigrammatic form of which he was a master, for example: "If virtue had everything her own way she would be as insufferable as dominant factions generally are. It is the function of vice to keep virtue within reasonable bounds."① The notes are indeed a harvest of ideas, for they probe and challenge people's ways of thinking. Many of them attracted early readers by what was at that time their shocking unconventionality; they still attract the modern reader because they are thought-provoking. They search for the meaning of life, religion, philosophy and education; they reach pragmatic, mediating positions, deriding all extremism, whether of honesty or dishonesty, virtue or immorality. However, this aspect of Butler's work is rarely acknowledged. This thesis also attempts to make up for this ignorance and draws upon them frequently as they convey Butler's ideas so well.

From the late 1930s onward, critics have qualified the originally high estimate he once enjoyed.② At the height of his fame, George Bernard Shaw regarded Butler as an important figure, a brilliant and unjustly neglected debunker of his age. In Shaw's preface to *Major Barbara* (1907), he praised Butler as "the

---

① Samuel Butler. *Note-Books of Samuel Butler*. Edited with a preface and biographical statement by Henry Festing Jones. London: A. C. Fifield, 1912. Edition in use: IndyPublish edition, 2007, p. 18.

② E. M. Forster (1879 – 1970) had been deeply influenced by Butler and became one of his great admirers. See *The Creator as Critic and Other Writings by E. M. Forster*. Edited by Jeffrey M. Heath. Toronto: Dundurn, 2008, pp. 45-49. This point has been discussed by Lee E. Holt. See Lee E. Holt. "E. M. Forster and Samuel Butler." In PMLA. Vol. 61 No. 3 (September, 1946), published by Modern Language Associations, pp. 804-819.

greatest English writer of the latter half of the XIX century", for Shaw saw in him the earliest and most brilliant exponent of the anti-Darwinian spirit gathering strength at the turn of the century, the courageous prophet of Mammon, and the enlightened morality of good health.[①] Today Butler no longer commands so central a position in the world of literature. Though *Erewhon* and *The Way of All Flesh* continue to attend critical interest, Butler's other works are considered minor, partly because much of what he attacked has vanished and partly because his subjects are specialized and remote. However, it is significant that his excursion into scientific criticism echoes the conclusions of his secular humanism. Therefore, as a late Victorian who anticipated modern attitudes, he remains important. As a social critic and satirist, much of what he said delights and instructs modern readers. More than mere literary entertainment, *The Way of All Flesh*, I argue, is in fact a case study in which Butler poured his life experience to illustrate his central arguments on evolution. A coherent exploration of Butler's way of thinking and a precise and complete analysis of the connection between his evolutionary treatises on evolution and his literary works remain an unfinished project. Hence, in this work, my aim is to do this project, with my arguments of close connection between Butler's four treatises on evolution and *The Way of All Flesh.*

---

① Bernard Shaw. The preface of *Major Barbara*. In *Selected Plays of Bernard Shaw, with Prefaces.* New York: Dood Mead Company, 1898, p. 313.

Chapter One *The Way of All Flesh* (1903): a summary

Samuel Butler began to write *The Way of All Flesh* about the year 1872. Many of its details had been drawn from his own family experience, and so he also felt that publication would hurt the feelings of his closest relatives. The one book that might have been a commercial triumph in his lifetime thus did not appear until a year after his death. Unlike most biographical fictions, *The Way of All Flesh* does not begin with the birth of the protagonist (Ernest Pontifex). Edward Overton, the principal narrator, begins Ernest's story by describing three generations of his paternal forebears. Overton belongs to the generation of Ernest's father, but unlike Theobald Pontifex (Ernest's father), he is a relaxed, worldly, imaginative man, though a trifle stuffy; thus he can interpret and to some extent empathize with the tense and sometimes tragic events he narrates and can take Ernest's side. Many passages have an omniscient narrator who reports inner thoughts and has a wider view and greater knowledge than the thoughtful but complacent Overton, it seems that the novel's implications reach beyond the ken of its elderly narrator. This is no mere authorial vanity—the satirical depiction of the Pontifexes in the first quarter of the novel provides an essential background and is consistent with the author's desire to concentrate on Ernest's story. Butler's intention is not simply to provide a genealogy of the Pontifex line for its own sake; in keeping with the intellectual climate of his age, he is ardently engaged in weighing the consequences of evolutionary theories and doctrines made popular by Charles Darwin and other naturalists. Butler's interests in evolutionary theories are, in fact, presented so intensely in the novel accompanying his four books on evolution.

Since *The Way of All Flesh* is about the evolutionary development of a family and about the unconscious but devastating influence of thoughts, Butler proceeds from Ernest's great-grandfather John Pontifex, a gentle and unpretentious carpenter, who lives a humble life with his wife in the village of Paleham until his death in 1812. Besides his admirable character, John Pontifex is also an amateur artist and musician.

Unfortunately, his one and only son, George, possesses the characteristics of his obstinate and humourless mother. After being apprenticed to an uncle in London, George assumes control of his uncle's publishing house. He eventually becomes the sole proprietor of his uncle's business. Then describing the gradual decay of this pastoral mode of life in the successful career of Ernest's grandfather, George Pontifex, whose one aim in life is money and achievement, and who becomes a big-city man. Outwardly a respectable businessman, as a father, his main objective is to break the will of his children's, particularly his youngest son, Theobald. ①

Theobald, whom Overton knew as a childhood acquaintance, wishes to be a seafaring man. However, being weak-willed, he lacks the convictions and self-determination to realize his ambition, capitulating without a fight to his father's insistence that he enter the Anglican ministry. After taking his orders, Theobald become an assistant to the Reverend Allaby, the father of five daughters of marriageable age, and meets Christina Allaby, the second oldest daughter who is four years older than him. His engagement with Christina is only due to her luck at a game of cards-and the miserable marriage as well as the miserable career as a

① In the feeble attempt of the son, to defy his father George Pontifex and not become a clergyman, the reader sees what Ernest's life would have been had he not reincarnated some of his great-grandfather's strength.

clergyman, a life for which he had no inner calling or talent. Theobald realizes he feels little genuine affection for Christina, the couple settle into a strict and stern routine that would characterize their entire married life in Battersby-on-the-Hill.

The birth of Ernest during the fifth year of Theobald and Christina's marriage is especially welcome news to George Pontifex, for Ernest is his first grandson. Theobald inherits, however, his father's authoritarian streak being just as determined to seek out and destroy any signs of free will in his children, with most of his assault befalling the oldest child Ernest. Ernest is constantly beaten for failing to learn his lessons, "denied pocket money, and given 'pleasure' by being allowed to select his own hymn to sing at Sunday evening service". ① Theobald is not fond of children, and Christina wishes that they could be born as "full-grown clergymen," and to obey his father's will and to suppress his own. For his parents think they are doing all in the name of love and duty so as to achieve their children's breeding and growth.

At the age of 12, Ernest is enrolled in a grammar school at Roughborough, located about 50 miles from Battersby. Ernest's headmaster, Dr. Skinner, treats his pupil sin much the same way that Theobald treats his children. When Alethea Pontifex, the unmarried younger sister of Theobald, moves to Roughborough, she is much attracted to Ernest. Being wealthy and independent, Alethea befriends her nephew and for a time counteracts the misery of his childhood. Unfortunately, she is suddenly stricken with typhoid fever and dies, but not before making a will that arranges for the bulk of her estate to be left in trust with Overton for Ernest until his twenty-eighth birthday.

Ernest survives the thumbscrews of parental inquisition, but just barely. After his graduation, Ernest leaves Roughborough, and he enters Emmanual College at

① Online source: "A Summary and Analysis of *The Way of All Flesh*." http://www.cliffsnotes.com/literature/w/the-way-of-all-flesh/book-summary.

Cambridge University where he has more freedom to grow. Thus, Ernest is conscious of being happy for the first time in his school life. Unfortunately, in the university, after showing his talent in literature and a sense of humour, Ernest "falls under the influence of the Simeonites, a small group of evangelistically fervent students". ①He takes an honors degree and, when he is twenty-two, comes into £ 5 000 left to him by his grandfather. Upon returning home a free and wealthy man, however, he still through habit defers to his father in all things and spends several hours a day studying the classics and his math. It is astonishing to see so wretchedly that he has been molded. Back in Cambridge, he prepares for ordination. Unlike his father, who had felt his faith fading as this event approached, Ernest, upon hearing an evangelical preacher, suddenly becomes more passionately devoted to Christ and with great zeal to save people's soul.

Soon after obtaining his degree and being ordained as a curate, Ernest is assigned to a London parish which is populated by lower classes. The newly ordained Ernest takes up his duties in central London where he becomes acquainted with a senior curate, Pryer, who moves him rapidly toward Rome. ② Pryer persuades Ernest to turn his money over to him to invest a College of Spiritual Pathology to regenerate the Church of England and treat disorders of the soul in much the same manner as physicians treat ailments of the body. When visiting Ernest, Overton is vexed to learn of Ernest's ill-conceived plans. ③To put his ideas into immediate practice, Ernest rents a room in the slums of London-

---

① See online source: http://www. cliffsnotes. com/literature/w/the-way-of-all-flesh/book-summary.

② Pryer, slightly older than Ernest, is a personable and persuasive conservative who holds High Church views.

③ Ernest is suddenly becoming religious. Overton apologizes for his godson by using an argument from biology: "The vagaries which it will now be my duty to chronicle", he says, are the result of "the shock of change", and are not surprising "when his antecedents are remembered". Since "circumstances had led to his being ordained". See Samuel Butler. *The Way of All Flesh.* London: Grant Richards, 1903, published posthumously. Edited with an introduction by V. S. Pritchett, London: Penguin English Library, 2012, Ch. 51, pp. 267-267.

Ashpit Place. His landlady Mrs. Jupp speaks of Ernest as knowing "no more than an unborn babe."① Then, Ernest meets a classmate from Cambridge, Towneley, by chance. Being wealthy, handsome, courteous, Towneley is Butler's portrait of a gentleman. Ernest soon permits Pryer to assume the absolute responsibility of investing his money in the stock market so that the intended profits of this venture will enable them to advance God's work in the world.

Unable to contain his enthusiasm, however, Ernest determines to begin a private evangelical campaign of saving souls by canvassing his own neighborhood at Ashpit Place. In an unfortunate incident, Ernest mistakes a decent young woman for a prostitute. Finding that Towneley already has an appointment with Miss Snow, he enters into the room of Miss Maitland, whom he supposes to be of the same moral persuasion as Miss Snow. However, Miss Maitland is terrified by the sudden intrusion, and flees in alarm to the street where an overly zealous police officer is stationed. As a result, Ernest is arrested for assault, and sentenced to six months in prison because, as the judge says, he did not have "the common sense to be able to distinguish between a respectable girl and a prostitute."②

In prison, Ernest has an attack of brain fever, like John Pickard Owen before him, though unlike Owen he does not die. Having recovered, he is informed that his fellow curate, Pryer, has absconded with his money. Ernest learns to be a tailor and on leaving prison sets up an old-clothes shop. He marries Ellen, a servant girl who had been expelled from Theobald's house when she became pregnant.③ Overton is upset by Ernest's decision to marry with Ellen, but he offers financial help to the young couple so that they can buy a shop-cum-living quarters.

① *Ibid.*, Ch. 55, p. 287.

② *Ibid.*, Ch. 62, p. 319.

③ This marriage is later proved to be illegal because Ellen is already married.

After the marriage, the couple's efforts are quickly rewarded with prosperity. Both the marriage and the business thrive at first; however, Ellen starts to feel the pressure of being the wife of a well-educated and refined husband and begins to drink heavily, a habit that she conceals from Ernest.① Without realizing that she is alcoholic, Ernest attributes this strange behaviour to her pregnant state, and it is only after she lapses into drinking a second time, when with her second child, that the naive Ernest recognizes the true cause of her distress. Faced with "a burdensome marriage and almost certain penury", Ernest's physical and mental conditions deteriorate.② He has a chance encounter with John, his father's former coachman, who informs Ernest that he married Ellen shortly after they left the service of Ernest's parents. This news prompts Ernest to arrange a separation from his supposed wife and to place his children first in the care of Overton's laundress and later in a foster home.

After being saved from a disastrous marriage, Ernest suffers an attack of nervous prostration from his ordeal. An eminent London physician prescribes his treatment by visiting the Zoological Gardens, as a method of rest and recover for Ernest. In three weeks' time, he is sufficiently recovered to travel across France to Italy with Overton. Overton decides that Ernest has suffered enough and employs him as his secretary. His main charge is to manage the sums of money which, though he does not know it, would be later his own. Upon reaching the age of 28, Ernest receives his inheritance. Then, Overton comments again by using Butler's words, "poverty is very wearing; it is a quasi-embryonic condition through which a man had better pass if he is to hold his later developments securely."③

---

① See online source: http://www.cliffsnotes.com/literature/w/the-way-of-all-flesh/book-summary.

② *Ibid.*

③ Samuel Butler. *The Way of All Flesh*. London: Grant Richards, 1903, published posthumously. Edited with an introduction by V. S. Pritchett, London: Penguin English Library, 2012, Ch. 78, p. 405.

Now financially able to do as he pleases, Ernest goes abroad for a number of years in search of societies with the best, comeliest and nicest people. At the end of three years of globetrotting, he resumes life in England well supplied with notes with which to fuel his literary ambitions. His first book is a collection of essays on a variety of topics, ostensibly written by separate authors and published anonymously. The subject matter and ironical nature of these essays are reminiscent of Butler's own earlier literary efforts. Ernest then decides to set himself up as an intellectual gadfly, determined to attack the shams of a society that he deems in need of his corrective treatment.① Unfortunately, his subsequent writings meet with much less success because of their controversial nature.

Ernest's two children, Georgie and Alice, prosper from being placed with foster parents who treat them as their own. To free the two children from the dangers of parental abuse, Ernest insists that they be brought up by others and is pleased when his son becomes a boatman and his daughter marries one of her playfellows. They grow up to be handsome, healthy and responsible adults, unencumbered by a formal education. Overton who is by now 80 years old, continues to dispense advice to his charge. He urges Ernest to write with the general public in mind, but Ernest, like Butler, goes his own way, heedless of others' opinions in the belief that a later generation of readers will reward him with the recognition he lacks during his own lifetime. The novel moves rapidly to a close.

① Online source: http://www.cliffsnotes.com/literature/w/the-way-of-all-flesh/book-summary.

Chapter Two *The Way of All Flesh* as a Lamarckian novel of inheritance

2.1 Lamarckian essence in the novel: change, will and environment

> Every man's work, whether it be literature or music or pictures or architecture or anything else, is always a portrait of himself, and the more he tries to conceal himself the more clearly will his character appear in spite of him. I may very likely be condemning myself, all the time that I am writing this book, for I know that whether I like it or not I am portraying myself more surely than I am portraying any of the characters whom I set before the reader. ①

Butler's words above can be understood in two ways. Firstly, Samuel Butler started to write *The Way of All Flesh* in 1872, after 15 years of evolutionary debate. He put it aside to pursue his interest in human evolution in a whole series of texts—*Life and Habit* (1878), *Evolution, Old and New* (1879), *Unconscious Memory* (1880), and *Luck, or Cunning* (1887)—terminating *The*

① Samuel Butler. *The Way of All Flesh*. London: Grant Richards, 1903, published posthumously. Edited with an introduction by V. S. Pritchett, London: Penguin English Library, 2012, Ch. 14, pp. 72-73.

Way of All Flesh only in 1884. As I have argued, there exists an intimate connection between the novel and his four books on evolution. The writing of *The Way of All Flesh* and *Life and Habit* were roughly coeval, and Butler's central argument is still that memory is the basis of all the phenomena of heredity, as he insists:

> The processes of embryonic development, and instinctive actions, might be now seen as repetitions of the same kind of action by the same individual in successive generations. It was natural; therefore, that they should come in the course of time to be doneunconsciously and a consideration of the most obvious facts of memory removed all further doubt that habit—which is based on memory—was at the bottom of all the phenomena of heredity. ①

Butler had reached this conclusion by the spring of 1874 and traced the genesis of his latter text to a note made in June 1874, after his arrival in Canada:

> It is one against legion when a man tries to differ from his own past selves. He must yield or die if he wants to differ widely, so as to lack natural instincts, such as hunger or thirst, and not to gratify them. It is more righteous in a man that he should "eat strange food", and that his cheek should "so much as lank not", than that he should starve if the strange food be at his command. His past selves are living in him at this moment with the accumulated life of centuries. "Do this, this, this, which we too have done, and found out profit in it", cry the souls of his forefathers within him. Faint are the far ones, coming and going as the sound of bells wafted on to a high

① Samuel Butler. *Unconscious Memory*. London: David Bogue, 1880. New edition with a note by R. A. Streatfeild and introduction by Marcus Hartog, London: A. C. Fifield, 1910. The edition in use: The Echo Library edition, 2006, p. 10. Chapter 2 of this work is titled "How I came to write 'Life and Habit' and the circumstances of its completion".

mountain; loud and clear are the near ones, urgent as an alarm of fire. ①

Sally Shuttleworth argues: "It is this sense of the power of hereditary memory, and the consequent difficulties of defining or maintaining a unified sense of selfhood, that lies at the heart of both *Life and Habit* and *The Way of All Flesh*." ② The novel has been read as a direct expression of Butler's evolutionary conception, but I would argue that the relationship between the novel and Butler's evolutionary theory is more complex and problematic than critics have suggested. In this dissertation, I aim to prove the connections between *The Way of All Flesh* and Butler's four books on evolution with textual analysis and contextual analysis. This thesis is supported by C. E. M. Joad, who points out that "Many of the ideas suggested in *Erewhon* and *The Way of All Flesh* are worked out fully in his biological writings, and some account of them and of the attitude to life which they implied is an indispensable preliminary to a consideration of Butler's work as a whole." ③ Indeed, Butler is not a man of science. Butler's objective was to produce a plausible illustration of his theory as a perfect deduction to his hypothesis, for no-one has seen unconscious memory working, and there was, therefore, no direct scientific evidence for it. In order to avoid his theory of unconscious memory being taken as a piece of pure speculation, Butler wanted to prove that it was a highly probable inference from evidence by extract of man's experience. So as to explain with facts how evolution works in mankind, Butler then formulated his position as follows: "We must try to explain the facts somehow. Does not my theory of unconscious memory, admittedly only a guess, explain most of them well, and all of them

---

① *Ibid.*, pp. 10-11.

② Sally Shuttleworth. "Evolutionary Psychology and *The Way of All Flesh*." In *Samuel Butler: Victorian Against the Grain, A Critical Overview*. Edited by James G. Paradis. Toronto, Buffalo and London: University of Toronto Press, 2007, p. 144.

③ C. E. M. Joad. *Samuel Butler (1835 – 1902)*. London: L. Parsons, 1924, p. 19.

tolerably well? What is more, are there any facts which definitely contradict it?"①

Secondly, the novel exhibits clear if few signs of angoras are common to many other autobiographies. Setting aside reductive evolutionary arguments, it makes sense to think of *The Way of All Flesh* as a precise kind of autobiography that Butler would have written. Butler conceived of his ideas on evolution in a fundamentally expressive way, and it is in his novel that he expresses himself through the narrator of the story. As one of Butler's few idealized characters, Edward Overton is essentially a mouthpiece of the author in his older and more mature years. Butler admitted to substantial parallels between himself and Ernest (the protagonist), aiming at the same time for the detachment of the narrator as an alter ego who could assess his life with unsentimental regard. Even the chronology and dates line up. Samuel Butler began to write *The Way of All Flesh* in 1872, and was engaged with it intermittently until its completion in 1884.② Butler himself points out how the novel echoed his life:

> The preceding chapter was written soon after the events it records—that is to say in the spring of 1867. By that time my story had been written up to this point; but it has been altered here and there from time to time occasionally. It is now the autumn of 1882, and if I am to say more I should do so quickly, for I am eighty years old and though well in health cannot conceal from myself that I am no longer young. Ernest himself is forty-seven, though he hardly looks it.③

① *Ibid.*, pp. 58-59.

② See the Preface of *The Way of all Flesh* written by R. A. Streatfeild, in Samuel Butler. *The Way of All Flesh.* First published in 1903. London: A. C. Fifield, 1908.

③ Samuel Butler. *The Way of All Flesh.* London: Grant Richards, 1903, published posthumously. Edited with an introduction by V. S. Pritchett, London: Penguin English Library, 2012, Ch. 86, p. 463.

The mindful reader will recall that Ernest was born in the year 1835—the same year as Butler. The novel spans over 150 years, from the birth of Old John Pontifex in 1727 to the death of Theobald Pontifex in 1881. However, it would be inadequate to understand the novel as merely an ordinary autobiography charting the growth of an individual (Butler-Ernest).

Butler sets the tone of his fictional work at the outset with an evocation of the evolutionary perspective; the third paragraph of *The Way of All Flesh* is very revealing of the construction of memory and evolution, especially the last sentence:

> Mr Pontifex was a carpenter by trade; he was also at one time parish clerk; when I remember him, however, he had so far risen in life as to be no longer compelled to work with his own hands. In his earlier days he had taught himself to draw. I do not say he drew well, but it was surprising he should draw as well as he did. My father, who took the living of Paleham about the year 1797, became possessed of a good many of old Mr Pontifex's drawings, which were always of local subjects, and so unaffectedly painstaking that they might have passed for the work of some good early master. I remember them as hanging up framed and glazed in the study at the Rectory, and tinted, as all else in the room was tinted, with the green reflected from the fringe of ivy leaves that grew around the windows. I wonder how they will actually cease and come to an end as drawings, and into what new phases of being they will then enter. ①

Butler digs a trap for his readers here: we are plunged simultaneously into an imaginable future state. Memory does not only connect with the past; however, as Gillian Beer says, "it seems that this whole exercise of memory has been at

---

① *Ibid.*, Ch. 1, pp. 1-2.

the service of implying a new phase of being...memory is intimately bound up for Butler with future states."① Butler's contradictory vision, as presented by Overton—"that it is the young and fair who are the truly old and truly experienced inasmuch as it is they who alone have a living memory to guide them"—calls attention to the conflict between progressive nineteenth-century assumptions on individual growth as played out in the *Bildungsroman*, and Butler's retrogressive notions of remembering.② This gives rise to Butler's vision of life as slow accumulation or accommodation, as an individual's responds to his changing world, setting the framework for a work about growth, change and development.

> "My boy," returned my father, "you must not judge by the work, but by the work in connection with the surroundings..." Continued he, waxing warm, "if old Pontifex had had Cromwell's chances he would have done all that Cromwell did, and have done it better; if he had had Giotto's chances he would have done all that Giotto did, and done it no worse; as it was, he was a village carpenter, and I will undertake to say he never scamped a job in the whole course of his life."③

As I have explained previously, Butler's views on evolution are close to those of Lamarck, who points out that the chief factor in the cause of variation is the environment. Changes in their environment bring about changes in living

① Gillian Beer. "Butler, Memory, and the Future." In *Samuel Butler: Victorian Against the Grain, A Critical Overview.* Edited by James G. Paradis. Toronto, Buffalo and London: University of Toronto Press, 2007, p. 48.

② Carl Dawson. "Strange Metamorphoses: Samuel Butler's 'Unconscious Memory' and *The Way of All Flesh.*" In *Prophets of Past Time: Seven British Autobiographers, 1880 – 1914* . London: Johns Hopkins University Press, 1988, p. 89.

③ Samuel Butler. *The Way of All Flesh.* London: Grant Richards, 1903, published posthumously. Edited with an introduction by V. S. Pritchett, London: Penguin English Library, 2012, Ch. 1, pp. 4-5.

organisms, who in order to adapt are compelled to evolve. Those who are successful in adapting themselves to the changes will survive and transmit the traits of the adaptation to their descendants. The adaptations envisaged by Lamarck concern the development of new organs and the lapsing of old ones: changes in the environment and surroundings lead to new needs in organisms, these new needs lead to new habits, which lead in turn to changes in organs. For Butler, acquired characteristics can be and are inherited. In *The Way of All Flesh*, Overton declares:

> Fortune, we are told, is a blind and fickle foster-mother, who showers her gifts at random upon her nurslings. But we do her a grave injustice if we believe such an accusation. Trace a man's career from his cradle to his grave and mark how Fortune has treated him. You will find that when he is once dead she can for the most part be vindicated from the charge of any but very superficial fickleness. Her blindness is the merest fable; she can espy her favourites long before they are born. We are as days and have had our parents for our yesterdays, but through all the fair weather of a clear parental sky the eye of Fortune can discern the coming storm, and she laughs as she places her favourites it may be in a London alley or those whom she is resolved to ruin in kings' palaces. Seldom does she relent towards those whom she has suckled unkindly and seldom does she completely fail a favoured nursling. ①

Here, Butler's paradoxes are presented but not sufficiently dramatized by Overton. Chance plays a very important role in the individual's life, but its role usually works after change has happened. To put it another way, chance only benefits individuals who are in a position to receive it. Life, for Butler, centers on largely unconscious intelligence and cunning, as opposed to the Darwinian

① *Ibid.*, Ch. 5 p. 21.

nightmare of chance and luck.[①] As Overton remarks:

> To me it seems that youth is like spring, an over praised season—delightful if it happen to be a favoured one, but in practice very rarely favoured and more remarkable, as a general rule, for biting east winds than genial breezes. Autumn is the mellower season, and what we lose in flowers we more than gain in fruits. Fontenelle at the age of ninety, being asked what was the happiest time of his life, said he did not know that he had ever been much happier than he then was, but that perhaps his best years had been those when he was between fifty-five and seventy-five, and Dr Johnson placed the pleasures of old age far higher than those of youth. True, in old age we live under the shadow of Death, which, like a sword of Damocles, may descend at any moment, but we have so long found life to be an affair of being rather frightened than hurt that we have become like the people who live under Vesuvius, and chance it without much misgiving.[②]

The evolution of man, no less than organic, is about growth, change and development.[③] By the time men arrive at old age, their developments would have achieved the mature stage. In Butler's works, any speculations about life derive in the main from his studies of inherited memory (The development of Ernest, the hero of the novel, seems like an exception or anomaly). While in prison, Ernest realizes the importance of carving out an independent course of action for himself. This marks the awakening of his self-consciousness. He makes efforts to

① Carl Dawson. "Strange Metamorphoses: Samuel Butler's 'Unconscious Memory' and *The Way of All Flesh*." In *Prophets of Past Time: Seven British Autobiographers, 1880 – 1914* . London: Johns Hopkins University Press, 1988, p. 96.

② Samuel Butler. *The Way of All Flesh*. London: Grant Richards, 1903, published posthumously. Edited with an introduction by V. S. Pritchett, London: Penguin English Library, 2012, Ch. 6 pp. 31-32.

③ Peter Morton. "Butler on Heredity." In *The Vital Science: Biology and the Literary Imagination: 1860 – 1900* . London: Allen and Unwin, 1984, p. 188.

disavow his hitherto passive self and assert his own judgment; such a change also liberates him from most of the external and internal forces that made him unhappy in the past.① Perhaps the most beneficial aspect of his confinement is the time it accorded him to reflect upon the new life he must begin when he regains his freedom. When Ernest is released after six months of imprisonment, he finds himself in his old surroundings, he feels dragged back into his old self, "the effect of unchanged surroundings upon the unchanged part of him".② But there is a changed part in himself, and "the effect of unchanged surroundings upon this was to make everything seem almost as strange as though he had never had any life but his prison one, and was now born into a new world."③

This undoubtedly constitutes the crisis of the protagonist's life and the climax of the novel, and one can quite safely say, distinctly reveals Butler's deviation from orthodoxy over the evolutionary significance of the potency of the individual will as presented as a power of vital force. For Darwinians, as Butler understood, each organism is entirely a product, "first of a random permutation from among a near-infinite number of genetic variables", and then of an environment that moulds its behaviour; thus they subscribe to the belief that "when put under stress the organism can do nothing but die and clear the field for the better-adapted".④ *The Way of All Flesh*, on the other hand, as a neo-Lamarckian novel, gives readers the overall impression of freedom instead of determinism.⑤ Ernest is a wretched creature with both an unstable ancestry and a miserable

① Online Source: *The Way of All Flesh*: Summary and Analysis: http://www.cliffsnotes.com/literature/w/the-way-of-all-flesh/summary-and-analysis/chapters-6771-6669

② Samuel Butler. *The Way of All Flesh.* London: Grant Richards, 1903, published posthumously. Edited with an introduction by V. S. Pritchett, London: Penguin English Library, 2012, Ch. 69, p. 356.

③ *Ibid.*, Ch. 69, p. 356.

④ Peter Morton. "Butler on Heredity." In *The Vital Science: Biology and the Literary Imagination: 1860 – 1900*. London: Allen and Unwin, 1984, p. 188.

⑤ *Ibid.*, p. 188.

home life bearing down on him—in other words, he has not been blessed by way of nature and nurture. One of the most important paragraphs in *The Way of All Flesh* sums up Butler's most important philosophy of life:

> All our lives long, every day and every hour, we are engaged in the process of accommodating our changed and unchanged selves to changed and unchanged surroundings; living, in fact, in nothing else than this process of accommodation; when we fail in it a little we are stupid, when we fail flagrantly we are mad, when we suspend it temporarily we sleep, when we give up the attempt altogether we die. In quiet, uneventful lives the changes internal and external are so small that there is little or no strain in the process of fusion and accommodation; in other lives there is great strain, but there is also great fusing and accommodating power; in others great strain with little accommodating power. A life will be successful or not according as the power of accommodation is equal to or unequal to the strain of fusing and adjusting internal and external changes [emphasis my own]. ①

Butler, following his Lamarckian way of thinking, believes in nature imbued with and full of desire and purposiveness. In his opinion, evolution, for individuals, is a process of interacting with the internal and external world. Moreover, the personal identity is extended to include elements of the external world that has become joined to the individual. It can be argued that in the novel Butler wrestles with both the personal and dramatized applications of his theories. ②

---

① Samuel Butler. *The Way of All Flesh.* London: Grant Richards, 1903, published posthumously. Edited with an introduction by V. S. Pritchett, London: Penguin English Library, 2012, Ch. 69, pp. 356-357.

② Carl Dawson. "Strange Metamorphoses: Samuel Butler's 'Unconscious Memory' and *The Way of All Flesh.*" In *Prophets of Past Time: Seven British Autobiographers, 1880 – 1914* . London: Johns Hopkins University Press, 1988, p. 80.

2.2 Heredity: "the oneness of personality between parents and offspring"

2.2.1 Heredity in *The Way of All Flesh*

Hereditary memory is Butler's improvement on Lamarckism: the novel is an experimental text almost his evolutionary theories concerning the growth and development of an individual, in this case, Ernest Pontifex. Unlike most fictional autobiographies, instead of beginning with the birth of the protagonist, *The Way of All Flesh* begins with an account of his paternal forebears of the preceding three generations. Butler's purpose, however, is not simply to provide a genealogy of the Pontifex line for its own sake. ① Butler was so preoccupied with his evolutionary theories that he wrote four books in which he presented his own views on evolution. Ernest's antecedents, therefore, "take on a special significance as biological prefiguration of Ernest's own delayed groping and struggling to attain manhood". ② Therefore, as R. A. Streatfield said *The Way of All Flesh* is "to a great extent, contemporaneous with *Life and Habit*, [and] may be taken as a practical illustration of the theory of heredity embodied in that book." ③ Indeed, the most important clue remains about the intersection of Butler's theories of memory and its experiment on an individual's life. Butler

---

① "Butler, in keeping with the intellectual climate of his age, is ardently engaged in weighing the consequences of evolutionary doctrines that were made popular by Charles Darwin and others". See online source: http://www.cliffsnotes.com/literature/w/the-way-of-all-flesh/summary-and-analysis/chapters-116

② *Ibid.*

③ See the Preface of *The Way of all Flesh* by R. A. Streatfield in Samuel Butler. *The Way of All Flesh.* London: Grant Richards, 1903; published posthumously, as edited by R. A. Streatfield. London: A. C. Fifield, 1908. The 5th impression of 2nd edition: London, A. C. Fifield, 1912.

concluded all his belief about continued identity between parents and children within *The Way of All Flesh* and his four books on evolution. Overton more than once cites his author to suggest the absurdity of theory without experience:

> Theorists may say what they like about a man's children being a continuation of his own identity, but it will generally be found that those who talk this way have no children of their own. Practical family men know better. "①

Perhaps for this reason, U C. Knoepflmacher argues that the novel becomes "a private experience, within and re-written to test Butler's theories about heredity, theories which were themselves an attempt to free himself from his personal doubts. "② To be more prudent, I insist that *The Way of All Flesh* includes or tries to include all that had concerned Butler, and nearly all that he had written about both in fiction and in science. ③

The theorist, alluded to in the citation above, is of course Butler himself, who had no children of his own, but was far more understanding than the protagonist' father, who would have preferred his children to arrive as "full-grown clergyman in priest's orders", and who was closer to the violent father-type of the eighteenth or nineteenth century, as described by Fielding, Richardson, Smollett and Sheridan, or even Jane Austen. ④ Concerning the relation between parents and children, as Butler reminds us in *The Way of All Flesh*, "It must be remembered

① Samuel Butler. *The Way of All Flesh.* London: Grant Richards, 1903, published posthumously. Edited with an introduction by V. S. Pritchett, London: Penguin English Library, 2012, Ch. 20, p. 101.

② U. C. Knoepflmacher. *Religious Humanism and the Victorian Novel: George Eliot, Walter Pater, and Samuel Butler.* Princeton: Princeton University Press, 1965, p. 226.

③ Carl Dawson. "Strange Metamorphoses: Samuel Butler's 'Unconscious Memory' and *The Way of All Flesh.*" In *Prophets of Past Time: Seven British Autobiographers, 1880 – 1914* . London: Johns Hopkins University Press, 1988, p. 87.

④ "*Le père de familleest capable de tout*" is sufficiently apparent throughout in Jane Austen's novels.

that at the beginning of the nineteenth century the relations between parents and children were still far from satisfactory. "[①] In the novel, the same as in Butler's real life experience, the painful relationship between father and son, especially over the question of money, is a leitmotiv. As Mrs. R S Garnett pointed out, it is "a deep underlying bitterness of pain. His [Butler's] many and incessant efforts to reach an understanding—his long letters with their pages upon pages of explanation and defense—his offerings of plants and ferns all tell the same story". [②] In the novel, "A man first quarrels with his father about three-quarters of a year before he is born," declares Ernest, "It is then he insists on setting up a separate establishment; when this has been once agreed to, the more complete the separation for ever after the better for both. "[③] In fact, the struggle is rendered all the more difficult by Butler's belief that the child is at one with its parents in terms of experience and memories. At that time, Lamarckians, like Herbert Spencer, had paved the way for ideas on instinctive actions, inherited traits and organic memory. On the issue of heredity, Butler tends towards the immediate and specific transfer of individual memory. [④] As he remarked in *Life*

---

① Samuel Butler. *The Way of All Flesh.* London: Grant Richards, 1903, published posthumously. Edited with an introduction by V. S. Pritchett, London: Penguin English Library edition, 2012, Ch. 5, p. 25.

② Martha Roscoe, Garnett. *Samuel Butler and His Family Relations.* London: J. M. Dent and sons, 1926, pp. 223-224.

③ Samuel Butler. *The Way of All Flesh.* London: Grant Richards, 1903, published posthumously. Edited with an introduction by V. S. Pritchett, London: Penguin English Library, 2012, Ch. 79, p. 410.

④ "In order to understand what Butler meant by his assertions of the oneness of parents and offspring, it will be helpful to look briefly at the contemporary scientific context. The physiological psychology of Herbert Spencer and George Henry Lewes had prepared the way for ideas of instinctive actions, inherited traits, and organic memory, which were reinforced by Ernest Haeckel's theory articulated in 1866 that 'ontogeny recapitulates phylogeny' (the pattern of the individual life follows that of the species) , and by publication of Darwin's *Descent of Man* (1871) . Butler explored these

and Habit, "A hen is only an egg's way of making another egg."① For Butler, habit-memories are at the bottom of all the phenomena of heredity. Butler's ideas of inherited memory give rise to the first principle of *Life and Habit*: "the oneness of personality between parents and offspring", which is the core biological principle at the heart of *The Way of All Flesh* and his evolutionary works.②

---

theories in his attempt to work and what evolutionary theory might mean for the experience of the individual life, but is repeatedly dismissive. 'What is this talk that is made about the experience of the race,' he demands in *Life and Habit*, 'as though the experience of one man could profit another who knows noting about him?' (*Life and Habit*, 49). His own impulses are to dwell on the immediate and specific transfer of individual memories. He was to find a confirmation of his theories in the work of the German scientist Ewald Hering, which, as Otis notes, was to make theories of organic memory respectable. Butler wrote *Life and Habit* in ignorance of Hering's lecture 'On Memory as a Function of Organised Matter,' but subsequently translated it in *Unconscious Memory* in support of his own position." See Sally Shuttleworth. "Evolutionary Psychology and *The Way of All Flesh*." In *Samuel Butler, Victorian Against the Grain: A Critic Overview*. Edited by James G. Paradis. Toronto and London: University of Toronto Press, 2007, pp. 155-156.

① Samuel Butler. *Life and Habit*. London: Trübner, 1878. Revised edition, with author's addenda and a preface by R. A. Streatfeild, London: A. C. Fifield, 1910. The Echo Library edition, 2007, Ch. VIII, p. 70. Butler wrote in his *Note-Books*, "The Egg that Hen Belonged to" I got some new-laid eggs a few Sundays ago. The landlady said they were her own, and talked about them a good deal. She pointed to one of them and said: "Now, would you believe it? The egg that hen belonged to laid 53 hens running and never stopped." She called the egg a hen and the hen an egg. One would have thought she had been reading *Life and Habit* [p. 134 and passim]. See Samuel Butler. *The Note-Books of Samuel Butler*. Edited with a preface and biographical statement by Henry Festing Jones. London: A. C. Fifield, 1912. Edition in use: IndyPublish edition, 2007, p. 210.

② Samuel Butler. *Evolution Old and New*. London: Hardwicke and Bogue, 1879. Ch. XIII, p. 198. Butler deduced his theory in *Life and Habit* in four principles: 1. The oneness of personality between parents and offspring. 2. Memory on the part of offspring of certain actions which it did when in the person of its forefathers. 3. The latency of that memory until it is rekindled by a recurrence of the associated ideas. 4. The unconsciousness with which habitual actions come to be performed. See Petronella Jacoba de, Lange. *Samuel Butler, Critic and Philosopher*. Zutphen, Netherlands: W. J. Thieme, 1925, p. 92.

Butler maintains strongly that there is a continuity of personal identity between man and his ancestors.① With this hereditary memory, each individual carries the accumulated experience of all the past generations of his ancestor. In the novel, we are required to accept the oneness of personality between the four generations of the Pontifexes. Ernest is the same person as his father, and no less his great-grandfather and their personalities are fully, though latently, part of his own. Personality has been transmitted through Ernest's ancestors and Ernest's own experience will contribute to the further development of it. The habit and instinct of individuals, as well as the unconscious physiological activities of their bodies, are memories from the lives of their ancestors awakened by the association of ideas.②For Butler, Heredity is an affair of memory: all habitual actions based on memory; besides, "this feature of memory is manifested in heredity by the way in which offspring [for example, Ernest] commonly resembles most its nearer ancestors [his father Theobald], but sometimes reverts to earlier ones [his grandfather John Pontifex]."③ One may speculate the connection between novel and theory, but it is reasonable to suppose that Butler

---

① Samuel Butler. *Life and Habit*. London: Trübner, 1878. Revised edition, with author's addenda and a preface by R. A. Streatfeild, London: A. C. Fifield, 1910. The Echo Library edition, 2007, Ch. VIII, p. 71.

② Frank Miller Turner. "Samuel Butler: The Man of Temper." In *Between Science and Religion: The Reaction to Scientific Naturalism in Late Victorian England*. New Haven: Yale University Press, 1974, p. 182.

③ Samuel Butler. "The Deadlock in Darwinism." In *Essays on Life, Art and Science*. Edited by R. A. Streatfeild. London: A. C. Fifield, 1908, pp. 332-334. For the second aspect of Butler's evolutionary doctrine, "if heredity is memory there must be a somatic equivalent to forgetfulness. The cumulative experience of past generations is available to the child only until he reaches the age when his parents conceived him; after that point he is thrown back on to his own resources. By the end of his life even his basal metabolism 'forgets' how to regulate itself—cellular repair fails because the body can no longer recall what healthy cells should be like. Forgetfulness, then, equals senescence; and amnesia, death". Peter Morton. "Butler on Heredity." In *The Vital Science: biology and the literary imagination: 1860 – 1900*. London: Allen and Unwin, 1984, p. 181.

had his complete but unpublished novel in mind when he wrote this. ① Hereditary memories enable individuals to deal with most of the problems that they would encounter during their lives.

According to Butler, the process of evolution is as he presented in *The Way of All Flesh*:

> Embryo minds, like embryo bodies, pass through a number of strange metamorphoses before they adopt their final shape... Ernest, however, could not be expected to know this; embryos never do. Embryos think with each stage of their development that they have now reached the only condition which really suits them. This, they say, must certainly be their last, inasmuch as its close will be so great a shock that nothing can survive it. Every change is a shock; every shock is a pro tan to death. What we call death is only a shock great enough to destroy our power to recognise a past and a present as resembling one another. It is the making us consider the points of difference between our present and our past greater than the points of resemblance, so that we can no longer call the former of these two in any proper sense a continuation of the second, but find it less trouble to think of it as something that we choose to call new. ②

Butler held that life is a journey implying a kind of programmed development, as he says in *Life and Habit*. Ernest is a passive traveller whose life is "slowly

① *Ibid.*, p. 208.

② Samuel Butler. *The Way of All Flesh*. London: Grant Richards, 1903, published posthumously. Edited with an introduction by V. S. Pritchett, London: Penguin English Library edition, 2012, Ch.53, p. 276.

coming into focus as Overton guides his looking back". ① According to Butler, memories are normally latent in each individual, and can be roused from dormancy only by environmental shock or "crossing", ② since in a permanent evolving world; no new situation could exactly resemble a past situation retained in memories. ③ When theses shocks are not violent enough to damage or destroy the organism, their effect can be beneficial. It may just as well be argued that it is precisely by this unwelcome "crossing"—by the difficulties he has to surmount-that a man attains strength, dexterity and self-confidence. ④

In *The Way of All Flesh*, Edward Overton, as an alter ego of Samuel Butler, is the commentator of the story of five generations of the Pontifex family. Overton is also the mouthpiece for certain of Butler's evolutionary ideas and their potential rebuttal. Here it is necessary to mention that in the chapter "Our Subordinate Personalities" in *Life and Habit*, Butler asserts:

> It is within the common scope of meaning of the words 'personal identity,' not only that once creature can become many as the moth becomes manifold in her eggs, but that each individual may be manifold in the sense of being compounded of vast numbers of subordinate individualities, which have their

---

① Carl Dawson. "Strange Metamorphoses: Samuel Butler's 'Unconscious Memory' and *The Way of All Flesh*." In *Prophets of Past Time: Seven British Autobiographers, 1880 – 1914* . London: Johns Hopkins University Press, 1988, p. 92.

② Peter Morton. "Butler on Heredity." In *The Vital Science: Biology and the Literary Imagination: 1860 – 1900* . London: Allen and Unwin, 1984, p. 182. "Crossing" is Butler's own idiosyncratic term for it. Presumably "crossing" is analogous to the hardening-off process used on tomatoes to prepare them for a cool climate.

③ Samuel Butler. *Unconscious Memory*. London: David Bogue, 1880. The Echo Library edition, 2006, Ch. XII.

④ Martha Roscoe, Garnett. *Samuel Butler and His Family Relations*. London: J. M. Dent and sons, 1926, p. 188.

separate lives within him."①

For Butler, each individual is a compound creature.② In *The Way of All Flesh*, Overton is, in fact, Ernest in his final stage of development. This explains Ernest's multiple roles as "student, clergyman, prisoner, businessman, writer, man of the world, as well as son, husband, father, friend, bachelor—and the role of Overton in recording his life".③ Ernest-Overton is the same hero in Butler's evolutionary cosmos.

Overton has been educated by a sage parent, as commented by U. C. Knoepflmacher, Overton's father, who resembles the genial Owen Senior in *The Fair Haven*, inculcates in his son a respect for the intuitive wisdom of the species.④ Overton is the figure described in 'Darwin on The Origin of the Species' as the man of science who must also be "a man of other things besides science".⑤ Thus, Overton, an independent free thinker like Butler, could view Ernest from the point of view of Butler's evolutionary theories. In *The Way of All Flesh*, Overton is even capable of quoting from *Life and Habit*. The next-to-last paragraph in Chapter 33 of the novel is taken directly from Chapter 15 of *Life and*

① Samuel Butler. *Life and Habit*. London: Trübner, 1878. Revised edition, with author's addenda and a preface by R. A. Streatfeild, London: A. C. Fifield, 1910. The Echo Library edition, 2007, Ch. VII, p. 65.

② *Ibid.*, Ch. VII, p. 56.

③ Carl Dawson. "Strange Metamorphoses: Samuel Butler's 'Unconscious Memory' and *The Way of All Flesh*." In *Prophets of Past Time: Seven British Autobiographers, 1880 – 1914*. London: Johns Hopkins University Press, 1988, p. 91. In continuing, Carl Dawson explains, "Like a latter-day Tristram Shandy, Ernest enters his own book well into the narrative, in fact, after three generations; by the close of the novel, the narrator can speak of Ernest and himself as *we*, even appropriating Ernest's children as 'our own two'. Since Butler conceives of the individual enacting all the stages of life before him—going 'through the embryonic stages an infinite number of times'."

④ U. C. Knoepflmacher. *Religious Humanism and the Victorian Novel: George Eliot, Walter Pater, and Samuel Butler*. Princeton: Princeton University Press, 1965, p. 260.

⑤ *Ibid.*, p. 260.

Habit:

> "I believe it has been lately maintained that it is the young and fair who are the truly old and truly experienced, inasmuch as it is they who alone have a living memory to guide them; "the whole charm," it has been said, "of youth lies in its advantage over age in respect of experience, and when this has for some reason failed or been misapplied, the charm is broken. When we say that we are getting old, we should say rather that we are getting new or young, and are suffering from inexperience; trying to do things which we have never done before, and failing worse and worse, till in the end we are landed in the utter impotence of death."①

Moreover, Overton is never lacking humour. In the novel, John, Alethea and Ernest all share this sense of humour; however, it is conspicuously absent in Mrs. John Pontifex, George and Theobald. On Overton's characterization, U. C. Knoepflmacher remarks:

> Overton's tone also provides a perfect vehicle for the aphorisms, inverted quotations, and bon mots which had been so conspicuously out of place in Butler's "serious" works. Butler realized the value of this tone and promptly added "love of fun" to the desirable eugenic qualities he had enumerated in *Life and Habit*.②

John Pontifex, as Overton described distinctly at the beginning of the novel, represents the highest form of evolutionary development. A man of good qualities

---

① Samuel Butler. *The Way of All Flesh*. London: Grant Richards, 1903, published posthumously. Edited with an introduction by V. S. Pritchett. London: Penguin English Library, 2012, Ch33, p. 165.

② U. C. Knoepflmacher. *Religious Humanism and the Victorian Novel: George Eliot, Walter Pater, and Samuel Butler*. Princeton: Princeton University Press, 1965, p. 261.

and modest attainments, John is nevertheless the version of "mute, inglorious Milton" eulogized by Thomas Gray in his famous *Elegy*. John's genius as a carpenter and musician, as an example of his highest creativity, are lauded by Overton's father in the novel:

> If a man has done enough either in painting, music or the affairs of life, to make me feel that I might trust him in an emergency he has done enough. It is not by what a man has actually put upon his canvas, nor yet by the acts which he has set down, so to speak, upon the canvas of his life that I will judge him, but by what he makes me feel that he felt and aimed at. If he has made me feel that he felt those things to be loveable which I hold loveable myself I ask no more; his grammar may have been imperfect, but still I have understood him; he and I are *en rapport*; and I say again, Edward, that old Pontifex was not only an able man, but one of the very ablest men I ever knew. ①

Absorbed in his world as an artisan, John finds greatest satisfaction in playing his own hand-built organ and in sketching and painting. He is unconsciously adapted to his rural life, just as he is unconsciously an adept in his supremely practical skills of master carpenter, artist and musician. ② Though beginning his life "with no other capital than his good sense and good constitution", John Pontifex measures up in every way to an evolutionary ideal of unconscious grace, for he

① Samuel Butler. *The Way of All Flesh*. London: Grant Richards, 1903, published posthumously. Edited with an introduction by V. S. Pritchett. London: Penguin English Library, 2012, Ch. 1, p. 5.

② Peter Morton. "Butler on Heredity." In *The Vital Science: Biology and the Literary Imagination: 1860–1900*. London: Allen and Unwin, 1984, p. 185.

has constructed a balanced and harmonious life instinctively. ①His closeness to nature is symbolized by his words, "Good-bye, sun," uttered softly on the eve of his peaceful death. This instinctive attunement to nature is what Overton's father retains when he sees Old John the day before the old man dies. ②

John dies at the age of 85 years old. John's wife, Ruth Pontifex, is equally hearty and long-lived. However, she is humourless and has a stormy temper. The couple married in the year 1750, but for 15 years the wife bore no baby. She bears her husband an only son when she is 38 years old. Her strange behaviour and odd temperature during her pregnancy is described in the following paragraph:

> At the end of that time Mrs Pontifex astonished the whole village by showing unmistakable signs of a disposition to present her husband with an heir or heiress. Hers had long ago been considered a hopeless case, and when on consulting the doctor concerning the meaning of certain symptoms she was informed of their significance, she became very angry and abused the doctor roundly for talking nonsense. She refused to put so much as a piece of thread into a needle in anticipation of her confinement and would have been absolutely unprepared, if her neighbours had not been better judges of her condition than she was, and got things ready without telling her anything about it. Perhaps she feared Nemesis, though assuredly she knew not who

---

① Samuel Butler. *The Way of All Flesh*. London: Grant Richards, 1903, published posthumously. Edited with an introduction by V. S. Pritchett. London: Penguin English Library edition, 2012, Ch. 1 p. 3.

② "The old man had a theory about sunsets, and had had two steps built up against a wall in the kitchen garden on which he used to stand and watch the sun go down whenever it was clear. My father came on him in the afternoon, just as the sun was setting, and saw him with his arms resting on the top of the wall looking towards the sun over a field through which there was a path on which my father was. My father heard him say 'Good-bye, sun; good-bye, sun,' as the sun sank, and saw by his tone and manner that he was feeling very feeble. Before the next sunset he was gone." *Ibid.*, Ch. 3, p. 14.

> or what Nemesis was; perhaps she feared the doctor had made a mistake and she should be laughed at; from whatever cause, however, her refusal to recognise the obvious arose, she certainly refused to recognise it, until one snowy night in January the doctor was sent for with all urgent speed across the rough country roads. When he arrived he found two patients, not one, in need of his assistance, for a boy had been born who was in due time christened George, in honour of his then reigning majesty. ①

Due to the intromission of his bossy wife's genetic and characteristic factors, John's grace eludes in the next few generations of Pontifexes. John's son, George Pontifex, encapsulates the very qualities detested by Butler. George has derived "the greater part of his nature from this obstinate old lady, his mother". ②Thus George has inherited the unfavorable characteristics from his mother's part. This is in spite of the fact that, "she saw, or thought she saw, with pleasure, that he [George] resembled her and her family in feature as well as in disposition rather than her husband and his." ③ Though Mrs. Pontifex "felt nothing of this; to her George was pure and absolute perfection", it is she who introduces the unnatural strain that affects the identity of John's offspring. ④

When it comes to George, although "in those days fathers were always thrashing their boys", being aggressive, obstinate and conventionally pious, George is "a little sterner with his children than some of his neighbours", for he "thrashed his boys two or three times a week and some weeks a good deal oftener". ⑤ George surpasses the habits at that time, which were "universally admitted that to spare the rod was to spoil the child, and St Paul had placed

① *Ibid.*, Ch. 2 p. 6.
② *Ibid.*, Ch. 2 p. 6.
③ *I Ibid.*, Ch. 2 pp. 9-10.
④ *Ibid.*, Ch. 2 pp. 9-10.
⑤ *Ibid.*, Ch. 5 pp. 25-26.

disobedience to parents in very ugly company". ① It is in the depiction of George Pontifex that Butler unleashes his irony: "If his children did anything which Mr Pontifex disliked they were clearly disobedient to their father". ②When Overton advises parents who wish to lead a quiet life to insist on their own perfection and to make their children believe themselves to be inferior and depraved, he is, in some sense, using George as a satiric target:

> It consisted in checking the first signs of self-will while his children were too young to offer serious resistance. If their wills were "well broken" in childhood, to use an expression then much in vogue, they would acquire habits of obedience which they would not venture to break through till they were over twenty-one years old. ③

Overton's final comments on George Pontifex remained rational, pointing out what could be called atavism in George's heredity:

> Where then was the weak place in George Pontifex's armour? I suppose in the fact that he had risen too rapidly... It is their children of the first, or first and second, generation who are in greater danger, for the race can no more repeat its most successful performances suddenly and without its ebbings and flowings of success than the individual can do so, and the more brilliant the success in any one generation, the greater as a general rule the subsequent exhaustion until time has been allowed for recovery. Hence it oftens happens

---

① *Ibid.*, Ch. 5 p. 26. Here Butler refers to Paul the Apostle (Greek: Παῦλος *Paulos*, c. 5-c. 67), original name Saul of Tarsus (Greek: Σαῦλος *Saulos*), was an apostle (though not one of the Twelve Apostles) who taught the gospel of Christ to the first-century world. Biblical scholars are in general agreement that *Philippians*, the eleventh book in the New Testament, was written by St. Paul. See online Source: http://en.wikipedia.org/wiki/Paul_the_Apostle. We can find a greatly developed meaning of suffering in St. Paul's writings.

② *Ibid.*, Ch. 5, pp. 25-26.

③ *Ibid.*, Ch. 5, p. 26.

> that the grandson of a successful man will be more successful than the son—the spirit that actuated the grandfather having lain fallow in the son and being refreshed by repose so as to be ready for fresh exertion in the grandson. ①

Due to his mother's interference, George is considered to be a "hybrid" by Butler. ② Butler explains that the phenomena of atavism are caused by "some disorders of memory like fixations and obsessions and phobias are characterised by the upheaval of old, forgotten and obsolete memories." ③ Thus, changed and disappeared genius characteristics of the first generation can be only recovered in the third or later generations. The passage above also foreshadows later events in the novel, as George engages in another profession and builds up a more successful career than his father's, although Mrs. Pontifex also plays a part in George's transplantation with a corresponding alteration in the family's religious outlook. ④ When George is 15 years old, he starts to work for Mr Fairlie, a publisher of religious books. ⑤ He then moves to London, and his succession to Mr. Fairlie's business begins a new step in the Pontifex line. Old John's

---

① *Ibid.*, Ch. 5, P. 23.

② *Ibid.*, Ch. 5, p. 23.

③ Peter Morton. "Butler on Heredity." In *The Vital Science: Biology and the Literary Imagination: 1860 - 1900*. London: Allen and Unwin, 1984, p. 161.

④ U. C. Knoepflmacher. *Religious Humanism and the Victorian Novel: George Eliot, Walter Pater, and Samuel Butler*. Princeton: Princeton University Press, 1965, p. 267.

⑤ Butler writes, "George Pontifex might have been brought up as a carpenter and succeeded in no other way than as succeeding his father as one of the minor magnates of Paleham, and yet have been a more truly successful man than he actually was—for I take it there is not much more solid success in this world than what fell to the lot of old Mr and Mrs Pontifex; it happened, however, that about the year 1780, when George was a boy of fifteen, a sister of Mrs Pontifex's, who had married a Mr Fairlie, came to pay a few days' visit at Paleham. Mr Fairlie was a publisher, chiefly of religious works, and had an establishment in Paternoster Row; he had risen in life, and his wife had risen with him." See Samuel Butler. *The Way of All Flesh*. London: Grant Richards, 1903, published posthumously. Edited with an introduction by V. S. Pritchett, London: Penguin English Library, 2012, Ch. 2, p. 7.

primitive faith is replaced by the religious cant of his son. This complete change of tone can be seen in a poem composed during his journey to the Montanvert to see the *Mer de Glace*:

Lord, while these wonders of thy hand I see,
My soul in holy reverence bends to thee.
These awful solitudes, this dread repose,
Yon pyramid sublime of spotless snows,
These spiry pinnacles, those smiling plains,
This sea where one eternal winter reigns,
These are thy works, and while on them I gaze
I hear a silent tongue that speaks thy praise. ①

George starts to "look at nature and art only through the spectacles that had been handed down to him by generation after generation of prigs and impostors". ② He adopts the conscious hypocrisy of religious conduct instead of his father's healthy "habit". George is a mutated variation that impresses a dangerous change on the Pontifex line, and Butler employs his most potent metaphors and most suggestive analogies. Therefore, George is "a new animal, arising from the coming together of many unfamiliar elements"; however, "it is well known that the reproduction of abnormal growths, whether animal or vegetable, is irregular and not to be depended upon, even when they are not absolutely sterile." ③ Extracting this sentence from the elaborate context in which it appears reveals more clearly the narrative's intrusiveness and shift in gear at

① *Ibid.*, Ch. 4 p. 17.
② *Ibid.*, Ch. 4 p. 16.
③ *Ibid.*, Ch. 5 p. 23.

this point. When the reader is told that "it is well known that ...", the confidence in tone causes him to quieten his critical faculties and to take the biological fact without a quibble, just as Butler argued in *Life and Habit* that hybrids are either sterile or do not breed true with successive generations. ①

But "[A] very successful man... has something of the hybrid in him." ② Here it is the author's metaphorical transformation from businessman to hybrid. George's intelligence is connected with his business success. When George first

① Butler explains the sterility of hybrids with his memory theories: "Or, perhaps, more seriously, the memory of every impregnate ovum from which every ancestor of a mule, for example, has sprung, has reverted to a very long period of time during which its forefathers have been creatures like that which it is itself now going to become: thus, the impregnate ovum from which the mule's father was developed remembered nothing but horse memories; but it felt its faith in these supported by the recollection of a *vast number* of previous generations, in which it was, to all intents and purposes, what it now is. In like manner, the impregnate ovum from which the mule's mother was developed would be backed by the assurance that it had done what it is going to do now a hundred thousand times already. All would thus be plain sailing. A horse and a donkey would result. These two are brought together; an impregnate ovum is produced which finds an unusual conflict of memory between the two lines of its ancestors, nevertheless, being accustomed to *some* conflict, it manages to get over the difficulty, *as on either side it finds itself backed by a very long series of sufficiently steady memory.* A mule results—a creature so distinctly different from either horse or donkey, that reproduction is baffled, owing to the creature's having nothing but its own knowledge of itself to fall back upon, behind which there comes an immediate dislocation, or fault of memory, which is sufficient to bar identity, and hence reproduction, by rendering too severe an appeal to reason necessary—for no creature can reproduce itself on the shallow foundation which reason can alone give. Ordinarily, therefore, the hybrid, or the spermatozoon or ovum, which it may throw off (as the case may be), finds one single experience too small to give it the necessary faith, on the strength of which even to try to reproduce itself. In other cases the hybrid itself has failed to be developed; in others the hybrid, or first cross, is almost fertile; in others it is fertile, but produces depraved issue. The result will vary with the capacities of the creatures crossed, and the amount of conflict between their several experiences." See Samuel Butler. *Life and Habit.* London: Trübner, 1878. Revised edition, with author's addenda and a preface by R. A. Streatfeild, London: A. C. Fifield, 1910. The Echo Library edition, 2007, Ch. X, p. 92.

② Samuel Butler. *The Way of All Flesh.* London: Grant Richards, 1903, published posthumously. Edited with an introduction by V. S. Pritchett, London: Penguin English Library, 2012, Ch. 5, p. 23.

becomes a partner, an advertisement for his publishing house runs thus:

Books proper to be given away at this Season:

> The Pious Country Parishioner, being directions how a Christian may manage every day in the course of his whole life with safety and success; how to spend the Sabbath Day; what books of the Holy Scripture ought to be read first; the whole method of education; collects for the most important virtues that adorn the soul; a discourse on the Lord's Supper; rules to set the soul right in sickness; so that in this treatise are contained all the rules requisite for salvation. The 8th edition with additions. Price 10d.
>
> *** An allowance will be made to those who give them away. ①

Several years later, George changes his advertisement to be in keeping with modern times:

> The Pious Country Parishioner. A complete manual of Christian Devotion. Price 10d.
>
> A reduction will be made to purchasers for gratuitous distribution. ②

At this point in the novel, George is redeemed only by his ability to make money and to leave most of it to his heirs. He transplants his family from their rural abode to London. Although George adapted well to his new social environment, compared to his father, he is a failure. He is not concerned about the well-being of his offspring. Butler observes wryly that "when a man is very fond of his money it is not easy for him at all times to be very fond of his children

① *Ibid.*, Ch. 5 p. 22.
② *Ibid.*, Ch. 5 p. 23.

also ... the two are like God and Mammon."[①] He overeats, over drinks and overvalues the worth of his money. George's disastrous transplantation has a bad influence on his weakly son Theobald.

Theobald isa timid boy who is "dull and deficient in animal spirits".[②] Unlike his brother John and his sisters Eliza and Mary, he has inherited all the traits of George and old Mrs. Pontifex, excepting his father's camouflaging abilities. He could not be more different than his lively sister Alethea, who has inherited the genuine vitality of John Pontifex.[③] As a result, Theobald quickly falls under the control of his father:

> It was seemly that Mr Pontifex, the well-known publisher of religious books, should devote at least one of his sons to the Church; this might tend to bring business, or at any rate to keep it in the firm; besides, Mr Pontifex had more or less interest with bishops and Church dignitaries and might hope that some preferment would be offered to his son through his influence. The boy's future destiny was kept well before his eyes from his earliest childhood and was treated as a matter which he had already virtually settled by his acquiescence.[④]

Theobald accepts the faith imposed by his father and makes it his duty "to see the honour and glory of God through the eyes of a Church which had lived three hundred years without finding reason to change a single one of its opinions".[⑤]

---

① *Ibid.*, Ch. 5 p. 24.

② *Ibid.*, Ch. 7, p. 34.

③ U. C. Knoepflmacher. *Religious Humanism and the Victorian Novel: George Eliot, Walter Pater, and Samuel Butler.* Princeton: Princeton University Press, 1965, p. 270.

④ Samuel Butler. *The Way of All Flesh.* London: Grant Richards, 1903, published posthumously. Edited with an introduction by V. S. Pritchett, London: Penguin English Library, 2012, Ch. 7, pp. 34-35.

⑤ *Ibid.*, Ch. 26, p. 128.

Because "performing uneasily those ecclesiastical duties which call for human conduct, Theobald finds relief in pasting snippets of the Old Testament against their counterparts in the New."① Theobald's passive nature and weakness are reinforced by an education that strips away his meager ration of instinctive wisdom and restrains his self-awareness. He is forced to obey his father and his self-consciousness and free will are oppressed to the point of being totally destroyed. Eventually, Theobald Pontifex becomes a pale shadow of his father. Lacking both convictions and the determination to carry out his self-will, he accedes to his father's choice of a profession for him even as he allows himself to be drawn into marrying Christina for whom he feels little genuine attachment.

2.2.2 Ernest's parents—Theobald and Christina

Religion is the only meeting-ground for Christina and Theobald. When Christina meets Theobald, she is 27 years old and 4 years older than him. Theobald meets her when as a young clergyman, he works as an assistant to Mr. Allaby, rector of Crampsford, who is a father of five unmarried daughters. A storm soon arises in Mr Allaby's family as to "which of them it should be who should become Mrs Pontifex."② Christina, the second daughter in line, "wins his hand" in a game of cards with her sister, a marriage is arranged. It is at this point that we see exactly what Butler meant when he said that Darwinism filled him with loathing, for Theobald has to "bear the brunt of surviving in a blackly Darwinian world of random events untransfigured by the chance of personal

① U. C. Knoepflmacher. *Religious Humanism and the Victorian Novel: George Eliot, Walter Pater, and Samuel Butler*. Princeton: Princeton University Press, 1965, p. 271.

② Samuel Butler. *The Way of All Flesh*. London: Grant Richards, 1903, published posthumously. Edited with an introduction by V. S. Pritchett, London: Penguin English Library, 2012, Ch. 10, p. 50.

striving to grow".[①] Critics have argued that the card-playing and dicing are Butler's contrivances to show up Darwinian evolution, bringing events and the theory together.[②] Consequently, Theobald is drawn into his fate; after all, as Butler said, "What does a fish's best come to when the fish is out of water?"[③] Thus, "going about his distasteful pastoral duties he [Theobald] sinks into a dreadful spiritual exhaustion, almost asphyxiated by being cut off from his oxygenating past identities".[④] Overton's judgement of him is stern, he is convinced that Theobald is "no pawn of circumstances but a free moral being who has repudiated his sacred genetic obligations" and "flinched away from the stimulating 'crossings', which might have forced him to put out new shoots".[⑤] Instead Theobald fails in his development on both cerebral and instinctual levels:

> The habit of not admitting things to himself has become a confirmed one with him. Nevertheless there haunts him an ill defined sense that life would be pleasanter if there were no sick sinners, or if they would at any rate face an eternity of torture with more indifference. He does not feel that he is in his element. The farmers look as if they were in their element. They are full-

① Peter Morton. "Butler on Heredity." In *The Vital Science: Biology and the Literary Imagination: 1860–1900*. London: Allen and Unwin, 1984, p. 187.

② *Ibid.*, p. 208. Indeed, Butler wrote, "According to Messrs. Darwin and Wallace, we may have evolution, but are on no account to have it as mainly due to intelligent effort, guided by ever higher and higher range of sensations, perceptions, and ideas. We are to set it down to the shuffling of cards, or the throwing of dice without the play." See Samuel Butler. "The Deadlock in Darwinism." In *Essays on Life, Art and Science*. Edited by R. A. Streatfeild. London: A. C. Fifield, 1908, p. 247. The same comparison can also be found in *Luck, or Cunning?* Ch. VIII.

③ Samuel Butler. *The Way of All Flesh*. London: Grant Richards, 1903, published posthumously. Edited with an introduction by V. S. Pritchett, London: Penguin English Library, 2012, Ch. 15, p. 78.

④ Peter Morton. "Butler on Heredity." In *The Vital Science: Biology and the Literary Imagination: 1860–1900*. London: Allen and Unwin, 1984, p. 187.

⑤ *Ibid.*, p. 187.

> bodied, healthy and contented; but between him and them there is a great gulf fixed. A hard and drawn look begins to settle about the corners of his mouth, so that even if he were not in a black coat and white tie a child might know him for a parson. ①

As described above, it is the arduous intellectual training that has effectively destroyed Theobald as a healthy man. ② Christina is clear-eyed in her assessment that Theobald is not "the ideal she had dreamed of when reading Byron upstairs with her sisters, but he was an actual within the bounds of possibility", but consoles herself that "after all not a bad actual as actuals went". ③ After a long six-year engagement, they get married when Christina is 33 years old. Their personalities and life together are vividly represented in their conversations about the glory of God, and the wholeheartedness with which they would devote themselves to religion. ④ Christina is also a weak person; however, she is better

---

① Samuel Butler. *The Way of All Flesh.* London: Grant Richards, 1903, published posthumously. Edited with an introduction by V. S. Pritchett, London: Penguin English Library edition, 2012, Ch. 16, p. 79.

② Peter Morton. "Butler on Heredity." In *The Vital Science: Biology and the Literary Imagination: 1860 – 1900* . London: Allen and Unwin, 1984, p. 187.

③ Samuel Butler. *The Way of All Flesh.* London: Grant Richards, 1903, published posthumously. Edited with an introduction by V. S. Pritchett, London: Penguin English Library, 2012, Ch. 11, p. 52.

④ "We, dearest Theobald," she exclaimed, "will be ever faithful. We will stand firm and support one another even in the hour of death itself. God in his mercy may spare us from being burnt alive. He may or may not do so. Oh Lord" (and she turned her eyes prayerfully to Heaven), "spare my Theobald, or grant that he may be beheaded." "My dearest," said Theobald gravely, "do not let us agitate ourselves unduly. If the hour of trial comes we shall be best prepared to meet it by having led a quiet unobtrusive life of self-denial and devotion to God's glory. Such a life let us pray God that it may please Him to enable us to pray that we may lead." "Dearest Theobald," exclaimed Christina, drying the tears that had gathered in her eyes, "you are always, always right. Let us be self-denying, pure, upright, truthful in word and deed." She clasped her hands and looked up to Heaven as she spoke. "Dearest," rejoined her lover, "we have ever hitherto endeavoured to be all of these things; we have not been worldly people; let us watch and pray that we may so continue to the end." See *Ibid.*, Ch. 12, p. 62.

natured than Theobald and more amiable in her faults. Her precarious balance between loyalty to her husband and abandonment of her ideals is exceptionally well presented in the fiction. The marriage of Theobald and Christina represents the patriarchal authority prevalent in Victorian society:

> And thus this worthy couple jogged on from month to month and from year to year. The reader, if he has passed middle life and has a clerical connection, will probably remember scores and scores of rectors and rectors' wives who differed in no material respect from Theobald and Christina. Speaking from a recollection and experience extending over nearly eighty years from the time when I was myself a child in the nursery of a vicarage, I should say I had drawn the better rather than the worse side of the life of an English country parson of some fifty years ago. I admit, however, that there are no such people to be found nowadays. A more united or, on the whole, happier, couple could not have been found in England. One grief only overshadowed the early years of their married life: I mean the fact that no living children were born to them.①

Soon after their marriage, their eldest son Ernest is born. Like his father, Theobald "had never liked children. He had always got away from them as soon as he could, and so had they from him."② Though Christina is totally obedient towards her husband, her "motherly instincts" nonetheless prevailed:

> Christina did not remonstrate with Theobald concerning the severity of the tasks imposed upon their boy, nor yet as to the continual whippings that were found necessary at lesson times [...] nevertheless she was fond of her boy, which Theobald never was, and it was long before she could destroy all

① *Ibid.*, Ch. 16, p. 85.

② *Ibid.*, Ch. 20, pp. 101-102.

> affection for herself in the mind of her first-born. But she persevered.[①]

"Blood is blood as much through the female line as the male."[②] UC. Knoepflmacher remarks that "Christina endows Ernest with the power of feeling so manifestly absent in her husband."[③] She "who, when not frightened, and when there was nothing on the horizon which might cross the slightest whim of her husband, was an amiable, good-natured woman,"[④] passes her temper to Ernest, described as "naturally of an even temper, he doted upon his nurse, on kittens and puppies, and on all things that would do him the kindness of allowing him to be fond of them."[⑤] Overton repeatedly describes Ernest as his mother's son, Christina has a beneficent effect on her children.

With hindsight, after the appearance of the last two generations of the Pontfixes. Butler softens his judgment of George Pontifex.[⑥]Butler gives us the impression that no matter how bad a father George was, Theobald is worse. Having been brought up to obey his father's will and to suppress his own, Theobald resolves to stifle any signs of self-will in his children. Thus, Ernest is destined to suffer Theobald's self-righteous paternal resolution:

> He (Ernest) disliked the games worse even than the squalls of the class-room and hall, for he was still feeble, not filling out and attaining his full strength

① *Ibid.*, Ch. 20, pp. 103-104.

② *Ibid.*, Ch. 29, p. 144.

③ U. C. Knoepflmacher. *Religious Humanism and the Victorian Novel: George Eliot, Walter Pater, and Samuel Butler*. Princeton: Princeton University Press, 1965, p. 275.

④ Samuel Butler. *The Way of All Flesh*. London: Grant Richards, 1903, published posthumously. Edited with an introduction by V. S. Pritchett, London: Penguin English Library edition, 2012, Ch. 30, p. 173.

⑤ *Ibid.*, Ch. 20, p. 103.

⑥ Butler might have been influenced in this respect by the writing of his grandfather's biography, a man of whom he had no personal recollection.

> till a much later age than most boys. This was perhaps due to the closeness with which his father had kept him to his books in childhood, but I think in part also to a tendency towards lateness in attaining maturity, hereditary in the Pontifex family, which was one also of unusual longevity. At thirteen or fourteen he was a mere bag of bones, with upper arms about as thick as the wrists of other boys of his age. ①

From the above passage, Theobald's sole emotional outlet seems to be the sadistic training he inflicts on Ernest to make the same kind of failure of him, as if "inherited decay once set in motion is self-perpetuating". ② Of Ernest's childhood suffice to say that his entire upbringing supports *Life and Habit*'s dictum that birth is "commonly considered as the point at which we begin to live. More truly it is the point at which we leave off knowing how to live. "③

2.2.3 Ernest's childhood in a God-fearing family

Butler believes that "the Church Catechism has a good deal to do with the unhappy relations which commonly even now exist between parents and children", for it leaves a general impression that wickedness of young men at birth was "but very imperfectly wiped out at baptism, and that the mere fact of being young at all has something with it that savours more or less distinctly of the

① Samuel Butler. *The Way of All Flesh*. London: Grant Richards, 1903, published posthumously. Edited with an introduction by V. S. Pritchett, London: Penguin English Library, 2012, Ch. 30, p. 150.

② Peter Morton. "Butler on Heredity." In *The Vital Science: Biology and the Literary Imagination: 1860 – 1900* . London: Allen and Unwin, 1984, p. 187.

③ Samuel Butler. *Life and Habit*. London: Trübner, 1878. Revised edition, with author's addenda and a preface by R. A. Streatfeild, London: A. C. Fifield, 1910. The Echo Library edition, 2007, Ch. IV, p. 34.

nature of sin".[①] A common observation in England was that "the sons of clergymen are frequently unsatisfactory".[②]Ernest is scarcely a toddler when his parents begin the regimen that continues throughout his childhood. Theobald has never liked children, and Christina wishes that they could be born as "full-grown clergymen".[③] Constantly on guard against leniency, Theobald gives Ernest daily lessons and beatings to eradicate any signs of self-will in him. Christina obediently tries to follow her husband's ways in child rearing, for she "dreams herself to be a possible Madonna and Ernest as a reincarnation of Christ".[④] In *The Way of All Flesh*, Butler devotes approximately half of the novel to Theobald and Christina's wrangling for the possession of their son. However, the clergy is the least attractive option for Ernest, since "things must not be done in him which are venial in the week-day classes. He is paid for this business of leading a stricter life than other people. It is his *raison d' être.* "[⑤]

The clerical profession usually causes problems for the family of the clergyman. If he holds certain opinions when he is ordained, the clergyman must "either forego change and development or become a hypocrite".[⑥] Clergymen are prohibited from either freethinking or free actions, and "their minds are atrophied and their lives are starved".[⑦] Yet, Butler is adamant that free will, change and development are essential processes for any individual. Again Butler

---

① Samuel Butler. *The Way of All Flesh.* London: Grant Richards, 1903, published posthumously. Edited with an introduction by V. S. Pritchett, London: Penguin English Library, 2012, Ch. 7, p. 36.

② *Ibid.*, Ch. 26, p. 127.

③ *Ibid.*, Ch. 20, p. 102.

④ Source online: www. cliffsnotes. com/literature/w/the-way-of-all-flesh/summary-and-analysis/chapters-1721.

⑤ Samuel Butler. *The Way of All Flesh.* London: Grant Richards, 1903; published posthumously. Edited with an introduction by V. S. Pritchett, London: Penguin English Library, 2012, Ch. 26, p. 127.

⑥ C. E. M. Joad. *Samuel Butler (1835 – 1902)*. London: L. Parsons, 1924, p. 116.

⑦ *Ibid.*, p. 117.

says, "A clergyman... can hardly ever allow himself to look facts fairly in the face. It is his profession to support one side."①As such, it is impossible for the clergyman to make an unbiased examination of the other. The clergyman's family is also involved; family members must "devote themselves to the honour and glory of God".② The outcome of a God-fearing family is described as follows:

> This was how it came to pass that their children were white and puny; they were suffering from *home-sickness*. They were starving, through being over-crammed with the wrong things. Nature came down upon them, but she did not come down on Theobald and Christina. Why should she? They were not leading a starved existence. There are two classes of people in this world, those who sin, and those who are sinned against; if a man must belong to either, he had better belong to the first than to the second.③

Thus we learn that little Ernest is suffering from "home-sickness".④At the tender age of three, he is already being whipped for being "self-willed and naughty", when he cannot correctly pronounce the word "come". A measure of relief from this oppressive existence only occurs on Sunday evenings when the children are permitted to select their own hymns to sing.⑤ A mother's love and kindness could have tempered this severity, but Christina is mostly an accomplice to her husband's tyranny. Unfortunately for the children, her

---

① Samuel Butler. *The Way of All Flesh*. London: Grant Richards, 1903; published posthumously. Edited with an introduction by V. S. Pritchett, London: Penguin English Library, 2012, Ch. 26, p. 127-128.

② *Ibid.*, Ch. 26, p. 128.

③ *Ibid.*, Ch. 26, p. 129.

④ *Ibid.*, Ch. 26, p. 129.

⑤ Source online: www. cliffsnotes. com/literature/w/the-way-of-all-flesh/summary-and-analysis/chapters-2226. In *The Way of All Flesh*, Ernest's childhood is recollected as an unrelieved succession of Victorian Sundays.

solicitude for their welfare consists of admonishing them to be obedient to their father. ① Overton relates with some relish an anecdote that is revealing of the atmosphere reigning in Battersby, home of the Pontifexes, ② and admits that "the sight of so much suffering" prevents him from visiting the Pontifexes more often, where there is no reference to children's happiness. ③

On the identity of parent and offspring, Butler observes in *Life and Habit* that "Nor, again, does it depend upon sameness of form or fashion; for the personality is felt to survive frequent and radical modification of structure, as in

① This point is well borne out by the reproduction of a letter written by Christina to her children at a time of confinement when she feared that she would not survive the delivery of another baby. See Christina's letter to her children in Appendix VI.

② This story goes like this: "Next day I was to go back to London, but before I went I said I should like to take some new-laid eggs back with me, so Theobald took me to the house of a labourer in the village who lived a stone's throw from the Rectory as being likely to supply me with them. Ernest, for some reason or other, was allowed to come too. I think the hens had begun to sit, but at any rate eggs were scarce, and the cottager's wife could not find me more than seven or eight, which we proceeded to wrap up in separate pieces of paper so that I might take them to town safely. This operation was carried on upon the ground in front of the cottage door, and while we were in the midst of it the cottager's little boy, a lad much about Ernest's age, trod upon one of the eggs that was wrapped up in paper and broke it. 'There now, Jack,' said his mother, 'see what you've done, you've broken a nice egg and cost me a penny—Here, Emma,' she added, calling her daughter, 'take the child away, there's a dear.' Emma came at once, and walked off with the youngster, taking him out of harm's way. 'Papa,' said Ernest, after we had left the house, 'Why didn't Mrs Heaton whip Jack when he trod on the egg?' I was spiteful enough to give Theobald a grim smile which said as plainly as words could have done that I thought Ernest had hit him rather hard. Theobald coloured and looked angry. 'I dare say,' he said quickly, 'that his mother will whip him now that we are gone.' I was not going to have this and said I did not believe it, and so the matter dropped, but Theobald did not forget it and my visits to Battersby were henceforth less frequent." See Samuel Butler. *The Way of All Flesh.* London: Grant Richards, 1903; published posthumously, as edited by R. A. Streatfield. London: A. C. Fifield, 1908. Edited with an introduction by V. S. Pritchett, London: Penguin English Library edition, 2012, Ch. 23, pp. 116-117.

③ *Ibid.*, Ch. 23, p. 118.

the case of caterpillars and other insects."① Hence, he quotes from *The Variation of Plants and Animals under Domestication* (1868) that in the case of what is called metagenetic development, Darwin informs us that "the new parts are not moulded upon the inner surfaces of the old ones. The plastic force has changed its mode of operation. The outer case, and all that gave form and character to the precedent individual, perish, and are cast off; they are not changed into the corresponding parts of the same individual. These are due to a new and distinct developmental process."② For Butler, the evolution of the individual, no less than organic, is growth, change and development. He appreciated the importance of evolution for matters of self and identity, indeed for the very nature of human life.③ In chapter 11 of *Life and Habit* Butler draws extensively on Théodule Ribot's *L' Hérédité* and on Sydney Smith to supply him with facts about instinctive behaviour, which he used as proof of hereditary memory. For example, he quotes Smith on the sphex wasp's habit of laying it eggs beside the bodies of paralysed insects, thus guaranteeing its grubs a supply of food when they hatch after their parents' death. This example is reproduced in *The Way of All Flesh*:

> Writing as I do by the light of a later knowledge, I suppose I should have seen nothing in this but the world's growing pains, the disturbance inseparable from transition in human things. I suppose in reality not a leaf goes yellow in autumn without ceasing to care about its sap and making the

① Samuel Butler. *Life and Habit*. London: Trübner, 1878. Revised edition, with author's addenda and a preface by R. A. Streatfeild, London: A. C. Fifield, 1910. The Echo Library edition, 2007, p. 52.

② *Ibid.*, p. 52. The original version of the quotation is marked by Butler "Plants and Animals under Domestication", vol. ii, p. 362 ed. 1875.

③ Carl Dawson. "Strange Metamorphoses: Samuel Butler's 'Unconscious Memory' and *The Way of All Flesh.*" In *Prophets of Past Time: Seven British Autobiographers, 1880 – 1914*. London: Johns Hopkins University Press, 1988, p. 73.

> parent tree very uncomfortable by long growling and grumbling—but surely nature might find some less irritating way of carrying on business if she would give her mind to it. Why should the generations overlap one another at all? Why cannot we be buried as eggs in neat little cells with ten or twenty thousand pounds each wrapped round us in Bank of England notes, and wake up, as the sphex wasp does, to find that its papa and mamma have not only left ample provision at its elbow, but have been eaten by sparrows some weeks before it began to live consciously on its own account?①

In a sense, Butler's vision of fatherhood as a mere "old husk" to be cast off is replicated in *Life and Habit* where in another act of filial insubordination, he draws on Darwin's writings to vindicate his position. Butler finds the most striking illustration of this is in Darwin's account of some Echinoderms—"the animal in the second stage of development is formed almost like a bud within the animal of the first stage, the latter being then cast off like an old vestment, yet sometimes maintaining for a short period an independent vitality". ② For Butler, the parent is a mere "husk" or "old vestment" of its offspring. Two or more persons may unite and become one person, melding the memories and experiences of the one and the other. ③ Butler is aware of the difficulty of separating the offspring's personality from that of the parent, since parent and offspring become a union in memory, experience and personality. Here, it is necessary to quote Butler's comments on this point in *Life and Habit* at some

---

① Samuel Butler. *The Way of All Flesh*. London: Grant Richards, 1903; published posthumously. Edited with an introduction by V. S. Pritchett, London: Penguin English Library edition, 2012. Ch. 18, p. 93.

② Samuel Butler. *Life and Habit*. London: Trübner, 1878. Revised edition, with author's addenda and a preface by R. A. Streatfeild, London: A. C. Fifield, 1910. The Echo Library edition, 2007, p. 52. The original version of the quotation is marked by Butler "Plants and Animals under Domestication", vol. ii, P. 362 ed. 1875.

③ *Ibid.*, p. 51.

length:

> Wherever there is a separate centre of thought and action, we see that it is connected with its successive stages of being, by a series of infinitely small changes from moment to moment, with, perhaps, at times more startling and rapid changes, but, nevertheless, with no such sudden, complete, and unrepaired break up of the preceding condition, as we shall agree in calling death. The branching out from it at different times of new centres of thought and action, has commonly as little appreciable effect upon the parent-stock as the fall of an apple full of ripe seeds has upon an apple-tree; and though the life of the parent, from the date of the branching off of such personalities, is more truly continued in these than in the residuum of its own life, we should find ourselves involved in a good deal of trouble if we were commonly to take this view of the matter. The residuum has generally the upper hand. He has more money, and can eat up his new life more easily than his new life, him. A moral residuum will therefore prefer to see the remainder of his life in his own person, than in that of his descendants, and will act accordingly. Hence we, in common with most other living beings, ignore the offspring as forming part of the personality of the parent, except in so far as that we make the father liable for its support and for its extravagances (than which no greater proof need be wished that the law is at heart a philosopher, and perceives the completeness of the personal identity between father and son) for twenty-one years from birth. In other respects we are accustomed, probably rather from considerations of practical convenience than as the result of pure reason, to ignore the identity between parent and offspring as completely as we ignore personality before birth. With these exceptions, however, the common opinion concerning personal identity is reasonable enough, and is found to consist neither in consciousness of such identity, nor yet in the power of recollecting its various phases (for it is plain that identity survives the distinction or suspension of both these), but in the fact that the various

> stages appear to the majority of people to have been in some way or other linked together. ①

Butler was at pains to emphasize the oneness of personality between generations. Heredity is memory, forcing him to reconsider "his sense of memory and self as personal recollection vied with an inherently untellable past". ② This prepares us for Ernest's diatribe towards the family in *The Way of All Flesh*:

> A survival of the principle which is more logically embodied in the compound animal—and the compound animal is a form of life which has been found incompatible with high development. I would do with the family among mankind what nature has done with the compound animal, and confine it to the lower and less progressive races. Certainly there is no inherent love for the family system on the part of nature herself. Poll the forms of life and you will find it in a ridiculously small minority. The fishes know it not, and they get along quite nicely. The ants and the bees, who far outnumber man, sting their fathers to death as a matter of course, and are given to the atrocious mutilation of nine-tenths of the offspring committed to their charge, yet where shall we find communities more universally respected?③

When questioned by Overton in his later years about his childhood, Ernest is quite emphatic in his insistence that the family as an institution should be confined to a lower species. Although no social psychologist, Butler was very

---

① *Ibid.*, pp. 51-52.

② Carl Dawson. "Strange Metamorphoses: Samuel Butler's 'Unconscious Memory' and *The Way of All Flesh.*" In *Prophets of Past Time: Seven British Autobiographers, 1880 – 1914*. London: Johns Hopkins University Press, 1988, p. 83.

③ Samuel Butler. *The Way of All Flesh.* London: Grant Richards, 1903; published posthumously. Edited with an introduction by V. S. Pritchett, London: Penguin English Library, 2012, Ch. 24, p. 120.

perceptive in his analysis of Ernest's childhood.[①] Both the Freudian struggle between father and son and Darwin's survival of the fittest are played out in *The Way of All Flesh* through Butler's engagement with evolutionary theory. As he says in his *Note-Books*:

> I believe that more unhappiness comes from this source than from any other—I mean from the attempt to prolong family connection unduly and to make people hang together artificially who would never naturally do so. The mischief among the lower classes is not so great, but among the middle and upper classes it is killing a large number daily. And the old people do not really like it much better than the young.[②]

The overwhelming impression that family leaves on young Ernest is unhappiness, due largely to the omnipresence of the Old Testament in his household. For Overton, Theobald's Old Testament readings in the novel find their parallel in the bees that mistake the Pontifex drawing room wallpaper design of roses for actual flowers.[③] The bees traverse the walls "without ever suspecting that so many of the associated ideas could be present, and yet the main idea be wanting hopelessly, and for ever."[④] Theobald symbolizes the man "dedicated to defending an institution which for three hundred years had not changed a single

---

① As demonstrated by his observation, at a time when psychology was not yet generally regarded as a scientific discipline.

② Samuel Butler. *The Note-Books of Samuel Butler*. Edited with a preface and biographical statement by Henry Festing Jones. London: A. C. Fifield, 1912. Edition in use: IndyPublish edition, 2007, p. 20.

③ Online summary and analysis of *The Way of All Flesh*: http://www.cliffsnotes.com/literature/w/the-way-of-all-flesh/summary-and-analysis/chapters-2226.

④ Samuel Butler. *The Way of All Flesh*. London: Grant Richards, 1903; published posthumously. Edited with an introduction by V. S. Pritchett, London: Penguin English Library, 2012. Ch. 23, p. 116.

one of its opinions" and is thus "obviously unsuited for the role of father".[①] As C. E. M. Joad observes, Anglican clergymen are victims of much repressed tension and take it out on their defenceless children:

> The dullness of clergymen, their stupidity and the unhappiness of their homes, where they privately revenge themselves upon the community for demanding of them an impossible standard of conduct in public, and at the same time find an outlet for their thwarted desires by bullying their offspring. For this occupation they have exceptional opportunities, since their poor wretches of children can never get away from fathers who, alone among male parents, have no official place of business outside the home.[②]

Life in a clergyman's family is far less happy than in other families. Be it for Ernest or for his creator Butler, the family, is a most undesirable and unnatural institution.

2.2.4 Alethea and Overton

Alethea and Overton are two important persons for Ernest's growth. They represent, in fact, Ernest's ideal mother and father. Alethea Pontifex, the unmarried younger sister of Theobald and Ernest's aunt, visits Roughborough and feels much fondness for Ernest because of his agreeable nature and his extraordinary interest in music. Aware of the lamentable effects of his upbringing, Alethea decides to take an active interest in her nephew. Seeking a more healthful place to live outside London, Alethea takes up a small residence in Roughborough; there she ingratiates herself with Ernest's schoolmates and at

---

① The summary and analysis of *The Way of All Flesh* source on line: http://www.cliffsnotes.com/literature/w/the-way-of-all-flesh/summary-and-analysis/chapters-2226.

② C. E. M. Joad. *Samuel Butler (1835 – 1902)*. London: L. Parsons, 1924, p. 117.

the same time affords Ernest a happy shelter from his oppressive school life. Alethea's residency in Roughborough probably marks the happiest period in Ernest's young life. He is provided with lessons in carpentry and all the necessary tools and materials to construct a musical organ. A few days is enough for him to flourish in health and spirit while engaged in these activities under the cheerful guidance of his aunt.

After having shown that Ernest's better self has been thoroughly suppressed by his parents and schoolmasters, Overton presents Ernest's hope for the future in the form of Alethea. ① Unfortunately, Alethea is suddenly stricken with typhoid fever and, summoning Overton and her solicitor, dictates a will that provides for the bulk of her estate to be left in trust with Overton for Ernest until he reaches the age of 28. Butler shows his high regard for women's intelligence in *The Way of All Flesh*:

> The insight of women upon matters of this sort was deeper and more unerring than that of men. It was a woman and not a man who had been filled most completely with the whole fullness of the Deity. ②

Alethea's death, however, delays the fulfillment of her expectations. Ernest, who had not been told of the actual terms of his aunt's will, is once again forced to endure oppressive and damaging environments that he eventually overcomes only after suffering a series of calamities.

---

① Being a highly idealized characters in the novel, Alethea, whose name is taken from the pagan Greek word for truth, represents the unconscious perfection of character reminiscent of old John Pontifex, Alethea's grandfather and Ernest's great-grandfather. Her attempt to interest Ernest in the construction of an organ characterizes Alethea's way of attempting to develop the finest traits of the Pontifex heritage in Ernest, whom she presumes to be the most likely of the younger members of the family to keep them alive.

② Samuel Butler. *The Way of All Flesh.* London: Grant Richards, 1903; published posthumously. Edited with an introduction by V. S. Pritchett, London: Penguin English Library, 2012, Ch. 21, p. 106.

Not only does Alethea stand apart from her family, she is also an important example of the free woman:

> [She] railed at matrimony as women seldom do unless they have a comfortable income of their own. She by no means, however, railed at man as she railed at matrimony, and though living after a fashion in which even the most censorious could find nothing to complain of, as far as she properly could she defended those of her own sex whom the world condemned most severely. In religion she was, I should think, as nearly a freethinker as anyone could be whose mind seldom turned upon the subject. She went to church, but disliked equally those who aired either religion or irreligion. ①

Alethea rails against matrimony—not against men. Overton is deeply fond of Alethea. He "admires her more and more as the best, kindest, wittiest, most lovable...and the handsomest woman"② he has ever seen. She is equally fond of him, and between the two prevailed "the most perfect sympathy and understanding between us". ③ Overton and Alethea, just as Butler and Miss Savage, share an untold story. Unconventionally this deep friendship does not lead to marriage, although both also knew that neither of them would marry anyone else. ④

Although Overton admits that "it is impossible for me to explain how it was

① *Ibid.*, Ch. 32, p. 157.

② *Ibid.*, Ch. 18, p. 90.

③ *Ibid.*, Ch. 18, p. 91.

④ *Ibid.*, Ch. 18, p. 91. In continuing, Butler says: "I had asked her to marry me a dozen times over; having said this much I will say no more upon a point which is in no way necessary for the development of my story. For the last few years there had been difficulties in the way of our meeting, and I had not seen her, though, as I have said, keeping up a close correspondence with her."

that she and I never married," the answer lies in the author's intentions.[①] Alethea is a positive influence on young Ernest, who throughout his life frequently thinks of her kindness. Moreover, by following her advice "kissing the soil", Ernest finds a complete new direction in the trajectory of childhood. Unlike his father, Ernest does not see women as primarily sexual creatures, subordinate to and economically dependent on man. Apart from his aunt, Ernest has no experience with women. Since his childhood, he has been prepared for a vocation that frowns upon the sexuality. This explains Ernest's predicament:

> This was deplorable. The only way out of it that Ernest could see was that he should get married at once. But then he did not know any one whom he wanted to marry. He did not know any woman, in fact, whom he would not rather die than marry. It had been one of Theobald's and Christina's main objects to keep him out of the way of women, and they had so far succeeded that women had become to him mysterious, inscrutable objects to be tolerated when it was impossible to avoid them, but never to be sought out or encouraged. As for any man loving, or even being at all fond of any woman, he supposed it was so, but he believed the greater number of those who professed such sentiments were liars. Now, however, it was clear that he had hoped against hope too long, and that the only thing to do was to go and ask the first woman who would listen to him to come and be married to him as soon as possible.[②]

Theobald's and Christina's interest in keeping Ernest away from women represents the Victorian enforcement of sexual segregation. Women were economically dependent on men in Victorian society and financial support was the main reason for women to marry. But why did a man like Ernest get married at that time?

---

① *Ibid.*, Ch. 18, p. 91.

② *Ibid.*, Ch. 51, p. 270.

Ernest marries Ellen out of subservience to Christian morality, which implicates pessimistic prospects of his marriage. ① As Peter Morton argued: "If the game were being played out to Weismannian rules, Ernest would succumb; instead he resists and struggles to remark himself into something nearer society's desire-not his own heart's." ②

① Annette R. Federico. "Samuel Butler's *The Way of All Flesh*: Rewriting the Family." In *English Literature in Transition, 1880 – 1920*, Vol. 38, No. 4, 1995, pp. 476.

② Peter Morton. "Butler on Heredity." In *The Vital Science: Biology and the Literary Imagination: 1860 – 1900*. London: Allen and Unwin, 1984, p. 188.

Chapter Three Ainsi va toute evolution—Butler's utilitarian taste①

3.1 Butler and God

It is notable that Butler writes in his *Note-Books*, "God and Man—to love God is to have good health, good looks, good sense, experience, a kindly nature and a fair balance of cash in hand."② It is thus interesting to explore the role of God in Butler's world. Butler, like Ernest, was born into a family whose parents lived for the love of God. Ernest's mother Christina, as well as his father Theobald, was of the mind that "Religion... had long since attained its final development, nor could it enter into the heart of reasonable man to conceive any faith more perfect than was inculcated by the Church of England."③

Butler used Ernest Pontifex to illustrate the variation introduced by an offspring who improves on his heredity by deliberately altering the climate of his Christian

---

① The French version of *The Way of All Flesh* is translated as "Ainsi Va Toute Chair". See Samuel Butler. *Ainsivatoute chair*. Traduit de l'anglais par Valéry Larbaud. Paris: Gallimard, 1936.

② Samuel Butler. *The Note-Books of Samuel Butler*. Edited with a preface and biographical statement by Henry Festing Jones. London: A. C. Fifield, 1912. Edition in use: IndyPublish edition, 2007, p. 22.

③ Samuel Butler. *The Way of All Flesh*. London: Grant Richards, 1903; published posthumously. Edited with an introduction by V. S. Pritchett, London: Penguin English Library, 2012, Ch. 16 p. 83.

upbringing. [①] Sally Shuttleworth explains that "Love of God becomes a mode of parental self-justification that takes away any need for self-questioning or doubt, creating 'the atmosphere of lying and self-laudatory hallucination' within which Ernest was raised." [②] Theobald wishes to stamp out Ernest's "true self", as his had been, suffering the unrelenting pressure of paternal rule in a "God fearing family":

> I wish he was not so fond of music, it will interfere with his Latin and Greek. I will stop it as much as I can. Why, when he was translating Livy the other day he slipped out Handel's name in mistake for Hannibal's, and his mother tells me he knows half the tunes in the "Messiah" by heart. What should a boy of his age know about the "Messiah"? If I had shown half as many dangerous tendencies when I was a boy, my father would have apprenticed me to a greengrocer, of that I'm very sure. [③]

With his selfhood suppressed, Theobald's "past self", his heritage, comes to dominate him and he seeks to replicate this with his children. One of the parental rules in this "God-fearing family" is that "the first signs of self-will must be carefully looked for, and plucked up by the roots at once before they had time to grow". [④] As Theobald failed to stand up to the weight of his own father, he leaves his offspring unable to develop his or her selfhood. In Theobald, we can see Ernest's future if Ernest has no strength to rebel. Thus Theobald's failures are seen as capable of ruining Ernest's life. Sally Shuttleworth

---

① U. C. Knoepflmacher. *Religious Humanism and the Victorian Novel: George Eliot, Walter Pater, and Samuel Butler.* Princeton: Princeton University Press, 1965, pp. 233-234

② Sally Shuttleworth. "Evolutionary Psychology and *The Way of All Flesh.*" In *Samuel Butler: Victorian Against the Grain, A Critical Overview.* Edited by James G. Paradis. Toronto, Buffalo and London: University of Toronto Press, 2007. p. 150. We know that all things work together for good to them that love God (Rom. viii, 28).

③ Samuel Butler. *The Way of All Flesh.* London: Grant Richards, 1903; published posthumously. Edited with an introduction by V. S. Pritchett, London: Penguin English Library, 2012, Ch. 29, p. 144.

④ *Ibid.*, Ch. 20, p. 103.

infers thus:

> Paradoxically, given the explicit anticlerical nature of the text, Butler draws repeatedly on the Old Testament to express his sense of the unremitting power of biological inheritance: the sins of the fathers will be visited on the sons. Theobald meanwhile meditates, as he returns from delivering Ernest to school, on the tenth plague of Egypt (the slaughter of the first born): "if the little Egyptians had been anything like Ernest, the plague must have been a very doubtful one". The reflection is simultaneously comic and chilling: the tenth plague becomes an expression of the Victorian paterfamilias's infanticidal impulses. ①

The Old Testament texts, which dominate Ernest's childhood, ironically have a subversive influence on this Victorian family. Fortunately, the young Ernest prefers to define his own moral conduct instead of following the religion of his parents. He questions:

> Is there any religion whose followers can be pointed to as distinctly more amiable and trustworthy than those of any other? If so, this should be enough. I find the nicest and best people generally profess no religion at all, but are ready to like the best men of all religions. ②

Unfortunately, influenced by such God-fearing circumstances for a long period in Ernest's life, his belated discovery of his abilities as a student at Cambridge

---

① Sally Shuttleworth. "Evolutionary Psychology and *The Way of All Flesh*." In *Samuel Butler: Victorian Against the Grain, A Critical Overview*. Edited by James G. Paradis. Toronto, Buffalo and London: University of Toronto Press, 2007, pp. 153-154.

② Samuel Butler. *The Note-Books of Samuel Butler*. Edited with a preface and biographical statement by Henry Festing Jones. London: A. C. Fifield, 1912. Edition in use: IndyPublish edition, 2007, p. 23.

and his growth are likely, as Overton observes, to be "nipped ... by a late frost."① Later, the novel demonstrates again the severe handicap of a young man who enters the practical world insufficiently prepared. Like Butler himself, soon after graduating from Cambridge and being ordained as a curate, Ernest is assigned to a London parish. Pryer, the senior curate, is a conservative whose High Church views gain Ernest's support, and they soon agree on founding a School of Spiritual Pathology.② Having caught the fever of evangelism, Ernest welcomes ordination as a curate only to save people's souls. Cynically, Ernest's only angelic qualities are an apparently limitless naiveté and blind trust in anyone to whom he takes a fancy. Worst of all, Ernest allows Pryer to manage his financial resources, only to end up being deceived when Pryer disappears with all his money.

So instead of saving souls, Ernest finds himself sentenced to six months in prison. He decides while in prison that his fellow countrymen must be persuaded for their own good to stop believing in the supernatural element in Christianity.③

---

① Samuel Butler. *The Way of All Flesh*. London: Grant Richards, 1903; published posthumously. Edited with an introduction by V. S. Pritchett, London: Penguin English Library edition, 2012, Ch. 51, p. 267.

② "They intend to treat people's souls in the manner that physicians treat bodies and thereby bring church practices up-to-date with developments in the field of science." See online source: http://www.cliffsnotes.com/literature/w/the-way-of-all-flesh/summary-and-analysis/chapters-5155

③ While these reflections are rolling upon Ernest's mind: "Looking at the matter from a practical point of view he thought the Archbishop of Canterbury afforded the most promising key to the situation. It lay between him and the Pope. The Pope was perhaps best in theory, but in practice the Archbishop of Canterbury would do sufficiently well. If he could only manage to sprinkle a pinch of salt, as it were, on the Archbishop's tail, he might convert the whole Church of England to free thought by a coup de main. There must be an amount of cogency which even an Archbishop—an Archbishop whose perceptions had never been quickened by imprisonment for assault—would not be able to withstand. When brought face to face with the facts, as he, Ernest, could arrange them; his Grace would have no resource but to admit them; being an honourable man he would at once resign his Archbishopric, and Christianity would become extinct in England within a few months' time." See Samuel Butler. *The Way of All Flesh*. London: Grant Richards, 1903; published posthumously. Edited with an introduction by V. S. Pritchett, London: Penguin English Library, 2012, Ch. 65, p. 332.

There is a tug-of war within Ernest:

> You are surrounded on every side by lies which would deceive even the elect, if the elect were not generally so uncommonly wide awake; the self of which you are conscious, your reasoning and reflecting self, will believe these lies and bid you act in accordance with them. This conscious self of yours, Ernest, is a prig begotten of prigs and trained in priggishness; I will not allow it to shape your actions, though it will doubtless shape your words for many a year to come. Your papa is not here to beat you now; this is a change in the conditions of your existence, and should be followed by changed actions. Obey me, your true self, and things will go tolerably well with you, but only listen to that outward and visible old husk of yours which is called your father, and I will rend you in pieces even unto the third and fourth generation as one who has hated God; for I, Ernest, am the God who made you. ①

Ernest, being persuaded with his inarticulate feelings, which are translated as words as above, this, is also the true thing that he wants to insist on in practice. Ernest must divest himself from the conscious "reasoning and reflecting self" and follow instead his "true self", the "God who made him". ② God or Butler's God here has been transmuted into a progressive force of evolution. It is his inheritance, accumulated over past generations, that allows Ernest to unconsciously access his "true self" and lead him later to cut his parents out of his life.

When Theobald and Christina confront him upon his release, Ernest curtly tells them to think of him as one who is dead and asks them to forget him. Instead, he very soon visits the only person in whom he can confide, his friend and godfather Edward Overton. When Overton has heard all about Ernest's prison

① *Ibid.*, Ch. 31, pp. 153-154.

② *Ibid.*, Ch. 31, pp. 153-154.

meditations, he mulls over the matter for a long time and concludes:

> It occurs to me that in reality he was wanting to do the very last thing which it would have entered into his head to think of wanting. I mean that he was trying to give up father and mother for Christ's sake. He would have said he was giving them up because he thought they hindered him in the pursuit of his truest and most lasting happiness. ①

But he then asks himself:

> Granted, but what is this if it is not Christ? What is Christ if He is not this? He who takes the highest and most self-respecting view of his own welfare which it is in his power to conceive, and adheres to it in spite of conventionality, is a Christian whether he knows it and calls himself one, or whether he does not. A rose is not the less a rose because it does not know its own name. ②

Ernest, determined to be independent, reaches the conclusion that he must give up his parents for Christ's sake, and he does just that. In making a complete break with his parents, Ernest executes his conviction that the highest possible religious principle is the pursuit of self-satisfaction, for Butler believes that "[t]he true laws of God are the laws of our own well-being."③ Consequently, Ernest makes a fresh start by redefining Christianity to serve his own interests and affirms that this is the only tenable philosophy by which one could live.

---

① *Ibid.*, Ch. 68, p. 347.

② *Ibid.*, Ch. 68, p. 347.

③ Samuel Butler. *The Note-Books of Samuel Butler*. Edited with a preface and biographical statement by Henry Festing Jones. London: A. C. Fifield, 1912. Edition in use: IndyPublish edition, 2007, p. 16.

In later chapters of *The Way of All Flesh*, Overton points out his disappointment with the Church of England, which "looks with no friendly eyes upon the theory of evolution or Descent with Modification". ① Butler has already suggested why in an earlier passage of the novel, when Theobald's unquestioning attitude and hypocrisy lead Overton to declare that, "It is his profession to know how to shut his eyes to things that were inconvenient—no clergyman could keep his benefice for a month if he could not do this." ② Ernest is the pitiable son of a cruel and self-righteous Anglican clergyman. It is no coincidence that Butler himself was the son of an Anglican cleric, once again reinforcing the autobiographical nature of the novel.

We can see how Ernest grows, matures and develops in *The Way of All Flesh*. Though at birth Ernest is endowed with many positive qualities common to children, such as cheerfulness and self-confidence, over time these qualities are stamped out by his bullying father, so that by the age of 20 he has utterly lost sight of his "true self". This he will recover only by abandoning the path traced out for him by his father to map his own way of life. ③ Therefore *The Way of All Flesh* depicts of two sets of forces, one set (the conscious self) furthering Ernest's deterioration, the other set (the true self or unconscious self) contributing to his recovery. The immediate cause of Ernest's decline is his father, Theobald, who bullies him into becoming a clergyman. Going further down the family tree, we recall Theobald's own father, the miserly publisher who had broken his son's spirit. And throughout the Pontifex line looms the Anglican Church, a vastly more powerful force. As presented in *The Way of All Flesh*, the Church, staffed by careerist clergymen with no interest in spiritual salvation, exists not to guide the wayward nor to comfort the distraught but to maintain an

① Samuel Butler. *The Way of All Flesh*. London: Grant Richards, 1903; published posthumously. Edited with an introduction by V. S. Pritchett, London: Penguin English Library, 2012, Ch. 83, p. 446.

② *Ibid.*, Ch. 44, p. 224.

③ Ordination, marriage and respectability as a clergyman.

unjust social order.[①] In a sense, the Anglican Church espouses a strictly hierarchical view of human existence—God through the Bible dictates to the clergyman, the clergyman dictates to the parent, and the parent dictates to the child, with the entire system demanding blind obedience by subordinate parties. In *The Way of All Flesh*, the harmfulness of church doctrine is evident; the parent is duty-bound under all circumstances to crush the child's will, the ultimate justification being that obedience is a virtue pleasing to God.

The novel depicts important social institutions, such as the family, the Anglican Church and the educational systems as unjust and un-nurturing. Nonetheless, *The Way of All Flesh* is far from pessimistic. The novel ends up with Ernest not defeated but triumphant, and what is more, in a state of emotional, intellectual and spiritual equilibrium. How Ernest reaches this state is the novel's focus of interest. It is achieved neither by chance nor a miracle. In fact, Butler does not believe in miracles, just as he was skeptical about the Resurrection of Jesus Christ.[②] For "the essence of a miracle", as he argued "lay not in the fact that means had been dispensed with, but in the adoption of means

---

① "The set has been steadily in one direction. A few men who knew what they wanted made cats' paws of the Christmas and the Charlottes, and the Christmas and the Charlottes made cats' paws of the Mrs Goodhews and the old Miss Wrights, and Mrs Goodhews and old Miss Wrights told the Mr Goodhews and young Miss Wrights what they should do, and when the Mr Goodhews and the young Miss Wrights did it the little Goodhews and the rest of the spiritual flock did as they did, and the Theobalds went for nothing; step by step, day by day, year by year, parish by parish, diocese by diocese this was how it was done." See Samuel Butler. *The Way of All Flesh.* London: Grant Richards, 1903; published posthumously, as edited by R. A. Streatfield. London: A. C. Fifield, 1908. Edited with an introduction by V. S. Pritchett, London: Penguin English Library edition, 2012, Ch. 83, p. 446.

② Butler wrote a book questioned about the evidence for The Resurrection of Jesus Christ. See Samuel Butler. *The Evidence for the Resurrection of Jesus Christ as Given by the Four Evangelists, Critically Examined.* London: William and Norgate, 1865.

to a great end that had not been available without interference." [1] Having fallen as far as an honest man can fall—shunned by his parents, disgraced in his profession and imprisoned for a sordid crime—Ernest takes stock of himself, working out how he, an unselfish man who only wanted to do good, ended up a felon and an outcast. In brief, Ernest grasps that he has trusted too much and thought too little, mindlessly adopting his father's understanding inherited from the Anglican Church rather than reasoning on his own, especially on the matter of evolution.

The following paragraph in which Ernest thinks over his life after death is interesting:

> Soon after his father and mother had left him Ernest dropped asleep over a book which Mrs Jay had given him, and he did not awake till dusk. Then he sat down on a stool in front of the fire, which showed pleasantly in the late January twilight, and began to muse. He felt weak, feeble, ill at ease and unable to see his way out of the innumerable troubles that were before him. Perhaps, he said to himself, he might even die, but this, far from being an end of his troubles, would prove the beginning of new ones; for at the best he would only go to Grandpapa Pontifex and Grandmamma Allaby, and though they would perhaps be more easy to get on with than Papa and Mamma, yet they were undoubtedly not so really good, and were more worldly; moreover they were grown-up people—especially Grandpapa Pontifex, who so far as he could understand had been very much grown-up, and he did not know why, but there was always something that kept him from loving any grown-up people very much—except one or two of the servants, who had indeed been as nice as anything that he could imagine. Besides even if he were to die and go to

[1] Samuel Butler. *The Way of All Flesh*. London: Grant Richards, 1903; published posthumously. Edited with an introduction by V. S. Pritchett, London: Penguin English Library, 2012, Ch. 21, p. 106.

> Heaven he supposed he should have to complete his education somewhere. ①

For Butler, death is not to be thought of as the final interruption of the identity of individuals existing exclusively in their memories. Personality cannot be cut off by death. P. N. Furbank perfectly illustrates Butler's assumption: "There is ... a continuous identity between the child and the man, and the embryo and the child... Identity...is to be seen to continue uninterrupted from generation to generation—and if identity, then memory." ② Furthermore, Gillian Beer argues that Butler removes the barriers of birth and death and imagines memory freely traversing present and past identity, which manifests itself in unknowable yet implicit future forms. ③ This is in contrast with the body, which as the President Gurgoyle in *Erewhon Revisited* points out, is unconscious of its own processes and is at its most unconscious when most healthy. He declares: "The part of our bodily life that enters into our consciousness is very small as compared with that of which we have no consciousness." ④ Entering into his argument about continuance through life and after death, he continues:

> A man, we will say, has written a book which delights or displeases thousands of whom he knows nothing, and who know nothing of him. The book, we will suppose, has considerable, or at any rate some influence on the action of these people. Let us suppose the writer fast asleep while others are enjoying his work, and acting in consequence of it, perhaps at long distances from him. Which is his truest life—the one he is leading in them,

---

① *Ibid.*, Ch. 29, p. 142.

② P. N. Furbank. *Samuel Butler (1835 – 1902)*. Cambridge: Cambridge University Press, 1948, pp. 54-55.

③ Gillian Beer. "Butler, Memory and the Future." In *Samuel Butler: Victorian Against the Grain, A Critical Overview*. Edited by James G. Paradis. Toronto, Buffalo and London: University of Toronto Press, 2007, p. 51.

④ Samuel Butler. *Erewhon Revisited*. London: A. C. Fifield, 1901, p. 130.

> or that equally unconscious life residing in his own sleeping body? Can there be a doubt that the vicarious life is the more efficient. [1]

The Erewhonian view of death is deeply sympathetic to their author. Memory carries those who are dead into the future through others.

In *The Way of All Flesh*, there is a highly ironical scene when the "converted" Ernest faces his dying mother. Christina is ill and frightened by the approach of death. Although genuinely cheered by Ernest's return, she "often said how thankful she was to be surrounded on her death-bed by a family so happy, so God-fearing, so united". [2] She begins to wonder about the remission of her worldly sins and worries whether she will get a pass to heaven on the Day of Judgment. Christina "hinted that she considered his [Theobald's] professional reputation was at stake; it would never do for his own wife to fail in securing at any rate a pass". [3] Consequently, "this was touching Theobald on a tender spot". [4] Neither Theobald nor Joey, Ernest's brother and also a clergyman, succeed in allaying Christina's fears. It is left to Ernest, a renegade clergyman and "convert" to vitality, to listen to his mother's confession and sooth her:

> Ernest interrupted: "My dear mother," he said, "you are ill and your mind is unstrung; others can now judge better about you than you can; I assure you that to me you seem to have been the most devotedly unselfish wife and mother that ever lived. Even if you have not literally given up all for Christ's sake, you have done so practically as far as it was in your power, and more than this is not required of anyone. I believe you will not only be a saint, but

---

① *Ibid.*, pp. 131-132.

② Samuel Butler. *The Way of All Flesh.* London: Grant Richards, 1903; published posthumously. Edited with an introduction by V. S. Pritchett, London: Penguin English Library, 2012, Ch. 83, p. 441.

③ *Ibid.*, Ch. 83, p. 441.

④ *Ibid.*, Ch. 83, p. 441.

> a very distinguished one." At these words Christina brightened. "You give me hope, you give me hope," she cried, and dried her eyes. She made him assure her over and over again that this was his solemn conviction; she did not care about being a distinguished saint now; she would be quite content to be among the meanest who actually got into heaven, provided she could make sure of escaping that awful Hell. The fear of this evidently was omnipresent with her, and in spite of all Ernest could say he did not quite dispel it. She was rather ungrateful, I must confess, for after more than an hour's consolation from Ernest she prayed for him that he might have every blessing in this world, inasmuch as she always feared that he was the only one of her children whom she should never meet in heaven; but she was then wandering, and was hardly aware of his presence; her mind in fact was reverting to states in which it had been before her illness. ①

Ernest, as the beneficiary of the vitality that his mother has stifled throughout her life, is able to allay her fears. Ernest possesses the optimism of this vitality, therefore he seems to be more merciful than his clergyman father. However, Christina does not know that the immortality promised to her by Ernest does not mean the Christian resurrection from the dead. In accordance with his memory theories, Butler believes in the possibility of immortality and even a mode of resurrection. ② As he confidently recorded in his *Note-Books*: "Life is the

① *Ibid.*, Ch. 83, p. 443.

② Butler conceives a threefold immortality: "First, men are immortal through the memory they have passed to their offspring. Second, immortality may be achieved by men whose lives, thoughts, and deeds come to live in and inspire the lives of other men. Finally, Butler declared that there could be no death in a universe of creative life. The living matter of our bodies reentered the universe at large.... Though our personal consciousness was dissolved, its constituent parts lived in the ever-evolving grandeur of the living universe and might again in the future enter into a human consciousness." See Frank Miller Turner. "Samuel Butler: The Man of Temper." In *Between Science and Religion: The Reaction to Scientific Naturalism in Late Victorian England.* New Haven: Yale University Press, 1974, p. 199.

gathering of waves to a head, at death they break into a million fragments each one of which, however, is absorbed at one into the sea of life and helps to form a later generation which comes rolling on till it too breaks. "① Thus Christina's redemption can be ensured. As U C. Knoepflmacher asserts, "In the shape of

---

① Samuel Butler. *The Note-Books of Samuel Butler*. Edited with a preface and biographical statement by Henry Festing Jones. London: A. C. Fifield, 1912. Edition in use: IndyPublish edition, 2007, p. 7. It is significant that Butler's point of views instead of being spiritual, is material. During the 1870s Butler accepted the protoplasmic theory and believed that life and mind existed only where protoplasm was present. As Butler writes: "I pointed out another consequence, which, again, was cruelly the reverse of what the promoters of the protoplasm movement might be supposed anxious to arrive at, in a series of articles which appeared in the *Examiner* during the summer of 1879, and showed that if protoplasm were held to be the sole seat of life, then this unity in the substance vivifying all, both animals and plants, must be held as uniting them into a single corporation or body—especially when their community of descent is borne in mind—more effectually than any merely superficial separation into individuals can be held to disunite them, and that thus protoplasm must be seen as the life of the world—as a vast body corporate, never dying till the earth itself shall pass away. This came practically to saying that protoplasm was God Almighty, who, of all the forms open to Him, had chosen this singularly unattractive one as the channel through which to make Himself manifest in the flesh by taking our nature upon Him, and animating us with His own Spirit. Our biologists, in fact, were fast nearing the conception of a God who was both personal and material, but who could not be made to square with pantheistic notions inasmuch as no provision was made for the inorganic world; and, indeed, they seem to have become alarmed at the grotesqueness of the position in which they must ere long have found themselves, for in the autumn of 1879 the boom collapsed, and thenceforth the leading reviews and magazines have known protoplasm no more. About the same time bathybius, which at one time bade fair to supplant it upon the throne of popularity, died suddenly, as I am told, at Norwich, under circumstances which did not transpire, nor has its name, so far as I am aware, been ever again mentioned." See Samuel Butler. *Luck, or Cunning as the Main Means of Organic Modification*? London: Trübner, 1887. The Echo Library edition, 2007, Ch. IX, pp. 70-71. Henry Festing Jones writes, "He often spoke of his religion as 'a modest Pantheism', and, if he had rewritten the articles, I think the re-casting would have been confined to showing in what way his idea of Pantheism differed from that usually underlying the word; and to his pointing out that, although we cannot see the bowl and the water as part of the goldfish, yet that their material is not without intelligence, and that God, who is Life, is in everything." See Henry Festing Jones. *Samuel Butler: Author of Erewhon (1835 – 1902), A Memoir*. London: Macmillan and Co., Limited. 1919, vol. I, p. 303.

Ernest's future 'selves', a generation of better Pontifexes, Christina can live on. Though not a saint, she is among the mean who are allowed to enter Butler's evolutionary heaven."①

For Butler, each organism perceives its present condition in terms of inherited memory and creation occurs when that memory is applied. Once assimilated into memory, these creative actions appear as natural law. They are never perfectly uniform nor are they eternal, for in future they will be modified by the same kind of evolutionary development. Thus, for Butler, evolution stems from the fulfillment of primitive desire.② In the concluding chapter of *Unconscious Memory*, Butler asserts that inherited memory assures that each purposive step would become cumulative and thus a succession of deterministic cycles would not ensure:

> There is life infinitely lower and more minute than any which our most powerful microscopes reveal to us, but let us leave this upon one side and begin with the amoeba. Let us suppose that this structureless morsel of protoplasm is, for all its structurelessness, composed of an infinite number of living molecules, each one of them with hopes and fears of its own, and all dwelling together like Tekke Turcomans, of whom we read that they live for plunder only, and that each man of them is entirely independent, acknowledging no constituted authority, but that some among them exercise a tacit and undefined influence over the others. Let us suppose these molecules capable of memory, both in their capacity as individuals, and as societies, and able to transmit their memories to their descendants, from the traditions

① U. C. Knoepflmacher. *Religious Humanism and the Victorian Novel: George Eliot, Walter Pater, and Samuel Butler.* Princeton: Princeton University Press, 1965, p. 277. Here he say: Thus, for a brief moment, Butler suggests that the vitalist creed of Ernest and the "Christ-Ideal" of his mother can merge one into another; that they are, in effect, one and the same.

② For Butler, this is also the significance of design.

> of the dimmest past to the experiences of their own lifetime. Some of these societies will remain simple, as having had no history, but to the greater number unfamiliar, and therefore striking, incidents will from time to time occur, which, when they do not disturb memory so greatly as to kill, will leave their impression upon it. The body or society will remember these incidents, and be modified by them in its conduct, and therefore more or less in its internal arrangements, which will tend inevitably to specialisation. This memory of the most striking events of varied lifetimes I maintain, with Professor Hering, to be the differentiating cause, which, accumulated in countless generations, has led up from the amoeba to man. If there had been no such memory, the amoeba of one generation would have exactly resembled time amoeba of the preceding, and a perfect cycle would have been established; the modifying effects of an additional memory in each generation have made the cycle into a spiral, and into a spiral whose eccentricity, in the outset hardly perceptible, is becoming greater and greater with increasing longevity and more complex social and mechanical inventions. ①

Hence Butler supposes the existence of the protoplasm as living molecules, containing and transferring memories, which leads to further development through evolution under changed conditions in accordance to new needs and desires. The world that Butler envisioned is one "without fixed entities in which all living things, at least in part, created their own essence from the circumstances of their existence. Such evolution was self-determining action in touch with the unseen kingdom."②

In *The Way of All Flesh*, by the time Ernest is ordained, he has learned to

① Samuel Butler. *Unconscious Memory*. London: David Bogue, 1880. The Echo Library edition 2006, Ch. XIII, p. 99.

② Frank Miller Turner. "Samuel Butler: The Man of Temper." In *Between Science and Religion: The Reaction to Scientific Naturalism in Late Victorian England*. New Haven: Yale University Press, 1974, p. 192.

distinguish between high and low Anglicanism, Anglicanism and Roman Catholicism, and ritualism and evangelicalism. What is Butler most concerned about was not so much the condemnation of Anglicanism as the exaltation of his own version of Christianity. ① As we know, all religions require faith. In effect, the Anglican Church requires adherents to eschew rationality, accepting even those Church teachings that defy science or logic. In the novel, the church doctrine is painted as a hive of unreason and incoherence. In place of this blind religious faith, Butler proposes faith in one's self. Ernest's intellectual pilgrimage leads him ultimately to a faith that is life-affirming, one that embraces pleasure and rejects suffering, as God is within each individual. Butler's concept of God, therefore, caps his view of evolution. Butler believed in a beloved and worshipped Unknown God that exists harmoniously with men and the material world. ② This God provides "the instinct of the universe", and God's "conscious life reached its earthly maturity in man". ③ Moreover, this God depends upon man, "as man cannot live without God in the world, so neither can God live in

---

① Anglicanism as portrayed in the novel is arrogant in its demands and contemptuous in its offerings, demanding absolute faith while offering only a mishmash of unscientific and self-contradictory teachings.

② "[We] enthrone Him upon the wings of birds, on the petals of flowers, on the faces of our friends, and upon whatever we most delight in of all that lives upon the earth. We then can not only love Him, but we can do that without which love has neither power nor sweetness, but is a phantom only, an impersonal person, a vain stretching forth of arms towards something that can never fill them—we can express our love and have it expressed to us in return. And this not in the uprearing of stone temples—for the Lord dwelleth [sic] in temples made with other organs than hands-nor yet in the cleansing of our hearts, but in the caress bestowed upon horse and dog, and kisses upon the lips of those we love." Samuel Butler. *The God Known and The God Unknown.* London, A. C. Fifield, 1909, Ch. VII, p. 67.

③ Frank Miller Turner. "Samuel Butler: The Man of Temper." In *Between Science and Religion: The Reaction to Scientific Naturalism in Late Victorian England.* New Haven: Yale University Press, 1974, p. 197.

this world without mankind."① In Butler's universe, creation and evolution, God and nature, mind and matter, life and death—all theses contradictions develop harmoniously and as a function of the other, and "the elements in each pair were so intrinsically related that neither could exist without the other".②

---

① *Erewhon Revisited.* First published in 1901. London: Jonathan Cape, 1925, pp. 150-151. On this point, Frank Miller Turner comments, "Butler's final thought represented an attempt to suggest the presence of a limited God who required the free cooperation of man in the evolution of the world." See Frank Miller Turner. "Samuel Butler: The Man of Temper." In *Between Science and Religion: The Reaction to Scientific Naturalism in Late Victorian England.* New Haven: Yale University Press, 1974, p. 197.

② Frank Miller Turner. "Samuel Butler: The Man of Temper." In *Between Science and Religion: The Reaction to Scientific Naturalism in Late Victorian England.* New Haven: Yale University Press, 1974, p. 190.

3.2 Vice and virtue

The Way of All Flesh also presents an orthodox view of vice and virtue, both of which I will analyze in the following sections. Vice and virtue, Butler argued should not be seen as polar opposites because:

> There is no useful virtue which has not some alloy of vice, and hardly any vice, if any, which carries not with it a little dash of virtue; virtue and vice are like life and death, or mind and matter—things which cannot exist without being qualified by their opposite. ①

For Butler, vice and virtue are like mind and matter, each work as a function of the other. In addition, Butler believes that nothing is cast in stone and everything evolves. In this section, I will discuss what Butler's true "faith" is.

Ernest's parents abide by the following rule in raising their children: "For no duty could be more important than that of teaching a child to obey its parents in all things. ② Theobald and Christina are convinced that their duty is to train up

① Samuel Butler. *The Way of All Flesh*. London: Grant Richards, 1903; published posthumously. Edited with an introduction by V. S. Pritchett, London: Penguin English Library, 2012, Ch. 19, pp. 98-99. In continuing, Butler writes, "The most absolute life contains death, and the corpse is still in many respects living; so also it has been said, 'If thou, Lord, wilt be extreme to mark what is done amiss,' which shows that even the highest ideal we can conceive will yet admit so much compromise with vice as shall countenance the poor abuses of the time, if they are not too outrageous. That vice pays homage to virtue is notorious; we call this hypocrisy; there should be a word found for the homage which virtue not unfrequently pays, or at any rate would be wise in paying, to vice."

② *Ibid.*, Ch. 20, p. 102.

their children in the way they should go. This necessitates that "[T]he first signs of self-will must be carefully looked for, and plucked up by the roots at once before they had time to grow."① Under such circumstances, children are surprisingly resilient, as Overton explains in Darwinian terms:

> Young people have a marvelous faculty of either dying or adapting themselves to circumstances. Even if they are unhappy—very unhappy—it is astonishing how easily they can be prevented from finding it out, or at any rate from attributing it to any other cause than their own sinfulness.②

This is not, however, an invocation of the survival of the fittest. Overton simply describes children's unhappy state in a world where "children's own perceptions are stifled at birth and replaced by the parental view of their own worthlessness and moral inferiority".③ Duty, as a Victorian imperative, is assumed to operate from children to parents. Overton suggests that the church catechism is in part to blame: "That work was written too exclusively from the parental point of view; the person who wrote it did not get a few children to come in and help him."④ Butler denounces fiercely how parents abuse the moral influence they exercise

① *Ibid.*, Ch. 20, p. 103.

② *Ibid.*, Ch. 6, p. 30

③ Sally Shuttleworth. "Evolutionary Psychology and *The Way of All Flesh.*" In *Samuel Butler: Victorian Against the Grain, A Critical Overview.* Edited by James G. Paradis. Toronto: University of Toronto, 2007, p. 151.

④ Samuel Butler. *The Way of All Flesh.* London: Grant Richards, 1903; published posthumously. Edited with an introduction by V. S. Pritchett, London: Penguin English Library, 2012, Ch. 7, p. 36.

over their children. ①

C. E. M. Joad maintains that "the whole function of the parent in his professional capacity is to impress upon the child a sense of his own sin and of his parent's virtue. ② Herewe should take note of an important conversation between Ernest and Overton in *The Way of All Flesh*, whereby Overton talks about the duty of a favourable father as he sees it:

> It was not much that was wanted. To make no mysteries where Nature has made none, to bring his conscience under something like reasonable control, to give Ernest his head a little more, to ask fewer questions, and to give him pocket money with a desire that it should be spent upon menus plaisirs...③

Ernest laughs and he asks, "Why it is the whole duty of a father, but it is the

---

① Butler claims: "To parents who wish to lead a quiet life I would say: Tell your children that they are naughty—much naughtier than most children. Point to the young people of some acquaintances as models of perfection and impress your own children with a deep sense of their own inferiority. You carry so many more guns than they do that they cannot fight you. This is called moral influence, and it will enable you to bounce them as much as you please. They think you know and they will not have yet caught you lying often enough to suspect that you are not the unworldly and scrupulously truthful person which you represent yourself to be; nor yet will they know how great a coward you are, nor how soon you will run away if they fight you with persistency and judgment. You keep the dice and throw them both for your children and yourself. Load them then, for you can easily manage to stop your children from examining them. Tell them how singularly indulgent you are; insist on the incalculable benefit you conferred upon them, firstly in bringing them into the world at all, but more particularly in bringing them into it as your own children rather than anyone else's [...] You hold all the trump cards, or if you do not you can filch them; if you play them with anything like judgment you will find yourselves heads of happy, united, God-fearing families [...] True, your children will probably find out all about it someday, but not until too late to be of much service to them or inconvenience to yourself". See *Ibid.*, Ch. 6, pp. 30-31.

② C. E. M. Joad. *Samuel Butler (1835 – 1902)*. London: L. Parsons, 1924, p. 114.

③ Samuel Butler. *The Way of All Flesh.* London: Grant Richards, 1903; published posthumously. Edited with an introduction by V. S. Pritchett, London: Penguin English Library, 2012, Ch. 44, p. 224.

mystery-making which is the worst evil. If people would dare to speak to one another unreservedly, there would be a good deal less sorrow in the world a hundred years hence."[①] We may ask, if the fulfillment of duty does not mean to be surly and virtuous, what then is the measure of true virtue? "For most men and most circumstances," Overton's answer, "pleasure—tangible material prosperity in this world," is "the safest test of virtue".[②] He states that "progress has ever been through the pleasures rather than through the extreme sharp virtues".[③]

Butler declares, "To me it seems that those who are happy in this world are better and more lovable people than those who are not."[④] Happy people are generally well-liked and a happy individual gives pleasure to others. Butler proceeds to show that the pursuit of pleasure enables the offspring to adjust successfully to ancestral memory. For Butler, what is morally right is that which provides the means of pleasing oneself. He would like to see children taught things that they really like instead of what adults think they should like. The individual concludes that its means of pleasure is the same as ancestor, so as to avoid pain. Butler insists that "the seeking all reasonable pleasure and avoiding all pain can be honourably avoided" is the most important duty.[⑤] He expounds:

> Being in this world is it not our most obvious business to make the most of it—to observe what things do *bona fide* tend to long life and comfort, and to act accordingly? All animals, except man, know that the principal business of life is to enjoy it—and they do enjoy it as much as man and other circumstances will allow. He has spent his life best who has enjoyed it most;

---

① *Ibid.*, Ch. 44, p. 224.

② *Ibid.*, Ch. 19, p. 99.

③ *Ibid.*, Ch. 19, p. 99.

④ *Ibid.*, Ch. 26, p. 126.

⑤ *Ibid.*, Ch. 7, p. 36.

> God will take care that we do not enjoy it any more than is good for us. Goodness is naught unless it tends towards old age and sufficiency of means. I speak broadly and *exceptis excipiendis*. So the psalmist says, "The righteous shall not lack anything that is good." Either this is mere poetical license, or it follows that he who lacks anything that is good is not righteous; there is a presumption also that he who has passed a long life without lacking anything that is good has himself also been good enough for practical purposes. ①

According to Butler, pleasure is a safer guide than either right or duty. ② Following sound utilitarian principles, Butler is convinced that virtue is meaningless except in its procurement of happiness. Moreover, Virtue, for Butler, is never unalloyed: ③

> It is involved in the very essence of things that rich men who die old shall have been mean. The greatest and wisest of mankind will be almost always found to be the meanest—the ones who have kept the "mean" best between excess either of virtue or vice. ④

Being a clergyman, Theobald's duty is to "see the honour and glory of God through the eyes of a Church which had lived three hundred years without finding reason to change a single one of its opinions". ⑤ Theobald and Christina have been so immured in their thinking that they are persuaded beyond

---

① *Ibid.*, Ch. 19, p. 96.

② *Ibid.*, Ch. 19, p. 99.

③ Samuel Butler. *The Note-Books of Samuel Butler*. Edited with a preface and biographical statement by Henry Festing Jones. London: A. C. Fifield, 1912. Edition in use: IndyPublish edition, 2007, under the title of "Vice and Virtue", pp. 16-19.

④ Samuel Butler. *The Way of All Flesh*. London: Grant Richards, 1903; published posthumously. Edited with an introduction by V. S. Pritchett, London: Penguin English Library, 2012, Ch. 19, p. 98.

⑤ *Ibid.*, Ch. 26, p. 128.

unconsciousness that theirs is the only possible path. ① The phrase "even to unconsciousness" is very important and sums up the essence of Theobald and Christina. They are led by the habits of their forefathers with no self-reflections and self-awareness on their part. As a result, there is neither progress nor happiness in their life—such is the tragedy of Ernest's parents. By following this unconsciousness, Theobald's unquestioning obedience to duty causes him to avoid thought and feeling.

In the late chapters of the novel, there is a morally abused scene when Ernest confronts with his father as his mother lies dying, Theobald regards that his son looks healthy and affluent:

> Here he was swaggering in grey Ulster and blue and white neck-tie, and looking better than Theobald had ever seen him in his life. It was unprincipled... Well, he would not go a penny beyond the eight or nine pounds which he had promised [...] Why he, Theobald, had never been able to afford such a portmanteau in his life [...] Ernest saw what was passing through his father's mind and felt that he ought to have prepared him in some way for what he now saw [...] He put out his hand and said

① Butler says, "I should doubt whether he ever got as far as doubting the wisdom of his Church upon any single matter. His scent for possible mischief was tolerably keen; so was Christina's, and it is likely that if either of them detected in him or herself the first faint symptoms of a want of faith they were nipped no less peremptorily in the bud, than signs of self—will in Ernest were—and I should imagine more successfully. Yet Theobald considered himself, and was generally considered to be, and indeed perhaps was, an exceptionally truthful person; indeed he was generally looked upon as an embodiment of all those virtues which make the poor respectable and the rich respected. In the course of time he and his wife became persuaded even to unconsciousness, that no one could even dwell under their roof without deep cause for thankfulness. Their children, their servants, their parishioners must be fortunate *ipso facto* that they were theirs. There was no road to happiness here or hereafter, but the road that they had themselves travelled, no good people who did not think as they did upon every subject, and no reasonable person who had wants the gratification of which would be inconvenient to them—Theobald and Christina." *Ibid.*, Ch. 26, pp. 128-129.

> laughingly, "Oh it's all paid for—I am afraid you do not know that Mr. Overton has handed over to me Aunt Alethea's money." Theobald flushed scarlet...①

The passage above shows that Theobald's delusion of duty obstructs his consciousness of his own selfishness and cruelty. ② Theobald develops according to Butler's conception of evolution, which apparently challenged the natural selection

---

① *Ibid.*, Ch. 82, p. 430.

② J. W. Yarbrough. "Autobiography and Artistic Sensibility in Samuel Butler's *The Way of All Flesh.*" In *The Bulletin of the Rocky Mountain Modern Language Association*, Vol. 25, No. 1 (Mar., 1971), p. 24. On altruism and selfishness: "If Theobald and his wife had but known more of the world and of the things that are therein, they would have done little harm to anyone. Selfish they would have always been, but not more so than may very well be pardoned, and not more than other people would be. As it was, the case was hopeless; it would be no use their even entering into their mothers' wombs and being born again. They must not only be born again but they must be born again each one of them of a new father and of a new mother and of a different line of ancestry for many generations before their minds could become supple enough to learn anew." (See *The Way of all Flesh.* Ch. 63, p. 321) J. W. Yarbrough points out: "Something more than the Johannean "new birth" will be required to save them, to enable cunning to bridge the gap between the duty and humanity." He continues that "Butler's hope apparently was that even the Theobald's, confronted with the true picture of duty as a sleazy avoidance of Natural humanity, might bridge the gap between habit and conscious humanity, in order that what is patently irrational and vicious might be replaced by sympathetic, creative relationships." (See J. W. Yarbrough, Autobiography and Artistic Sensibility in Samuel Butler's "The Way of All Flesh". *The Bulletin of the Rocky Mountain Modern Language Association*, Vol. 25, No. 1 (Mar., 1971), p. 27) The selfish parents will lead to bad impact on their children's lifetime. Butler gives his argument on the evolution and ethics in chapter nineteen of *The Way of All Flesh*, he submits it that "a good deal of unkindness and selfishness on the part of parents towards children is not generally followed by ill consequences to the parents themselves. They may cast a gloom over their children's lives for many years without having to suffer anything that will hurt them". (See *The Way of all Flesh.* Ch. 19, p. 97) A selfish person is someone who cares only about themselves, but an altruist cares about others. When distinguishing the selfish persons with the altruist, we consider something about their motivation. The selfish parents usually consider their own happiness instead of considering what is exactly wanted by the children. Therefore, to claim about altruism or selfishness is to make a psychological judgment. According to Darwin, has evolution made man selfish? Tim Lewens discusses the psychological altruistic mechanism with the biological selfish

of Darwin. Cole breaks down Butler's doctrine of evolution into two main aspects: "inherited memory, which was habit, and 'cunning', or will, or

---

behaviours in his recent Darwin studies book. For example, looking after children is usually a mother's duty. This caring behaviour could be caused by the psychological selfishness. Perhaps mothers care only about their own happiness, because they know that if their offspring is injured this will make them unhappy. Nevertheless, the caring behaviour could also be brought about by psychological altruism. There are also possibilities that mothers care not for their own happiness and welfare, but for the welfare of their children. However, as Tim Lewens argued, natural selection is more likely to favour psychological altruism. The psychological altruistic mother may in fact be fitter than the psychological selfish mother. We might expect strong viable children to be reared more effectively by mothers who are directly concerned for the welfare of children, than by a mother who is primarily concerned about her own welfare, and who assists her children only in so far as she calculates that this will promote her welfare. In Darwin's views, the evolution can have a real impact upon ethics. Darwin argued that natural selection has equipped human being with many social instincts that prompt beneficent action with no prior calculation of the pain or pleasure, "Many a civilised man, or even boy, who never before risked his life for another, but full of courage and sympathy, has disregarded the instinct of self-preservation, and plunged at once into a torrent to save a drowning man, though a stranger...Such actions as the above appear to be the simple result of the greater strength of the social or maternal instincts rather than that of any other instinct or motive; for they are performed too instantaneously for reflection, or for pleasure or pain to be felt at the time". (See Charles Darwin. *The Descent of Man, and Selection in Relation to Sex.* With an introduction by James Moore and Adrian Desmond. London: Penguin Classic, first published 1877, second edition, 2004. P. 134) That is what can be brought as the way of moral evaluation. Darwin discusses the evolution of the moral sense in chapter four and five of *The Descent of Man.* Tim Lewens argues that Darwin's interests in evolution and morality focus mainly on an attempt to give an historical explanation for the emergence of our moral sense—for the sense of what is right and what is wrong. His story is one of the progress of morality, nevertheless, driven by group selection. "The survival for fittest" between communities initially favours those communities whose members feel sympathy for each other, and those who are consequently motivated to act in ways that strengthen the community as a whole. Tim Lewens continues his arguments: "As time goes by, experience and reason cause the domain of sympathy to expand, encompassing humans from other communities, and eventually non-human animals. We also gain the ability to formulate, disseminate and enforce rules of good conduct generated by reason and experience. In these respects Darwin's account of the evolution of the emotions: Natural selection is part of the story, but by no means the only part of that story." (See Tim Lewens. *Darwin.* London and New York: Routledge, 2007, P. 187) However, it is important to mention here, as discussed in *The Selfish Gene*, that Richard Dawkins, being a Darwinian, argues that the process of evolution will result in altruism.

striving, in place of the blind chance of 'natural selection', as the basis of variation and therefore of evolutionary progress." ① Theobald fails to evolve due to his passivity. There is no "cunning" to enable an alteration to occur; as a result, he adds nothing to the collective unconsciousness. Butler comments on the inability of both Theobald and Christina to develop:

> Poor people! They had tried to keep their ignorance of the world from themselves by calling it the pursuit of heavenly things, and then shutting their eyes to anything that might give them trouble. A son having been born to them they had shut his eyes also as far as was practicable. Who could blame them? They had chapter and verse for everything they had either done or left undone; there is no better thumbed precedent than that for being a clergyman and a clergyman's wife. In what respect had they differed from their neighbours? How did their household differ from that of any other clergyman of the better sort from one end of England to the other? ②

Thus, any theory of evolution should not limit itself to being a scientific theory about animals, instead it should be a practical working notion about and for man. ③ For Butler, the development and evolution of the individuals lay at the seeking for pleasure and avoiding of pains.

---

① G. D. H. Cole. *Samuel Butler and The Way of All Flesh.* London: Home and Van Thal LTD., 1947, p. 26.

② Samuel Butler. *The Way of All Flesh.* London: Grant Richards, 1903; published posthumously. Edited with an introduction by V. S. Pritchett, London: Penguin English Library, 2012, Ch. 63, p. 321.

③ G. D. H. Cole. *Samuel Butler and The Way of All Flesh.* London: Home and Van Thal LTD., 1947, p. 26.

3.3 Butler and utilitarianism

> Nature has placed mankind under the governance of two sovereign masters, *pain* and *pleasure.* It is for them alone to point out what we ought to do, as well as to determine what we shall do. On the one hand the standard of right and wrong, on the other the chain of causes and effects, are fastened to their throne. They govern us in all we do, in all we say, in all we think: every effort we can make to throw off our subjection, will serve but to demonstrate and confirm it. In words a man may pretend to abjure their empire: but in reality he will remain subject to it all the while. The *principle of utility* recognizes this subjection, and assumes it for the foundation of that system, the object of which is to rear the fabric of felicity by the hands of reason and of law. Systems which attempt to question it, deal in sounds instead of sense, in caprice instead of reason, in darkness instead of light. ①

Butler's ideas on evolution are diametrically opposed to the Enlightenment tradition of reason as the guiding principle of life. ② Butler argues that "virtue's true lineage is older and more respectable than any that can be invented for her", for "she springs from man's experience concerning his own well-being—and this, though not infallible, is still the least fallible thing we have". ③For

① Jeremy Bentham. *An Introduction to the Principles of Morals and Legislation*, an authoritative ed. by J. H. Burns and H. L. A. Hart; with a new introduction by F. Rosen; and an interpretative essay by H. L. A. Hart. Oxford: Clarendon press, 1996, p. 11.

② Frank Miller Turner. "Samuel Butler: The Man of Temper." In *Between Science and Religion: The Reaction to Scientific Naturalism in Late Victorian England.* New Haven: Yale University Press, 1974, p. 182.

③ Samuel Butler. *The Way of All Flesh.* London: Grant Richards, 1903; published posthumously. Edited with an introduction by V. S. Pritchett, London: Penguin English Library, 2012, Ch. 19, p. 97.

John Locke (1632 – 1704), one of the most important Enlightenment thinkers, the starting-point in constructing a theory of knowledge is the experience of the individual. Butler, on the other hand, believes that the unknown and instinctive action is just as important. Wittily he declares, "Mr. Locke has been greatly praised for his essay upon human understanding. An essay on human misunderstanding should be no less interesting and important."① This "misunderstanding", he maintains, is crucial since it is precisely incomprehension and random "stabs in the dark" that allow individuals to act, to adapt to their present and to evolve in the future:

> Action is taken in the dark, which sometimes succeeds and becomes a fertile source of further combinations; or we are brought to a dead stop. All action is random in respect of any of the minute actions which compose it that are not done in consequence of memory, real or supposed. So that random, or action taken in the dark, or illusion, lies at the very root of progress. ②

To some extent, illusion by means of memories of the past is one of the main causes of progress. ③ For Butler, such illusory and speculative development is the result of cunning action instead of reason represented in a form of faith. ④ It is the key point that allows living organisms to successfully adapt to their changing environment:

---

① Samuel Butler. *Alps and Sanctuaries of Piedmont and the Canton Ticino*. London: David Bogue, 1882, Ch. III, p. 36.

② Samuel Butler. *Unconscious Memory*. London: David Bogue, 1880. The Echo Library edition, 2006, Ch. XII p. 95.

③ Samuel Butler. *Alps and Sanctuaries of Piedmont and the Canton Ticino*. London: David Bogue, 1882, Ch. III, p. 36.

④ Frank Miller Turner. "Samuel Butler: The Man of Temper." In *Between Science and Religion: The Reaction to Scientific Naturalism in Late Victorian England*. New Haven: Yale University Press, 1974, p. 183.

> Action is the connecting link between the physical and psychical worlds; it is a kind of mean proportional between body and mind; it is the invisible immaterial opinion that belongs to the spiritual world, taking material shape, coming among us, and revealing itself to us in the only way in which we can understand anything about it. ①

Butler believes that cunning action is the point of connection between individuals and the unseen kingdom. Actions originate from individuals in response to their circumstances, and are stimulated by a sense of need, desire and will, because by their very nature they show "the influence of the invisible world that touched men who were acting". ②

In *The Way of All Flesh*, Butler recognises the value of virtue—in its promotion of pleasure, which in turns enables the progress of human world. With this background, therefore, Samuel Butler seems to be the earliest exponent of the new interpretation of evolution and he forged a new link between Lamarckism and the liberal ideology which emerged. ③ Although Samuel Butler is not known as a Utilitarian or political economist, the novel contains many ideas close to Utilitarianism, namely that virtue is meaningless except in terms of the happiness it helps to procure. ④ Utilitarianism, is a normative ethics theory that encompasses the Utilitarian doctrine of Jeremy Bentham (1748 – 1832), and a series of history ideas by other thinkers such as the philosophers James Mill (1773 – 1836) and

---

① Samuel Butler. *Collected Essays*, vol. I of *The Shrewsbury Edition of the Works of Samuel Butler*. Edited by Henry Festing Jones and A. T. Bartholomew. London: Johathan Cape, 1925, p. 197.

② Frank Miller Turner. "Samuel Butler: The Man of Temper." In *Between Science and Religion: The Reaction to Scientific Naturalism in Late Victorian England.* New Haven: Yale University Press, 1974, p. 184.

③ Peter J. Bowler. *Charles Darwin. The Man and His Influence.* Oxford: Basil Blackwell Ltd, 1990, p. 172.

④ After exploring the relations between duty and pleasure in Butler's views, I find there is evidence of Butler's Benthamite connections in *The Way of All Flesh.*

John Stuart Mill (1806 – 1873). Another important thinker in English history that needs to be mentioned here is Thomas Hobbes (1588 – 1679). Hobbes can be considered as a pre-liberal, since he espoused the idea that desire is the source of the dynamics of human action and "to have no desire is to be dead".① In other words, it is desire that pushes the individual to achieve his or her autonomy. For both Hobbes and Bentham, desires enjoy a kind of independence that places them outside the province of morality. Desire in itself is something positive and should not be judged from a morality point of view. Liberals did not question how desires come about and generally ignored the social origins of desire. For them, desires are simply part of human nature. What is more important is that each individual should be the most reliable judge of his or her own desires. Liberal thinkers believe that if this notion is not accepted, the way is open to despotism of some kind of enlightened morality which claims to know better than a society what it wants. In a sense, the individual must construct his or her own morality.

Liberal thought on desires implies some kind of equality between individuals. Each individual possesses certain rights on an equal footing with other individuals. At the same time, the individual is naturally selfish and tends to use other individuals as means to achieving their own ends. This selfishness is freely acknowledged but not blamed by liberals;② nonetheless it inevitably leads to some individuals dominating others. At the end of the day, the sum of each individual's egoism forms the basis for an active and coherent society. For both Hobbes and Adam Smith, selfishness, far from being distractive, contributes to the general well-being of society. Though desire is the source of all human

① Hobbes, Thomas. *Leviathan*. First published in 1651. A critical edition by G. A. J. Rogers and Karl Schuhmann, 2 vols. Bristol: Thoemmes continuum, 2003, Vol. 2, Ch. XI, p. 79.

② Adam Smith, with his most famous work *The Wealth of Nations* (1776) believed that one's selfishness would lead to the benefit of the others. Everybody will be happier if everybody is selfish, as if there were an invisible hands. Charity is not sufficient but entrepreneurs' selfishness works.

activities, there is a counter—weight to desire that prevents society from collapsing into chaos—reason. Importantly, for the liberals, reason and desire do not stand on the same footing: desire comes first and reason plays second fiddle. It is not reason that determines the individual's acts or purposes, but desire that actuates the individual and provides the impetus to move in one direction rather than another.① The function of reason is to work out how desires can be satisfied. Liberal philosophy also did not accept the heritage of the past without questioning.

In this section I suggest that Bentham might have influenced Butler. It is worth going back to Bentham to take measure of his pleasure principle, which is the promotion of the greatest happiness for the greatest numbers. Though Bentham has been identified with carceral panopticism, he can be seen as a spokesman for pleasures of all sorts. In her recent book, Kathleen Blake makes an incisive analysis of Benthamian pleasures in connection with Victorian literature, which is worth quoting at some length:

> For Bentham utility is "benefit, advantage, pleasure, good or happiness" or, alternatively, prevention of "mischief, pain, evil, or unhappiness to the party whose interest is considered" (*An Introduction to the Principles of Morals and Legislation*, 12). In political economy utility is value-in-use, in Mill's definition, invoking Smith, "capacity to satisfy a desire" (*Principles of Political Economy*, iii. 456, and see *Wealth of Nations*, i. 44-45) Smith pronounces consumption to be the sole end of production, and he calls "every man...rich or poor according to the degree in which he can afford to enjoy the necessaries, conveniencies, and amusements of human life" (ii. 60, i. 47). Smith sees no limit to desire. While "the desire of food is limited in every man by the narrow capacity of the human stomach [...] the desire of the conveniencies and ornaments of building, dress, equipage, and

① If desire is what to do, reason is how to do it.

> household furniture, seems to have no limit or certain boundary" (i. 181)
>
> Utility or value-in-use as satisfaction of desire, as consumption, enjoyment, amusement, may or may not bear a price on the market and carry second-level value-in-exchange. But utility or value-in-use is primary. Bentham conceives of himself as a student and ally of smith ... Smith and Bentham join in their insistence on self-interest ... Bentham's analysis is wider, encompassing applications beyond market exchange. He asserts "the general predominance of personal interest over every other interest" (*Rationale of Judicial Evidence*, vii. 329), as this motivates the seeking of value-in-use, utility, pleasure.
>
> Utility or value-in-use connotes avoiding pain as part and parcel of gaining pleasure. The greatest happiness principle involves a perpetual cost-benefit analysis. To calculation on behalf of each individual add calculation of the greatest happiness of the greatest number. The more happiness and the less unhappiness the better—in one, and all. "*Sum up*", says Bentham in *The Principles of Morals and Legislation* (p. 40). ①

According to Bentham's principle of utility, the cause of any action is to get pleasure and avoid pain. When the individual makes a decision, he or she assesses how much happiness, and how much pain it would produce, in a cost-benefit analysis that Bentham called felicific calculus. Utility is thus this ability to produce happiness. ② It is interesting to find that there exists a commonality

---

① See the chapter "Pleasures of Benthamism-Utility, or, 'Peolemutht be amuthed: Bentham and *Hard Times*.'" In Kathleen Blake. *Pleasures of Benthamism: Victorian Literature, Utility, Political Economy*. Oxford: Oxford University Press. 2009, pp. 42-43.

② "Utility, *what*. By utility is meant that property in any object, whereby it tends to produce benefit, advantage, pleasure, good, or happiness (all this in the present case comes to the same thing) or (what comes again to the same thing) to prevent the happening of mischief, pain, evil, or unhappiness to the party whose interest is considered." See Jeremy Bentham. *An Introduction to the Principles of Morals and Legislation*, an authoritative ed. by J. H. Burns and H. L. A. Hart; with a new introduction by F. Rosen; and an interpretative essay by H. L. A. Hart. Oxford: Clarendon press, 1996, p. 12.

between Butler's views and Utilitarianism. C. E. M. Joad has argued that it was Bentham's brand of Utilitarianism rather than Mill's brand that influences Butler.[①] Bentham's ideas on pleasure are in accordance with Butler's theory of evolution. For Butler, desire is the core element of evolution, and progress is made in the fulfilment of desires of individuals.

① C. E. M. Joad explains, "Both Bentham and Mill agreed that one's duty was to promote the greatest happiness of the greatest number, but while Mill held that in case of conflict between the individual and the community it was the duty of the former to prefer the happiness of the community to his own, Bentham held that no such conflict could possible arise; and it could not arise because in promoting the greatest happiness of the greatest number the individual was automatically promoting his own. Bentham was led to this rather surprising view by an inspection of his own psychology; he was a benevolent gentleman who liked doing good, and found, or persuaded himself that found, his greatest happiness in philanthropy". See C. E. M. Joad. *Samuel Butler (1835 – 1902)*. London: L. Parsons, 1924, p. 147.

3.4 Butler and money

In this brand of utilitarianism, there is a transition from biology into economics and it is expressed in monetary terms: "if society is indeed a single organism, or one great polyp, then the reward for private virtue is going to be expressed, typically, in money terms."① Thus, poverty is virtueless a proof of evolutionary failure. Once again I have to rummage in *Life and Habit* to illustrate Butler's thought on failure. He makes a connection between the slow accumulations of human capital investment with the gradual improvement of organic function:

> Our own riches grow with our desires and the pains we take in pursuit of them, and our desires vary and increase with our means of gratifying them; but unless with men of exceptional business aptitude, wealth grows gradually by the adding field to field and farm to farm; so with the limbs and instincts of animals; these are but the things they have made or bought with their money, or with money that has been left them by their forefathers, which, though it is neither silver nor gold, but faith and protoplasm only, is good money and capital notwithstanding.②

In Butler's views, money itself is a sign of evolutionary progress; conversely, it also stands that "A man can stand being told that he must submit to a severe surgical operation, or that he has some disease which will shortly kill him...but the strongest quail before financial ruin, and the better men they are, the more

① Peter Morton. "Butler on Heredity." In *The Vital Science: Biology and the Literary Imagination: 1860 – 1900*. London: Allen and Unwin, 1984, p. 186.

② Samuel Butler. *Life and Habit*. London: Trübner, 1878. Revised edition, with author's addenda and a preface by R. A. Streatfeild, London: A. C. Fifield, 1910. The Echo Library edition, 2007, Ch. XII, p. 125.

complete, as a general rule, is their prostration."① Evolution, for men, is a process of interacts with internal and external world. The personal identity is also extended to include elements of the external world that become joined to the individual. On this point, my analysis in this section will be focused on Butler's ideas about money. "Money," as Butler wrote in his *Notebooks*, "is the last enemy that shall never be subdued. While there is flesh there is money—or the want of money; but money is always on the brain so long as there is a brain in reasonable order."②

This pervasive role of money in Butler's writing can very likely be traced to his personal experience. As Jill Rubenstein remarks: "Butler's background created a healthy respect for money and an inevitable awareness of its potential perversions, especially as an instrument of parental tyranny."③ This awareness probably began in 1859, when Butler clashed with his father over his choice of career. Butler refused to be ordained and turned down Canon Butler's suggestion of law or teaching as an alternative, since neither of them appealed to Butler himself. Canon Butler immediately threatened to withdraw financial support, but this only strengthened Butler's resolve to be true to himself and reinforced his

---

① Samuel Butler. *The Way of All Flesh*. London: Grant Richards, 1903; published posthumously. Edited with an introduction by V. S. Pritchett, London: Penguin English Library, 2012, Ch. 66, p. 338.

② Samuel Butler. *The Note-Books of Samuel Butler*. Edited with a preface and biographical statement by Henry Festing Jones. London: A. C. Fifield, 1912. Edition in use: IndyPublish edition, 2007, p. 24.

③ Jill Rubenstein. "'Business is Business': The Money Ethic of Samuel Butler." In *English Literature in Transition, 1880 – 1920*, Volume 19, Number 4, 1976, p. 237. She continues, "Until his father died in 1886, when Butler was fifty-one, his financial status was at best uncertain and often quite precarious. In reconstructing and judging the financial relationship between Canon Butler and his prodigal son, one is tempted to award the verdict to the son, but fairness demands some equivocation. At various times both were at fault. The father vitiated originally good intentions with inflexibility and self-righteousness, while Butler allowed youthful pride and the desire for independence to be transformed into hypersensitivity."

keen desire for freedom:

> You would with the best intention in the world make me a bed that I know very well will not fit me. I know that when I am in, escape is impossible; and knowing that I have duties to myself to perform even more binding on me than those to my parents, with all respect, adopt the alternative of rejecting the pounds shilling and pence and going in search of my own bread my own way. ①

Money might well have been the crux of Butler's antagonistic relationship with his father. Later on, Canon Butler promised his son £ 5 000 as capital to establish his sheep farming business in New Zealand in 1859. However, his father never paid the last £ 1 000 and Butler, who had assumed obligations on the strength of it, was seriously hindered in his enterprise and might have failed completely had the market gone against him. Even though far removed from this homeland, Clara. G Stillman notes that:

> The long arm of paternal sabotage could still reach out to cripple him... The spiritual ignominy of financial dependence was born in upon him. He saw that freedom of soul depended on freedom of pocket. He saw wealth as the great liberator—from parents first, since parents were that he wanted to be free of, but he soon generalized the conception as he always did his own experience. This is the meaning of the frequent references to the importance of the wealth scattered through his books, which have sometimes been misunderstood as a base for truckling to riches. Wealth frees the soul. ②

① Letter of 10 May 1859. In *The Family Letters of Samuel Butler*. Edited by Arnold Silver. London: J. Cape, 1962, p. 76.

② Clara G. Stillman. *Samuel Butler: A Mid-Victorian Modern*. London: Martin Secker, 1932, pp. 49-50.

Butler found himself physically and spiritually in a new world. Contrary to everyone's expectations, Butler made a remarkable success of his sheep farming in New Zealand and returned to England in the autumn of 1868 with an excellent profit on his initial investment. Unfortunately, a series of speculative investments caused him to lose a considerable sum and led once again to a rift between Butler and his father. ① Money is usually the bond that creates and fosters the connection between parents and offspring. For Butler, money is a most taboo and sensitive topic between father and son as he observed wryly in his *Note-Books*:

> Next to sexual matters there are none upon which there is such complete reserve between parents and children as on those connected with money. The father keeps his affairs as closely as he can to himself and is most jealous of letting his children into a knowledge of how he manages his money. His children are like monks in a monastery as regards money and he calls this training them up with the strictest regard to principle. Nevertheless he thinks himself ill-used if his son, on entering life, falls a victim to designing persons whose knowledge of how money is made and lost is greater than his own. ②

This is precisely the situation Butler landed in when several companies, including the Canada Tanning Extract Company, into which he had sunk money on the advice of Henry Hoare and Pauli, failed in 1874. ③ Butler found himself once again impecunious. Consequently his hope of earning a comfortable living through writing and painting remained unrealized, and his quarrel with his father continued. In the autumn of 1879, Butler decided to borrow money on a property

① Canon Butler did not intend to provide his son with any substantial monetary assistance.

② Samuel Butler. *The Note-Books of Samuel Butler*. Edited with a preface and biographical statement by Henry Festing Jones. London: A. C. Fifield, 1912. Edition in use: IndyPublish edition, 2007, p. 20.

③ Henry FestingJones. *Samuel Butler: Author of Erewhon (1835 – 1902), A Memoir*. London: Macmillan and Co., Limited. 1919, vol. I.

left to him in his grandfather's will:

> This necessitated Canon Butler's changing his own will to make Samuel's reversion absolute rather than contingent on his father's death. However, he refused to effect the change, and he forced Butler to submit a minutely detailed and, considering the son was forty-four years old at the time, humiliating account of how he had spent his money since returning from New Zealand. In return he granted Butler an allowance of £ 300 per year, contingent on Butler's promise to stop contributing to the maintenance of Charles Paine Pauli. ①

Canon Butler did not yield until 1881, and the bitterness of this quarrel remained with Butler for the rest of his life.

It is not surprising then that Money became almost an obsession with Butler. The author's quarrel with his father on the issue of money is closely reflected in *The Way of All Flesh*, where George and Theobald Pontifex indulge in frequent "will-shakings" to intimidate their children. Butler insists that greed and parental affection are incompatible: "when a man is very fond of his money it is not easy for him at all times to be very fond of his children also. The two are like God and Mammon. "② Fortunately, Alethea Pontifex, who "knew the power and value of money exceedingly well", is the only member of the family with a sensible attitude toward bequeathing money. She wants "those to have it who would be most likely to use it genially and sensibly, and whom it would thus be likely to make most happy". ③

---

① Jill Rubenstein. "'Business is Business': The Money Ethic of Samuel Butler." In *English Literature in Transition, 1880 – 1920*, vol. 19, No. 4, 1976, p. 238.

② Samuel Butler. *The Way of All Flesh*. London: Grant Richards, 1903; published posthumously. Edited with an introduction by V. S. Pritchett, London: Penguin English Library, 2012, Ch. 5, p. 24.

③ *Ibid.*, Ch. 33, p. 162

Because of his father's preoccupation with money and his own financial struggles during those years of financial dependence on his father, Butler became acutely aware of the importance of money. Partly as a result of this experience, money is closely connected to two of his favourite subjects, evolution and art. Putting together Butler's theory of cumulative change and his preoccupation with money, it seems almost inevitable that Butler should construct "a working analogy between evolutionary development and the accumulation of capital and property". ① Property also lies at the core of liberal values. Butler makes a clear analogy between evolutionary development and accumulation of property in *Luck, or Cunning*? (1887)

> Variations are an organism's way of getting over an unexpected discrepancy between its resources as shown by the fly-leaves of its own cheques and the universe's passbook; the universe is generally right, or would be upheld as right if the matter were to come before the not too incorruptible courts of nature, and in nine cases out of ten the organism has made the error in its own favour, so that it must now pay or die. ②

In the comparison above, Butler reduces the organism's struggle with a hostile environment to the individual's struggle with his bank statement. He offers another economic parable in the following paragraph in which he hypothesizes on the difference between a settlement of Irish Celts and one of Germans. Though both settlements started equally poor, "on the German side there is comfort, thrift, peace, but on the other side the spectacle is very different." ③ Why? The

① Jill Rubenstein. "'Business is Business': The Money Ethic of Samuel Butler." In *English Literature in Transition, 1880 – 1920*, vol. 19, No. 4, 1976, pp. 240-241.

② Samuel Butler. *Luck, or Cunning as the Main Means of Organic Modification*? London: Trübner, 1887. The Echo Library edition, 2007, Ch. VIII, p. 59.

③ *Ibid.*, Ch. VIII, p. 60.

difference is not attributed to mere chance or luck, "for luck is blind". [①] In his explanation of the factors that contribute to development, Butler believes that "cunning is the one more proper to be insisted on as determining the physical and psychical well or ill being, and hence, ere long, the future form of the organism." [②] Thus, the "abiding memory between successive generations" allows the organism to adapt exactly as it allows the one colony to create economic well-being. [③] The differences between individuals or groups cannot be attributed to mere chance or luck. Consequently, material success, the same as felicitous evolutionary development, "becomes a tangible sign of the accumulated unconscious wisdom of generations". [④] To transmit one's money intact to one's offspring is to contribute to progress, and it is on these grounds that I should mention George Pontifex in *The Way of All Flesh*. Ernest's grandfather, of whom Butler says:

> Over and above his having lived long and prosperously, he left numerous offspring, to all of whom he communicated not only his physical and mental characteristics, with no more than the usual amount of modification, but also no small share of characteristics which are less easily transmitted—I mean his pecuniary characteristics. It may be said that he acquired these by sitting still and letting money run, as it were, right up against him, but against how many does not money run who do not take it when it does, or who, even if they hold it for a little while, cannot so incorporate it with themselves that it shall descend through them to their offspring? Mr Pontifex did this. He kept what he may be said to have made, and money is like a reputation for

---

① *Ibid.*, p. 60.

② *Ibid.*, pp. 59-60.

③ *Ibid.*, p. 60.

④ Jill Rubenstein. "'Business is Business': The Money Ethic of Samuel Butler." In *English Literature in Transition, 1880 – 1920*, vol. 19, No. 4, 1976, p. 241.

ability—more easily made than kept. ①

Like a fool and his money, Butler says:

> A foolish organism and its fortuitous variation will be soon parted, for, as a general rule, unless the variation has so much connection with the organism's past habits and ways of thought as to be in no proper sense of the word "fortuitous", the organism will not know what to do with it when it has got it, no matter how favourable it may be, and it is little likely to be handed down to descendants. ②

Moreover, cunning, rather than luck is as important to "the kind of people who get on best in the world" as it is to the ultimate improvement of the species. ③ This "fortuitous variation", which allows an organism to adapt to its environment, is equivalent in Butler's mind to the accumulation of capital, which allows the individual, such as Alethea, Overton, and finally Ernest in *The Way of All Flesh*, to function independently. In Butler's views, the unconsciousness is the accumulation of evolutionary process. However, this progress demands conscious efforts and intellectual decisions of the individual to access the assimilated knowledge of ancestors. According to Butler, cunning or individual effort is more correctly said to be the main means of the development of capital,

---

① Samuel Butler. *The Way of All Flesh.* London: Grant Richards, 1903; published posthumously. Edited with an introduction by V. S. Pritchett, London: Penguin English Library, 2012, Ch. 19, p. 100.

② Samuel Butler. *Luck, or Cunning as the Main Means of Organic Modification*? London: Trübner, 1887. The Echo Library edition, 2007, Ch. VIII, p. 61.

③ *Ibid.*, p. 61. Here Butler continues his attack on Darwin's natural selection: he argues "what test to a Darwinian can be comparable to this? Commonly do insist on cunning rather than on luck, sometimes perhaps even unduly; speaking, at least, from experience, I have generally found myself more or less of a failure with those Darwinians to whom I have endeavoured to excuse my shortcomings on the score of luck."

furthermore, the development of the organism:

> It is one of the commonplaces of biology that the nature of the organism (which is mainly determined by ancestral antecedents) is greatly more important in determining its future than the conditions of its environment, provided, of course, that these are not too cruelly abnormal, so that good seed will do better on rather poor soil, than bad seed on rather good soil; this alone should be enough to show that cunning, or individual effort, is more important in determining organic results than luck is, and therefore that if either is to be insisted on to the exclusion of the other, it should be cunning, not luck.①

This is also valid, Butler asserts, for the capital accumulation: "Cunning is in the long run mightier than luck as regards the acquisition of property."② Butler expands on the analogy between evolution and property. The same law which applies to property also applies to organism. The same laws also govern health and wealth, because one's stomach is actually a "living sack, or purse of untanned leather" and one's purse is "a kind of abridged extracorporeal stomach wherein we keep the money which we convert by purchase into food, as we presently convert the food by digestion into flesh and blood".③ Property becomes not merely acquisition but also "a kind of extension of the personality into the outside world."④ At the core of what Jill Rubenstein calls his "theory of the continuous evolutionary personality" is Butler's obsession with money and the question of inheritance.⑤ This can be traced to how his personal experience "continually reinforced the awareness that financial bequests are at least as

① *Ibid.*, Ch. VIII, p. 60.

② *Ibid.*, Ch. VIII, p. 62.

③ *Ibid.*, p. 62.

④ *Ibid.*, p. 62.

⑤ Jill Rubenstein. "'Business is Business': The Money Ethic of Samuel Butler." In *English Literature in Transition, 1880 – 1920*, vol. 19, No. 4, 1976, pp. 241-242.

important as genetic bequests in determining the bounds of one's life. "①

Butler's Utilitarian point of view remains notwithstanding, he did not believe that money was the be-all and end-all of existence. Instead, as useful legs or tools, money is necessary and indispensable for the good fortune of individual. Butler did wish to earn more money from his books. However, he did not believe that the necessity between money, art and literature exist. Certainly for the *bona fide* writer it is not a worthy consideration. According to Butler, "the principle business of life is to enjoy it". ② Freedom to act is essential and imperative for the self-development of the individual, yet Butler was pragmatic enough to acknowledge that both enjoyment and self-fulfillment require money. Butler's ideal, as illustrated in the novel through Alethea and Overton, who lead congenial and independent lives, is not possible without material well-being, which guarantees independence. Butler's ideal of the gentleman also depends on this concept of well-endowed freedom. ③Money, to some degree, is the guarantee for the independence of the individual. Indeed, in Butler's assessment, "money losses are the worst, loss of health is the next worst and loss of reputation comes in a bad third. "④ The fate of Butler's alter ego at the end of *The Way of All Flesh* is revealing. Henry Festing Jones remarks on the novel's happy ending in his *A Memoir*:

> Had Butler re-written the book he might have thought it worthwhile to emphasise Ernest's final success and happiness which, it may be, is

① *Ibid.*, pp. 241-242.

② Samuel Butler. *The Way of All Flesh.* London: Grant Richards, 1903; published posthumously. Edited with an introduction by V. S. Pritchett, London: Penguin English Library, 2012, Ch. 19, p. 100.

③ Jill Rubenstein. "'Business is Business': The Money Ethic of Samuel Butler." In *English Literature in Transition, 1880 – 1920*, vol. 19, No. 4, 1976, p. 244.

④ Samuel Butler. *The Note-Books of Samuel Butler.* Edited with a preface and biographical statement by Henry Festing Jones. London: A. C. Fifield, 1912. Edition in use: IndyPublish edition, 2007, p. 25.

presented in a form that may strike some readers as not unlike failure. But I do not think he would have altered it, for we all know that happiness consists in doing what a man likes and not in doing what other people think he ought to like. Writing about his own literary position in 1893 he said:

> I should have liked notoriety and financial success well enough if they could have been had for the asking, but I was not going to take any trouble about them and, as a natural consequence, I did not get them. If I had wanted them with the same passionate longing that has led me to pursue every inquiry that I have pursued, I should have got them fast enough. It is very rarely that I have failed to get what I have really tried for and, as a matter of fact, I believe I have been a great deal happier for not trying than I should have been if I had had notoriety thrust upon me.

And so, having made Ernest as like himself as he could, he left him in the happy position of being free, like himself, to do and say the things he considered best worth doing and saying. ①

Ernest ultimately achieves the "discretaposizionina" thanks to his Aunt Alethea's money and to Overton's prudence. ② He lives the life of a gentleman and

① Henry Festing Jones. *Samuel Butler: Author of Erewhon (1835 – 1902) A Memoir.* Vol. II London: Macmillan and Co. Ltd, 1919, pp. 16-17.

② Butler wrote about money, art and artists in his *Note-Books*: "It is curious that money, which is the most valuable thing in life, *exceptis excipiendis*, should be the most fatal corrupter of music, literature, painting and all the arts. As soon as any art is pursued with a view to money, then farewell, in ninety-nine cases out of a hundred, all hope of genuine good work. If a man has money at his back, he may touch these things and do something which will live a long while, and he may be very happy in doing it; if he has no money, he may do good work, but the chances are he will be killed in doing it and for having done it; or he may make himself happy by doing bad work and getting money out of it, and there is no great harm in this, provided he knows his work is done in this spirit and rates it for its commercial value only. Still, as a rule, a man should not touch any of the arts as a creator unless be has a *discretaposizionina* behind him." See Samuel Butler. *The Note-Books of Samuel Butler*. Edited with a preface and biographical statement by Henry Festing Jones. London: A. C. Fifield, 1912. Edition in use: IndyPublish edition, 2007, p. 140.

writes a series of unsuccessful books in blissful indifference to the verdict of critics. Money is essential and fundamental to the survival of art and artists. Although Ernest has "never asked a reviewer to dinner in his life", [①] it is his material wealth that gives him the intellectual and artistic independence which Butler regards as the *sine qua non* of truly creative work. [②] Claude Bissell aptly remarks that *The Way of All Flesh* "is a study of the redemptive powers of the unconscious. But it might also be defined as a study of the redemptive powers of money."[③] For Butler, to have money and become rich, whether by personal effort or by inheritance, is a sign of evolutionary grace. [④]

---

① Samuel Butler. *The Way of All Flesh.* London: Grant Richards, 1903; published posthumously. Edited with an introduction by V. S. Pritchett, London: Penguin English Library, 2012, Ch. 86, p. 474.

② "sine qua non" means a condition without which it could not be. "What can it matter to me," he says, "whether people read my books or not? It may matter to them—but I have too much money to want more, and if the books have any stuff in them it will work by and by." *Ibid.*, Ch. 86, p. 474.

③ Claude, Bissell. "A Study of *The Way of All Flesh.*" In *Nineteenth-Century Studies*, collected and edited by Herbert Davis, William C. De Vane, and R. C. Bald. New York: Cornell University Press, 1940, p. 287.

④ Peter Morton. "Butler on Heredity." In *The Vital Science: Biology and the Literary Imagination: 1860 – 1900*. London: Allen and Unwin, 1984, p. 189.

Chapter Four Self-help and free-will: the reconstruction of personal identity[①]

4.1 Unconscious memory and cunning as two limbs of man—Ernest's growth

> Although there are undoubtedly similarities of ideas between *Life and Habit* and *The Way of All Flesh*, and indeed direct quotation from one to the other, the primary link is a shared motivating energy—a desire to explore, in all its bewildering and contradictory aspects, the nature of identity.[②]

Critics argue that Butler's initial differences with Darwin are motivated by his desire to introduce a more Lamarckian sense of the power of human agency within evolutionary development.[③] In this section, I will analyse how the ideas Butler held in this respect are based again on his theory of evolution.

---

① "The spirit of self-help is the root of all genuine growth in the individual." See Samuel Smiles. *Self-Helps, with Illustrations of Character, Conduct and Perseverance*. First published in 1859. Edited with an Introduction and Notes by Peter W. Sinnema. Oxford: Oxford University Press, 2002, p. 17.

② Sally Shuttleworth. "Evolutionary Psychology and *The Way of All Flesh*." In *Samuel Butler: Victorian Against the Grain, A Critical Overview*. Edited by James G. Paradis. Toronto, Buffalo and London: University of Toronto Press, 2007, p. 155.

③ *Ibid.*, p. 152.

At times *The Way of All Flesh* seems to reflect an almost overwhelming sense of biological, psychological and cultural determinism. For example, it is revealed by Ernest's statement that: "I shall be just as unkind to my children [...] as my grandfather was to my father, or my father to me. If they did not succeed in making their children love them, neither shall I." ① Ernest observes that children are oppressed not only by their psychological inheritance of parental patterns of behaviour, but also by their parents' habitual repetition of the oppressive patterns they had experienced when they were young. Moreover, Butler's paradox on the implications of evolutionary theory provides an opportunity for our understanding of the nature of personal identity and the individual selfhood. ② According to Butler's evolutionary theory, parents are the past selves of the individual. As Ernest remarked:

> A man first quarrels with his father about three-quarters of a year before he is born. It is then he insists on setting up a separate establishment; when this has been once agreed to, the more complete the separation for ever after the better for both. ③

Thus for Butler, evolution in a way is all about breaking the ties between the self and the past self. This struggle is rendered all the more monumental since Butler considers that children are at one with their parents in terms of experience

① Samuel Butler. *The Way of All Flesh.* London: Grant Richards, 1903; published posthumously. Edited with an introduction by V. S. Pritchett, London: Penguin English Library, 2012, Ch. 79, p. 409.

② "It is this sense of the power of hereditary memory, and the consequent difficulties of defining or maintaining a unified sense of selfhood, that lies at the heart of both *Life and Habit* and *The Way of All Flesh.*" See Sally Shuttleworth. "Evolutionary Psychology and *The Way of All Flesh.*" In *Samuel Butler: Victorian Against the Grain, A Critical Overview.* Edited by James G. Paradis. Toronto, Buffalo and London: University of Toronto, 2007, p. 144.

③ Samuel Butler. *The Way of All Flesh.* London: Grant Richards, 1903; published posthumously. Edited with an introduction by V. S. Pritchett, London: Penguin English Library, 2012, Ch. 79, p. 410.

and memories. In the novel, Butler introduces a few significant changes in Ernest's growth. He aims to prove that it is the conscious effort or will that must overcome the burden of inheritance. Here, it would be impossible not to mention Sigmund Freud's assertion that the maturity of individual identity is in some sense achieved through the separation with parents. Indeed, Butler precedes Freud, and Sally Shuttleworth argues that the Freudian struggle between father and son is played out in *The Way of All Flesh* through Butler's engagement with evolutionary theory. ①

The narrator of the fiction Overton knows what has happened and what will happen to Ernest as well. The past is to some degree an important source of one's futurity. "This is the deathly aspect of Butler's insistence on lineage as pre-enactment," as Gillian Beer remarked, "in contrast, the undescribed future is for him a form of liberation, since memory may by then have undergone a process of transformation akin to the activity that moves caterpillar into butterfly." ② By way of illustration, I quote an important passage from *Life and Habit* (1878) in which Butler describes personal identity:

> Personal identity, then, is much like species itself. It is now, thanks to Mr. Darwin, generally held that species blend or have blended into one another; so that any possibility of arrangement and apparent subdivision into definite groups, is due to the suppression by death both of individuals and whole genera, which, had they been now existing, would have linked all living beings by a series of gradations so subtle that little classification could have

① Sally Shuttleworth. "Evolutionary Psychology and *The Way of All Flesh*." In *Samuel Butler: Victorian Against the Grain, A Critical Overview*. Edited by James G. Paradis. Toronto, Buffalo and London: University of Toronto Press, 2007, p. 155. In parallel with the *Life and Habit*, Butler's narrative outcome in *The Way of All Flesh* seemed to be a redeemed version of the father and son antagonistic performance.

② Gillian Beer. "Butler, Memory, and the Future." In *Samuel Butler: Victorian Against the Grain, A Critical Overview*. Edited by James G. Paradis. Toronto, Buffalo and London: University of Toronto Press, 2007, p. 49.

> been attempted. How it is that the one great personality of life as a whole, should have split itself up into so many centres of thought and action, each one of which is wholly, or at any rate nearly, unconscious of its connection with the other members, instead of having grown up into a huge polyp, or as it were coral reef or compound animal over the whole world, which should be conscious but of its own one single existence; how it is that the daily waste of this creature should be carried on by the conscious death of its individual members, instead of by the unconscious waste of tissue which goes on in the bodies of each individual (if indeed the tissue which we waste daily in our own bodies is so unconscious of its birth and death as we suppose); how, again, that the daily repair of this huge creature life should have become decentralised, and be carried on by conscious reproduction on the part of its component items, instead of by the unconscious nutrition of the whole from a single centre, as the nutrition of our own bodies would appear (though perhaps falsely) to be carried on; these are matters upon which I dare not speculate here, but on which some reflections may follow in subsequent chapters. ①

Butler's concept of personal identity is associated with Darwin's early writing in *The Voyage of the Beagle*, with the polyp, the coral and the compound animal. The behaviour of men must have roots in the communal memory of the human race. For Butler, the family of human beings is only one kind of hereditary organization. He intends to "escape from the strictures of familial shared identity by imaging life as a lateral organization associated by unconscious ties performed through the persistent activity of waste and repair."② Here Butler's key point is that "the

① Samuel Butler. *Life and Habit*. London: Trübner, 1878. Revised edition, with author's addenda and a preface by R. A. Streatfeild, London: A. C. Fifield, 1910. The Echo Library edition, 2007, Ch. VI, p. 55.

② Gillian Beer. "Butler, Memory, and the Future." In *Samuel Butler: Victorian Against the Grain, A Critical Overview*. Edited by James G. Paradis. Toronto, Buffalo and London: University of Toronto Press, 2007, p. 49.

unconsciousness of connection has allowed diversity to thrive in 'the one great personality of life'."① Thus, Gillian Beer points out that "improvement, progress, future life all fall to his pen, yet he [Butler] hopes for transformation."②

There is a kind of vertical split in the mind that makes for delusion and their defensive equivalents—Ernest of *The Way of All Flesh* experiences this split self between ego and superego, the self versus the conscious.③ As a schoolboy, Ernest becomes aware of the "other Ernest that dwelt within him and was so much stronger and more real than the Ernest of which he was conscious".④ This is in fact his ego, his unconscious true self. The unarticulated struggle inside Ernest's mind is presented an intropsychic dialogue in which the true self of Ernest says,

> You are surrounded on every side by lies which would deceive even the elect, if the elect were not generally so uncommonly wide awake; the self of which you are conscious, your reasoning and reflecting self, will believe these lies and bid you act in accordance with them. This conscious self of yours, Ernest, is a prig begotten of prigs and trained in priggishness; I will not allow it to shape your actions, though it will doubtless shape your words for many a year to come. Your papa is not here to beat you now; this is a change in the conditions of your existence, and should be followed by changed actions. Obey me, your true self, and things will go tolerably well with you, but only listen to that outward and visible old husk of yours which is called your father, and I will rend you in pieces even unto the third and fourth generation as one who has hated God; for I, Ernest, am the God who made you.⑤

---

① *Ibid.*, p. 49.

② *Ibid.*, p. 51.

③ Leonard Shengold. *Delusions of Everyday Life*. New Haven: Yale University Press, 1995, pp. 142-143.

④ Samuel Butler. *The Way of All Flesh*. London: Grant Richards, 1903; published posthumously. Edited with an introduction by V. S. Pritchett, London: Penguin English Library, 2012, Ch. 31, p. 153.

⑤ *Ibid.*, Ch. 31, pp. 153-154.

Here Butler shows Ernest's awareness of the intropsychic conflict both between ego and superego (self and consciousness) and within ego and superego (by providing two competing versions of self and consciousness). ① This unconscious self urges Ernest to disobedience, to discard his consciously and priggishly trained self. Ernest, for the first time, recognizes this inner voice of Butler's evolutionary personality as "the God who made him". Ernest, of course, is never an "elect". The "elect" are those fortunate beings who, like Old John, Towneley, Overton and Aunt Alethea are protected by their ever-wakeful instincts. Instead, Ernest, argues U. C. Knoepflmacher, "must act through his 'reasoning and reflecting self'. He must rely on consciousness in order to recall his ancestral experience, to induce a modification, and to pass it one to his descendants as a 'law'. Ernest's children, or rather his children's children, will again be able to revert to 'habit' and join the elect. "②

Ernest's first traumatic experience occurs during his house-to-house visitation at Ashpit Place. He witnesses the different habits, thoughts and conditions of life of his neighbors. Unfortunately, the visit goes awry. Mr. Holt threatens to harm him physically; Mr and Mrs Baxter try to persuade him to Methodism; Mr. Shaw

① Leonard Shengold. *Delusions of Everyday Life*. New Haven: Yale University Press, 1995, pp. 143-144. The real self of Ernest is the one that is separated from his father, thus Shengold says, "In a narcissistically delusional mode, part of him [Ernest] has become God and another (the father part) is Satan. (These are of course entirely reversible roles)."

② U. C. Knoepflmacher. *Religious Humanism and the Victorian Novel: George Eliot, Walter Pater, and Samuel Butler*. Princeton: Princeton University Press, 1965, pp. 278-279. According to U. C. Knoepflmacher, Ernest's reconversion to his "true self" is depicted in three separate stages. The first stage portrays Ernest at Battersby and at Roughborough as the victim of the heritage introduced by George Pontifex. The second stage depicts the adolescent at Cambridge and in London, where he is imposed upon by a succession of false prophets. Still misusing the changed "conditions of his existence". Ernest finally succumbs to a crisis that illustrates the insufficiency of his training. In the third stage of his career, to be examined in the last section of this chapter, Ernest finally tries to unlearn the false habits of the past two generations. This final schooling produces Ernest's misguided marriage, but ends "tolerably well" with a "pontifex" who can build a bridge from the past into the future.

undermines his faith in the Resurrection; Miss Snow, a charming young woman, nearly ruins his moral character; Miss Maitland, whom he supposes to be of the same moral persuasion as Miss Snow, causes a huge misunderstanding that leads to irreparable damage. The only lodger who has done no harm to Ernest is the bellows' mender—whom he has not visited. ①Due to his naïveté, Ernest fails to see that Miss Maitland is not a prostitute like Miss Snow. It is while he is speaking to the latter that Ernest is startled by the arrival of Towneley at his appointed time. Then Ernest enters Miss Maitland's room, only to be carried off by two policemen ten minutes later. Overton recounts afterwards for the reader the unfortunate turn of events:

> Miss Maitland had had no intention of giving Ernest in charge when she ran out of Mrs Jupp's house. She was running away because she was frightened, but almost the first person whom she ran against had happened to be a policeman of a serious turn of mind, who wished to gain a reputation for activity. He stopped her, questioned her, frightened her still more, and it was he rather than Miss Maitland, who insisted on giving my hero in charge to himself and another constable. ②

Here, Butler quotes Shakespeare to express the irony of chance and luck:

> O Opportunity, thy guilt is great
> 'Tis thou that execut'st the traitor's treason:
> Thou set'st the wolf where he the lamb may get;
> Whoever plots the sin, thou 'point'st the season;

① Samuel Butler. *The Way of All Flesh*. London: Grant Richards, 1903; published posthumously. Edited with an introduction by V. S. Pritchett, London: Penguin English Library, 2012, Ch. 61, p. 312.

② *Ibid.*, Ch. 61 p. 313.

> 'Tis thou that spurn'st at right, at law, at reason;
> And in thy shady cell, where none may spy him,
> Sits Sin, to seize the souls that wander by him. ①

Still in Mrs. Jupp's house, Towneley comes running at the sound of the commotion. Even at this moment of crisis, even at his reputation is being slandered, Ernest shows his instinctive sense of humour when Towneley asks him who are his friends in London. Ernest reluctantly mentions Overton. Towneley then asks, "Does he write comedy?" Ernest thinks, "Towneley meant that he ought to write tragedy, and said he was afraid I wrote burlesque. "② Soon after Ernest is sent to the police court. The magistrate considers this one of the most painful cases that he has ever had to deal with and sentences Ernest to six months of hard labor at Coldbath Fields Prison. He even reprimands Ernest for having betrayed his genteel upbringing, which is worth quoting at length:

> You have been singularly favoured in your parentage and education. You have had before you the example of blameless parents, who doubtless instilled into you from childhood the enormity of the offence which by your own confession you have committed. You were sent to one of the best public schools in England. It is not likely that in the healthy atmosphere of such a

① *Ibid.*, Ch. 60 p. 311. See also Shakespeare's poem "Tarquin and Lucrece" ("The Rape of Lucrece" 1594) in *Poems by William Shakespeare*, with illustrative remarks, original and selected. London: James Cundee, 1804, vol. I, p. 88. Then Butler makes Overton to ask, "If the guilt of opportunity is great, how much greater is the guilt of that which is believed to be opportunity, but in reality is no opportunity at all. If the better part of valour is discretion, how much more is not discretion the better part of vice?" See Samuel Butler. *The Way of All Flesh.* London: Grant Richards, 1903; published posthumously. Edited with an introduction by V. S. Pritchett, London: Penguin English Library, 2012, Ch. 60, p. 311.

② Samuel Butler. *The Way of All Flesh.* London: Grant Richards, 1903; published posthumously. Edited with an introduction by V. S. Pritchett, London: Penguin English Library, 2012, Ch. 61, pp. 313-314.

> school as Roughborough you can have come across contaminating influences; you were probably, I may say certainly, impressed at school with the heinousness of any attempt to depart from the strictest chastity until such time as you had entered into a state of matrimony. At Cambridge you were shielded from impurity by every obstacle which virtuous and vigilant authorities could devise, and even had the obstacles been fewer, your parents probably took care that your means should not admit of your throwing money away upon abandoned characters. At night proctors patrolled the street and dogged your steps if you tried to go into any haunt where the presence of vice was suspected. By day the females who were admitted within the college walls were selected mainly on the score of age and ugliness. It is hard to see what more can be done for any young man than this. For the last four or five months you have been a clergyman, and if a single impure thought had still remained within your mind, ordination should have removed it: nevertheless, not only does it appear that your mind is as impure as though none of the influences to which I have referred had been brought to bear upon it, but it seems as though their only result had been this—that you have not even the common sense to be able to distinguish between a respectable girl and a prostitute. ①

The speech alone establishes Butler as a brilliant satirist. It is actually a denunciation of the institutions of family, education and religion in keeping young people ignorant in sexual matters. The magistrate's reason is that since Ernest has been protected from "contaminating influences" since birth and can be assumed to be free of any impure thoughts by virtue of ordination, he should not be subject to any improper carnal desires. Ernest's upbringing is not only autobiographical but has also been arranged to support the dictumin *Life and Habit* that "It [birth] is commonly considered as the point at which we begin to

① *Ibid.*, Ch. 62, pp. 318-319.

live. More truly it is the point at which we leave off knowing how to live."[1]

The disastrous ending of Ernest's short-lived evangelistic campaign is the climactic event that reveals his increasingly befuddlement over his personal identity and development. It also exposes all the deficiencies of Ernest's education at Battersby, Roughborough, and even Cambridge. Ernest's education has not even taught him how to "distinguish between a respectable girl and a prostitute."[2] The only excuse Overton can make for Ernest is that "he was very young [...] and that in mind as in body [...] he was a slow grower. By far the greater part of his education had been an attempt, not so much to keep him in blinkers as to gouge his eyes out altogether."[3] Overton speculates that no one is really to blame: neither Theobald for his treatment of his son, considering how badly his father treated him, nor Ernest for his actions, considering how he has been brought up. He puts the matter in a biological framework, reflecting Butler's theory in *Life and Habit*:

> If a man is to enter into the Kingdom of Heaven, he must do so, not only as a little child, but as a little embryo, or rather as a little zoosperm—and not only this, but as one that has come of zoosperms which have entered into the Kingdom of Heaven before him for many generations.[4]

Even before reaching prison, Ernest collapses with an incipient attack of brain fever that leaves him bedridden for nearly two months in the prison

① Samuel Butler. *Life and Habit*. London: Trübner, 1878. Revised edition, with author's addenda and a preface by R. A. Streatfeild, London: A. C. Fifield, 1910. The Echo Library edition, 2007, Ch. IV, p. 34.

② Samuel Butler. *The Way of All Flesh*. London: Grant Richards, 1903; published posthumously. Edited with an introduction by V. S. Pritchett, London: Penguin English Library, 2012, Ch. 62, p. 319.

③ *Ibid.*, Ch. 61, p. 313.

④ *Ibid.*, Ch. 63, p. 323.

infirmary. During his slow recovery, Ernest realizes his mistake in becoming a clergyman and convinces himself that all the Christian miracles, including the Resurrection, are false. Overton remarks that Ernest has been shorn of his brainwashing:

> Perhaps the shock of so great a change in his surroundings had accelerated changes in his opinions, just as the cocoons of silkworms, when sent in baskets by rail, hatch before their time through the novelty of heat and jolting. But however this may be, his belief in the stories concerning the Death, Resurrection and Ascension of Jesus Christ, and hence his faith in all the other Christian miracles, had dropped off him once and for ever. ①

Ernest's meditation during this period purges away the "reasonable" religious faith implanted by two generations of his family. "Never in full possession of his reason" for two months, Ernest recovers at last with consciousness and even laughs at a "rallying sally" made by his nurse who promptly predicts that "he would be a man again". ② In the meantime, however, Theobald has already renounced Ernest as his son. Overton, who assumed the burden of bearing the bad news of Ernest's misfortune to Theobald, is pleased by this development, for he is certain that Ernest's chances for straightening himself out are much better without further parental interference. Ironically, it is in prison where is isolated from his parents and allies that Ernest finally recovers his freedom. It is the loosening of these ties that enables him to adapt and evolve. ③ As U. C. Knoepflmacher points out, "for his [Ernest's] cell provides him with the abruptly altered environment he needs in order to undo the work of parents and

---

① *Ibid.*, Ch. 64, p. 326.

② *Ibid.*, Ch. 64, pp. 324-325.

③ Danielle Nielsen. "Samuel Butler's *Life and Habit* and *The Way of All Flesh*: Traumatic Evolution." In *English literature in Transition, 1880 – 1920*, vol. 54, No. 1, 2011, p. 96.

institutions who 'hated change of all sorts'."[1]

This event in Ernest's life marks the start of his recovery and the reconstruction of his identity. Ernest's trust in the morality and the truth of Battersby, Roughborough and Cambridge is shattered forever, but he has yet to learn that truth does not come in the form of moral absolutes. Convinced that he needs a faith to negate the "past selves" of George, Theobald and Christina, Ernest searches for a "criterion of truth" to guide his future actions: "decision was difficult—so difficult that a man had better follow his instinct than attempt to decide them by any process of reasoning."[2] Ernest determines to make a clear break with his past and rely on his instincts. In so doing he unwittingly revives his true heredity, the creed of John Pontifex: "Instinct then is the ultimate court of appeal. And what is instinct? It is a mode of faith in the evidence of things not actually seen."[3] Henceforth Ernest "decides to rely on the unseen 'power' which he now feels "to be in him", this vital principle described in *Life and Habit* as 'the desire to know, or do, or live at all.'"[4] Butler compares this desire with reason or discursive knowledge:

> One neither finds nor expects much*a priori* knowledge, whether in man or beast; but one does find some little in the beginnings of, and throughout the development of, every habit, at the commencement of which, and on every successive improvement in which, deductive and inductive methods are, as it were, fused. Thus the effect, where we can best watch its causes, seems

---

① U. C. Knoepflmacher. *Religious Humanism and the Victorian Novel: George Eliot, Walter Pater, and Samuel Butler.* Princeton: Princeton University Press, 1965, p. 288.

② Samuel Butler. *The Way of All Flesh.* London: Grant Richards, 1903; published posthumously. Edited with an introduction by V. S. Pritchett, London: Penguin English Library, 2012, Ch. 65, p. 331.

③ *Ibid.*, Ch. 65, p. 331

④ U. C. Knoepflmacher. *Religious Humanism and the Victorian Novel: George Eliot, Walter Pater, and Samuel Butler.* Princeton: Princeton University Press, 1965, p. 289.

> mainly produced by a desire for a definite object—in some cases a serious and sensible desire. ①

Butler insists that faith rather than reason guides individuals as they act to fulfill their desire and will, and it is by faith too that man dealt with the circumstances and conditions of their existence. ② In accordance with Butler's evolutionary theories, Ernest's passive recollection of the instinctual "grace" of his great-grandfather, John Pontifex, must be translated into action. Ernest enacts the precepts of his instinctive faith and his optimism overcomes all of his earlier doubts and hesitations: "He had lost his faith in Christianity, but his faith in something—he knew not what, but that there was as something as yet but darkly known which made right right and wrong wrong—his faith in this grew stronger and stronger daily." ③ For Overton, the loss of money is far worse than the loss of one's health or reputation; Ernest, on the other hand, is far more concerned with the threat to his welfare posed by his parents. In a vivid passage in *Life and Habit*, Butler describes the internal battle fought by the individual who, like Ernest Pontifex, must defy the identity forced upon him by his ancestors and parents:

> It is one against legion when a creature tries to differ from his own past selves. He must yield or die if he wants to differ widely, so as to lack natural instincts, such as hunger or thirst, or not to gratify them. It is more righteous

① Samuel Butler. *Life and Habit*. London: Trübner, 1878. Revised edition, with author's addenda and a preface by R. A. Streatfeild, London: A. C. Fifield, 1910. The Echo Library edition, 2007, Ch. XIII, p. 137.

② For Samuel Butler's pondering on faith and reason see Samuel Butler. *Alps and Sanctuaries of Piedmont and the Canton Ticino*. London: David Bogue, 1882.

③ Samuel Butler. *The Way of All Flesh*. London: Grant Richards, 1903; published posthumously. Edited with an introduction by V. S. Pritchett, London: Penguin English Library, 2012, Ch. 68, p. 350.

> in a man that he should "eat strange food," and that his cheek should "so much as lank not," than that he should starve if the strange food be at his command. His past selves are living in him at this moment with the accumulated life of centuries. "Do this, this, this, which we too have done, and found our profit in it," cry the souls of his forefathers within him. Faint are the far ones, coming and going as the sound of bells wafted on to a high mountain; loud and clear are the near ones, urgent as an alarm of fire. "Withhold," cry some. "Go on boldly," cry others. "Me, me, me, revert hitherward, my descendant," shouts one as it were from some high vantage-ground over the heads of the clamorous multitude. "Nay, but me, me, me," echoes another; and our former selves fight within us and wrangle for our possession. Have we not here what is commonly called an *internal tumult*, when dead pleasures and pains tug within us hither and thither? Then may the battle be decided by what people are pleased to call our own experience. ①

In *The Way of All Flesh*, Butler's analysis of a continuous personality is confined to a study of five generations of the Pontifex line; moreover, the reconstruction of the personal identity is centered on the development of Ernest. Old John, George, Theobald and Christina are merely Ernest's past selves, the "past existences" described in *Life and Habit*. "He [Ernest] is the victim of John Pontifex's injudicious marriage, of George Pontifex's transplantation, of Theobald Pontifex's timidity and weakness. He is the accumulation of their mistakes."②

Ernest's "internal tumult" is depicted through both an internal and an external

① Samuel Butler. *Life and Habit*. London: Trübner, 1878. Revised edition, with author's addenda and a preface by R. A. Streatfeild, London: A. C. Fifield, 1910. The Echo Library edition, 2007, Ch. III, p. 30.

② U. C. Knoepflmacher. *Religious Humanism and the Victorian Novel: George Eliot, Walter Pater, and Samuel Butler*. Princeton: Princeton University Press, 1965, p. 259.

struggle with his "past selves". Overton, Butler's alter ego, gives his reinterpretation of the notion of salvation as opposed to that of New Testament:

> Accidents which happen to a man before he is born, in the persons of his ancestors, will, if he remembers them at all, leave an indelible impression on him; they will have moulded his character so that, do what he will, it is hardly possible for him to escape their consequences. If a man is to enter into the kingdom of heaven, he must do so, not only as a little child, but as a little embryo, or rather as a little zoosperm—and not only this, but as one that has come of zoosperms which have entered into the Kingdom of Heaven before him for many generations. Accidents which occur for the first time, and belong to the period since a man's last birth, are not, as a general rule, so permanent in their effects, though of course they may sometimes be so. ①

Ernest determines to be independent. It is no wonder then that Ernest has to pay for the "consequences" of his heredity and must make a complete break with his parents. Ernest's growth and development occur in a process where: "[e]very change is a shock". ② Change and shock are prompted by an alteration in surroundings, material or spiritual, and Ernest's mind moves by fits and starts on its path of evolution. In the last stage of evolution, in order to recover a healthy ancestral memory, Ernest must, like any organism described in *Life and Habit*, induce a conscious modification which is to alter the habits of his past self and create a "law" for his future self. ③ Here Butler advises to obey one's own

---

① Samuel Butler. *The Way of All Flesh.* London: Grant Richards, 1903. Edited with an introduction by V. S. Pritchett, London: Penguin English Library, 2012, Ch. 63, p. 323.

② *Ibid.*, Ch. 53, p. 276.

③ U. C. Knoepflmacher. *Religious Humanism and the Victorian Novel: George Eliot, Walter Pater, and Samuel Butler.* Princeton: Princeton University Press, 1965, p. 289.

conscience (the true self).[①] For individuals, obeying one's own conscience rather than the dictates of others is the best way to guarantee one's own welfare. We can observe how, in attempting to combat the mechanistic, arbitrary aspects of Darwinian theory of evolution, Butler emphasizes notions of consciousness and unconscious memory through his theories of inherited memory and oneness of personality between parents and offspring. He wrote *The Way of All Flesh* from the perspective of the individual life and created the main character Ernest with a greater sense of personal identity.

Butler also differed from other nineteenth-century writers in how he presents Coldbath Fields as perhaps the most enjoyable and beneficial environment in Ernest's life, in contrast to the conventional portrayal of the horrors of English prisons. This innovation ensues from Butler's evolutionary thoughts. Ernest actually finds prison life more to his liking than any of his previous residences, especially Battersby and Roughborough. The prison chaplain wisely directs his charge to consider what he will do after he is released from prison. While in prison, Ernest learns the rudiments of tailoring and is allowed to play the chapel organ. He realizes that the prison chaplain is much more effective in ministering to his needs than the many clergymen who were associated with him in the past. He understands for the first time in his life that he must acquire new knowledge and habits to replace those that he has unlearned. Ernest's subsequent actions show the power of his new faith.

Butler's works bear the stamp of his opposition to absolute truth or morality. For Butler, all extremes are absurd.[②] As for the judgement of the effect of one's

---

① Petronella Jacoba de. Lange. *Samuel Butler, Critic and Philosopher*. Zutphen, Netherlands: W. J. Thieme, 1925, p. 138.

② Butler wrote in *Erewhon Revisited*, why is it so necessary to avoid extremes of truthfulness? because "extremes meet, and extremes truth will be mixed with extreme falsehood". See Samuel Butler. *Erewhon and Erewhon Revisited*, with an introduction by Lewis Mumford. New York: The Modern Library, 1927, Ch. XIII, p. 457.

action in general, whether right or wrong, Butler believed that this should be judged according to the result. He gives a striking example in his *Note-Books*: "Turns on whether the pleasure precedes or follows the pain. Thus, it is immoral to get drunk because the headache comes after the drinking, but if the headache came first, and the drunkenness afterwards, it would be moral to get drunk."① According to Butler, the result is all that matters while the motive is inconsequent.② Since there are no absolute and unshakable principles, the only practical way of existing and thinking is by means of compromise and by acting on a balance of considerations.③

Butler's ideas on truth sprung from his conception of the relativity of vice and virtue, reason and faith. For too long people have followed a "will-o-the wisp" in their desire for "a single spot of absolutely unassailable ground" based on reason. Butler contends, "we have been penny-wise in the matter of risk, and prove pound-foolish in the end; we have tried to get rid of faith altogether as involving uncertainty, and behold, when our faith was dead, our reason was dead also."④ In Butler's views, the intrinsically interdependent relationship of reason and faith liberates himself from any professional truth tellers who interpret life by mechanic doctrine or abstract formulae. Truth must "never be allowed to

① Samuel Butler. *The Note-Books of Samuel Butler*. Edited with a preface and biographical statement by Henry Festing Jones. London: A. C. Fifield, 1912. Edition in use: IndyPublish edition, 2007, p. 18.

② The same idea is also expressed in *The Way of All Flesh*. See Samuel Butler. *The Way of All Flesh*. London: Grant Richards, 1903. Edited with an introduction by V. S. Pritchett, London: Penguin English Library edition, 2012, Ch. 80, pp. 418-419.

③ Petronella Jacoba de, Lange. *Samuel Butler, Critic and Philosopher*. Zutphen, Netherlands: W. J. Thieme, 1925, p. 151.

④ Samuel Butler. *Collected Essays. The Shrewsbury Edition of the Works of Samuel Butler*. Edited by Henry Festing Jones and A. T. Bartholomew. London: Jonathan Cape, 1925, vol. I, p, 152.

become extreme; otherwise it will be apt to meet and to run into the extreme of falsehood."① Butler was convinced that truth is provisional and relative, and that morality must be judged by results—what is upheld of morality being also true of truth.②

This notion of truth is certainly debated in *The Way of All Flesh*, where Butler muses that "truth is what commends itself to the great majority of sensible and successful people—is not infallible".③ Ernest asks himself:

> What were they? Ah! That was a difficult matter; there were so many, and the rules which governed them were sometimes so subtle, that mistakes always had and always would be made; it was just this that made it impossible to reduce life to an exact science.④

There is a rough and ready rule-of-thumb test that one could apply, yet there is always a residue of cases "in which decision was difficult—so difficult that a man had better follow his instinct than attempt to decide them by any process of reasoning".⑤ For a clergyman like Ernest's father, Butler had this piece of advice:

> If "an Earnest Clergyman" has not cheated himself into thinking he is telling the truth, he will do no great harm by stopping where he is. Do not

---

① Samuel Butler. *The Note-Books of Samuel Butler*. Edited with a preface and biographical statement by Henry Festing Jones. London: A. C. Fifield, 1912. Edition in use: IndyPublish edition, 2007, p. 256.

② C E. Joad discusses Butler's attitude towards morality, see C. E. M. Joad. *Samuel Butler (1835 – 1902)*. London: L. Parsons, 1924, p. 107.

③ Samuel Butler. *The Way of All Flesh*. London: Grant Richards, 1903. Edited with an introduction by V. S. Pritchett, London: Penguin English Library edition, 2012, Ch. 65, p. 330.

④ *Ibid.*, Ch. 65, p. 330.

⑤ *Ibid.*, Ch. 65, p. 331.

> let him make too much fuss about trifles. The solemnity of the truths which he professes to uphold is very doubtful; there is a tacit consent that it exists more on paper than in reality. If he is a man of any tact, he can say all he is compelled to say and do all the Church requires of him—like a gentleman, with neither undue slovenliness nor undue unction—yet it shall be perfectly plain to all his parishioners who are worth considering that he is acting as a mouthpiece and that his words are spoken dramatically.①

The misfortune of the clergyman is that he has lost his own belief and has no means of his own to support the needs of his wife and children. In general, if a tact man, "like a gentleman, with neither undue slovenliness nor undue unction", who also holds the wisdom of the common sense. This man, whether he is a clergyman or not, we could not blame him on account of his profession. For Butler, this is a kind of improvement. The only way to such improvement as Butler considered is through good breeding. According to Butler, vice and crime are mainly a result of impractical education and bad environment. Hereditary defects and unsound surroundings that lead to crime can be considered as a kind of misfortune, and just as it is illogical to reward people for their sheer good luck, it is equally unfair to punish people for their misfortunes.② Butler makes the malcontents in *Erewhon* his mouthpiece. They assert that:

> Illness is the inevitable result of certain antecedent causes, which, in the great majority of cases, were beyond the control of the individual, and that

① Samuel Butler. *The Note-Books of Samuel Butler*. Edited with a preface and biographical statement by Henry Festing Jones. London: A. C. Fifield, 1912. Edition in use: IndyPublish edition, 2007, p. 263.

② Samuel Butler. *Erewhon*. First published in 1872. Edited with an introduction by Peter Mudford. London: Penguin, 1985, p. 120.

> therefore a man is only guilty for being in a consumption in the same way as rotten fruit is guilty for having gone rotten... But these radicals would not punish him further than by loss of liberty and a strict surveillance. So long as he was prevented from injuring society, they would allow him to make himself useful by supplying whatever of society's wants he could supply. If he succeeded in thus earning money, they would have him made as comfortable in prison as possible... deduct from his earnings the expenses of his board, lodging, surveillance, and half those of his conviction... The main argument on which they rely is that of economy; for they know that they will sooner gain their end by appealing to men's pockets, in which they have generally something of their own, than to their heads, which contain for the most part little but borrowed or stolen property; and also, they believe it to be the readiest test and the one which has most to show for itself. ①

From this passage, we learn that Butler's tolerant attitudes towards prisoners are in accordance with liberal values. It also illustrates Butler's favourite tenet: money, like machine, is the way in which the human race varies at present. ② Butler feels that inmates ought to be allowed to tend to their own welfare in prison and make themselves useful to society. This also confirms Butler's adherence to Utilitarian principles.

As for Ernest, the most significant aspect of his prison experience is the realization that it was vitally important for him to carve out an independent course of action for himself. He disavows his previous self and resolves to assert his own judgment. He begins by redefining Christianity to serve his own interests and

---

① *Ibid.*, pp. 123-125.

② Petronella Jacoba de, Lange. *Samuel Butler*, *Critic and Philosopher*. Zutphen, Netherlands: W. J. Thieme, 1925, pp. 143-144. Butler's opinion, as Petronella Jacoba de. Lange concluded: "the man who has most money and machines at his disposal has the best chance of surviving and of producing a well-bred offspring."

concludes that the only tenable philosophy to live by is one that is consistent in its inconsistency. He will "kiss the soil" in the manner prescribed by his Aunt Alethea by becoming a tailor and by shedding all pretensions to gentility. This experience liberates Ernest from most of the external and internal strains that have ill-served him in the past.

Ernest's trials and tribulations, however, are not over. Although he has realized the impracticality of his religious and educational training and the harm caused by his parents' influence, Ernest has not yet acquired common sense in the choice of a mate. It is possibly that here he has been affected by John Pontifex's injudicious choice. Ernest's deficiency in this matter is dryly remarked upon by Overton, "What he wanted was in reality so easily to be found that it took a highly educated scholar like himself to be unable to find it."[①] Just as he could not tell a respectable girl from a prostitute, he rashly proposes marriage to Ellen. Overton dislikes Ellen "instinctively", for he is aware that Ernest's future status as a gentleman is seriously threatened by this unsuitable marriage.[②] For Butler, the only thing that guides us through this puzzling world full of contradictions is common sense.[③] In *Luck or Cunning*? Butler argues, "We cannot serve the God of philosophy and the Mammon of common sense at one and the same time, and yet it would seem as though the best that can be made of both these worlds were the whole duty of organism."[④] Common sense is even more

① Samuel Butler. *The Way of All Flesh.* London: Grant Richards, 1903. Edited with an introduction by V. S. Pritchett, London: Penguin English Library, 2012, Ch. 71, p. 364.

② Overton knows that Ernest will receive a fortune of seventy-thousand pounds on his twenty-eighth birthday.

③ Petronella Jacoba de, Lange. *Samuel Butler, Critic and Philosopher.* Zutphen, Netherlands: W. J. Thieme, 1925, p. 152.

④ Samuel Butler. *Luck, or Cunning as the Main Means of Organic Modification*? London: Trübner, 1887. The Echo Library edition, 2007, Ch. XI, pp. 80-81.

important than philosophy in practice. [①] It has the power to keep the world sane and safe, since it is accumulated knowledge through generations.

It is significant that Butler's opinion on life is compatible with his evolutionary theory. In light of the illusory nature of truth and the inseparatible nature of reason and faith, Butler defends what could act as guides to life. From his Lamarckian perspective, life is a continual process of accommodation, which can only be arrived at through compromise. [②] For Butler, life is not one of the exact sciences and living is essentially an art, everything addressed to human minds at all must be more or less of a compromise. Here, the individual reaches a compromise by relying on either reason or instinct as a final court of appeal. [③] What then is the place of instinct in Butler's conception of evolution? Butler views instinct as "a mode of faith in the evidence of things not actually seen",

① Butler wrote in *Erewhon*, "It will be seen from the foregoing chapters that the Erewhonians are a meek and long-suffering people, easily led by the nose, and quick to offer up common sense at the shrine of logic, when a philosopher arises among them, who carries them away through his reputation for especial learning, or by convincing them that their existing institutions are not based on the strictest principles of morality...Happily common sense, though she is by nature the gentlest creature living, when she feels the knife at her throat, is apt to develop unexpected powers of resistance, and to send doctrinaires flying, even when they have bound her down and think they have her at their mercy." See Samuel Butler. *Erewhon*. First published in 1872. Edited with an introduction by Peter Mudford. London: Penguin, 1985, p. 227.

② For "All our lives long, every day and every hour, we are engaged in the process of accommodating our changed and unchanged selves to changed and unchanged surroundings [...] A life will successful or not, according as the power of accommodating is equal to, or unequal to the strain of fusing and adjusting internal and external changes." See Samuel Butler. *The Way of All Flesh*. London: Grant Richards, 1903; published posthumously, as edited by R. A. Streatfield. London: A. C. Fifield, 1908. Edited with an introduction by V. S. Pritchett, London: Penguin English Library edition, 2012, Ch. 69, pp. 356-357.

③ Petronella Jacoba de, Lange. *Samuel Butler, Critic and Philosopher*. Zutphen, Netherlands: W. J. Thieme, 1925, p. 153. Butler argued: "Reason uncorrected by instinct is as bad as instinct uncorrected by reason." See Samuel Butler. *Erewhon*. First published in 1872. Edited with an introduction by Peter Mudford. London: Penguin, 1985, Ch. XXVII, p. 242.

but he believes that instinct is the ultimate court of appeal. ① Instinct, according to Butler, combines two aspects of the individual-unconscious memory and intelligence (cunning or will). Hence our unconscious thinking, in a sense, is no different from our conscious thinking—in both, we are able to develop rapid decision-making with training and experience. Learning should also be taken into practice. Underlining the importance of instinct as the accumulated wisdom of people's ancestors, Butler argues, "The just shall live by the conduct of faith." ② And who are the just? Butler would answer: "reasonable people". ③ He continues:

> They settle smaller matters by the exercise of their own deliberation. More important ones, such as the cure of their own bodies and the bodies of those whom they love, the investment of their money, the extrication of their affairs from any serious mess—these things they generally entrust to others of whose capacity they know little save from general report; they act therefore on the strength of faith, not of knowledge. So the English nation entrusts the welfare of its fleet and naval defences to a First Lord of the Admiralty, who, not being a sailor can know nothing about these matters except by acts of faith. There can be no doubt about faith and not reason being the *ultima ratio*. ④

From the passage above, we learn that Ernest finally understands that there is no system of perfect rules or guides to life. While Butler places instinct and reason on an equal footing, should the two conflict with each other, to trust instinct—the inherited experience of generations embedded within each individual—is

---

① Samuel Butler. *The Way of All Flesh.* London: Grant Richards, 1903. Edited with an introduction by V. S. Pritchett, London: Penguin English Library, 2012, Ch. 65, p. 331.

② *Ibid.*, Ch. 69, p. 357.

③ *Ibid.*, Ch. 65, p. 331.

④ *Ibid.*, Ch. 65, p. 331. The definition of ultima ratio: the final argument, also the last resort (as force) See source online: http://www.merriam-webster.com/dictionary/ultima%20ratio

one's surest guide, Butler would advise.

For Butler, there is no original sin; rather than bearing the Joad of self-condemnation, man carries within himself the seeds of his own salvation, based on the cunning faith of past generations and his own present faith.① Butler believes that instinct, as a mode of faith, exists in all living things as plants and animals are capable of acting on their volition. In *Life and Habit* Butler argues that "even the corn in the fields grows upon a superstitious basis as to its own existence, and only turns the earth and moisture into wheat through the conceit of its own ability to do so, without which faith it were powerless."② Likewise, Butler imagines that lichen on a rock, "only grows upon the granite rock by first saying to itself, 'I think I can do it'; so that it would not be able to grow unless it thought it could grow, and would not think it could grow unless it found itself able to grow."③ Butler suggests that will has its place in the development of individuals. As Gillian Beer remarks on Butler's theories:

> The spontaneous acts of an organism have already been performed by its progenitors, and re-enactment is inescapable. The idea that personal identity is already predicated in the parent form—that parents and children can never be divided—may seem acceptable in a discussion of other forms of life, but becomes claustrophobic when applied to the human, and almost unbearable when referred to Butler's own life. He seeks ways out of this

① Frank Miller Turner. "Samuel Butler: The Man of Temper." In *Between Science and Religion: The Reaction to Scientific Naturalism in Late Victorian England*. New Haven: Yale University Press, 1974, p. 186.

② Samuel Butler. *Life and Habit*. London: Trübner, 1878. Revised edition, with author's addenda and a preface by R. A. Streatfeild, London: A. C. Fifield, 1910. The Echo Library edition, 2007, Ch. V, p. 44.

③ *Ibid.*, p. 44.

dilemma by estranging the future and making it the bearer of unnamed transformation."①

What are the main tenets of this "faith" that underlines Butler's evolutionary theory? At the core lies Butler's belief in the oneness of personality and the unity of organic life. This oneness, according to Butler, holds not only between parents and offspring, but also between all species of a common ancestry. Just as cells make up the body of the individual, so are individuals themselves "only component atoms of a single compound creature, *life*, which has probably a distinct conception of its own personality though none whatever of ours".② Therefore, the identity of the individual is subordinated to the identity of the entire evolutionary organism. The personal identity is evolving with change as its dynamics. Chief among Butler's evolutionary ideas is his belief in "faith, or as the desire to know, or do, or live at all",③ and that "plants and animals are living forms of faith, or faiths of form".④ Life and death, for Butler, then, become "memory and forgetfulness ... matter which can remember is living; matter which cannot remember is dead."⑤ U. C. Knoepflmacher explains the mechanics of Butler's evolutionary concept:

To induce an organic change, matter like the Erewhonian "Unborn" must pass

---

① Gillian Beer. "Butler, Memory, and the Future." In *Samuel Butler: Victorian Against the Grain, A Critical Overview.* Edited by James G. Paradis. Toronto, Buffalo and London: University of Toronto Press, 2007, p. 48.

② Samuel Butler. *Life and Habit.* London: Trübner, 1878. Revised edition, with author's addenda and a preface by R. A. Streatfeild, London: A. C. Fifield, 1910. The Echo Library edition, 2007, Ch. VIII, p. 68.

③ *Ibid.*, Ch. VIII, p. 68.

④ Samuel Butler. *Evolution Old and New.* London: Hardwicke and Bogue, 1879, Ch. XIX, p. 339.

⑤ Samuel Butler. *Life and Habit.* London: Trübner, 1878. Revised edition, with author's addenda and a preface by R. A. Streatfeild, London: A. C. Fifield, 1910. The Echo Library edition, 2007, Ch. XV, p. 152.

> from an instinctive, unconscious stage to consciousness; it must transform the vital principle into an awareness of effort and power. Challenged by a new environment or a new climate, the awakened organism calls forth a conscious modification, solidifies it into a *law*, and passes it on to subsequent generations as a *habit*. If unable to perform this change, the organism becomes extinct; if successful, its relapse again into unconscious memory. ①

Thus, "faith" or the will to live is the initial stage of any organic change of a living organism. Butler's concept of the vital principle is tied to that of unconscious memory. "Faith" (cunning) and unconscious memory are both requisites for life, as the two limbs of man residing in man himself in the present and in the future.

---

① U. C. Knoepflmacher. *Religious Humanism and the Victorian Novel: George Eliot, Walter Pater, and Samuel Butler*. Princeton: Princeton University Press, 1965, p. 252.

4.2 Luck or cunning? Butler's ideal gentleman

> Prosperity depends, as we all know, in great measure upon energy and good sense, but it also depends not a little upon pure luck—that is to say, upon connections which are in such a tangle that it is more easy to say that they do not exist, than to try to trace them [...] so little, indeed, can be certainly known, that it is better not to try to know more than is in everybody's mouth, and to leave the rest to chance. ①

As we have seen, Butler believes that individual personality is fixed by heredity and the influence of one's surroundings. In this sense, birth can be regarded as a salient feature in a man's life. ② According to Butler, "The only thing that can produce a deep and permanently good influence upon a man's character is to have been begotten of good ancestors for many generations—or at any rate to have reverted to a good ancestor—and to live among nice people."③ Character is "human nature in its best form", and it is also "the crown and glory of life". ④ A gentleman must be of possession of a good character. On this issue, Butler echoes Samuel Smiles that character would be "strengthened and supported by

① Samuel Butler. *The Way of All Flesh*. London: Grant Richards, 1903. Edited with an introduction by V. S. Pritchett, London: Penguin English Library, 2012, Ch. 72, pp. 380-381.

② Samuel Butler. *Life and Habit*. London: Trübner, 1878. Revised edition, with author's addenda and a preface by R. A. Streatfeild, London: A. C. Fifield, 1910. The Echo Library edition, 2007, Ch. IV, p. 34.

③ Samuel Butler. *Alps and Sanctuaries of Piedmont and the Canton Ticino*. London: David Bogue, 1882, Ch. 23, p. 327.

④ Samuel Smiles. *Self-Help, with Illustrations of Character, Conduct and Perseverance*. First published in 1859. Edited with an Introduction and Notes by Peter W. Sinnema. Oxford: Oxford University Press, 2002, p. 314.

the cultivation of good habit", for "man... is a bundle of habits". ① Nice people and gentlemen are Butler's ideal and are only produced by good breeding. ② Butler's definition of what constitutes "ideal" and "good breeding" also stems from his concept of evolution. The ideal gentleman as Butler calls it, is characterized by his charity and kindness. ③ He records in his *Note-Books*, "If we are asked what is the most essential characteristic that underlies this word, the word itself will guide us to gentleness, to absence of such things as brow-beating, overbearing manners and fuss, and generally to consideration for other people. "④ A gentleman is thus set apart by his well-bred expression, physical well-being, self-respectfulness, genial manners, unconscious, instinctive knowledge and consideration for others. ⑤

Towneley and Ernest: Luck or Cunning?

Reflecting on the implications of evolutionary theory for our understanding of the identity of individuals, Butler suggests in *Life and Habit* that "[b]irth has been made too much of". ⑥ According to Butler, evolution involves a continuous process of derivation because of the "oneness of personality between parents and offspring". That is to say unconscious memory creates a sort of unchanging personal identity between parents and offspring; the latter are not wholly different individuals but can

---

① *Ibid.*, p. 319.

② Petronella Jacoba de, Lange. *Samuel Butler, Critic and Philosopher*. Zutphen, Netherlands: W. J. Thieme, 1925, p. 135.

③ *Ibid.*, p. 135.

④ Samuel Butler. *The Note-Books of Samuel Butler*. Edited with a preface and biographical statement by Henry Festing Jones. London: A. C. Fifield, 1912, 1918. IndyPublish edition: Boston, 2007, p. 24.

⑤ Petronella Jacoba de, Lange. *Samuel Butler, Critic and Philosopher*. Zutphen, Netherlands: W. J. Thieme, 1925, p. 136.

⑥ Samuel Butler. *Life and Habit*. London: Trübner, 1878. Revised edition, with author's addenda and a preface by R. A. Streatfeild, London: A. C. Fifield, 1910. The Echo Library edition, 2007, Ch. IV, p. 34.

be thought of as the parents at a later evolutionary stage. This personal identity, Butler maintains, is not bounded by birth and death, or even by material existence. To some degree, a newborn infant is part of an unbroken biological process, and not an utterly separate individual. Accordingly, there is a deep unity of all life, so that it constitutes a greater continuity between the embryo and past lives, than between the infant and the octogenarian which he will become. Therefore, we are "in reality, nothing but one single creature, of which the component members are but, as it were, blood corpuscles or individual cells."① There exists in reality an instinctive perpetuation of knowledge before birth.

In *The Way of All Flesh*, Butler makes Towneley the perfect representative of his ideal. He is described by Ernest as "not only a good fellow, but he is without exception the very best man I ever saw in my life [...] Towneley is my notion of everything which I should most like to be."② Towneley is a college friend of Ernest. When Ernest humps into him Towneley on a London street, he is suddenly aware of his inferiority compared to Towneley. The character of Towneley was probably based on one of Butler's contemporaries, an aristocratic elite, and incarnates the kind of individual who is perfectly, effortlessly and unconsciously adapted to the world. He is the man who "has been made too much of" since his birth, as well as the "gentleman in the full sense of the word". ③ His lack of questioning and self-doubt is "an Ideal which all may look upon for a shilling". ④

When considering his difference with Towneley, Ernest makes the following

---

① *Ibid.*, Ch. VI, p. 53.

② Samuel Butler. *The Way of All Flesh.* London: Grant Richards, 1903. Edited with an introduction by V. S. Pritchett, London: Penguin English Library, 2012, Ch. 80, p. 421.

③ Samuel Butler. *Erewhon, or Over the Range.* London: Trübner, 1872. The Penguin Classics edition, 1985, p. 157. Towneley is also the biological example of a gentleman as Butler described in his fiction.

④ *Ibid.*, p. 158.

observation to Overton after his enlightening passage in prison:

> The people like Towneley are the only ones who know anything that is worth knowing, and like that of course I can never be. But to make Towneley possible there must be hewers of wood and drawers of water—men in fact through whom conscious knowledge must pass before it can reach those who can apply it gracefully and instinctively like the Towneleys can. I am a hewer of wood, but if I accept the position frankly and do not set up to be a Towneley, it does not matter. ①

Ernest knows that, unlike Towneley, he is not one of the "elect". ② Thus, as a "hewer" and a "drawer" as opposed to the unconsciously perfect Towneley, he must learn about life by the hard way. Ernest must struggle for life and invent his personality as he proceeds, because "the life-force must periodically become aware of itself before relapsing into blessed instinctiveness". ③ Butler also emphasizes the Lamarckian inheritance of acquired characteristics in terms that admit self-help. The instinctive wisdom or "cunning", as the power of faith or desire within the individual, is venerated by Butler as a life force.

However, it must suffice to say that Butler's highest evolutionary ideal is not an intensification of consciousness but its replacement by "grace". ④ In the second chapter of *Life and Habit*, "Conscious and Unconscious Knowers—The Law and

---

① Samuel Butler. *The Way of All Flesh.* London: Grant Richards, 1903. Edited with an introduction by V. S. Pritchett, London: Penguin English Library, 2012, Ch. 73, p. 385.

② Here, From Butler's own personal experience, on Towneley, perhaps we see the shadow of Mr. Charles Darwin. Butler, himself, was also prevented from becoming the "elect" in the scientific atmosphere of evolution. However, Butler is assured of the transcendence, for even as a hewer of wood.

③ Peter Morton. "Butler on Heredity." In *The Vital Science: Biology and the Literary Imagination: 1860–1900*. London: Allen and Unwin, 1984, p. 182.

④ *Ibid.*, p. 182.

Grace", Butler develops his theories of grace in opposition to contemporary scientists and clergymen whose pursuit of knowledge he dismissed as worse than useless.① Any true knowledge, Butler argues, presupposes such total absorption and unconsciousness.② Man, like all organic life, "performs as a unit of complementary memories, accrued over centuries and shaping individuals with a kind of genetic predetermination".③ This is simply because we carry the physical, intellectual and psychic attributes and character of our ancestors:

> That a man should have been bred well and breed others well; that his figure, head, hands, feet, voice, manner and clothes should carry conviction upon this point, so that no one can look at him without seeing that he has come of good stock and is likely to throw good stock himself, this is the desiderandum.④

---

① For Butler, if a man holds the erroneous belief in absolute truth and absolute right, he is intolerant of other beliefs and makes things uncomfortable for those who do not hold it: he is thus no gentleman. Based on his evolutionary conception, and bearing in mind the professional tendency of both religion and science, as already described in previous chapters, as C. E. M. Joad asserts to "sacrifice men to institutions and people to principles, a tendency spring from the same erroneous belief in absolute truth and absolute right, we shall find Butler's outbursts against professionals and professionalism more readily intelligible than they are apt to be at a first reading." See C. E. M. Joad. *Samuel Butler (1835 – 1902)*. London: L. Parsons, 1924, pp. 112-113. C. E. M. Joad also discusses Butler's attitudes against those authorities and professionals—parents, schoolmasters, and parsons—whose complacencies are Butler's chief quarry in *The Way of All Flesh.*

② On this point, Butler's favorite illustrations of the working of unconscious memory is the analogy of the pianist who plays hundreds of notes a minute and who could not perform if he thinks about the process. A good pianist must learn too well to play habitually and unconsciously. See *Life and Habit*. Ch. I

③ Carl Dawson. "Strange Metamorphoses: Samuel Butler's 'Unconscious Memory' and *The Way of All Flesh.*" In *Prophets of Past Time: Seven British Autobiographers, 1880 – 1914*. London: Johns Hopkins University Press, 1988, p. 78.

④ Samuel Butler. *The Way of All Flesh.* London: Grant Richards, 1903. Edited with an introduction by V. S. Pritchett, London: Penguin English Library, 2012, Ch. 85, p. 459.

A gentleman must be a representative of good breeding with his knowledge accumulated through generations unconsciously stocked within him. Sally Shuttleworth maintains that Towneley can be seen as an expression of Butler's theories of "grace" outlined in *Life and Habit*—a state attained when knowledge, through generations of good breeding, becomes thoroughly unconscious and incarnate. ① Butler exalts a type of socially dominant figure in his characterizations of Towneley, in whom good breeding and knowledge are worked in perfect harmony. The gentleman is also the incarnation of graceful adaptation to environment, which Butler called "Habit", an instinctive conformity to his contemporaries and surroundings denied both to Ernest Pontifex and to Butler himself. ② On this point, Jill Rubenstein remarks:

> Butler regarded the unconscious as the culmination of the evolutionary process. Intellectual and moral principles function most effectively when they are unstated and unconscious. He "idealized the life founded on the virtues of grace, unconscious wisdom and beauty."—Grace describes those individuals who have so thoroughly assimilated knowledge as to be unaware of even possessing it. But even these favored few must confront new situations which the unconscious wisdom of the past cannot control; then they must depend on conscious knowledge and/or communal moral law. Progress, then, demands occasional conscious, intellectual moral decisions, but too much consciousness bars our access to the assimilated knowledge of past generations, the "continuous evolutionary personality". ③

---

① Sally Shuttleworth. "Evolutionary Psychology and *The Way of All Flesh.*" In *Samuel Butler: Victorian Against the Grain, A Critical Overview.* Edited by James G. Paradis. Toronto, Buffalo and London: University of Toronto Press, 2007, p. 161.

② Mr. Muggeridge calls this type "Nice Person" and makes much of Butler's sense of inferiority. See U. C. Knoepflmacher. *Religious Humanism and the Victorian Novel: George Eliot, Walter Pater, and Samuel Butler.* Princeton: Princeton University Press, 1965, p. 242.

③ Jill Rubenstein. "'Business is Business': The Money Ethic of Samuel Butler." In *English Literature in Transition, 1880 – 1920*, vol. 19, No. 4, 1976, p. 240.

For Butler, Knowledge is memory and inherited habit and experience that pass unconsciously through generations. Since "faith", according to Butler's vital principle, is applicable to men as well as animals and plants. The significance of knowledge as Butler argued in *Life and Habit* is that both plants and animals possess knowledge concerning their own history. Thus for him, memory becomes a process of sustained learning by forebears that declares itself in the individual organism. In some sense, heredity, for Butler, is a mode of memory. In one of Gillian Beer's recent essays named "Butler, Memory, and the Future", she explores Butler's thoughts on how change comes about and the degree to which future forms of life rely on unconscious memories and then outwit memory. Gillian Beer points out "He [Butler] centres *Life and Habit* on a series of statements whose sense relies upon his inversion of the usual assumption that the past has been left behind. Instead, his emphasis is that the past lies always in wait for us embedded in the future."① This is supported by the following passage in *Life and Habit*:

> A living creature well supported by a mass of healthy ancestral memory is a young and growing creature, free from ache or pain, and thoroughly acquainted with its business so far, but with much yet to be reminded of. A creature which finds itself and its surroundings not so unlike those of its parents about the time of their begetting it, as to be compelled to recognise that it never yet was in any such position, is a creature in the heyday of life. A creature which begins to be aware of itself is one which is beginning to recognize that the situation is a new one. It is the young and fair, then, who are the truly old and the truly experienced; it is they who alone have a

① Gillian Beer. "Butler, Memory, and the Future." In *Samuel Butler: Victorian Against the Grain, A Critical Overview*. Edited by James G. Paradis. Toronto, Buffalo and London: University of Toronto Press, 2007, p. 46.

trustworthy memory to guide them. ①

In brief, life in Butler's system is "memory", since it is "faith founded upon experience, which experience is in its turn founded upon faith". ② It follows therefore that the best example of life is that of a "creature well supported by a mass of healthy ancestral memory". ③ The growth and development of such an individual is attuned to the mechanics of evolution by virtue of his good breeding; he is in a state of grace as opposed to a state of law. It is this state, embodied by Towneley, Butler's ideal gentleman that Ernest finally manages to attain for his offspring. Experience or memory bridges past and future to sustain a small span of life: it is converted into a biological force perpetuated by breeding and heredity. It can be argued that this is Butler's attempt to extend Lamarck's doctrine by ascribing a role to unconscious memory in the phenomena of heredity. Towneley, in a way, is very lucky to "have been begotten of good ancestors for many generations". ④ Gillian Beer remarks that Butler "insisted on 'past selves' living 'at this moment with the accumulated life of centuries'." and that "action in his [Butler's] terms is a form of memory released from the labour of remembering". ⑤ We can imagine how the emerging discourse of

---

① Samuel Butler. *Life and Habit*. London: Trübner, 1878. Revised edition, with author's addenda and a preface by R. A. Streatfeild, London: A. C. Fifield, 1910. The Echo Library edition, 2007, Ch. XV, p. 152.

② *Ibid.*, Ch. XV p. 152. Butler wrote, "Life, then, is faith founded upon experience, which experience is in its turn founded upon faith—or more simply, it is memory. Plants and animals only differ from one another because they remember different things; plants and animals only grow up in the shapes they assume because this shape is their memory, their idea concerning their own past history."

③ *Ibid.*, p. 152

④ Samuel Butler. *Alps and Sanctuariesof Piedmont and the Canton Ticino*. London: David Bogue, 1882, Ch. 23, p. 327.

⑤ Gillian Beer. "Butler, Memory, and the Future." In *Samuel Butler: Victorian Against the Grain, A Critical Overview*. Edited by James G. Paradis. Toronto, Buffalo and London: University of Toronto Press, 2007, p. 51.

eugenics then could find fodder in Butler's preoccupation with the attainment of biological grace in both of his evolutionary treatises and in *The Way of All Flesh*.[①]

Birth, for Butler, rather than the point at which men begin to live, is the point at which men leave off knowing how to live.[②] In the line with his Lamarckian desire to imbue nature with purposiveness, Butler endows all organic nature with cunning or will. In fact, Butler's version of evolution leaped to two sweeping sides. With inheritance and memory on the one hand, on the other hand, it should be conscious effort, intelligence and cunning that exist throughout the whole organic world. "For the embryo of the chicken, we claim exactly the same kind of reasoning power and contrivance which we claim for the amoeba, or for our own intelligent performances in later life."[③] Butler wants to employ his "conscious knowledge" in the act of faith, and he finally becomes an unorthodox defender of faith.

Upon returning to England, however, Ernest is beset with feelings of guilt for resuming life as a "gentleman", since he cannot forget the sting of having been imprisoned. "He thought of the high resolves which he had made in prison about using his disgrace as a vantage ground of strength rather than trying to make people forget it," since the stimulation for change is a direct result of this traumatic event.[④] Danielle Nielsen argues that for Butler, it is precisely such

---

① Francis Galton had not yet coined the term "eugenics" when Butler composed *The Way of All Flesh*, but Galton had begun publishing in the field with *Hereditary Genius* (1869) and "Hereditary Improvement." In Fraser's *Magazine* 7 (1873).

② Samuel Butler. *Life and Habit*. London: Trübner, 1878. Revised edition, with author's addenda and a preface by R. A. Streatfeild, London: A. C. Fifield, 1910. The Echo Library edition, 2007, Ch. IV, p. 34.

③ *Ibid.*, Ch. IV, p. 40.

④ Samuel Butler. *The Way of All Flesh*. London: Grant Richards, 1903. Edited with an introduction by V. S. Pritchett, London: Penguin English Library, 2012, Ch. 80, p. 417.

trauma, shock or novelty that induces specific changes in one's habits. ① What is more, the shock must so greatly challenge memories as to break them and only in this way can the individual be completely adaptive. ② Only when the trauma causes tremors and chasms in one's memories will it bring about a change in personality. ③ Consequently, the free will of the individual will be activated and adaptation will be carried out.

Unfortunately, for Ernest, however, his physical recovery does not signal a commensurate spiritual recovery. One noteworthy case where Butler's own biological notion suffers analogical transformation in the novel is his use of his explanation of the consequences of breeding hybrid organisms, a tactic commonly called "crossing". Butler attributes the phenomenon of hybrid sterility to be the conflict between memories provided by each parent, thus the hybrid is rendered sexually ineffective by being "pulled hither and thither by two conflicting memories or advices". ④ In *The Way of All Flesh*, Butler makes a metaphorical transition between hybrid and "crossing"—an analogy between stockbreeding and the interaction between the individual and environment. ⑤ Both imprisonment and the false marriage with Ellen that Ernest experienced seem to have been altogether too great a cross. It is not until the dissolution of his marriage that Ernest gets a "relief from tension" as prescribed by the psychiatrist:

---

① Danielle Nielsen. "Samuel Butler's *Life and Habit* and *The Way of All Flesh*: Traumatic Evolution." In *English literature in Transition, 1880 – 1920*, vol. 54, No. 1, 2011, pp. 96-97.

② *Ibid.*, p. 97.

③ *Ibid.*, p. 97.

④ Samuel Butler. *Life and Habit*. London: Trübner, 1878. Revised edition, with author's addenda and a preface by R. A. Streatfeild, London: A. C. Fifield, 1910. The Echo Library edition, 2007, Ch. X, p. 89.

⑤ Peter Morton. "Butler on Heredity." In *The Vital Science: Biology and the Literary Imagination: 1860 – 1900*. London: Allen and Unwin, 1984, p. 191.

> Crossing is the great medical discovery of the age. Shake him out of himself by shaking something else into him [...] Seeing is a mode of touching, touching is a mode of feeding, feeding is a mode of assimilation, assimilation is a mode of re-creation and reproduction and this is crossing-shaking yourself into something else and something else into you. He spoke laughingly but it was plain he was serious. ①

Thus "crossing" as a method of the treatment is helpful for Ernest's slow recovery to full spiritual health. As part of his the treatment at the Zoological Gardens, Ernest saunters round the elephant-house and spiritual health improves for he seems to be "drinking in large draughts of their lives to the re-creation and regeneration of his own". ② The doctor insists that the big animals do his patient more good than the monkeys, which "are not a wide enough cross". ③ The interaction between the internal and external, self and environment, is necessary before self-recreation and reproduction can be achieved by "the individual's self-conscious selection of ideal forms of associates". ④ Later, Ernest begins his travels around the world and visits the place where "he found the inhabitants unusually good looking and agreeable." ⑤ Butler's idea of "crossing", as a critic argues, would offer "a kind of biological model of self-help that can work to counteract, if not entirely mitigate, the pressures of heredity, and offer some

---

① Samuel Butler. *The Way of All Flesh.* London: Grant Richards, 1903. Edited with an introduction by V. S. Pritchett, London: Penguin English Library, 2012, Ch. 79, p. 411.

② *Ibid.*, Ch. 79, p. 412.

③ *Ibid.*

④ Sally Shuttleworth. "Evolutionary Psychology and *The Way of All Flesh.*" In *Samuel Butler: Victorian Against the Grain, A Critical Overview.* Edited by James G. Paradis. Toronto, Buffalo and London: University of Toronto Press, 2007, p. 160.

⑤ Samuel Butler. *The Way of All Flesh.* London: Grant Richards, 1903. Edited with an introduction by V. S. Pritchett, London: Penguin English Library, 2012, Ch. 84, p. 452.

hope for redemption and self-determination". ①

Ernest finally attains physical and spiritual salvation, and becomes a contented bachelor and author. On the development of his mind, he grasps "the very essence of things"—to be mean: ②

> As the days went slowly by he came to see that Christianity and the denial of Christianity after all met as much as any other extremes do; it was a fight about names—not about things; practically the Church of Rome, the Church of England, and the freethinker have the same ideal standard and meet in the gentleman; for he is the most perfect saint who is the most perfect gentleman. Then he saw also that it matters little what profession, whether of religion or irreligion, a man may make, provided only he follows it out with charitable inconsistency, and without insisting on it to the bitter end. It is in the uncompromisingness with which dogma is held and not in the dogma or want of dogma that the danger lies. This was the crowning point of the edifice. ③

Ernest, like Butler, realized that "the greatest and wisest of mankind will be almost always found to be the meanest", ④ and that the quality of compromising, or what Butler calls compromisingness, is generally the only reasonable way of getting out of a difficulty. In Butler's philosophical outlook, inconsistency is

---

① Sally Shuttleworth. "Evolutionary Psychology and *The Way of All Flesh.*" In *Samuel Butler: Victorian Against the Grain, A Critical Overview.* Edited by James G. Paradis. Toronto, Buffalo and London: University of Toronto Press, 2007, p. 161. In continuing, Shuttleworth says, "Such hope seems deeply qualified, however, and its ideals, which focus on the power of money and virtues of good breeding, appear rather unappealing."

② Samuel Butler. *The Way of All Flesh.* London: Grant Richards, 1903. Edited with an introduction by V. S. Pritchett, London: Penguin English Library, 2012, Ch. 19, p. 98.

③ *Ibid.*, Ch. 68, p. 351.

④ *Ibid.*, Ch. 19, p. 98.

another of life's necessities. ① Petronella Jacoba Lange states:

> You can never follow up a principle to the end without coming into collision with established usage or differing from your fellowmen, so if there is no inner necessity that drives you to it, it is better to be inconsistent than to be consistent at the cost of unnecessary trouble or sorrow. ②

For Butler, habits do not randomly or unnecessarily mutate: therefore to adapt is to challenge stability, perfection, and generations of memories, with the life force of the individual. ③ The chapter on the "World of the Unborn" in *Erewhon* shows that Butler was fully aware of the drawbacks in life. Petronella Jacoba Lange argues that what Butler proposed is "the attitude of a man who appreciates the power of mind and will to overcome the difficulties of life and who believes in the tendency of everything in nature to strive towards improvement". ④ Butler has declared, "Life is, au fond, sensual." ⑤ Following the clue in most works by Butler, we learn that he insists on the inseparableness of life and death, of body and mind, of faith and reason, and most importantly, the power of will. Moreover, necessity and free will are, like life and death, faith and reason mutually destructive. For Butler, the contrasts cannot exist separately. Necessity and free will are bound up with each other as representatives of the seen and the

① Petronella Jacoba de, Lange. *Samuel Butler, Critic and Philosopher*. Zutphen, Netherlands: W. J. Thieme, 1925, p. 134.

② *Ibid.*, p. 135.

③ Danielle Nielsen. "Samuel Butler's *Life and Habit* and *The Way of All Flesh*: Traumatic Evolution." In *English literature in Transition, 1880 – 1920*, vol. 54, No. 1, 2011, p. 95.

④ Petronella Jacoba de. Lange. *Samuel Butler, Critic and Philosopher*. Zutphen, Netherlands: W. J. Thieme, 1925, p. 148.

⑤ Samuel Butler. *The Note-Books of Samuel Butler*. Edited with a preface and biographical statement by Henry Festing Jones. London: A. C. Fifield, 1912. Edition in use: IndyPublish edition, 2007, p. 188.

unseen world.[①] Echoing this is a suave passage from *Life and Habit*:

The phenomena of heredity, whether as regards instinct or structure were mainly due to memory of past experiences, accumulated and fused till they had become automatic, or quasi automatic, much in the same way as after a long life:

"Old experience do attain

① Petronella Jacoba de. Lange. *Samuel Butler, Critic and Philosopher*. Zutphen, Netherlands: W. J. Thieme, 1925, pp. 148-149. "Free-will otherwise cunning: The element of free-will, cunning, spontaneity, individuality—so omnipresent, so essential, yet so unreasonable, and so inconsistent with the other element not less omnipresent and not less essential, I mean necessity, luck, fate—this element of free-will, which comes from the unseen kingdom within which the writs of our thoughts run not, must be carried down to the most tenuous atoms whose action is supposed most purely chemical and mechanical; it can never be held as absolutely eliminated, for if it be so held, there is no getting it back again, and that it exists, even in the lowest forms of life, cannot be disputed. Its existence is one of the proofs of the existence of an unseen world, and a means whereby we know the little that we do know of that world". See *The Note-Books of Samuel Butler*. Edited with a preface and biographical statement by Henry Festing Jones. London: A. C. Fifield, 1912. IndyPublish edition, 2007, p. 275. Here, I quote the following passage titled "Necessity otherwise Luck" from *Note-Books of Samuel Butler*, which are helpful for our understanding of the relativity of luck and cunning lay at the heart of Butler's evolutionary outlook: "It is all very well to insist upon the free-will or cunning side of living action, more especially now when it has been so persistently ignored, but though the fortunes of birth and surroundings have all been built up by cunning, yet it is by ancestral, vicarious cunning, and this, to each individual, comes to much the same as luck pure and simple; in fact, luck is seldom seriously intended to mean a total denial of cunning, but is for the most part only an expression whereby we summarise and express our sense of a cunning too complex and impalpable for conscious following and apprehension. When we consider how little we have to do with our parentage, country and education, or even with our genus and species, how vitally these things affect us both in life and death...Cunning is nine-tenths luck, and luck is nine-tenths cunning; but the fact that nine-tenths of cunning is luck leaves still a tenth part unaccounted for." See Samuel Butler. *The Note-Books of Samuel Butler*. Edited with a preface and biographical statement by Henry Festing Jones. London: A. C. Fifield, 1912. IndyPublish edition, 2007, p. 276.

To something like prophetic strain. "①

Butler wished to illustrate his concept of evolution in contrast with Darwinism, which he understood and opposed as a kind of determinism, through Towneley-Ernest's example. For Butler, necessity and luck cannot deny the presence of free will and cunning, since there are no absolutes nor extremes and everything is in constant evoltion.

Looking back to the novel, Ernest once descends the social ladder when he opens an old clothes shop and marries Ellen. However, Ernest is not destined to remain a shopkeeper. Since "nature is eminently conservative", writes Butler in his last essay, which makes obvious references to the novel, "and fixity of type, even under considerable change of conditions, is surely more important for the well-being of any species than an over-ready power of adaptation to, it may be, passing changes. "② Indeed, Ernest's period of poverty is regarded by Overton as merely passing changes. ③ To be a rich man and to manipulate wealth is Ernest's final metamorphose, for " his great expectations are his most decisive

---

① Samuel Butler. *Life and Habit*. London: Trübner, 1878. Revised edition, with author's addenda and a preface by R. A. Streatfeild, London: A. C. Fifield, 1910. The Echo Library edition, 2007, Ch. XV, p. 150.

② Samuel Butler. "Deadlock in Darwinism. " In *Essays on Life*, *Art and Science*. Edited by R. A. Streatfield. London: A. C. Fifield, 1908, p. 317.

③ As Overton remarks that "His aunt had wished him to kiss the soil, and he had kissed it with a vengeance; but I did not like the notion of his coming suddenly from the position of a small shopkeeper to that of a man with an income of between three and four thousand a year. Too sudden a jump from bad fortune to good is just as dangerous as one from good to bad; besides, poverty is very wearing; it is a quasi-embryonic condition, through which a man had between pass if he is to hold his later developments securely, but like measles or scarlet fever, he had better have it mildly and get it over early. " See Samuel Butler. *The Way of All Flesh*. London: Grant Richards, 1903; published posthumously. Edited with an introduction by V. S. Pritchett, London: Penguin English Library, 2012, Ch. 78, p.405.

inheritance". ① Thanks to his aunt's money, Ernest's development is protected and guaranteed. ② With his inherited memory and wisdom, conscious effort plus cunning, Ernest overcomes the difficulties and obstacles of his biological inheritance to attain his state of perfection. Ultimately he is not far off from Towenely:

> Towneley himself could not have been appointed more becomingly. His portmanteau, his railway wrapper, everything he had about him, was in keeping. I thought he had grown much better-looking than he had been at two or three and twenty. His year and a half of peace had effaced all the ill effects of his previous suffering, and now that he had become actually rich there was an air of *insouciance* and good humour upon his face, as of a man with whom everything was going perfectly right, which would have made a much plainer man good-looking. ③

---

① Peter Morton. "Butler on Heredity." In *The Vital Science: Biology and the Literary Imagination: 1860 – 1900*. London: Allen and Unwin, 1984, p. 189.

② Henry Festing Jones wrote in his *Memoir*: "We may not always know very clearly what is meant by God, and things may not always work together for the particular kind of good that we desire; but there is 'a something as yet but darkly known which makes right right and wrong wrong,' and no man can ultimately fail who obeys the dictates of that voice which we can all hear within us if we will but listen. But he must obey without regard to theological dogmas or social conventions; he must never allow mistakes to dishearten him—mistakes made in good faith will teach him more than anything else; and he must never grow weary of taking pains. Then each difficulty will vanish like a morning mist, and his nest step will be made clear...Alethea realized that Ernest had this faith and that he was the sort of boy who would act steadfastly upon it, therefore she left him her money; and this led to Ernest's experiencing the trial of wealth, as well as that of poverty, if he had had no Aunt Alethea, or if Edward Overton had lost the money, that would only have given rise to different incidents and, after some other trials, some other kind of happiness would have been reached in the end." See Henry Festing Jones. *Samuel Butler: Author of Erewhon (1835 – 1902) A Memoir*, vol. II London: Macmillan and Co. Ltd, 1919, p. 16.

③ Samuel Butler. *The Way of All Flesh*. London: Grant Richards, 1903. Edited with an introduction by V. S. Pritchett, London: Penguin English Library, 2012, Ch. 82, p. 428.

It is with the power of mind and intelligence that an individual can improve his development and state fixed by birth. ① This powerful mental power is "the unseen kingdom which the writ of our thoughts runs not", as Gillian Beer believes, it is both individual unconsciousness and the material world beyond the human. ② Butler's contribution to the theory of evolution was to have replaced hereditary instinct with the notion of inherited memory, and he laid the greatest stress on cunning as the more important element. In views of Butler's interests, critics have argued that the name "Pontifex" echoes biological nomenclature to remind readers of "such forms of life, of the living and environmentally sensitive family organism which transcends its members and is effectively immortal". ③ The

① Butler also uses his favorite composer Handel as an example: "Handel was not an Englishman by birth, but no one was ever more thoroughly English in respect of all the best and most distinguishing features of Englishmen" SeeSamuel Butler. *The Note-Books of Samuel Butler*. Edited with a preface and biographical statement by Henry Festing Jones. London: A. C. Fifield, 1912. Edition in use: IndyPublish edition, 2007, p. 103. Being Butler's favorite, George Frideric Handel (1685 – 1759) was a German-born British Baroque composer, famous for his operas and oratorios. From Handel's experience, it seems to tell us, in the journey of life, the "failure" is not necessarily negative, the failure of the Handel operas career, made him to remember his passion for oratorios when he was young. The script of "Messiah", like a timely rain. Which is Handel's heart. Perhaps no Saviour "Messiah", the true meaning is understood and clear Handel, now get the help of Jane's deeply appreciate the authenticity of the "Savior"; when he moved, smooth Le pen steady stream spectrum of sacred music; many of writing skills, it is also effective to continue to write the opera hone. This brings us understand: the Christian life is not necessarily well, it is important to bear in mind the experience of "failure" to regain strength, the twinkling of an eye to God, and then re-start to live for Him. Handel began writing in 1741, 22, 2011 (Saturday) afternoon "Messiah", to be completed within six days of the first part of September 6 to complete the second part, 12 September to complete the whole song the structure, and then write the orchestral part and trimmed, before and after a total of only 24 days, it is amazing fast is inspired.

② Gillian Beer. "Butler, Memory, and the Future." In *Samuel Butler: Victorian Against the Grain, A Critical Overview*. Edited by James G. Paradis. Toronto, Buffalo and London: University of Toronto Press, 2007, p. 47.

③ Peter Morton. "Butler on Heredity." In *The Vital Science: Biology and the Literary Imagination: 1860 – 1900*. London: Allen and Unwin, 1984, p. 183.

derivation "-fex" from Ernest's family name gives him a role of " bridgemaker", signifying that the Pontifexes would reach into the future across five generations with its health restored, as incarnated in Ernest's children.[①] Indeed, today is yesterday's tomorrow. Butler's evolutionary theories thus give us helpful reflections on education.

① *Ibid.*, p. 183.

4.3 "Sensible teaching" in *The Way of All Flesh*

As we may already know, Butler draws on the subject of *Bildungsroman* which was invented by the Germans but practised by French novelists as well: indeed, Butler's work reveals a greater influence by Flaubert's *Education Sentimentale* (1869), and the novels by Dickens are also closer to Butler's inspiration.① The *Bildungsroman*, like the biography, deals with the moral and psychological development of the individual. Being a Lamarckian, Butler placed much emphasis on the surroundings of individuals. Hence, in this context, "education" is defined in a broad sense as referring to all personal, social and political influences that may exert pressure on and shape the emerging personality of individuals. Thus not only were Butler's opinions on education shaped by his engagement in revising and supplementing Darwin's theories, but they also encompassed biological and hereditary factors. Therefore, for Butler, "education" comprised all of those processes by which personal identity is acquired. Education also plays a highly important role in the reconstruction of the personal identity—this is not always an easy accomplishment. In *The Way of All Flesh* (1903), Butler views the main social entities of his day—the church, school and family, institutions which have so much to do with inculcating values and shaping identity—as unmitigated disasters.② In the novel, the narrative thus carries its readers through the nineteenth century to the brink of modern times and indeed delivers a contemporary message—one almost too prophetic to be appreciated in Butler's time.

---

① Sally Shuttleworth. "Evolutionary Psychology and *The Way of All Flesh.*" In *Samuel Butler. Victorian Against the Grain: A Critical Overview.* Edited by James G. Paradis. Toronto: Univeristy of Toronto Press, 2007, p. 148.

② John Douglas Grant has given a precise analysis on this point, in John Douglas Grant, *Samuel Butler as a Critic of Victorian England.* Toronto: University of Toronto, 1947.

What should an individual's essence be? Asked Butler. How can the individual be his or her true self? How can a young man save himself from parental or any other kind of tyranny, and what is more, free himself from the burden of heredity? And if all authority is suspect, how can a well-meaning individual who has survived the horrors of growing up, advise in turn a new generation? The most convincing explanations, as I shall argue in this section, are that Butler's opinions on education could be traced back to his evolutionary theories.[①] Moreover, as I have shown, throughout *The Way of All Flesh* (1903), the spiritual and intellectual life and development of the main character are all basically drawn from Butler's own experience. In order to gain more comprehensive understanding of Butler's implications and what he really believed in, I shall then start from Ernest's educational background and his personal experience.

4.3.1 On childhood

Ernest's childhood is filled with unforgettable bitterness. As I have analysed in the previous section, Ernest's father, Theobald, manages to instill in his children a deep sense of personal worthlessness—one of the weaknesses that nearly destroys Ernest later. The slightest failure to comply is rewarded with a beating, to the greater glory of God of course. For example, when little Ernest lisps, pronouncing "tom" instead of "come" (it seems that /t/ is easier for children than /k/). Theobald, in an attempt to correct this "perverse" error reprimands him, "Now Ernest...you are not taking pains: you are not trying as you ought to. It is high time you learned to say 'come'..."[②] Little Ernest, after several more tries and as many failures, is dragged off for a summary spanking in a retrograde

① Petronella Jacoba de. Lange. *Samuel Butler, Critic and Philosopher*. Zutphen, Netherlands: W. J. Thieme, 1925, pp. 123-124.

② Samuel Butler. *The Way of All Flesh*. London: Grant Richards, 1903. Edited with an introduction by V. S. Pritchett, London: Penguin English Library, 2012, Ch. 22, p. 112.

demonstration of "applied linguistics". Such beatings become a regularly horrible feature in Ernest's upbringing. Butler wishes his readers to note that it is not as if Theobald, a sincerely devout man "generally considered to be [...] an embodiment of all those virtues which make the poor respectable and the rich respected", is actually evil. ①It is a case, rather of the Victorian virtue being upheld to the extreme degenerating into bigotry. The virtuous man, as the God-fearing man, is he who wants his children to follow him in his ways of virtues, to be "obedient, affectionate, attentive to his wishes, self-denying and diligent". ② For Butler, such virtues, which are "most convenient to parents" are however largely irrelevant to children's happiness. The trouble with such a virtue, Butler argues, is that it is basically self-serving. "With what he did not like, however it was different; the more he disliked a thing the greater the presumption that it was right."③ In Butler's opinion, the legacy of Ernest's joyless upbringing is a great deal of self-distrust, in order to reveal the main feature of the fundamental system of Victorian morality. Having been taught that pleasure is evil, young Ernest regards everything he likes as essentially sinful. Growing up under such circumstances, Ernest suffers psychologically whenever he tries to feel or think for himself. In summarizing Ernest's childhood, Butler asks:

> How was it possible that such a child only a little five years old, trained in such an atmosphere of prayers and hymns and sums and happy Sunday evenings—to say nothing of daily repeated beating over the said prayers and hymns, etc., about which our authoress is silent—how was it possible that a lad so trained should grow up in any healthy or vigorous development...?④

---

① *Ibid.*, Ch. 26, p. 128.
② *Ibid.*, Ch. 26, p. 126.
③ *Ibid.*, Ch. 31, p. 152.
④ *Ibid.*, Ch. 26, p. 127.

Butler's description will induce the reader into wondering about Ernest's children. The horrors of family life are so strongly imprinted in Ernest's memory that the converted Ernest consciously refuses to repeat his father's mistakes in raising his own offspring. When Ernest discusses with Overton about how to take care of his two children Georgie and Alice, he says with grim resignation:

> I shall be just as unkind to my children [...] as my grandfather was to my father, or my father to me. If they did not succeed in making their children love them, neither shall I. I say to myself that I should like to do so, but so did they. I can make sure that they shall not know how much they would have hated me if they had had much to do with me, but this is all I can do. If I must ruin their prospects, let me do so at a reasonable time before they are old enough to feel it. ①

Reading *The Way of All Flesh*, we learn that Ernest does not usually spend too much time with his offspring, going as far as to keep a distance from his own children. In a sense, Ernest cannot shake off his personal fears that he is at one with his father and grandfather and doomed to repeat the self-righteous tyranny of fatherhood that was imposed on him.

In *Unconscious Memory* (1880), Butler outlines the four main principles behind *Life and Habit* (1878): "the oneness of personality between parents and offspring; memory on the part of offspring of certain actions which it did when in the persons of its forefathers; the latency of that memory until it is rekindled by a recurrence of the associated ideas; and the unconsciousness with which habitual actions come to be performed."② According to Butler's theory of inherited memory and oneness of personality between parents and offspring, children are

① *Ibid.*, Ch. 79, p. 409.

② Samuel Butler. *Unconscious Memory*. London: David Bogue, 1880. The Echo Library edition 2006, p. 11.

not to be visited in infancy with memories of old age, but they could be forced to experience the enactment of the similarity of order which leads to their own conception. For Butler, those would be the difficulties of a young individual life, because he or she seemed to be weighed down by the burden of inheritance.

In anticipation of Freud, Butler suggests that enmity is a condition of the relationship between father and son as portrayed in *The Way of All Flesh*. That kind of enmity can be mitigated by distance, or a more positive inheritance of memories (in Towneley's case): nonetheless, it can never be overcome. For fear of damaging them, Ernest has to forego personal involvement in the upbringing of his children. The novel replicates this distance, with the children first being placed with his laundress and then at Gravesend, where they are brought up in the healthy country air by a bargeman and his wife. When Ernest returns from his journey, one of the first things he does is to go to Gravesend with Overton to visit his children; Overton describes the place where the children live:

> It was a lovely April morning, but with a fresh air blowing from off the sea; the tide was high, and the river was alive with shipping coming up with wind and tide. Sea-gulls wheeled around us overhead, sea-weed clung everywhere to the banks which the advancing tide had not yet covered, everything was of the sea sea-ey, and the fine bracing air which blew over the water made me feel more hungry than I had done for many a day; I did not see how children could live in a better physical atmosphere than this, and applauded the selection which Ernest had made on behalf of his youngsters. ①

Ernest chose such surroundings for his children so that they may come into

① Samuel Butler. *The Way of All Flesh*. London: Grant Richards, 1903. Edited with an introduction by V. S. Pritchett, London: Penguin English Library, 2012, Ch. 84, p. 453.

close contact with nature. Georgie and Alice live happily together with the seven children of Mr and Mrs Rollings. The couple is very kind, and they have five healthy boys and two pretty girls, all of which enthuses Overton:

> I never saw a finer lot of children than the young Rollings, the boys were hardy, robust, fearless little fellows with eyes as clear as hawks; the elder girl was exquisitely pretty, but the younger one was a mere baby. I felt as I looked at them, that if I had had children of my own I could have wished no better home for them, nor better companions. ①

When Mr Rollings talks about his eldest son Jack and his other children with Ernest, he looks fondly and tenderly at them. His only complaint is that, although the children are fast learners in general, they do not take to reading and writing. Nonetheless, Mr Rollings feels very proud because his Jack is almost as good a bargeman as himself. ② Mr Rollings is very fond of his children and adopts a tolerant attitude on the issue of their education. Ernest agrees with him on this point and he wishes to let his own children develop just as freely and spontaneously. When talking about the future career of the child with Mr Rollings, Ernest says: "Georgie wants to be a bargeman, let him begin as one, the sooner the better [...] then if he shows developments I can be on the look-out to encourage them and make things easy for him; while if he shows no desire to go ahead, what on earth is the good of trying to shove him forward?" ③ Both fathers wish to provide their sons with free environment and necessary support for their future.

Ernest wishes for his offspring to live happily and freely in their childhood, and to grow up and develop according to their own desires and interests. That

① *Ibid.*, Ch. 84, pp. 453-454.

② *Ibid.*, Ch. 84, pp. 454-455.

③ *Ibid.*, Ch. 84, p. 455.

they should grow up in the country and be materially less well-off is a deliberate choice by Ernest. This is his hope that these children, freed from any paternal influence and brought up in poverty so that they can make their own way, if they wish, up the social scale, will offer a fresh start for the Pontifex line. ①In *The Way of All Flesh*, Ernest gives voice to Butler's ideas that children need to be placed in a humble social position and "go through the embryonic stages with their money as much as with their limbs". ② Furthermore, parents should, as Ernest has done, be open-minded with regards to the education of their children. Ernest wishes for his children to lead a happy life and permits them to choose the profession of their own desire, going further by encouraging and supporting them materially. Hence, in a text preoccupied with the workings of heredity, Ernest's conscious and diligent effort to counteract the forces of heredity paves the way for the happy and free lives of successive generations:

> Ernest's daughter Alice married the boy who had been her playmate more than a year ago. Ernest gave them all they said they wanted and a good deal more. They have already presented him with a grandson, and I doubt not, will do so with many more. Georgie though only twenty-one is owner of a fine steamer which his father has bought for him. He began when about thirteen going with old Rollings and Jack in the barge from Rochester to the upper Thames with bricks; then his father bought him and Jack barges of their own, and then he bought them both ships, and then steamers. I do not exactly know how people make money by having a steamer, but he does whatever is usual, and from all I can gather makes it pay extremely well. He is a good deal like his father in the face, but without a spark—so far as I have been

---

① Sally Shuttleworth. "Evolutionary Psychology and *The Way of All Flesh.*" In *Samuel Butler: Victorian Against the Grain, A Critical Overview*. Edited by James G. Paradis. Toronto, Buffalo and London: University of Toronto Press, 2007, p. 162.

② Samuel Butler. *The Way of All Flesh*. London: Grant Richards, 1903. Edited with an introduction by V. S. Pritchett, London: Penguin English Library, 2012, Ch. 84, p. 455.

> able to observe—any literary ability; he has a fair sense of humour and abundance of common sense, but his instinct is clearly a practical one. I am not sure that he does not put me in mind almost more of what Theobald would have been if he had been a sailor, than of Ernest.①

In brief, for Ernest's children, the fifth generation of the Pontifex line, their future developments toward perfection would be guaranteed in this way.

4.3.2 About Dr. Skinner's school at Roughborough

As we learn from the image of the future of Ernest's children, a better fortune than their father's and grandfather's is assured, which is thanks to Ernest's educational method. Ernest's opinion on the education of children is mainly gained from the consideration of his own experience, with reflection about the old generations. In fact, in *The Way of All Flesh*, Ernest's upbringing story is basically an adaptation of Samuel Butler's own experience. At the age of 12, Ernest is enrolled in a grammar school at Roughborough, located about 50 miles from Battersby.② Dr. Skinner, the headmaster, has a reputation as a man of genius by virtue of his undergraduate debating record and his biblical scholarship. Ernest dutifully writes to his parents as though he enjoys his time at Roughborough, when in true, he is always unhappy during his first two years there. Although Ernest shows little enthusiasm in the novel for Victorian public school education, Ernest feels slightly better at Roughborough than at Battersby. At least, he is free of his father's control, and Dr. Skinner only occasionally

① Samuel Butler. *The Way of All Flesh*. London: Grant Richards, 1903. Edited with an introduction by V. S. Pritchett, London: Penguin English Library, 2012. Ch. 86, pp. 465-466.

② This alsocoincides with Butler's own experience: in 1848, Butler attended Shrewsbury School, under headmaster Benjamin Hall Kennedy.

makes his menacing presence felt. ①In fact, Ernest's removal to the school at Roughborough is beneficial, as U. C. Knoepflmacher remarked: "Although the eminent theologian proves to be a magnified Theobald and his schooling a mere extension of the Battersby education, Ernest's growth is given a definite impetus by the intervention of his aunt."② Alethea moves to Roughborough and trains Ernest to build a musical organ in the fashion of her grandfather, old John Pontifex. It is a mnemonic association with the "past self" of the Pontifexes that spurs Alethea to make such a decision. Believing that recollections can transcend the span of the life of individuals, Butler asserts in *Life and Habit*: "Our memory is mainly called into action by force of association and similarity in the surroundings. We want to go on doing what we did when we were last as we are now."③ In this way, Alethea's practical training partially offsets the instruction offered by Dr. Skinner. As a result, Ernest is trained to re-enact the "habit" lost by George and Theobald Pontifex. Hence Ernest's "true self" reawakens:

> Of course, the boy said yes; then she told him about her grandfather and the organs he had built. It had never entered into his head that he could make one, but when he gathered from what his aunt had said that this was not out of the question, he rose as eagerly to the bait as she could have desired, and wanted to begin learning to saw and plane so that he might make the wooden pipes at once. ④

---

① Dr. Skinner is described as a "God-fearing earnest Christian"—a carbon copy of Ernest's father in his handling of children.

② U. C. Knoepflmacher. *Religious Humanism and the Victorian Novel*: *George Eliot*, *Walter Pater*, *and Samuel Butler*. Princeton: Princeton University Press, 1965, p. 281.

③ Samuel Butler. *Life and Habit*. London: Trübner, 1878. Revised edition, with author's addenda and a preface by R. A. Streatfeild, London: A. C. Fifield, 1910. The Echo Library edition, 2007, Ch. X, P. 86.

④ Samuel Butler. *The Way of All Flesh*. London: Grant Richards, 1903. Edited with an introduction by V. S. Pritchett, London: Penguin English Library, 2012, Ch. 34. p. 167.

Alethea has found out that Ernest does not like games; she therefore devises this plan to develop her nephew's physical strength. Her plan works as the effort of "a little plain carpentering, so as to get to know how to use his tools" and it leaves Ernest flushed with excitement:①

> What boy would not take kindly to almost anything with such assistance? All boys like making things; the exercise of sawing, planing and hammering, proved exactly what his aunt had wanted to find—something that should exercise, but not too much, and at the same time amuse him; when Ernest's sallow face was flushed with his work, and his eyes were sparkling with pleasure, he looked quite a different boy from the one his aunt had taken in hand only a few months earlier. His inner self never told him that this was humbug, as it did about Latin and Greek ... His aunt let him invite his friends, encouraging him to bring those whom her quick sense told her were the most desirable. ②

In *The Way of All Flesh*, Alethea's approach towards education would have been fully endorsed by Butler. Thus, during the construction of the music organ, Ernest receives a parallel education through Alethea's method of "kissing the soil". ③ Alethea detects Ernest's true interests and labours to create the means by which he can indulge in these interests and realize his inner desires. Alethea's character is a device to return Ernest to his "true self". As her Greek name indicates, she embodies a truth opposed to that preached by the professional truth-tellers she detests. ④ Ultimately, Ernest discovers the best method to

---

① *Ibid.*, Ch. 34, p. 171.

② *Ibid.*, Ch. 34, p. 171.

③ *Ibid.*, Ch. 67, p. 342. The symbolic meaning of "kissing the soil" is to keep the children in touch with the realities of life.

④ U. C. Knoepflmacher. *Religious Humanism and the Victorian Novel: George Eliot, Walter Pater, and Samuel Butler*. Princeton: Princeton University Press, 1965, p. 280.

acquire knowledge: "The way to get them is to study something of which one is fond, and to note down whatever crosses one's mind in reference to it, either during study or relaxation, in a little note-book kept always in the waistcoat pocket."① It takes him a while to arrive at this conclusion for, as Butler demonstrated this is not the kind of thing that was taught at Victorian schools and universities.②

Hence Butler argues that the study cannot be forced by a standard of reason. Moreover, it is important to note that Alethea's method of education makes an effort to alter Ernest's heredity "undo[ing] the effect of such surroundings as the boy had had at Battersby."③ When Ernest graduates from the school, his last day at Roughborough is depicted as follows:

> Just before saying good-bye the Doctor actually took down a volume from those shelves which had seemed so awful six years previously, and gave it to him after having written his name in it, and the words φιλιας και ευνοιας χαριν, which I believe means "with all kind wishes from the donor." The book was one written in Latin by a German—Schömann: "De comitiis Atheniensibus"—not exactly light and cheerful reading, but Ernest felt it was high time he got to understand the Athenian constitution and manner of voting; he had got them up a great many times already, but had forgotten them as fast as he had learned them; now, however, that the Doctor had given him this book, he would master the subject once for all. How strange it was! He wanted to remember these things very badly; he knew he did, but he could never retain them; in spite of himself they no sooner fell upon his mind than they fell off it again, he had such a dreadful memory; whereas, if

① Samuel Butler. *The Way of All Flesh*. London: Grant Richards, 1903. Edited with an introduction by V. S. Pritchett, London: Penguin English Library, 2012, Ch. 46, p. 237.

② *Ibid.*, Ch. 46, p. 237.

③ *Ibid.*, Ch. 35, p. 173.

> anyone played him a piece of music and told him where it came from, he never forgot that, though he made no effort to retain it, and was not even conscious of trying to remember it at all. His mind must be badly formed and he was no good. ①

As portrayed by Butler, Dr. Skinner is a benevolent but pompous windbag who has nothing to offer to his students that they really want. The headmaster's gift to Ernest at his graduation is a book in Latin on the Athenian constitution. It symbolizes the irrelevance of the genteel and useless learning dispensed at Dr. Skinner's school. Butler particularly despises the popular emphasis on Latin and Greek precisely, since both of them present a consuming and purely "hypothetical" nature. Instead of learning the dead languages, Ernest could spend his time more profitably in "growing bone and muscle", which is much more useful in one's life than Latin or Greek. In contrast, Ernest prefers to play the musical organ for pleasure in the following paragraph:

> Having still a short time to spare, he got the keys of St Michael's church and went to have a farewell practice upon the organ, which he could now play fairly well. He walked up and down the aisle for a while in a meditative mood, and then, settling down to the organ, played "They loathed to drink of the river" about six times over, after which he felt more composed and happier; then, tearing himself away from the instrument he loved so well, he hurried to the station. ②

Thus we become aware that Ernest dislikes Dr. Skinner's classical studies and

① *Ibid.*, Ch. 44, p. 225.
② *Ibid.*, Ch. 44, p. 225.

likes music instinctively. ① The instinct "which made him [Ernest] keep out of games [at Roughborough] for which he was ill adapted" serves him well in the end. ② Hence this pragmatic aspect of education according to Butler's evolutionary principles may be inferred as John Douglas Grant argued: "do not force the child to learn what its instincts make clear is unattractive to it; even what seems valuable by the standards of reason should give way to the instinctive preference." ③ For Butler, this refers to things with which we are more familiar and of which we are less conscious.

Ernest leaves Dr. Skinner's school and meditates over his past and present calamities. Sitting in the departing train, he gazes at the mist-covered sun, as if looking at the face of one whom he knows and is fond of, and suddenly breaks out into a smile:

> At first his face was grave, but kindly, as of a tired man who feels that a long task is over; but in a few seconds the more humorous side of his misfortunes presented itself to him, and he smiled half reproachfully, half merrily, as thinking how little all that had happened to him really mattered, and how small were his hardships as compared with those of most people. Still looking into the eye of the sun and smiling dreamily, he thought how he had helped

---

① Like Ernest, Butler "took every opportunity to play music, either on St Mary's church organ, or surreptitiously on the piano in the Shrewsbury music-seller's shop". See Peter Raby. *Samuel Butler: A Biography*. London: The Hogarth Press, 1991, p. 37. Moreover, "Samuel Butler's love of music developed early in his life. As a schoolboy he looked forward to hearing his favourite aunt playing Handel overtures on the piano, and soon learned to play them himself. He would sell his school books to finance his collection of Handel's music, published in cheap editions." See online source: the article "Samuel Butler and Music: An Introduction" from the website of St John's college at Cambridge University http://www. joh. cam. ac. uk/samuel-butler-and-music-introduction.

② *Ibid.*, Ch. 30, p. 151.

③ John Douglas Grant, *Samuel Butler as a Critic of Victorian England.* Toronto: University of Toronto, 1947, p. 61.

> to burn his father in effigy, and his look grew merrier, till at last he broke out into a laugh. Exactly at this moment the light veil of cloud parted from the sun, and he was brought to *terra firma* by the breaking forth of the sunshine. On this he became aware that he was being watched attentively by a fellow-traveller opposite to him, an elderly gentleman with a large head and iron-grey hair.
>
> "My young friend," said he, good-naturedly, "you really must not carry on conversations with people in the sun, while you are in a public railway carriage."①

Ernest's meditation recalls that of his grandfather, "who also addressed the sun as a symbol for his confidence in the benignity of nature".② However, here, Butler means that, even graduated from the school of Roughborough, Ernest still has a long way to go to return to his ancestor's faith.

In brief, in the eyes of Overton, the headmaster at Roughborough, like Ernest's grandfather and father is an example of the pompous pedant.③ Regarding on the early school years of Ernest, Overton claims that Ernest is difficult to be delivered out of the bondage to such a routine that deprives him of discovering his true self.④ Since "surrounded by prigs after birth, Ernest cannot avoid taking on the characteristics of priggishness".⑤ Here, Overton implicates that Ernest has little opportunity at Roughborough to rid himself of his father's influence.

---

① *Ibid.*, Ch. 44, pp. 226-227.

② U. C. Knoepflmacher. *Religious Humanism and the Victorian Novel: George Eliot, Walter Pater, and Samuel Butler*. Princeton: Princeton University Press, 1965, p. 283.

③ In *The Way of All Flesh*, Overton, Ernest's biographer, claims that the schoolmasters should not abuse his charges.

④ See online source: *The Way of All Flesh*: Summary and Analysis Chapter 27-31. http://www.cliffsnotes.com/literature/w/the-way-of-all-flesh/summary-and-analysis/chapters-2731.

⑤ *Ibid.* Priggishness: "a term used by Overton to indicate all that is wrong with pursuing life as a duty and not as a pleasure".

Unfortunately, he is fated to perpetuate his ignorance of the world and of his best possible his natural self. ① Hence Overton strongly reflects Butler's own deeply held attitudes of the importance of the environment and surrounding in the development of individuals.

4.3.3 Ernest's Cambridge years

After the graduation from the school of Roughborough, Ernest gains entry into the shrine of British classical education, Cambridge University. ② This is an important stage in Ernest's growth. As a student at Emmanuel College at Cambridge University being far away from his family and the oppressive schoolmaster, Ernest feels happy for the first time in his life. There, Ernest is surrounded by "freedom of movement, comfortable surroundings and the companionship of friends", all of which contributes to his sense of well-being. ③ Then, Ernest begins to write in a literary journal that the reputations of some of the classical Greek dramatists—Aeschylus, Sophocles, and Euripides, are greatly exaggerated. ④ It is at Cambridge that Ernest's true calling—that of a writer—makes

① *Ibid.*

② Here, it would be in the year 1854. It is in the same year that Butler attended St John's College, University of Cambridge.

③ See online source: *The Way of All Flesh*: Summary and Analysis Chapter 45-50. http://www.cliffsnotes.com/literature/w/the-way-of-all-flesh/summary-and-analysis/chapters-4550.

④ In fact, in 1858, Butler helped found and wrote for the *Eagle* and his first contribution was entitled "On English Composition and Other Matters". This essay is believed to be the first composition by Samuel Butler that appeared in print. It was published in the first number of the *Eagle*, a student literary journal written and edited by members of St. John's College, Cambridge, when Butler was in his fourth and last year of residence. In this essay, Butler expressed his admiration for a "masculine" style, compound of "vigour, straightforwardness, and conciseness"; This style is remarkable "for its statement of the principles of style that Butler had thus early evolved for himself and which he struck to all his life, It expresses admiration for simplicity and terseness and maintains that the best styles are based on intuition". For Butler, this is true of subjects. See Clara G. Stillman. *Samuel Butler*: *A Mid-Victorian Modern*. London: Martin Secker, 1932, p. 38. In this essay, Butler argued, "so rules, for the most part, are but useful to the weaker among us.

its first appearance with some small literary success. However, his interpretation of the classical Greek dramatists is important to his contemporaries in the very limited way that most Victorian clergymen are to their congregations. Cambridge, on the whole, does little damage to Ernest, but Butler put his finger at it as a serious failing—because it failed to stimulate intellectual originality in students. ①

Butler does not present us too much about life at Cambridge in *The Way of All*

Our greatest masters in language, whether prose or verse, in painting, music, architecture, or the like, have been those who preceded the rule and whose excellence gave rise thereto; men who preceded, I should rather say, not the rule, but the discovery of the rule, men whose intuitive perception led them to right practice. We cannot imagine Homer to have studied rules, and the infant genius of those giants of their art, Handel, Mozart, and Beethoven, who composed at the ages of seven, five, and ten, must certainly have been unfettered by them." See Samuel Butler. "On English Composition and Other Matters", From the *Eagle*, vol. 1, No. 1, Lent Term, 1858, p. 41. This essay is collected in Samuel Butler. *Canterbury Pieces & Cambridge Pieces*, published by the Echo Library, 2006, pp. 1-3.

① Butler believed that the best work and wonderful ideas were the products that naturally came from instincts of the individuals. In the choice of subjects, Butler argued there be need no pressure for the writer to be daringly original. Butler also insisted that ideas spur most easily when not consciously sought after, he says, "...The best rule is not to write concerning that about which we cannot at our present age know anything save by a process which is commonly called cram; on all such matters there are abler writers than ourselves; the men, in fact, from whom we cram. Never let us hunt after a subject; unless we have something which we feel urged on to say, it is better to say nothing". See Samuel Butler "On English Composition and Other Matters", From the *Eagle*, Vol. 1, No. 1, Lent Term, 1858, p. 41. This essay is collected in Samuel Butler. *Canterbury Pieces & Cambridge Pieces*, published by the Echo Library, 2006, pp. 1-3. These ideas contained in this youthful essay of Butler, later appeared in many guises in *The Note-Books of Samuel Butler*, and are exemplified in his writings. Therefore, Butler's own subject of writings "grew always out of the organic structure of his life, forced upon him by the needs of his own development". See Clara G. Stillman. Samuel Butler: *A Mid-Victorian Modern.* London: Martin Secker, 1932, p. 38. For more about Butler's critiques on Victorian educational system, see F. A. Cavenagh. "Samuel Butler and Education." *The Monist*, vol. 32, No. 2, (April, 1922), pp. 307-313.

Flesh, because, as he says, undergraduate life has been described in a score of novels. ① The Erewhonians, under Butler's pens, are a vivid mirror image of the Victorian colleges. In *Erewhon* (1872), they have an absurd educational system "Colleges of Unreason", with the main feature of "hypothetics" in their system, so that the university's concern is to "incapacitate young people so that they will be unable to lead useful lives". ② Since Victorian education formula largely insisted on Latin and Greek instead of paying attention to the practical knowledge. Mr Thims, a professor at "Colleges of Unreason" in *Erewhon*, by explaining that to drill students in "hypothetics" would enlarge their horizons by leading them to consider " a set of utterly strange and impossible contingencies", which reveals the educational system that is practiced there. ③ Meanwhile, the students, being trained with a synthetic language of no use, are drilled in the doctrine of "unreason" on the premise that "there is hardly an error into which men may not easily be led if they base their conduct upon reason only". ④ In Butler's vivid descriptions, the aim of the educators in "Colleges of Unreason" "seemed to devote themselves to the avoidance of every opinion with which they were not perfectly familiar, and regarded their brains as a sort of sanctuary, to which if an opinion had once resorted, non other was to attack it". ⑤

During his last year at Cambridge, Ernest, along with his other classmates who also plan to enter the Anglican ministry, become more attentive to religious topics. Supported by the family tradition, inevitably, it is the accompaniment of college fellowship or school headmastership, since a third of Cambridge

① See Philip Henderson. *Samuel Butler, the Incarnate Bachelor*. London: Cohen and West, 1953, p. 16.

② Lee E. Holt. *Samuel Butler*. New York: Twayne Publishers, 1964. Revised edition, 1989, p. 23.

③ Samuel Butler. *Erewhon*. London: Trübner, 1872. Edited with an introduction by Peter Mudford. London: Penguin, 1985. Ch. 21, p. 185.

④ *Ibid.*, Ch. 21, p. 187.

⑤ *Ibid.*, Ch. 22, p. 194.

undergraduates of Butler's contemporaries came from clergy families. ① Ernest's religious enthusiasm comes at a period in English history when skeptical currents were becoming popular with the public, with the new intellectual trends rising all around it:

> Ernest returned to Cambridge for the May term of 1858... Up to this time, though not religiously inclined, he had never doubted the truth of anything that had been told him about Christianity. He had never seen anyone who doubted, nor read anything that raised a suspicion in his mind as to the historical character of the miracles recorded in the Old and New Testaments.
>
> It must be remembered that the year 1858 was the last of a term during which the peace of the Church of England was singularly unbroken. Between 1844, when *Vestiges of Creation* appeared, and 1859, when *Essays and Reviews* marked the commencement of that storm which raged until many years afterwards, there was not a single book published in England that caused serious commotion within the bosom of the Church. Perhaps Buckle's *History of Civilisation* and Mill's *On Liberty* were the most alarming, but neither of them reached the substratum of the reading public, and Ernest and his friends were ignorant of their very existence.
>
> I need hardly say that the calm was only on the surface... Ernest had hardly been ordained before three works in quick succession arrested the attention even of those who paid least heed to theological controversy. I mean *Essays and Reviews*, Charles Darwin's *Origin of Species*, and Bishop Colenso's *Criticisms on the Pentateuch*. ②

① Peter Raby. *Samuel Butler: A Biography*. London: The Hogarth Press, 1991, p. 51.

② However, *Essays and Reviews*, edited by John William Parker, was published in March 1860. See Samuel Butler. *The Way of All Flesh*. London: Grant Richards, 1903. Edited with an introduction by V. S. Pritchett, London: Penguin English Library, 2012, Ch. 47, pp. 240-241.

Those are the most important events in his days that Butler has recorded in the novel. In coincidence with Butler's own experience, it is at Cambridge that Ernest starts to examine critically the theology in which he has been nurtured, and this takes him to face the first important crisis of his life. ① In the last year at Cambridge, for Ernest, there can be no doubt that the ordination would follow. ②

At Cambridge, Ernest is especially courted by the Simeonites, "Sims", in fact, as they are called, who were remainders of the evangelical awakening of more than a generation before. ③ They are a group of evangelistically fervent students of all ages who eschew the comforts of ordinary society to live piously among themselves in extreme poverty. Butler's dislike of religion and all that went with it was summed up for him in their personal descriptions:

> Behind the then chapel of this last-named college, there was a "labyrinth" (this was the name it bore) of dingy, tumble-down rooms, tenanted exclusively by the poorest undergraduates, who were dependent upon sizarships and scholarships for the means of taking their degrees. To many, even at St John's, the existence and whereabouts of the labyrinth in which the sizars chiefly lived was unknown; some men in Ernest's time, who had rooms in the first court, had never found their way through the sinuous passage which led to it.
>
> In the labyrinth there dwelt men of all ages, from mere lads to grey-haired old men who had entered late in life. They were rarely seen except in hall or

① Clara G. Stillman. *Samuel Butler: A Mid-Victorian Modern*. London: Martin Secker, 1932, p. 41.

② Butler's experience was also on the same routine, he had to follow his father and grandfather into the church.

③ Although Charles Simeon had died in 1836, his influence in the university was still strong when Butler at St John's college at Cambridge. See Peter Raby. *Samuel Butler: A Biography*. London: The Hogarth Press, 1991, p. 51.

> chapel or at lecture, where their manners of feeding, praying and studying, were considered alike objectionable; no one knew whence they came, whither they went, nor what they did, for they never showed at cricket or the boats; they were a gloomy, seedy-looking *confrérie*, who had as little to glory in clothes and manners as in the flesh itself.
>
> Unprepossessing then, in feature, gait and manners, unkempt and ill-dressed beyond what can be easily described, these poor fellows formed a class apart, whose thoughts and ways were not as the thoughts and ways of Ernest and his friends, and it was among them that Simeonism chiefly flourished. ①

From above, we learn that the Simeonites lived in quarters which were known as the labyrinth. As Philip Henderson remarked, "when the seedy-looking Simeonities had the temerity to drop their tracts into the letter-boxes of the nice people, Butler wrote parodies of them which he dropped into the letter-boxes of the labyrinth." ② This leads one to suppose that Ernest, from the first, looks on the Simeonites with a sardonic eye. ③ It might well be prudent to suppose that, regarding the Simeonites, ordination, the personal implications for Butler, therefore, "became synonymous with associating with men who would never be accepted by 'nice people'—that is, the healthy, the good-looking and the elegant, people who gave the impression that they were on good terms both with themselves and with the world". ④

However, there is a sharp contrast between the Simeonites and Ernest's

① Samuel Butler. *The Way of All Flesh.* London: Grant Richards, 1903. Edited with an introduction by V. S. Pritchett, London: Penguin English Library, 2012, Ch. 47, pp. 242-243.

② Philip Henderson. *Samuel Butler, the Incarnate Bachelor.* London: Cohen and West, 1953, p. 19.

③ The Simeonites ways were not of the ways of Butler and his friends, for "they would meet in one another's rooms for tea and prayer". Moreover, Butler's friends revealed that Butler's dislike of the Simeonites was due to his being the son of a clergyman. *Ibid.*, p. 19.

④ *Ibid.*, p. 19.

excellent college fellow, Towneley, whom I have discussed in the previous section. Here, it may be suggested that Ernest is instinctively attracted to Towneley, who is "the most handsome man whom he ever had seen or ever could see" and "good at cricket and boating, very good-natured, singularly free from conceit, not clever but very sensible".[①] At Cambridge, Towneley, who becomes Ernest's especial hero, lost his parents when he was only two years old, and has the fortune to be left as "their only child and heir to one of the finest estates in the South of England."[②]

Unfortunately, as naively as Ernest, he soon turns to the spiritual blandishments of the Simeonites. As a result, Ernest becomes a religious enthusiast.[③] When he writes to his parents about his new awakening to Christ, they are greatly disturbed: "Even Christina refrained from ecstasy over her son's having discovered the power of Christ's word, while Theobald was frightened out of his wits."[④] Consequently, Ernest, far from discovering his vocation, errs by becoming a clergyman, just as a pale imitation of Theobald. The self-distrusting Ernest has been misled and misguided by his father and by the spirit of conformity at Cambridge into a profession that he should have avoided like the plague.

Ernest's golden time at Cambridge is drawing to an end as soon as he becomes aware that "the light of the happiness which he had known during his four years at Cambridge had been extinguished, and he was appalled by the irrevocable

---

① Samuel Butler. *The Way of All Flesh.* London: Grant Richards, 1903. Edited with an introduction by V. S. Pritchett, London: Penguin English Library, 2012, Ch.48, p. 251.

② *Ibid.*, Ch.48, p. 251.

③ In *The Way of All Flesh*, Ernest is also persuaded by Mr. Hawke. The Rev. Gideon Hawke is a handsome, courteous Evangelical preacher from London.

④ Samuel Butler. *The Way of All Flesh.* London: Grant Richards, 1903. Edited with an introduction by V. S. Pritchett, London: Penguin English Library, 2012, Ch.50, p. 264.

nature of the step which he now felt that he had taken much too hurriedly."① After the ordination to a curacy in London, Ernest's religious enthusiasm momently vanishes. Then, until this moment, Ernest is still dominated by his "conscious self" not his "true self":

> The sense of humour and tendency to think for himself, of which till a few months previously he had been showing fair promise, were nipped as though by a late frost, while his earlier habit of taking on trust everything that was told him by those in authority, and following everything out to the bitter end, no matter how preposterous, returned with redoubled strength.②

Ernest's inner self is still not strong enough, since "the circumstances had led to his being ordained; for the moment he was sorry they had."③ But Ernest thinks that since "he had done it and must go through with it. He therefore set himself to find out what was expected of him, and to act accordingly."④ In London, Ernest meets a senior curate, Pryer, who is "a personable and persuasive conservative whose High Church views appeal to Ernest as much as did the diametrically opposed views of the Simeonites".⑤ Ernest thus falls under the spell of the senior curate, Pryer, who successfully convinces Ernest that "the High Church party, and even Rome itself, had more to say for themselves than he had thought."⑥

Hence Overton has an excellent remark on the education of young men,

---

① *Ibid.*, Ch. 51, p. 267.

② *Ibid.*, Ch. 51, pp. 267-268.

③ *Ibid.*, Ch. 51, p. 268.

④ *Ibid.*, Ch. 51, p. 268.

⑤ See online source: *The Way of All Flesh*: Summary and Analysis Chapter 51-55. http://www.cliffsnotes.com/literature/w/the-way-of-all-flesh/summary-and-analysis/chapters-5155.

⑥ Samuel Butler. *The Way of All Flesh*. London: Grant Richards, 1903. Edited with an introduction by V. S. Pritchett, London: Penguin English Library, 2012, Ch. 51, p. 269.

especially regarding that of Ernest:

> Everyone has a mass of bad work in him which he will have to work off and get rid of before he can do better—and indeed, the more lasting a man's ultimate good work is, the more sure he is to pass through a time, and perhaps a very long one, in which there seems very little hope for him at all. We must all sow our spiritual wild oats. The fault I feel personally disposed to find with my godson is not that he had wild oats to sow, but that they were such an exceedingly tame and uninteresting crop. ①

With regard to Pryer, Overton "only saw him once for about five minutes, and then thought him odious both in manners and appearance". ② With a young man's zeal, Ernest takes to Pryer's plan of a "College of Spiritual Pathology", in which priests skilled in "soul craft" are to cure men of their spiritual ailments. ③ Ernest's intention is to treat people's souls in the manner that physicians treat bodies and thereby bring the Church and the nation to be regenerated up-to date with developments in the field of science. ④ Imprudently, Pryer invests Ernest's funds at "a place they call the Stock Exchange". ⑤ Later, Pryer disappears with all of Ernest's financial resources. Eventually, Ernest becomes aware that he was

---

① *Ibid.*, Ch. 51, p. 267.

② *Ibid.*, Ch. 51, P. 268.

③ U. C. Knoepflmacher remarks, Pryer's proposed "spiritual pathologists" reverse the principle of the Erewhonian "straighteners" who punish physical disease as a moral crime. The analogy remains the same, however; in each case Butler's irony revolves around the attempt to remedy "spiritual" ills by theoretical standards, removed from the ways of the flesh." See U. C. Knoepflmacher. *Religious Humanism and the Victorian Novel: George Eliot, Walter Pater, and Samuel Butler.* Princeton: Princeton University Press, 1965, p. 286.

④ See online source: *The Way of All Flesh*: Summary and Analysis Chapter 51-55. http://www.cliffsnotes.com/literature/w/the-way-of-all-flesh/summary-and-analysis/chapters-5155.

⑤ Samuel Butler. *The Way of All Flesh.* London: Grant Richards, 1903. Edited with an introduction by V. S. Pritchett, London: Penguin English Library, 2012, Ch. 53, p. 279.

cheated, due to his disregarding both of the questionable nature of Pryer's morality and his theology. Nevertheless, Ernest decides to carry out his plan for saving the souls of the poor, then, he rents a house in Ashipit Place among the poor in order to familiarize himself with their habits and thoughts. Then, after visiting Ernest in his living quarters, Overton learns all of Ernest's ill-conceived plans and begins to worry about this young man's future.

Ernest's years at Cambridge, though presented as a pleasant period of tranquility between periods of strife, actually complicates his ensuing years of early manhood. His flashes of brilliance are concealed and his intelligence is not yet developed either, moreover, he fails to gain the self-knowledge and knowledge about the world, with which he needs to attain manhood. Consequently, Ernest realizes that he lacks both the appreciation of his intellectual talent he possessed instinctively and the method by which he can develop it. After taking lodgings in Ashipit Place, he finds himself "in a new and quite unexpected world".① Although Ernest is "good at heart", his landlady; Mrs. Jupp's comment on her tenant is that "[He] didn't seem to know anything at all".② He is childish and inexperienced "in the ways of anything but those back eddies of the world, schools and universities".③

---

① Butler's personal implications are coming closer and closer to the surface. In one of Butler's biography, Peter Raby records, "He [Butler] sat for the Classical Tripos in 1858, and achieved his First Class, being placed 12th equal, good enough for an academic career should he wish one. For the last time he coxed the 1st boat in the Mays. He then moved down to London, and spent six months as an unpaid assistant to the Rev. Philip Perring, a former pupil of Dr Butler at Shrewsbury, and a curate at St James's, Piccadilly. Butler took lodgings in Heddon street, off Regent Street, and found himself in a new and quite unexpected would." See Peter Raby. *Samuel Butler: A Biography*. London: The Hogarth Press, 1991, pp. 51-52. Here, Butler had faced the same situation with which Ernest faces now, therefore, we may reasonably assume that Butler writes his own experience into *The Way of All Flesh* (1903).

② Samuel Butler. *The Way of All Flesh.* London: Grant Richards, 1903. Edited with an introduction by V. S. Pritchett, London: Penguin English Library, 2012, Ch. 61, pp. 314-315.

③ *Ibid.*, Ch. 57, p. 295.

Unfortunately, in abandoning his budding sense of humour and ability to think for himself by engaging in evangelical enthusiasms, Ernest renders himself susceptible to the follies which will burden him for the next five years of his life. ① Ernest's passage to manhood is considerably influenced by the Cambridge years, which presages a new crisis. I have argued this point in my previous section.

① See online source: *The Way of All Flesh*: Summary and Analysis Chapter 45-50. http://www.cliffsnotes.com/literature/w/the-way-of-all-flesh/summary-and-analysis/chapters-4550.

4.4 Samuel Butler on education

It should be stressed that, on the subject of education for childhood, Butler's advice to parents is a reaction to his own experience. He advocates giving children some measure of freedom, as well as some pocket money to spend on pleasures. A simple suggestion that Butler has for parents is "merely to remember how they felt when they were young". ① The most important aspect of the education of children is to "make the child feel that he is loved and that his natural feelings are respected". ② According to Butler, children "should find out the right way for themselves". ③ It is only on matters of sex and money that he insists on providing some instruction to the children, for the ignorance of either of the two would easily lead to disaster. ④ As a result of his own bitter experience with respect to money, Butler recommends introducing speculation as a subject of study at school, training boys on "how this making haste to get rich moneys out in actual practice". ⑤

In fact, both Shrewsbury and Cambridge struck Butler as forts of

① Samuel Butler. *Erewhon*. London: Trübner, 1872. Edited with an introduction by Peter Mudford. London: Penguin, 1985, Ch. 20, p. 175.

② Samuel Butler. *The Fair Haven*. First published in 1873. With an introduction by R. A. Streatfeild. London: A. C. Fifield, 1913, p. 9.

③ Petronella Jacoba de, Lange. *Samuel Butler, Critic and Philosopher*. Zutphen, Netherlands: W. J. Thieme, 1925, p. 124.

④ *Ibid.*, p. 124.

⑤ Samuel Butler. *The Way of All Flesh*. London: Grant Richards, 1903. Edited with an introduction by V. S. Pritchett, London: Penguin English Library, 2012, Ch. 78, p. 406.

impracticality. [1] On this point, John D. Grant asserts that, "Though their authorities might profess otherwise, the training was carried on in an academic vacuum; the curriculum was a pedantic routine of manoeuvrings that completely overlooked future application to the affairs of men."[2] In Butler's views, Victorian schools and colleges dispensed a "hypothetical" style of education and neglected the wisdom of common sense. In *The Way of All Flesh*, when Ernest is sinking into the chasm he has dug for himself, Overton and Mrs. Jupp, act as observers and commentators of the young man's folly. Mrs. Jupp is remarkable as a character type that dates back to Chaucer's Wife of Bath and includes the most celebrated bawds in English literature—Shakespeare's Mistress Quickly, Laurence Sterne's Mrs. Slip-Slop, and even Richard Sheridan's Mrs. Malaprop. Although of the lowest class and lacking a formal education, Mrs. Jupp possesses an instinctive wisdom that enables her to share Overton's skeptical attitude toward Ernest's situation. Of incidental importance to the central action of the novel, Mrs. Jupp is nevertheless a brilliant triumph of characterization and brings a comic relief in Butler's world of fiction.

Instead, in *Erewhon*, Butler advocates an ideal style of education, which is presented as follows:

> That to teach a boy merely the nature of the things that exist in the world around him, and about which he will have to be conversant during his whole life, would be giving him but a narrow and shallow conception of the

---

① Butler says, "If Universities were not the worst teachers in the world I should like to see professorships of speculation established at Oxford and Cambridge. When I reflect, however, that the only things worth doing which Oxford and Cambridge can do well are cooking, cricket, rowing and games, of which there is no professorship, I fear that the establishment of a professorial chair would end in teaching young men neither how to speculate, nor how not to speculate, but would simply turn them out as bad speculators". *Ibid.*, Ch. 78, p. 406.

② John Douglas Grant, *Samuel Butler as a Critic of Victorian England.* Toronto: University of Toronto, 1947, p. 45.

> universe, which it is urged might contain all manner of things which are not now to be found therein. To open his eyes to these possibilities, and so to prepare him for all sorts of emergencies, is the object of this system of hypothetics. To imagine a set of utterly strange and impossible contingencies, and require the youths to give intelligent answers to the questions that arise there from, is reckoned the fittest conceivable way of preparing them for the actual conduct of their affairs in after life. ①

The impractical nature of Victorian education Butler attributed mainly to the burdensome study of Greek and Latin of all his classical studies, since he believes both of them are hypothetical language. Here, Butler's biographer, also his close friend Henry Festing Jones has pointed out that, in all Butler's classical studies, he seems to have formed an attachment only to Homer. ② On this point, John D. Grant comments, "Few Victorians vindicated the claims of classical training solely on its technical usefulness to the lawyer, doctor and clergyman. But many in both camps of educational theory, "artificial" and "natural", argued that the classics, taught in a spirit of liberality, could illuminate the English language. "③ To continue, he emphasizes that John Stuart Mill (1806 – 1873) would retain that "Every word used by Homer, Thucydides, and Cicero added to the exactness and completeness of the whole; in them was no prolixity, only a highly polished beauty, the perfect medium of the sense. "④ It is worth mentioning here that Butler was highly influenced by Mill, who stated that the "great aim of all learning is to know something of all the great subjects of human

① Samuel Butler. *Erewhon, or Over the Range*. London: Trübner, 1872. Edited with an introduction by Peter Mudford. London: Penguin, 1985, Ch. 21, pp. 185-186.

② Henring Festing Jones. *Samuel Butler: Author of Erewhon (1835 – 1902), A Memoir.* London: MacMillan, 1919, vol. I, p. 232.

③ John Douglas Grant, *Samuel Butler as a Critic of Victorian England.* Toronto: University of Toronto, 1947, p. 51.

④ Here, argued by J. D. Grant, by quoting J. S. Mill. *Ibid.*, p. 51.

interest [...] to obtain a true view of nature and life in their broad outline," which is well implied in the liberal education. ①

It should be stressed that Butler's attack on nineteenth-century education in England is derived mostly from his own student days. ② He felt that his own educational background, which I outlined in the first part, was inadequate in training him for a successful living. Therefore, his personal experience is broadened into his most satirical statement: this is the usual manner in which his arguments developed. Butler concretizes a positive scheme of education fitted into his evolutionary outlook. ③

For Butler, knowledge and true learning can never be acquired as a result of a deliberate search nor are they found by luck. They must be the fruits of conscious efforts. Learning becomes an instinctive process that is achieved only with the cooperation of the student, as Butler explained in *Life and Habit* (1878):

> This might be done with the help of an inward desire on the part of the boy to learn, but never otherwise. If the boy wants to learn or to improve generally, he will do so in spite of every hindrance, till in time he becomes a very different being from what he was originally. If he does not want to learn, he will not do so for any wish of another person. If he feels he has the power he will wish, or if he wishes, he will begin to think he has the power, and try to fulfill his wishes; one cannot say which comes first, for the power and the

① James and John Stuart Mill on Education. F. A. Cavenagh, ed. Westport (Conn.): Greenwood press, 1979, p. 143.

② See John Douglas Grant, *Samuel Butler as a Critic of Victorian England.* Toronto: University of Toronto, 1947, p. 45.

③ Earlier than Freud, as a thinker and writer on evolution, in a sense, in *The Way of All Flesh*, Butler has set out for applying the evolutionary psychology and psychoanalysis on education.

desire go always hand in hand, or nearly so. ①

Hence, what Butler is at pains to emphasize is the power of will, or the power of faith. In *The Way of All Flesh*, Butler tries to define his fundamental principle of education: it is a process in which one does what one is fond of, that is to say, what gives one pleasure. ② In particular, one should undertake the learning of something for which one feels the strongest desire. Because "[I]f he likes his subject, he will try; if he tries, he will soon succeed in doing something which shall open a door. It does not matter what a man does; so long as he does it with the attention which affection engenders, he will come to see his way to something else." ③ For Butler, to increase a boy's desire to learn is highly important. Moreover, Butler insists on sparking off curiosity and giving children the liberty to develop their own taste by trial and error. As for the effectiveness and advantage of such an approach to education, Butler believes that young men will acquire knowledge and skill in the process of personal involvement, and they will learn more from their own mistakes than if they were simply taught the theory and rules of their profession. ④

---

① See Samuel Butler. *Life and Habit*. London: Trübner, 1878. Revised edition, with author's addenda and a preface by R. A. Streatfeild, London: A. C. Fifield, 1910. The Echo Library edition, 2007, Ch. XI, p. 103.

② When John Douglas Grant illustrates Butler's argument on Victorian education, he points out, "In short, education is a process in which doing what one likes, (that is, what gives one pleasure), as soon as one is able is a fundamental principle." See John Douglas Grant, *Samuel Butler as a Critic of Victorian England.* Toronto: University of Toronto, 1947, p. 57.

③ Samuel Butler. *Alps and Sanctuaries of Piedmont and the Canton Ticino*. London: David Bogue, 1882, Ch. XIII, p. 195.

④ Petronella Jacoba de, Lange. *Samuel Butler, Critic and Philosopher*. Zutphen, Netherlands: W. J. Thieme, 1925, p. 125. To continue, Petronella J. Lange says, "Butler...arguing that in our world young people are stuffed with unnecessary learning till they have lost the ability of producing anything themselves, and that being thrown upon their own resources at an early age will teach them the ways of the world better than all theoretic instruction, and will improve the relation between parents and children into the bargain."

According to Butler, learning or acquiring knowledge like breathing, can only be perfected by repeating something over and over until it is imprinted upon one's memory. Therefore, John Douglas Grant suggests to immerse the child as soon as possible in "the ways and farings of many men", preferably as an apprentice, in a profession close to that of his ancestors, following these inclinations.① Yet, it is precisely what these inclinations are, that constitutes the problem of such an education, for it seems that there are many young men who are not very clear about their own likes and dislikes. They do not know how to choose their subject when they are given the liberty to do so.② Therefore, in *The Way of All Flesh* (1903), Butler stresses that the duty of the educators lies in providing a direction "trying to find out what activity seems to suit a particular character best and suggesting means of fulfilling these unconscious wishes of a child without forcing it".③ Alethea's speculation about Ernest's inclinations and her canny nudging in the right direction would have been highly approved of by Butler, who insists that this style of education is "the way in which even the greatest men as a general rule begin to develop".④ For Butler, a good educator pays more attention to and is also more pleased by a student's "receptiveness and

---

① John Douglas Grant, *Samuel Butler as a Critic of Victorian England.* Toronto: University of Toronto, 1947, p. 62. "He [the writer of the *Odyssey*] assuredly hit the right nail on the head when he epitomisedhis typical wise man as knowing 'the ways and farings of many men'. What culture is comparable to this? What a lie, what a sickly debilitating debauch did not Ernest's school and university career now seem to him, in comparison with his life in prison and as a tailor in Blackfriars...What confidence again in his own power to swim if thrown into deep waters had not he won through his experiences during the last three years!" See Samuel Butler. *The Way of All Flesh.* London: Grant Richards, 1903. Edited with an introduction by V. S. Pritchett, London: Penguin English Library, 2012, Ch. 78, pp. 404-405.

② Petronella Jacoba de, Lange. *Samuel Butler, Critic and Philosopher.* Zutphen, Netherlands: W. J. Thieme, 1925, p. 126.

③ *Ibid.*, p. 126.

④ Samuel Butler. *The Way of All Flesh.* London: Grant Richards, 1903. Edited with an introduction by V. S. Pritchett, London: Penguin English Library, 2012, Ch. 35, p. 174.

reproductiveness than alarmed at the things he caught and reproduced". ①

Instruction, suggests Butler, should be given when the memory fails in the intimate relationship of teacher and learner:

> I am sure that the young of all animals often do want help upon matters about which anyone would say "a priori" that there should be no difficulty. One would think that a young seal would want no teaching how to swim, nor yet a bird to fly, but in practice a young seal drowns if put out of its depth before its parents have taught it to swim; and so again, even the young hawk must be taught to fly before it can do so...I grant that the tendency of the times is to exaggerate the good which teaching can do, but in trying to teach too much, in most matters, we have neglected others in respect of which a little sensible teaching would do no harm. ②

It should be stressed that Butler's account of "sensible teaching" has its origin in his evolutionary theories. The way of teaching should be in accordance of the need. Intervention occurs at the right moment in the development of an organism: just as animals instinctively teach their offspring crucial skills for their survival such as flying and swimming. For Butler, the continuity of work through generations and the intimate relationship between teacher and student, father and son, form the basic pattern of the learning system, as he outlines below:

> [Ernest did not yet] know that ideas, no less than the living beings in whose minds they arise, must be begotten by parents not very unlike themselves, the most original still differing but slightly from the parents that have given rise to them. Life is like a fugue, everything must grow

① *Ibid.*, Ch. 35, p. 174.

② Samuel Butler. *The Way of All Flesh.* London: Grant Richards, 1903. Edited with an introduction by V. S. Pritchett, London: Penguin English Library, 2012, Ch. 72, p. 373.

> out of the subject and there must be nothing new. Nor, again, did he see how hard it is to say where one idea ends and another begins, nor yet how closely this is paralleled in the difficulty of saying where a life begins or ends, or an action or indeed anything, there being an unity in spite of infinite multitude, and an infinite multitude in spite of unity. He thought that ideas came into clever people's heads by a kind of spontaneous germination, without parentage in the thoughts of others or the course of observation[...] So strong was the hold which habit and association held over both father and son, that the one considered he had as good a right as ever to dictate, and the other that he had as little right as ever to gainsay. ①

It would be impossible to exaggerate the importance of assimilation, for it is a process of "spontaneous germination" made to fit into knowledge already gained. I would maintain that Butler's concept of evolution obviously runs through much of his thinking about education. Therefore, John Douglas Grant points out "Building upon the work of Buffon, Erasmus Darwin, and Lamarck, his biology made the development of any organism dependent upon two principal factors: desire and memory."② By way of illustration, the unbornchild is the only being completely devoid of desire, thus it is only in the unborn state, Butler asserts, "were we blessed; we thought as every man thinks, and held the same opinions as our fathers and mothers had done upon nearly every subject."③ From the time the ovum is impregnated, conscious desire to evolve marks all the stages reached by the new organism. This process, however, is graduated and strictly limited by

① *Ibid.*, Ch. 46, p. 238.

② John Douglas Grant, *Samuel Butler as a Critic of Victorian England.* Toronto: University of Toronto, 1947, p. 58.

③ Samuel Butler. *Life and Habit.* London: Trübner, 1878. Revised edition, with author's addenda and a preface by R. A. Streatfeild, London: A. C. Fifield, 1910. The Echo Library edition, 2007, Ch. IV, p. 34.

what the organism remembers of its racial ancestry. The certainty of this memory ends with birth, then ensues "the beginning of doubt, the first hankering after scepticism the dreaming of a dawn of trouble, the end of certainty and of settled convictions". ①

In this uncertainty that surrounds the organism at birth, instincts acts as the surest guides for action, which is really the accumulated knowledge of past behaviour unconsciously called to mind in a certain situation. Digestion and circulation are most unconscious acts in the infant because they are habits of extreme antiquity which are shared with invertebrate ancestry. The infant is also less conscious of processes that are acquisitions of prehuman ancestry, such as eating and drinking, swallowing, breathing, seeing and hearing. Full consciousness is possible only in such habits as speech, the upright position, the arts and sciences, and the whole scheme of what is commonly called education. ② Over these, control is maintained by the deliberate use of conscious direction; learning takes place by imitation and repetition. Nevertheless, unconsciousness of performance remains the criterion by which true knowledge is evaluated. The earliest pattern of behaviour in the child is likely to be its most successful one because the child is at that stage closest to the common pool of hereditable memory—his or her parents—and little or no thought is given to behaviour: ③

> It is the young and fair, then, who are the truly old and the truly experienced; it is they who alone have a trustworthy memory to guide them; they alone know things as they are, and it is from them that, as we grow older, we must study if we would still cling to truth. The whole charm of youth lies in its advantage over age in respect of experience, and where this has for some reason failed, or been misapplied, the charm is broken. When

① *Ibid.*, Ch. IV, p. 34.

② *Ibid.*, Ch. III, p. 29.

③ *Ibid.*, Ch. I, pp. 10-13.

> we say that we are getting old, we should say rather that we are getting new or young, and are suffering from inexperience, which drives us into doing things which we do not understand, and lands us, eventually, in the utter impotence of death. ①

Then, I find John Douglas Grant has left us an excellent comment on that paragraph, what he asserted is that "nature operates on the principle of descent with modification, of which the essence is that every offspring resembles its parents, and yet, at the same time, that no offspring resembles its parents". ② Hence, the sole means of progress and of education lay in this paradox, he continues:

> The normal offspring, then, experiences a sense of need to advance beyond its parents, but to do so with success it must never at any one leap go too far beyond the limits of its inherited memory. An entirely new environment suddenly thrust upon the child leaves it with no remembered resources or skills with which to accommodate the unfamiliar to the familiar. ③

The difficulty with this view is that when the "cross" is too wide for the individual, it would result in a crisis. On this case, Butler says:

> The trouble is that in the end we shall be driven to admit the unity of the universe so completely as to be compelled to deny that there is either an external or an internal, but must see everything both as external and internal at one and the same time, subject and object—external and internal—being unified as much as everything else... Much the best way out of this difficulty

① *Ibid.*, Ch. XV, p. 152.

② John Douglas Grant, *Samuel Butler as a Critic of Victorian England.* Toronto: University of Toronto, 1947, pp. 60-61.

③ *Ibid.*, p. 60.

> is to go in for separation between internal and external—subject and object—when we find this convenient, and unity between the same when we find unity convenient...It is faith and not logic which is the supreme arbiter. ①

Since nature for Butler is "distinctly a fairly liberal conservative rather than a conservative liberal"② as he pithily summarised in the old couplet:

> Be not the first by whom the new is tried,
> Nor yet the last to throw the old aside. ③

The primary requisite in dealing with these changes is to admit a sense of continuity between the old and the new. "This should teach us moderation...she [nature] will not be hurried and will culla creature out even more surely for forestalling her wishes too readily, than for lagging a little behind them."④ For Butler, there should be a fundamental motive in the development of the individual along with the process of evolution. Due to the necessity of harmony in the transition between the old and new, internal and external, subject and object, it is important to be reasonable in seeking out novelty. Aspirations must be carefully fitted into past accomplishments. Taking the case of the artists, Butler elaborates the process of assimilation as follows:

> So the greatest musicians, painters, and poets owe their greatness rather to their fusion and assimilation of all the good that has been done up to, and

---

① Samuel Butler. *The Way of All Flesh.* London: Grant Richards, 1903. Edited with an introduction by V. S. Pritchett, London: Penguin English Library, 2012, Ch. 69, p. 357.

② Samuel Butler. *Life and Habit.* London: Trübner, 1878. Revised edition, with author's addenda and a preface by R. A. Streatfeild, London: A. C. Fifield, 1910. The Echo Library edition, 2007, Ch. XV, p. 155.

③ *Ibid.*, Ch. XV, p. 155.

④ *Ibid.*, Ch. XV, p. 155.

> especially near about, their own time, than to any very startling steps they have taken in advance. Such men will be sure to take some, and important, steps forward; for unless they have this power, they will not be able to assimilate well what has been done already, and if they have it, their study of older work will almost indefinitely assist it; but, on the whole, they owe their greatness to their completer fusion and assimilation of older ideas. ①

Butler argues that aspirations are fundamental elements to the whole process of assimilation. Consequently, in order to break through restrictions, the solution as John Douglas Grant demonstrated, is that "free will could operate, and here, from the choices made, progress took place, in accord with the organism's desires". ② There can beno doubt that such an apprentice system for art schools and academies recommended by Butler is in accordance with his evolutionary theory. By following Butler's suggestion, a man who wants to become a writer or an artist can only make progress by making a habit of jotting down anything that strikes him as noteworthy and trying to express plainly what he desires to show, instead of studying famous examples or being taught by rule by others. ③ In brief, it is the power of will or cunning that helps the individual to achieve in the process of fusion and assimilation and eventually make progress.

Particularly, Butler advocates the same approach for art education and the training of artists as he suggests for education in general, as outlined by Ernest in his Cambridge essay on literary composition. One particular issue raised by Butler that the most important guideline in education is: "depend upon strong-felt interest in choosing a subject; trust the instincts; pay attention to the

① *Ibid.*, Ch. XV, p. 155.

② John Douglas Grant, *Samuel Butler as a Critic of Victorian England.* Toronto: University of Toronto, 1947, p. 61.

③ Petronella Jacoba de. Lange. *Samuel Butler, Critic and Philosopher.* Zutphen, Netherlands: W. J. Thieme, 1925, p. 127.

promptings of the unconscious as the final arbiter of taste."[①] For "art for art's sake", that is to say, "a work of art should be produced for the pleasure it gives the producer, and the pleasure he thinks it will give to a few of whom he is fond."[②] As Butler demonstrates more precisely in his *Notes-Books*:

> Art has no end in view save the emphasizing and recording in the most effective way some strongly felt interest or affection...Let them [the subjects] choose you, not you them. Only do that which insists upon being done and runs right up against you, hitting you in the eye until you do it. This calls you and you had better attend to it, and do it as well as you can. But until called in this way do nothing...The arts of the musician, the painter, and the writer are essentially the same; ...each realizes moments of extreme issue are unconscious and must be left to take care of themselves.[③]

This could be taken to mean that, for Butler, the greatest secret behind a good work of art, whether in music, literature or painting, lies in not attempting too much. To the query, "What is too much?" Butler would answer, "Anything that we find difficult or unpleasant."[④] For Butler believed that "the greatest work cannot get beyond this and the least comes strangely near the greatest if this can

---

① John Douglas Grant, *Samuel Butler as a Critic of Victorian England.* Toronto: University of Toronto, 1947, p. 45.

② Samuel Butler. *Alps and Sanctuaries of Piedmont and the Canton Ticino.* London: David Bogue, 1882, p. 203.

③ Samuel Butler. *The Note-Books of Samuel Butler.* Edited with a preface and biographical statement by Henry Festing Jones. London: A. C. Fifield, 1912. Edition in use: IndyPublish edition, 2007, pp. 77-85.

④ In continuing, Butler wrote, "We should not ask whether others find this same thing difficult or not. If we find the difficulty so great that the overcoming it is a labour and not a pleasure, we should either change our aim altogether, or aim, at any rate for a time, at some lower point. It must be remembered that no work is required to be more than right as far as it goes." *Ibid.*, p. 83.

be said of it". [①] Furthermore, Butler argued that such masterpieces as *The Iliad* and The Odyssey could only be the result of the conscious efforts of one artist, drawing upon the well of his intelligence, not a product of chance, laboured upon by a great number of men over various periods. [②] On evaluation of the greatest artists and Englishmen, particularly, in comparing Handel with Shakespeare, Butler concludes, "He [Handel] is as much above Shakespeare as Shakespeare is above all other, except Handel himself." [③] Regarding reason, Butler says "Neither was self-conscious in production, but when the thing has come out Shakespeare looks at it and wonders, whereas Handel takes it as a matter of course." [④] Butler greatly admired such a decisive self-awareness in Handel's music. [⑤] For Handel was well known for his sturdy self-confidence and strong sense of humour. [⑥] The music of Handel becomes one of the major influences and accompanies Butler's life:

> ...of all dead men Handel has had the largest place in my thoughts. In fact I should say he and his music have been the central fact in my life ever since I was old enough to know of the existence of either music or life. All day long—whether I am writing or painting or walking—but always—I have his music in my head, and if I lose sight of it and of him for an hour or two, as

---

① *Ibid.*, p. 83.

② Petronella Jacoba de, Lange. *Samuel Butler, Critic and Philosopher.* Zutphen, Netherlands: W. J. Thieme, 1925, p. 128.

③ Samuel Butler. *Alps and Sanctuaries of Piedmont and the Canton Ticino.* London: David Bogue, 1882, p. 2.

④ Samuel Butler. *The Note-Books of Samuel Butler.* Edited with a preface and biographical statement by Henry Festing Jones. London: A. C. Fifield, 1912. Edition in use: IndyPublish edition, 2007, p. 92.

⑤ Ellen T. Harris, "Butler's Narcissus: 'A Tame Oratorio'." In *Samuel Butler, Victorian Against the Grain: A Critical Overview.* Edited by James G. Paradis. Toronto: University of Toronto Press, 2007, p. 289.

⑥ *Ibid.*, p. 313.

> of course I sometimes do, this is as much as I do. I believe I am not exaggerating when I say that I have never been a day since I was 13 without having had Handel in my mind many times over. ①

The *Way of All Flesh* (1903) is also connected with Handel's music. ② At the moment Overton talks about collaborating with Ernest on one of his theatrical projects, he says, "I was then at work upon my burlesque 'The Impatient Griselda', and was sometimes at my wits' end for a piece of business or a situation; he gave me many suggestions, all of which were marked by excellent good sense." ③ This point is much like Butler's musical collaboration with his friend Henry Festing Jones, and together they wrote the words and music for *Narcissus: A Dramatic Cantata* (1888). Furthermore, it should be stressed that in his own literary criticism Butler is led by the principle of the omnipresence and importance of the mind, which also stems from his evolutionary theories. ④

Butler's ideal system of education could never be achieved by the dull

---

① Samuel Butler. *The Note-Books of Samuel Butler.* Edited with a preface and biographical statement by Henry Festing Jones. London: A. C. Fifield, 1912. Edition in use: IndyPublish edition, 2007, p. 332.

② Rita Yeasted points out that Butler's obsession with Handel's music is not peripheral to an understanding of his writings. See Rita Yeasted. "The Handelian Quality of Butler's *The Way of All Flesh.*" In *Modern Language Studies*, vol. 9, No. 2 (Spring, 1979), pp. 23-32.

③ Samuel Butler. *The Way of All Flesh.* London: Grant Richards, 1903. Edited with an introduction by V. S. Pritchett, London: Penguin English Library, 2012, Ch. 73, p. 384. Overton also mentions in the novel that one of his burlesques was set to Handel's music: "It is true that in the intervals of business I had written a good deal but my works had been almost exclusively for the stage, and for those theatres that devoted themselves to extravaganza and burlesque. I had written many pieces of this description, full of puns and comic songs, and they had had a fair success...I had also dramatised "The Pilgrim's Progress" for a Christmas Pantomime...The orchestra played music taken from Handel's best-known works, but the time was a good deal altered, and altogether the tunes were not exactly as Handel left them". *Ibid.*, Ch. 27, p. 132.

④ Petronella Jacoba de, Lange. *Samuel Butler, Critic and Philosopher.* Zutphen, Netherlands: W. J. Thieme, 1925, p. 128.

machinery of Victorian schools and colleges, although "Colleges of Unreason", as Butler suggested in *Erewhon* (1872) did have some success, their academicism notwithstanding. Where there exists in a student a special taste, no amount of cramming with the "hypothetical languages" can prevent the "natural instinct" from asserting itself, thus enabling the youths to grow up "as sensible and goodly as they did". [①] Moreover, "those who had any special tastes could not be restrained from developing them: they would learn what they wanted to learn and liked." [②] Although this meant that the boys would have lost some time, being keen and intelligent, they keep their eyes and ears constantly open to everything that interests them, and will pick up all manner of really useful information unconsciously. The High Ydgrunites of *Erewhon* triumph in this way. Because their heredity has made them physically attractive, self-reliant in intellect, and generous in spirit, they manage to overcome the prejudices of their culture and bypass the attempted distortions of their educators. For Butler, they are the epitome of the English gentleman. He describes them thus:

> Being inured from youth to exercises and athletics of all sorts, and living fearlessly under the eye of their peers, among whom there exists a high standard of courage, generosity, honour, and every good and manly quality—what wonder that they should have become, so to speak, a law unto themselves; and while taking an elevated view of the goddess Ydgrun, they should have gradually lost all faith in the recognised deities of the country? These they do not openly disregard, for conformity until absolutely intolerable is a law of Ydgrun, yet they have no real belief in the objective existence of beings which so readily explain themselves as abstractions...They keep their

① Samuel Butler. *Erewhon, or Over the Range*. London: Trübner, 1872. Edited with an introduction by Peter Mudford. London: Penguin, 1985, Ch. 22, p. 192.

② *Ibid.*, Ch. 22, p. 192.

> opinions, however, greatly to themselves, inasmuch as most of their countrymen feel strongly about the gods, and they hold it wrong to give pain, unless for some greater good than seems likely to arise from their plain speaking. ①

According to Butler, the High Ydgrunites are "gentlemen in the full sense of the word". ② Being of the successive generations, they live harmoniously by their instincts. They are creatures of grace with good breeding. In them knowledge has become "perfect, assured, unhesitating", and "so-called earthly knowledge... passed through so many people as have become living and incarnate." ③ They are the products of "good forefathers for many generations", who "live much in the open air, and, as Lord Beaconsfield finely said, never read". ④ Strong and handsome, gently nurtured and well educated as they are, Butler also calls them ignorant and uncultivated—such a paradox allows them to fit neatly into his whole evolutionary outlook. However, their knowledge would unconsciously and instinctively guide them with a happy, realistic code of behaviour in their

① *Ibid.*, Ch. 17, pp. 157-158. To continue, Butler says, "In other respects they are more like the best class of Englishmen than any whom I have seen in other countries. I should have liked to have persuaded half-a-dozen of them to come over to England and go upon the state, for they had most of them a keen sense of humour and a taste for acting: they would be of great use to us. The example of a real gentleman is, if I may say so without profanity, the best of all gospels; such a man upon the stage, becomes a potent humanising influence, an Ideal which all may look upon for a shilling."

② *Ibid.*, Ch. 17, p. 157.

③ Samuel Butler. *Life and Habit*. London: Trübner, 1878. Revised edition, with author's addenda and a preface by R. A. Streatfeild, London: A. C. Fifield, 1910. The Echo Library edition, 2007. Ch. Ⅱ, p. 24.

④ *Ibid.*, Ch. Ⅱ, pp. 21-25.

development. ①

In brief, education, as the means of good breeding, is also set out in Ernest's essay on the various marriage systems of the world. He holds forth:

> If people require us to construct [...] we set good breeding as the corner-stone of our edifice. We would have it ever present consciously or unconsciously in the minds of all as the central faith in which they should live and move and have their being, as the touchstone of all things whereby they may be known as good or evil according as they make for good breeding or against it. That a man should have been bred well and breed others well;

① Take case of the High Ydgrunites, Butler intends to show "the importance of instinct as the accumulated wisdom of their ancestors in cases where reason fails." See Petronella Jacoba de, Lange. *Samuel Butler, Critic and Philosopher*. Zutphen, Netherlands: W. J. Thieme, 1925, p. 153. Since Butler believed that instinct is "a mode of faith in the evidence of things not actually seen." See Samuel Butler. *The Way of All Flesh*. London: Grant Richards, 1903. Edited with an introduction by V. S. Pritchett, London: Penguin English Library, 2012, Ch. 65, p. 331. I find this code of behaviour Butler has implicated in his *Note-Books*, involving with the artists, for it is especially the artist among men who is led by the faith or instinct towards the unseen world of which ordinary people are but faintly conscious, Butler says, "When I say the artist tends towards such a world, I mean not that he tends consciously and reasoningly, but that his instinct to take the direction will be strong to led him take any other. He is incapable of reasoning on the subject; if he could reason he would be lost *qua* artist; for, by every test that reason can apply, those who sell themselves for a price are in the right. The artist is guided by a faith that for him transcends all reason. Granted that this faith has been in great measure founded on reason, that it has grown up along with reason, that if it lose touch with reason it is no longer faith but madness; granted, again, that reason is in great measure founded on faith, that it has grown up along with faith, that if it lose touch with faith it is no longer reason but mechanism; granted, therefore, that faith grows with reason as will with power, as demand with supply, as mind with body, each stimulating and augmenting the other until an invisible, minute nucleus attains colossal growth—nevertheless the difference between the man of the world and the man who lives by faith is that the first is drawn towards the one and the second towards the other of two principles which, so far as we can see, are co-extensive and co-equal in importance." See Samuel Butler. *The Note-Books of Samuel Butler*. Edited with a preface and biographical statement by Henry Festing Jones. London: A. C. Fifield, 1912. IndyPublish edition, 2007, pp. 139-140.

> that his figure, head, hands, feet, voice, manner and clothes should carry conviction upon this point, so that no one can look at him without seeing that he has come of good stock and is likely to throw good stock himself, this is the desiderandum. And the same with a woman. The greatest number of these well-bred men and women, and the greatest happiness of these well-bred men and women, this is the highest good; towards this all government, all social conventions, all art, literature and science should directly or indirectly tend. Holy men and holy women are those who keep this unconsciously in view at all times whether of work or pastime. ①

Ernest spends his time as a writer composing works in the form of *Essays and Reviews*, which offered "good breeding" as the cornerstone of faith. The phrase, "good breeding", "in the unconsciously used double sense of the continuance of the race and grace of manner, is, in fact, one of the ultimates in Butler's thinking". ②

The issue then is how to educate young men? And what does Butler recommend to educators, parents and children some of whom might not be able to escape the problem of generation as closely as Ernest Pontifex does? In brief, the education that Butler pleaded for is a compound of a revolt against what had been forced on him, and approval of what he had acquired himself. In particular, his

---

① Samuel Butler. *The Way of All Flesh.* London: Grant Richards, 1903. Edited with an introduction by V. S. Pritchett, London: Penguin English Library, 2012, Ch. 85, p. 459. Thus, according to Butler, education shows its highest value in evolution and development of both individuals and societies.

② John Douglas Grant, *Samuel Butler as a Critic of Victorian England.* Toronto: University of Toronto, 1947, pp. 22-23. He continues, "It crystallizes many of Butler's final judgments on the family, education, biology, religion, ethics. The product of good breeding is a grand figure, like Towneley in *The Way*, or those supremely successful results of "nature" forces, like the Italian peasants or Breton fishermen. It is the "swell", created out of "good health, looks, temper, fortune", characterized by "gentleness, and consideration for other people, the absence of brow-beating, over-bearing manners and fuss".

system of education does not entail any forcing along of the process of development through inflexible rules and tyrannical discipline. The knowledge imparted should also be practical in nature. Butler suggests an education in which physical culture and economics play a large part such that the young man could adapt quickly to the real and imperfect world. There must be no unworldly professionalism or authorities removed from the instinctive behaviour of the majority of common people, who could well incapacitate the student as a craftsman. Moreover, education should take into consideration the needs and desires of young men and be attentive to individual talents. Butler would have leisurely progression in learning, guided by personal desires, and founded upon the accumulated wisdom and skill of ancestors, who were unconsciously versed in the practical affairs of the world. Ultimately, then, for Butler, the aim of a good educator is to build a bridge when it is necessary for the individuals to cross the distance between the old and new, internal and external, subject and object affairs, so as to help them to accomplish the development.

Thus I will end this section by a last reflection on Butler's most substantial work *The Way of All Flesh* (1903), since I would like to clearly lay out his final position. In a sense, Butler is, by nature, a skeptic, who questions intolerance, professionals and authorities of all stripes. In addition, Butler is strongly opposed to the view that actions are right or wrong in themselves; along with the Utilitarians, he held that rightness or wrongness can only be assessed in terms of their consequences, and of these consequences the only ones that mattered in practice were happiness and unhappiness. ① Ernest concludes in *The Way of All Flesh* in the same vein as Butler, "no man's opinions [...] can be worth holding unless he knows how to deny them easily and gracefully upon occasion in the

① C. E. M. Joad. *Samuel Butler (1835 – 1902)*. London: L. Parsons, 1924, p. 104.

cause of charity."[①] The novel therefore ends with the suggestion of a kind of triumph: Ernest, in pursuing his career as a writer, has achieved a state of mind that would be "Chinese" to his father and grandfather.[②] Ernest's instinct and free will have produced desired results. He has achieved the reconstruction of personal identity of the new generation and evolved as a gentleman. Ernest becomes Overton, and Overton reveals himself as a successful theorist and experimenter.[③] If Ernest's story is a spectacle of "the way of all flesh", it reveals us the function of instinct and the unconscious, the intellectual wisdom of generations, the power of self-consciousness and free will, and furthermore, the beneficence of good breeding. Then, this is the only logical conclusion we can reach that it is in this connection that Ernest and Overton are perfectly abreast of Butler's evolutionary theories, moreover, in *The Way of All Flesh* (1903), Butler *étaitl' acteur de sa vie.*

---

① Samuel Butler. *The Way of All Flesh.* London: Grant Richards, 1903. Edited with an introduction by V. S. Pritchett, London: Penguin English Library, 2012, Ch. 86, p. 476.

② "In politics he [Ernest] is a Conservative so far as his vote and interest are concerned. In all other respects he is an advanced Radical. His father and grandfather could probably no more understand his state of mind than they could understand Chinese, but those who know him intimately do not know that they wish him greatly different from what he actually is." *Ibid.*, Ch. 86, p. 476.

③ U. C. Knoepflmacher. "'Ishmael' or Anti-Hero? The Division of Self in *The Way of All Flesh.*" In *English Literature in Transition, 1880 – 1920*, vol. 4, No. 3, 1961, p. 33.

Conclusion

As Butler discussed his evolutionary theories at full in his four books on evolution, still he was full of this line of thought when he wrote his novel during the years he was most occupied with his most prominent ideas of evolution. It is in *The Way of All Flesh* that Butler illustrates further his theories of heredity and evolution. Ernest finally achieves the reconstruction of his personal identity, as Petronella J. Lange argued:

> A man's type may differ very much from that of his father and revert, like Ernest's, to a remote ancestor; yet in his early youth he is very much dependent on what his immediate ancestor, father and mother, have been like in their youths, and only his own conscious efforts can free him from this oppression and carry him carry him forwards on the path of evolution, helped by the innate general tendency of nature towards improvement under sense of need. ①

Ernest's son, Georgie's adoption of new habits is to involve a conversion or reconversion to the hidden aptitude for sailing of Theobald. Sailing is Theobald's own wish, however, he is bullied by his father and forced to become a clergyman. Ernest's predicament of self-help is likened to that of the fly's way to survive observed by Overton as it "crosses" a cup of coffee as follows:

> I once saw a fly alight on a cup of hot coffee on which the milk had formed a thin skin; he perceived his extreme danger, and I noted with what ample strides and almost super muscan effort he struck across the treacherous surface and made for the edge of the cup—for the ground was not solid enough to let him raise himself from it by his wings. As I watched him I

① Petronella Jacoba de, Lange. *Samuel Butler, Critic and Philosopher*. Zutphen, Netherlands: W. J. Thieme, 1925, p. 129.

> fancied that so supreme a moment of difficulty and danger might leave him with an increase of moral and physical power which might even descend in some measure to his offspring. But surely he would not have got the increased moral power if he could have helped it, and he will not knowingly alight upon another cup of hot coffee. ①

Like the fly observed by Overton, Ernest has to regain and generate his own "moral and physical power". For Butler, "A life will be successful or not according as the power of accommodation is equal to or unequal to the strain of fusing and adjusting internal and external changes."② Finally, Ernest successfully passes on the grace he has regained to his children.

Butler was successful in dissolving the boundaries of genre between *The Way of All Flesh* and his scientific volumes on evolution, by uniting "the *Bildungsroman* form with a biological and ontological theory that does not recognize the conventional boundaries of individual identity". ③ It is significant that the form of the novel breaks with the tradition. George Bernard Shaw, who had been a great supporter of Butler during his lifetime, appreciated *The Way of All Flesh* as "one

① Samuel Butler. *The Way of All Flesh.* London: Grant Richards, 1903; published posthumously. Edited with an introduction by V. S. Pritchett, London: Penguin English Library, 2012, Ch. 80, p. 418.

② *Ibid.*, Ch. 69, pp. 356-357.

③ It is impossible to separate Butler's scientific writings from his novel: the same anxieties, preoccupations, intellectual ambition, and sheer love of paradox fuel both forms of experiment. On reading *The Fair Haven*, Darwin had written to Butler, he records, "telling me he thought I should do well to turn my attention to novel-writing. All scientific people tell me to do this". (*Note-Books*, p. 131) Although Butler chooses to interpret the suggestion as a rebuff, from scientific expert to amateur, he nonetheless deliberately adopts in both *Life and Habit* and *The Way of All Flesh* a style that pushes at the boundaries of genre, whether novel or scientific thesis. "There is nothing", Butler observes in *Life and Habit*, in almost Wildean fashion, "in such complete harmony with itself as a flat contradiction in terms". See Sally Shuttleworth. "Evolutionary Psychology and *The Way of All Flesh.*" In *Samuel Butler: Victorian Against the Grain, A Critical Overview*. Edited by James G. Paradis. Toronto, Buffalo and London: University of Toronto Press, 2007, p. 148.

of the great books of the world". [1] Butler's original title of this novel is "*Ernest Pontifex*", or *The Way of All Flesh*", with its swift transplantation of the individual by the expression of many tensions within the text. What Shaw appreciated, is the positive Lamarckian image of creativity, of making bridges. Therefore, with overtones of the subtitle, Butler's theories challenge the concept of death: in his reworking of the idea of the primordial cell, all flesh is linked in one continuous life form, back to the dawn of time.

The name of our hero, Ernest, selected by his grandfather, is very close to the word "earnest". Pontifex, in its meaning of a creator of a bridge, gives voices to Christina's fantasies about Ernest's future destiny—although as Carlyle noted in *Sartor Resartus*, in some sense that Butler no doubt appreciated, the Pontifex, or bridge builders. For the implied meanings of Pontifex, there is no doubts reference backwards here to Butler's *The Fair Haven* (1873), where John Pickard Owen's mother has even more elaborate religious fantasies than Christina about her son's future religious glory and martyrdom. In *Sartor Resartus*, which like *The Fair Haven* is a fictional memoir, the supposed editor trying to make sense of Teufelsdröckh's life and writings, observes: "Never perhaps since our first Bridge-builders, Sin and Death, built that stupendous Arck from Hell-gate to the Earth, did any Pontifex, or Pontiff undertake such a task as the present Editor." [2]

Butler's experiment on the construction of the personal identity is successful,

---

① Bernard Shaw. The preface of *Major Barbara*. *Selected Plays, with Prefaces*. New York: Dood Mead Company, 1898, p. 313.

② Thomas Carlyle. *Sartor Resartus*. First published as a serial in 1833 – 1834 in *Fraser's Magazine*. London: Macmillan, 1901, P. 67.

for his training of Ernest's unconsciousness has produced desired results. ① Butler is always faithful in such a substitute myth of this construction of evolution. Ernest has experienced great success in his attempt. This is a myth, in which Ernest could be "shaken into something else". Though thrown into "deep waters," Ernest regains "his own power to swim". ② Having spanned the "great chasm" between his own "past and future", Ernest applies his acquired experience to ensure the preservation of the line of John Pontifex. Moreover, by giving up his offspring to a healthy circumstance, then "he can convert his own modification into a law". ③ Ernest children, apprenticed to a bargeman, can cross over to a better race and to a more natural faith.

Ernest, the bridge-builder has also provided for their crossing by trying to close the gap and to realize harmony between Darwin and Lamarck, evolutionist and creationist, between science and religion, between Overton and Theobald, between reason and faith, and between past and future.

---

① As Overton annotates the monologue in *The Way of All Flesh*: "After all I suppose I was right; I suppose things did turn out all the better in the end for having been left to settle themselves—at any rate whether they did or did not, the whole thing was in too great a muddle for me to venture to tackle it so long as Ellen was upon the scene; now, however, that she was removed, all my interest in my godson revived, and I turned over many times in my mind, what I had better do with him." See Samuel Butler. *The Way of All Flesh.* London: Grant Richards, 1903; published posthumously. Edited with an introduction by V. S. Pritchett, London: Penguin English Library, 2012, Ch. 78, p. 403.

② *Ibid.*, Ch. 78, p. 405.

③ U. C. Knoepflmacher remarks: "His [Ernest's] and Ellen's children are re-educated by 'sea-faring folk' well skilled in crossings. Ernest has done all he could do. He has built a bridge: 'Ernest's daughter Alice married the boy who had been her playmate more than a year ago. Ernest gave them all they said they wanted and a good deal more. They have already presented him with a grandson, and I doubt not, will do so with many more. Georgie though only twenty-one is owner of a fine steamer which his father has bought for him'." See U. C. Knoepflmacher. *Religious Humanism and the Victorian Novel: George Eliot, Walter Pater, and Samuel Butler.* Princeton: Princeton University Press, 1965, pp. 293-294. Knoepflmacher quotes from *The Way of All Flesh.* Ch. 86

Moreover, Ernest is happy in a life combining pleasure with utility. At the end, Ernest with his own life experience well illustrates the workings of Butler's evolutionary theories; he has proved the wisdom of instinct and the unconscious, the beneficence of good breeding. Ernest's maturity and development are perfectly evolved and presented by Butler in following the four principles of "Life and Habit". ① For the good *Bildungsroman* Butler hoped to make of *The Way of All Flesh*, he initiated perhaps the earliest case study of educational psychology.

Moreover, the harmony between Butler's evolutionary treatises and the novel embodies the same spirit of seeking the truth. According to Butler, Truth remained double-sided. This duality allows him to think in a paradoxical way, and he is too faithful in believing in his philosophy. Butler assumes that logic and morality could rely on the faith alone. Demanding an unquestioning faith in the natural instincts of the species, that should be the contribution in the history of ideas that Butler would have been the first to appreciate. ② He settles for an apotheosis of paradox: "there is no juxtaposition of things that differ too widely by omission of necessary links, or too sudden departure from recognised methods

---

① Here, I come to the four principles noted by Butler: "From these notes I find that by this time I had the theory contained in 'Life and Habit' completely before me, with the four main principles which it involves, namely, the oneness of personality between parents and offspring; memory on the part of offspring of certain actions which it did when in the persons of its forefathers; the latency of that memory until it is rekindled by a recurrence of the associated ideas; and the unconsciousness with which habitual actions come to be performed." See Samuel Butler. *Unconscious Memory*. London: David Bogue, 1880, The Echo Library edition 2006, Ch. II, p. 11.

② Knoepflmacher words here as I concluded. See U. C. Knoepflmacher. *Religious Humanism and the Victorian Novel: George Eliot, Walter Pater, and Samuel Butler*. Princeton: Princeton University Press, 1965, p. 256.

of procedure. "① Butler is too shrewd to believe in his "faith", and in his "faith" for truth. Ultimately, Butler's system yielded the relativism quite similar to that underlying the humanist creeds of other Victorian thinkers. ②

Furthermore, it seems that Butler was influenced by French voluntarist, in a similar vein, Félix Ravaisson (1813 - 1900) had written:

Le mouvement volontaire n'a donc pas seulement sa matière, sa substance,

---

① Butler says, "I know that contradiction in terms lurks within much that I have said, but the texture of the world is a warp and woof of contradiction in terms; of continuity in discontinuity, and discontinuity in continuity; of unity in diversity, and of diversity in unity. As in the development of a fugue, where, when the subject and counter subject have been enounced, there must henceforth be nothing new, and yet all must be new, so throughout organic life—which is as a fugue developed to great length from a very simple subject—everything is linked on to and grows out of that which comes next to it in order—errors and omissions excepted. It crosses and thwarts what comes next to it with difference that involves resemblance, and resemblance that involves difference. "See Samuel Butler. *Luck, or Cunning as the Main Means of Organic Modification?* London: Trübner, 1887. The Echo Library edition, 2007, Ch. XIX, p. 150.

② Knoepflmacher words here as I concluded. See U. C. Knoepflmacher. *Religious Humanism and the Victorian Novel: George Eliot, Walter Pater, and Samuel Butler.* Princeton: Princeton University Press, 1965, p. 255. Relativism is the concept that points of view have no absolute truth or validity, having only relative, subjective value according to differences in perception and consideration. See online source: http://en. wikipedia. org/wiki/Relativism. The most notable proponent of relativism in the early modern period is Michel de Montaigne (1533 - 1592), who was also considered as a major influence in the development of French Enlightenment. Relativism can also be found in the writings of key Enlightenment figures such as Voltaire (1694 - 1778) and Diderot (1713 - 1784). For a more detailed account of relativism see Maria Baghramian. *Relativism*. New York: Routledge, 2004. Christopher Herbert treats Darwin, Huxley, Spencer and James as Victorian relativists, and he suggests that the idea of relativity is fundamental to their philosophies. Importantly, Christopher Herbert argues that Darwin's *The Origin of Species* shows "the intimate historical bond linking the principles of evolution and relativity"; moreover, he says: "For Darwin, a biological species seen in evolutionary context is not so much an autonomous thing defined by an independent identity as it is a phenomenon expressing in every detail of its physical form and its instinctual codes the whole relational structure of the universe. " See Christopher Herbert. *Victorian Relativity: Radical Thought and Scientific Discovery*. Chicago: University of Chicago Press, 2001, p. 58.

> mais son origine et sa source dans le désir. Le désir est un instinct primordial, dans lequel le but de l' acte est confondu avec l' acte, l' idée avec la réalisation, la pensée avec l' élan de la spontanéité; c' est l' état de nature, c' est nature même. ①

That passage highlighted the exact image that Butler welcomed: it is cunning that is the core of man and nature. Butler's achievement of this concept of evolution is that such evolution is self-determining, in touch with a world "without fixed entities in which all living things, at least in part, created their own essence from the circumstances of their existence". ② For Butler, evolution stems from the fulfilment of primitive desire. Succession of deterministic cycles would not ensure, because each purposive step would become cumulative which is ensured by the inherited memory. Butler described this process in the conclusion of *Unconscious Memory* as follows:

> If there had been no such memory, the amoeba of one generation would have exactly resembled the amoeba of the preceding, and a perfect cycle would have been established; the modifying effects of an additional memory in each generation have made the cycle into a spiral, and into a spiral whose eccentricities, in the outset hardly perceptible, are becoming greater and greater with increasing longevity and more complex social and mechanical inventions. ③

---

① Félix Ravaisson-Mollien. *De L' Habitude*. Paris: Imprimerie de H. Fournier, 1838, p. 34. Voluntarism suggests that any metaphysical or psychological system that assigns to the will (Latin: *voluntas*) a more predominant role than that attributed to the intellect. See online source: http://global. britannica. com/EBchecked/topic/632605/voluntarism.

② Frank Miller Turner. "Samuel Butler: The Man of Temper." In *Between Science and Religion: the Reaction to Scientific Naturalism In Late Victorian*. London: Yale University Press, 1974, p. 192.

③ Samuel Butler. *Unconscious Memory*. London: David Bogue, 1880. The Echo Library edition 2006, Ch. XIII, p. 99.

Butler led up this assertion from the amoeba to man.① His concept of evolution proved nature to be creative and non-mechanical, furthermore, it proved culture to be nondeterministic. It is significant that Butler revised and developed Lamarckism with humanity. In *Luck or Cunning*? Butler quoted Claude Bernard's statement as his final position, "Rien ne nâit, rien ne se crée, tout se continue. La nature ne nous offre le spectacle d'aucune création, elle est d'une éternelle continuation." Considering this is only one side of the doctrine, Butler contended that Bernard might just as well have said, "Rien ne se continue, tout nâit, tout se crée, La nature ne nous offre le spectacle d'aucune continuation. Elle est d'une éternelle création; for change is no less patent a fact than continuity, and indeed, the two stand or fall together."② Finally, I will conclude my thesis with Butler's words: "Nevertheless a certain kind of good fortune generally attends self-made men to the last."③ That is the way that civilisation advances, as the "ruban de Möbius" demonstrated by Patrick Tort—the process of evolution is a process of interaction between nature and civilisation.

① *Ibid.*, Ch. XIII, p. 99. Butler states: "Let us suppose these molecules capable of memory, both in their capacity as individuals, and as societies, and able to transmit their memories to their descendants, form the traditions of the dimmest past to the experiences of their own lifetime."

② Samuel Butler. *Luck, or Cunning as the Main Means of Organic Modification*? London: Trübner, 1887. The Echo Library edition, 2007, Ch. II, p. 14. For Butler, discontinuity is also important.

③ Samuel Butler. *The Way of All Flesh*. London: Grant Richards, 1903; published posthumously. Edited with an introduction by V. S. Pritchett, London: Penguin English Library, 2012, Ch. 5, p. 23.

Bibliography

Primary sources

Writings by Samuel Butler

Novels

[1] Butler Samuel. The Way of All Flesh[M]. London: A. C. Fifield, 1908.

[2] Butler Samuel. The Way of All Flesh [M]. London: Grant Richards, 1903. Edited with an article by V S. Pritchett. London: Penguin English Library, 2012.

[3] Butler Samuel. Ainsivatoute Chair[M]. Traduit de l'anglais par Valéry Larbaud. Paris: Gallimard, 1936.

[4] 塞缪尔·巴特勒. 众生之路[M]. 黄雨石,译. 华夏出版社, 2008.

Satirical romances

[1] Butler Samuel. Erewhon, or Over the Range [M]. London: Trübner, 1872; published anonymously. Edited with an introduction by Peter Mudford. London: Penguin English Library, 1970. Reprinted in Penguin Classics, 1985.

[2] Butler Samuel. Erewhon Revisited[M]. London: A. C. Fifield, 1901. London: Jonathan Cape, 1925.

[3] Butler Samuel. Erewhon and Erewhon Revisited [M]. Edited with an introduction by Lewis Mumford. New York: The Modern Library, 1927.

Writings on Evolution

[1] Butler Samuel. Life and Habit [M]. London: Trübner, 1878. Revised edition, with author's addenda and a preface by R. A. Streatfeild, London:

A. C. Fifield, 1910. Teddington: The Echo Library, 2007.

[2] Butler Samuel. Evolution, Old and New, or the Theories of Buffon, Dr. Erasmus Darwin, and Lamarck, as Compared with that of Mr. Charles Darwin[A]. London: Hardwicke and Bogue, 1879.

[3] Butler Samuel. Unconscious Memory: A Comparison Between the Theory of Dr. Eward Hering, Professor of Physiology at the University of Prague, and the "Philosophy of the Unconscious" of Dr. Edward von Hartmann, with translations from these authors, and preliminary chapters bearing on "Life and Habit", "Evolution, Old and New", and Mr. Charles Darwin's edition of Dr. Krause's "Erasmus Darwin[A]." London: David Bogue, 1880. Teddington: The Echo Library, 2006.

[4] Samuel Butler. Luck or Cunning as the Main Means of Organic Modification? An attempt to throw additional light upon the late Mr. Charles Darwin's theory of natural selection[A]. London: Trübner, 1887. Teddington: The Echo Library, 2006.

Notebooks

[1] Butler Samuel. Butleriana[M]. Edited by A. T. Bartholomew. London: Nonesuch press, 1932.

[2] Butler Samuel. The Note-Books of Samuel Butler[M]. London: A. C. Fifield, 1912. IndyPublish edition, 2007.

Essays

[1] Butler Samuel. A First Year in Canterbury Settlement, with Other Early Essays[M]. London: A. C. Fifield, 1914.

[2] Butler Samuel. Alps and Sanctuaries of Piedmont and the Canton Ticino [M]. London: David Bogue, 1882.

[3] Butler Samuel. The Shrewsbury Edition of the Works of Samuel Butler[M].

Edited by London: Jonathan Cape, 1925.

[4] Butler Samuel. Essays on Life, Art and Science[M]. London: A. C. Fifield, 1908.

[5] Butler Samuel. God Known and God the Unknown[J]. Examiner, 1879 (21, 31); 1879 (14, 21, 28); 1879 (12, 19, 26). Published in pamphlet form, with prefatory note by R. A. Streatfeild. London: A. C. Fifield, 1909.

[6] Butler Samuel. On English Composition and Other Matters[J]. Eagle, 1858, 1 (1).

[7] Butler Samuel. The Evidence for the Resurrection of Jesus Christ as given by the Four Evangelists[M]. London: William and Norgate, 1865.

Letters

[1] Butler Samuel. The Life and Letters of Dr. Samuel Butler[M]. R A Streatfeild. London: John Murray, 1896.

[2] Butler Samuel. Letters Between Samuel Butler and E M A. Savage, 1871 – 1885[M]. Edited by Geoffrey Keynes, Brian Hill. London: Jonathan Cape, 1935.

[3] Butler Samuel. The Family Letters of Samuel Butler[M]. selected, edited and introduced by Arnold London: J. Cape, 1962.

Secondary Sources

Writings about Samuel Butler

Bibliographies

[1] Breuer Hans-Peter, Parsell Roger. Samuel Butler: An Annotated Bibliography of Writing About Him[M]. New York and London: Garland Publishing, INC, 1990.

[2] Harkness, Stanley Bates. The Career of Samuel Butler (1835 - 1902): A Bibliography[M]. London: Bodley Head, 1955.

Biographical and critical studies

[1] Cannan Gilbert. Samuel Butler: A Critical Study[M]. London: Martin Seeker, 1915.

[2] Cole G D H. Samuel Butler[M]. Denver: A Swallow, 1948.

[3] Cole G D H. Samuel Butler and *The Way of All Flesh*[M]. London: Home & Van Thal, 1947.

[4] Fort Joseph B. Samuel Butler (1835 - 1902)[M]. Etude d'un caractère et d'une intelligence. Thèse pour le doctorat, Présentée à la Faculté des lettres de l'Université de Paris, Bordeaux: J. Bière, 1934.

[5] Furbank P N. Samuel Butler, 1935 - 1902[M]. Cambridge: Cambridge University Press, 1948.

[6] Ganz Margaret. Humor, Irony, and the Realm of Madness: Psychological Studies in Dickens, Butler, and Others [M]. New York: AMS Press, 1990.

[7] Garnett R S. Samuel Butler and His Family Relations[M]. London and Toronto: J. M. Dent, 1926.

[8] Grant John Douglas. Samuel Butler As a Critic of Victorian England[M]. Toronto: Toronto University, 1947.

[9] Greenacre Phyllis. The Quest for the Father: A Study of the Darwin-Butler Controversy, as a Contribution to the Understanding of the Creative Individual[M]. New York: International University Press, 1963.

[10] Henderson Philip. Samuel Butler, the Incarnate Bachelor[M]. London: Cohen and West, 1953.

[11] Holt Lee E. Samuel Butler[M]. New York: Twayne Publishers, 1964. Revised edition, 1989.

[12] Joad C E M. Samuel Butler (1935 – 1902) [M]. London: L. Parsons, 1924.

[13] Jones Henry Festing. Charles Darwin and Samuel Butler: A Step Towards Reconciliation[M]. London: A. C. Fifield, 1911.

[14] Jones Henry Festing. Samuel Butler: Author of *Erewhon* (1835 – 1902): A Memoir[M]. 2 vols. London: Macmillan, 1919.

[15] Knoepflmacher U C. Religious Humanism and the Victorian Novel: George Eliot, Walter Pater, and Samuel Butler [M]. Princeton: Princeton University Press, 1965.

[16] Muggeridge Malcolm. The Earnest Atheist: A Study of Samuel Butler [M]. London: Eyre and Spottiswoode, 1936.

[17] Paradis James G. Samuel Butler, Victorian Against the Grain, a Critical Overview[M]. Toronto: University and Toronto Press, 2007.

[18] Petronella Jacoba de. Lange. Samuel Butler, Critic and Philosopher[M]. Zutphen, Netherlands: W. J. Thieme, 1925.

[19] Raby Peter. Samuel Butler: A Biography [M]. London: Chatto and Windus, 1991.

[20] Seimiya Michikio. The novelist who challenges Charles Darwin-Samuel Butler's Life and Works[M]. Tokyo: NANUN-DO, 2010.

[21] Stillman Clara G. Samuel Butler, a Mid-Victorian Modern[M]. London: Martin Secker, 1932.

[22] Turner Frank Miller. Between Science and Religion: the Reaction to Scientific Naturalism in late Victorian England [M]. New Haven; London: Yale university press, 1974.

[23] Willey Basil. Darwin and Butler: Two Versions of Evolution [M]. London: Chatto and Windus, 1960.

Books chapters and articles

[1] Beer Gillian. Butler, Memory, and the Future [M]//Samuel Butler: Victorian Against the Grain, A Critical Overview. Edited by James G. Paradis. Toronto, Buffalo and London: University of Toronto Press, 2007, 45-57.

[2] Bissell Claude. A Study of The Way of All Flesh[M]//Nineteenth-Century Studies, collected and edited by Herbert Davis, William C. De Vane, and R. C. Bald. New York: Cornell University Press, 1940, 277-303.

[3] Breuer Hans-Peter. Samuel Butler's *The Book of the Machines* and the *Argument Form Design*[M]//In Modern Philology 72, no. 4 (May 1975): 365-383.

[4] Breuer Hans-Peter. Samuel Butler and George Frideric Handel[M]//In Dalhousie Review 1975, 55(3): 467-490.

[5] Carey Glenn O. Samuel Butler's Theory of Evolution: A Summary [J]. English Literature in Transition, 1880 – 1920, 1964 (7): 230-233.

[6] Daniels Anthony. Butler's Unhappy Youth [M]//On Samuel Butler's Autobiographical Novel *The Way of all Flesh*. New Criterion, 2005, 23 (5): 11-17.

[7] Dawson Carl. Strange Metamorphoses: Samuel Butler's "Unconscious Memory" and *The Way of All Flesh* [M]//Prophets of Past Time: Seven British Autobiographers, 1880 – 1914. London: Johns Hopkins University Press, 1988: 70-97.

[8] Federico Annette R. Samuel Butler's *The Way of All Flesh*: Rewriting the Family [J]//English Literature in Transition, 1880 – 1920, 1995, 38 (4): 466-482.

[9] Forsdyke Donald R. Heredity as Transmission of Information: Butlerian "Intelligent Design" [J]. Centaurus, 2006 (48): 133-148.

[10] Ganz Margaret. Samuel Butler: Ironic Abdication and the Way to the Unconscious [J]. English Literature in Transition, 1880 – 1920, 1985, 28 (4): 366-394.

[11] Harris Ellen T. Butler's Narcissus: "A Tame Oratorio" [M]//Samuel Butler, Victorian Against the Grain: A Critical Overview. Edited by James G. Paradis. Toronto: University of Toronto Press, 2007: 287-316.

[12] Holt Lee E. E M Forster and Samuel Butler [J]. Publications Modern Language Associations. 1946, 61 (3): 804-819.

[13] Knoepflmacher U C. "Ishmael" or Anti-Hero? The Division of Self The Way of All Flesh [J]. English Literature in Transition, 1880 – 1920, 1961, 4 (3): 28-35.

[14] MacDonald W L. Samuel Butler and Evolution [J]. The North American Review, 1926, 223 (833): 626-637.

[15] Morton Peter. Butler on Heredity [M]//The Vital Science: Biology and

the Literary Imagination, 1860 – 1900. London: Allen and Unwin, 1984: 156-194.

[16] Nielsen Danielle. Samuel Butler's Life and Habit and *The Way of All Flesh*: Traumatic Evolution[J]. English literature in Transition, 1880 – 1920, 2011,54 (1): 79-100.

[17] Paradis James G. The Butler-Darwin Biographical Controversy in the Victorian Periodical Press[M]//Science Serialized: Representations of the Sciences in Nineteenth-Century Periodicals, edited by Geoffrey Cantor and Sally Shuttleworth. Cambridge, MA: MIT Press, 2004: 307-329.

[18] Prum Michel. Homme et machines chez Samuel Butler[J]. Cahiers Victoriens et édouardiens, 1990 (31): 111-118.

[19] Rattray Robert F. The Philosophy of Samuel Butler[J]. Mind, 1914 (23): 371-385.

[20] Rubenstein Jill. "Business is Business": The Money Ethic of Samuel Butler[J]. English Literature in Transition, 1880 – 1920, 1976, 19 (4): 237-147.

[21] Shaw George Bernard. Old Bachelor Sam Butler[J]. Observer, 1950 (26). Reprinted in Shavian, 1963 (7): 8-10.

[22] Shuttleworth Sally. Evolutionary Psychology and *The Way of All Flesh* [M]//Samuel Butler: Victorian Against the Grain, A Critical Overview. Edited by James G. Paradis. Toronto, Buffalo and London: University of Toronto Press, 2007: 143-169.

[23] Simpson George Gaylord. Lamarck, Darwin, and Butler: Three Approaches to Evolution[M]//The American Scholar, 1961, 30 (2): 238-249.

[24] Sussanman Herbert L. Evolution and the Machine: Samuel Butler[M]//

Victorians and the Machine: The Literary Response to Technology. Cambridge, MA: Harvard University Press, 1968: 135-161.

[25] Stuart Ross. Samuel Butler and Charles Paine Pauli: A Friendship Reconsidered[J]. English Literature in Transition, 1880 – 1920, 1985,8 (2): 145-161.

[26] Turner Frank Miller. Samuel Butler: The Man of Temper[M]//Between Science and Religion: The Reaction to Scientific Naturalism in Late Victorian England. New Haven: Yale University Press, 1974: 164-200.

[27] Yarbrough J W. Autobiography and Artistic Sensibility in Samuel Butler's *The Way of All Flesh*[J]. The Bulletin of the Rocky Mountain Modern Language Association, 1971, 25 (1): 22-27.

[28] Yeasted Rita. The Handelian Quality of Butler's *The Way of All Flesh*[J]. Modern Language Studies, 1979, 9 (2): 23-32.

[29] Zemka, Sue. Erewhon and the End of Utopian Humanism[J]. ELH, 2002, 69 (2): 439-72.

Darwin's works, and critics about Darwin and Darwinism

[1] Darwin Charles. On the Origin of Species by Means of Natural Selection [M]. London: Dover Giant Thrift Edition, 2006.

[2] Darwin Charles. L' Origine des espèces: par le moyen de la sélection naturelle[M]. ou la préservation des races favorisées dans la lutte pour la vie, sous la direction de Patrick Tort, traduction par Aurélien Berra, coordonnée par Michel Prum, préface de Patrick Tort, Paris: H. Champion, 2009.

[3] Darwin Charles. The Origin of Species: A Variorum Text[M]. Edited by Morse Peckham. Philadelphia: The University of Pennsylvania Press, first

paperback edition 2006.

[4] Darwin Charles. The Descent of Man, and Selection in Relation to Sex [M]. London: Murray, 1871.

[5] Darwin Charles. La Filiation de l'homme et la sélectionliée au sexe[1871] [M]. éditiondirigée par Patrick Tort, traductioncoordonnée par Michel Prum, préface de P. Tort. Paris, Syllepse, 1999.

[6] Darwin Charles. Esquisse au Crayon de ma Théorie des Espèces (Essay de 1842)[M]. Traduction de Jean-Michel Benayoun, Michel Prum et Patrick Tort. Paris: Honore Champion, 2007.

[7] Darwin Charles. Charles Darwin's Notebooks, 1836 - 1844 [M]. Transcribed and edited by Paul H Barrett, Peter J Gautrey, Sandra Herbert, David Kohn, and Sydney Smith. Cambridge: Cambridge University press, 2008.

[8] Darwin Charles. The Autobiography of Charles Darwin (1809 - 1982) [M]. First published in 1958. London: W. W. Norton and Company, 1969.

[9] Darwin Charles. Charles Darwin's The Life of Erasmus Darwin[M]. Edited by Desmond King-Hele. Cambridge: Cambridge University Press, 2003.

[10] Darwin Charles. The Life and Letters of Charles Darwin[M]. Edited by his son Francis Darwin. London: William Clowes and Sons, 1887.

[11] Darwin Charles. Metaphysics, Materialism, and the Evolution of Mind: Early Writings of Charles Darwin[M]. Transcribed and annotated by Paul H. Barrett. Chicago: The University of Chicago Press, 1980.

[12] Darwin Charles. The Correspondence of Charles Darwin [M]. Eds. Frederick H. Burkhardtm Sidney Smith, Duncan M Porter, et al, volume 1-19. Cambridge: Cambridge University Press, 1985 -2012.

[13] Darwin Charles. Origins: Selected Letters of Charles Darwin, 1822 – 1859 [M]. Edited by Frederick H Burkhardt. Cambridge: Cambridge University Press, 2008.

[14] Barnett S A. A Century of Darwin [M]. Cambridge, Massachusetts: Harvard University Press, 1958.

[15] Bowler Peter J. The Eclipse of Darwinism: Anti-Darwin Evolution Theories in the Decades Around 1900[M]. London: The Johns Hopkins University Press, 1983.

[16] Bowler Peter J. Evolution: The History of an Idea[M]. Berkeley and Los Angeles: University of California Press, 1983. Revised edition, 1989.

[17] Bowler Peter J. Charles Darwin: The Man and his Influence[M]. Oxford: Basil Blackwell, 1990.

[18] Browne Janet. Darwin's Origin of Species: A Biography[M]. New York: Atlantic Monthly press, 2006

[19] Dawkins Richard. The Selfish Gene [M]. Oxford: Oxford University Press, 2006.

[20] Dennett Daniel. Darwin's Dangerous Idea: Evolution and the Meanings of Life[M]. New York, London and Toronto: Simon and Schuster, 1995.

[21] Eiseley Loren. Darwin's Century, Evolution and the Man Who Discovered It[M]. London: Victor Gollancz, 1959.

[22] Ghiselin T Michael. The Triumph of the Darwinian Method[M]. Originally published: Berkeley: University of California Press, 1969. The Dover Edition: New York: Dover Publications, Inc. , 2003.

[23] Gruber E Howard. Darwin on Man: A Psychological Study of Scientific Creativity [M]. Second Edition: Chicago: The University of Chicago Press, 1981. First edition by Gruber E. Howard and Barrett, H.

Paul, 1974.

[24] Heiligman Deborah. Charles and Emma: The Darwins' Leap of Faith [M]. New York: Henry Holt and Company, 2009.

[25] Hösle Vittorio, Christian Illies. Darwinism and Philosophy[M]. Notre Dame: The University of Notre Dame, 2005.

[26] Lewens Tim. Darwin[M]. London and New York: Routledge, 2007.

[27] Morton Peter. The Vital Science: Biology and the Literary Imagination: 1860 – 1900[M]. London; Boston; Sydney: G. Allen and Unwin, 1984.

[28] Popper Karl. Of Clouds and Clocks: An Approach to the Problem of Rationality and the Freedom of Man[M]. St. Louis, Mo.: Washington University Press, 1966.

[29] Popper Karl. Objective Knowledge: An Evolutionary Approach[M]. Oxford: Clarendon Press, 1972.

[30] Popper Karl. Unended Quest: An Intellectual Biography[M]. London: Fontana, 1976.

[31] Popper Karl. Darwinism as a Metaphysical Research Programme[M]// Philosophy After Darwin: Classic and Contemporary Readings. Edited by Michael Ruse. Princeton and Oxford: Princeton University Press, 2009.

[32] Prum Michel et Letissier Georges dir. L'Héritage de Charles Darwin dans les cultures européennes[M]. Ouvrage publie avec le concours de l'Université de Nantes et de l'Université Paris Diderot. Collection Racisme et eugénisme. Paris: L'Harmattan, 2011

[33] Richards Robert J. Darwin and the Emergence of Evolutionary Theories of Mind and Behavior[M]. Chicago: University of Chicago Press, 1989.

[34] Ruse Michael, Richards Robert J. The Cambridge Companion to the "Origin of Species"[M]. Cambridge: Cambridge University Press, 2009.

[35] Sober E and Wilson D S. Unto Others: The Evolution and Psychology of Unselfish Behavior[M]. Cambridge MA: Harvard Unversity Press, 1998.

[36] Tort Patrick. Darwin et le darwinisme[M]. Paris, Presses Universitaires de France, 1997.

[37] Tort Patrick. Darwin et La philosophie: religion, morale, matérialisme [M]. Paris, KIME, 2004.

[38] Tort Patrick. Dictionnaire du darwinisme et de l'évolution[M]. Paris, PUF, 1996.

[39] Tort Patrick. L'Effet Darwin, sélection naturelle et naissance de la civilisation[M]. Paris, Editions du Seuil, 2008.

[40] Tort Patrick. Darwin n'est pas celui qu'on croit[M]. Paris, Le Cavalier Bleu, 2010.

[41] Tort Patrick. Darwin et la religion: la conversion matérialiste, avec la collaboration de Solange Willefert[M]. Paris, Ellipses, 2011.

[42] Vorzimmer Peter J. Charles Darwin: the Years of Controversy, the Origin of species and its Critics 1859 – 1882[M]. London: University of London Press, 1972.

[43] Young M Robert. Darwin's Metaphor: Nature's Place in Victorian Culture [M]. Cambridge: Cambridge Univerisity Press, 1985.

Other evolutionists

[1] Lamarck. "Discours de ouverture" of 1800, Système des animaux sans vertèbres[M]. Paris: Deterville, 1801.

[2] Darwin Erasmus. Zoonomia: or the Laws of Organic Life[M]. Vol. I New York: T. and J. Sword, 1796. Bristol: Thoemmes, 2004.

[3] Desmond King-Hele. Erasmus Darwin: a Life of Unequalled Achievement [M]. London: DLM, 1999.

[4] Laniel-Musitelli Sophie. Erasmus Darwin: de la métamorphose au transformisme[M]//Darwin Dans la Bataille des Idées, directed by Michel Prum and Sophie Geoffroy, ouvragepublié avec le concours du laboratoireIdentité, Cultures, Territoires (EA 337) de l'université Paris Diderot, Sorbonne Paris Cité, with a preface by Patrick Tort. Paris: L'Harmattan, 2012.

Herbert Spencer and critics

[1] Herbert Spencer. Principles of Biology [M]. London: Williams and Norgate, 1898.

[2] Mark Francis. Herbert Spencer and the Invention of Modern Life[M]. Ithaca, New York: Cornell University Press, 2007.

[3] Taylor Michael W. The Philosophy of Herbert Spencer[M]. London: Continuum, 2007.

[4] Tort Patrick. Spencer et L'évolutionnisme philosophique[M]. Paris, Presses Universitaires de France, 1996.

[5] Weinstein David. Equal Freedom and Utility: Herbert Spencer's Liberal Utilitarianism[M]. Cambridge: Cambridge University Press, 2006.

[6] Hartmann Eduard Von. Philosophy of the Unconscious[M]. First published in 1869. Translation by William Chatterton Coupland, 3 vols. London: Trübner, 1884.

[7] Huxley Thomas Henry. Method and Results: Essays[M]. New York: D. Appleton and Company, 1896.

Liberal ideas and Utilitarianism

[1] Bentham Jeremy. An Introduction to the Principles of Morals and Legislation [M]. Oxford: Clarendon press, 1996.

[2] Blake Kathleen. Pleasures of Benthamism: Victorian Literature, Utility, Political Economy[M]. Oxford: Oxford University Press, 2009.

[3] Roger Crisp. Mill on Utilitarianism. London: Routledge, 1997.

[4] Hobbes Thomas. Leviathan[M]. Bristol: Thoemmes continuum, 2003.

[5] Locke John. An Essay Concerning Human Understanding[M]. London: J. F. Dove, 1828.

[6] Malthus Thomas. An Essay on the Principle of Population[M]. London: Penguin, 1985.

[7] Mill James. James Mill on Education[M]. London: CUP, 1969.

[8] Mill John Stuart. Utilitarianism[M]. Oxford: B. Blackwell, 1949.

Other related studies

[1] Baghramian Maria. Relativism[M]. New York: Routledge, 2004.

[2] Briggs Asa. Victorian People: A Reassessment of Persons and Themes 1851 - 1867[M]. Chicago: The University of Chicago, 1955.

[3] Bristed Charles Astor. Five Years in an English University[M]. New York: G. D. Putnam, 1852.

[4] David J C. Utopia and the Ideal Society[M]. Cambridge: Cambridge University Press, 1981.

[5] David Philip. The Oxford English Literary History. The Victorians. Volume 8: 1830 - 1880[M]. Oxford: Oxford University, 2004.

[6] Edward S Reed. From Soul to Mind: The Emergence of Psychology From Erasmus Darwin to William James[M]. New Haven and London: Yale University Press, 1997.

[7] Herbert Christopher. Victorian Relativity: Radical Thought and Scientific Discovery[M]. Chicago: University of Chicago Press, 2001.

[8] Gilmour Robin. The Victorian Period: The Intellectual and Cultural Context of English Literature 1830 – 1890[M]. Longman Literature in English Series. Harlow: Pearson Education, 1993.

[9] James William. Great Men, Great Thoughts, and the Environment[J]. Atlantic Monthly, 1880 (66).

[10] Jay Elisabeth. Faith and Doubt in Victorian Britain. Basingstoke: Macmillan, 1986.

[11] Joad Cyril Edwin. Shaw[M]. London: Victor Gollancz Ltd, 1949.

[12] Morris William. News From Nowhere, or An Epoch of Rest[M]. Oxford: Oxford University Press, 2003.

[13] Paley William. Natural Theology[M]. A new edition: London: Longman, 1846.

[14] Ravaisson-Mollien Félix. De L'Habitude[M]. Paris: Imprimerie de H Fournier, 1838.

[15] Shaw Bernard. The preface of Major Barbara. Selected Plays, with Prefaces[M]. New York: Dood Mead Company, 1898.

[16] Smiles Samuel. Self-Help, with Illustrations of Character, Conduct, and Perseverance[M]. Edited with an Introduction and Notes by Peter W. Sinnema. Oxford: Oxford University Press, 2002.

[17] Wilson A N. The Victorians[M]. London: Arrow Books, 2003.

[18] Yeats John B. Essays Irish and American[M]. New York: Macmillan, 1918.

[19] Young G M. Victorian England: Portrait of an Age[M]. First published in 1936. Second edition. London: Oxford, 1960.

Online sources

[1] About Samuel Butler, St John's Colledge, Cambridge[EB/OL]. http://www.joh.cam.ac.uk/about-samuel-butler.

[2] A Summary and Analysis of The Way of All Flesh[EB/OL]. http://www.cliffsnotes.com/literature/w/the-way-of-all-flesh/book-summary.

[3] The reference of the Darwin Conference at Chicago 2009, a conference celebrating the 200th anniversary of Darwin's birth, the 150th anniversary of The Origin of Species, and the 50th anniversary of another remarkable Darwin conference at Chicago[EB/OL]. http://darwin-chicago.uchicago.edu/origin-of-species.html.

[4] The Complete Works of Herbert Spencer[EB/OL]. http://oll.libertyfund.org/index.php? option = com_staticxt&staticfile = show.php%3Fperson = 165&Itemid = 28.

[5] Encyclopedia Britannica[EB/OL]. http://www.britannica.com/.

[6] The Free Encyclopedia Wikipedia[EB/OL]. http://en.wikipedia.org/wiki/Main_Page.

[7] Site officiel de Patrick Tort[EB/OL]. http://www.patrick-tort.org/.

[8] Site Institut Charles Darwin International [EB/OL]. http://www.charlesdarwin.fr/index.htm.

Selected index and glossary of names

Bildungsroman, 16, 33, 164, 212, 215

Buffon Georges-Louis Leclerc Comte de, 8, 9, 196

Carlyle Thomas, 213

Clodd Edward, 7

Darwin Charles, Darwinism, 4-11, 14-15, 20-21, 34, 36, 38, 40, 42, 45, 56-57, 65-66, 69, 93, 98-99, 103, 115, 120, 122, 135, 149, 160, 164, 181, 196, 212, 214, 216

Darwin Erasmus (Dr.), 6, 8, 9, 196

Diderot Denis, 216

Flaubert Gustave, 164

Freud Sigmund (and Freudian psychology), 69, 122, 168, 192

Forster Edward Morgan, 19

Haeckel Ernest, 5, 40

Handel George Friedrich, 76, 162, 176, 179, 202-203

Hering Ewald, 9, 41, 89

Hobbes Thomas, 104

Huxley Thomas, 216

Kennedy Benjamin Dr, 17, 171

Lamarck, Jean-Baptiste, Lamarckism (and Neo-Lamarckism), Lamarckians (and Neo-Lamarckians), 4-9, 12, 28, 33-34, 36-38, 40, 103, 120, 141, 149, 153-154, 164, 196, 213-214, 218

Locke John, 102

Lewes George Henry, 40

Jones Henry Festing, 1, 3, 6, 8, 10, 12, 18-19, 41, 69, 75, 77, 80, 87, 96, 103, 109, 111, 117-118, 136-137

James Mill and James Stuart Mill, 103-105, 107, 181, 191-192

Mivart St. George, 7-8

Ribot Théodule, 65

Savage Eliza Mary Ann, 11-13, 72

Shaw George Bernard, 2, 4, 5, 19, 20, 126, 212-213

Shrewsbury, 3, 16-17, 103, 136, 171, 176, 187, 189

Simeonites, 24, 182-185

Smith Adam, 104-106

Smith Sydney, 65

Spencer Herbert, 4-5, 40, 216

Tort Patrick,218

Utilitarianism, (and Utilitarians), 101, 103, 107-108, 208

Ravaisson Félix, 216-217

Voltaire(François-Marie Arouet), 216

Wallace Alfred Russel, 57

Weismannian (Weismann August), 74

Appendix

I. Chronology

1831	Darwin begins voyage of the *Beagle*.
1835	Born on 4 December at Langar, near Nottingham.
1843	First visit to Italy.
1848 – 1854	Attends Shrewsbury School.
1851	Henry Festing Jones born.
	Herbert Spencer *Social Statics*
1853	Second visit to Italy.
1854	Goes to St John's College, Cambridge.
1858 – 1859	Working in parish of St James's, Piccadilly, as preparation for ordination.
	Returns to Cambridge and takes drawing lessons.
1859	Unable on principle to sign the *Thirty-Nine Articles*, refuses ordination.
	Emigrates, with financial backing from his father, to Canterbury Settlement, New Zealand.
	Charles Darwin *On the Origin of Species by Means of Natural Selection*.
	J. S. Mill On Liberty.
	Samuel Smiles *Self-Help*.
1860 – 1864	Reads Charles Darwin *On the Origin of Species by Means of Natural Selection*.

	Contributes to New Zealand Press (1862 – 1864).
	A First Year in Canterbury Settlement (1863) published by his father from material from his letter home.
	Meets Charles Paine Pauli.
	J. S. Mill *Utilitarianism*.
	Huxley *Man's Place in Nature* (1863).
1864	Return to England and settles in Clifford's Inn.
	Paints *Family Prayers*.
	Herbert Spencer *Principles of Biology*.
1865	*The Evidence for the Resurrection of Jesus Christ, As Given By The Four Evangelist, Critically Examined*, published anonymously as a pamphlet.
	"Lucubratio Ebria" in the Christchurch *Press* and "The Mechanical Creation" in George Jacob Holyyoake's journal of free thought, the *Reasoner*. Two reveries on evolution.
	Corresponds with Charles Darwin.
1867	Studying painting at Heatherley's School of Art, Newman Street.
	Meets fellow art student Eliza Mary Ann Savage at Heatherley's.
1870	Begins *Erewhon*.
1871	Begins extensive correspondence with Miss Savage.
	Charles Darwin *The Descent of Man*.
1872	*Erewhon*, or *Over the Range*, published anonymously.
	Begins *The Way of All Flesh*.

	Visits Charles Darwin at Down.
	Darwin *The Expression of the Emotions in Man.*
1873	*The Fair Haven*, published under the pseudonym "William Bickersteth Owen".
	His mother dies in Mentone, Southern France.
	Recalls interest-bearing investments from New Zealand to Speculate banker Henry Hoare's companies.
1874 – 1875	Collapse of Henry Hoare's companies. Goes to Canada.
	Mr Heatherley's Holiday, his most polished painting, exhibited at Royal Academy.
	Begins writing his aphoristic Note-Books, a lifelong undertaking.
1876	Begins *Life and Habit: An Essay After a Completer View of Evolution.*
	Meets Henry Festing Jones.
1877	His art career wanes.
	Begins using the British Museum Reading Room regularly.
1878	*Life and Habit* published.
	A Psalm Montreal published in *The Spectator*.
	Completes draft of the novel *The Way of All Flesh*.
1879	*Evolution, Old and New: Or, the Theories of Buffon, Dr Erasmus Darwin and Lamarck, as compared with that of Mr Charles Darwin* published.
	A Clergyman's Doubts (letter series under various pseudonyms) and *God the Known and God the Unknown* (an article series) published in the *Examiner*.

1880	Quarrels with Darwin. Letter to *Athenaeum* 31 January. *Unconscious Memory* published.
1882	*Alps and Sanctuaries* published, with illustrations by Butler, Jones and Gogin.
1883	Begins writing music.
1884	*Selections from Previous Works, with Remarks on Mr. G. H Romanes' Mental Evolution in Animals* published. Completes final revisions of *Ernest Pontifex; or The Way of All Flesh*.
1885	Death of Miss Savage, his literary confidante, close friend, and correspondent.
1886	Death of Rev. Thomas Butler, his father, and inheritance of substantial financial legacy.
1887	*Luck, or Cunning as the Main Means of Organic Modification?* Takes Alfred Cathie into service as clerk and domestic aide. Engages Henry Festing Jones as paid musical collaborator and companion. Revives interests in photography. Darwin *Autobiography*.
1888	*Ex Voto: An Account of the Sacro Monte or New Jerusalem at Varallo-Sesia.* Illustrated with his own photographs.
1888 – 1889	Occasional essays, including "The Deadlock in Darwinism" in the *Universal Review*. Later collected as *Essays on Life, Art, and Science* (1904).

1892	Deliver lecture *The Humour of Homer* at the Working Men's College, Great Ormond Street.
	Death of Lucie Dumas.
	First visit to Sicily.
1893	Meets Hans Faesch, young Swiss man and business apprentice in London.
1895	Visits Greece and Troad.
1896	*The Life and Letters of Dr. Samuel Butler.*
1897	*The Authoress of the Odyssey.*
	Death of Charles Paine Pauli, friend, literary adviser, barrister, and financial dependent.
1898	*The Iliad Rendered into English Prose.*
1899	*Shakespeare's Sonnets reconsidered and in part rearranged*, with a reprint of the original edition of 1609.
1900	*The Odyssey rendered into English Prose.*
1901	*Erewhon Revisited Twenty Years Later.*
	Erewhon, or over the Range. New and revised edition of *Erewhon.*
1902	Last visit to Sicily, collapses in Palermo, brought back to London by Alfred Cathie.
	Last illness and death, 18 June, in London hospice.
1903	*The Way of All Flesh*, edited by R. A. Streatfeild.
	Death of Hans Faesch.
1904	*Essays on Life, Art and Science.*

	Ulysses: A Dramatic Oratorio, in collaboration with Henry Festing Jones.
1909	*God the Known and God the Unknown*, articles from *The Examiner*.
1912	*The Note-Books of Samuel Butler*, edited by Henry Festing Jones.
1919	*Samuel Butler: Author of Erewhon: A Memoir*. By Henry Festing Jones.
1928	Death of Henry Festing Jones.

Ⅱ. Chronology and addenda for *The Way of All Flesh* (1903)

1727	Old Mr. and Mrs. Pontifex born.
1750	Old Pontifex married.
1765	George Pontifex born in January.
1780	Mrs. Fairlie came to stay with old P.
1790	G. P. went into partnership.
1797	He married a woman 7 years younger than himself.
1798	Xtina born.
1800	Christina born chap. ix.
1801	John Pontifex born.
1802	I born p. I, and Theobald (my name is Edward p. 7).
1805	Alethaea Pontifex born and her mother died.
1811	Old Mrs. Pontifex died aged 84.
1812	Old Mr. Pontifex died aged 85.
	Theobald's correspondence with his father found by Ernest and given to myself on Theobald's death.
1825	spring Theobald took his degree p. 58.
	Autumn was ordained p. 58.
1825	Nov. went over first to the Allabys.
1831	July married.
1832	January. I go and stay with them. Ellen born.

1835	Ernest born Sep. 6.
1838	Old Pontifex died at 73 or in the 73d year.
1836	Sep. Joseph Pontifex born Vol. I. pt. 2. p. 18.
1837	Aug. The daughter born.
1848	Jan. He is 12 and goes to school. Chap, xxii.
1848	Jan. He goes to school.
1849	Aug. His aunt Alethea goes down.
1850	Easter she dies.
	Ellen went to Battersby aged 18, born 1832.
1851	Mids. His bad character.
	The Ellen row.
1854	Oct. He goes to Cambridge.
1856	Sep. 6. came of age.
1858	Feb. took his degree.
	Ember weeks was ordained and goes up to London.
1859	Spring, wrote his mad letters.
	Mar. 26 was arrested.
	Sep. 28 released.
	Oct. 15 married he just turned 24.
1860	Easter prosperous—his wife begins to drink.
1860	Sep. a girl born.
1861	A boy born.

	All his prosperity now at an end. His wife ruins him.
	Then he saw what the devil had been at with him.
1862	Mar. 25. he sees John and finds out that he is not married.
1862	Ap. 15. Goes abroad with me.
1863	Sep. 5 is 28 yrs. old and comes into his money.
	November. Xtina dies.
1867	Chap. xlvi. and chap. lxxxxix.
1881	Theobald died.

Source: Henry Festing Jones. *Samuel Butler, Author of Erewhon (1835 – 1902) A Memoir*. Vol. Ⅱ, Appendix D, pp. 468-469.

Ⅲ. Main characters list of *The Way of All Flesh* (1903)

Pontifex family

First generation

- "Old" John Pontifex (16 August 1727 –8 February 1812)
- Ruth Pontifex (13 October 1727 – 10 January 1811; wife of Old Pontifex; married 1750)

Second generation

- George Pontifex (c. 1765 – 1838; son of Old John and Ruth Pontifex; married c. 1792 to unnamed woman who died 1805)

Third generation

- Eliza (179? –18??; George Pontifex's eldest child; never marries)
- Maria (179? –18??; George Pontifex's second child; never marries)
- John (ca. 1800 – 18??; George Pontifex's third child; marries and has unnamed son early 1837)
- Theobald (1802 – 1881; George Pontifex's fourth child; marries Christina Allaby July 1831; has 3 children)
- Alethea Pontifex (1805 – 1850; George Pontifex's fifth child; loves Overton but never marries him).
- Christina Pontifex (nee Allaby; wife of Theobald Pontifex; married July 1831; died ca. 1863 –1865).

Fourth generation

- Ernest Pontifex, the central character (born 6 September 1835; eldest child of Theobald and Christina Pontifex)
- Ellen Pontifex (born ca. 1831; housemaid of Theobald and Christina; pregnant to John the coachman & married him 15 August 1851; separated; married bigamously to Ernest late 1850s; annulled 1862)
- Joseph (born 1836; second child of Theobald & Christina; married between 1875 & 1876)
- Charlotte (born 1837; third child of Theobald & Christina; married between 1876 & 1882)

Fifth generation

- Alice (born September 1860; illegitimate daughter of Ellen and Ernest; married Jack Rowlings (born 1855))
- Georgie (born late 1861; illegitimate son of Ernest and Ellen)
- Ted (born 1870s; son of Ernest and an unnamed mistress. Mention of Ted in the final chapter of the manuscript was removed by the editor in the posthumous published edition)

Others

- Dr Skinner (Ernest's teacher)
- John (Theobald & Christina's family coachman. Gets Ellen pregnant; marries her 15 August 1851. Later separated due to her drunkenness)
- Mr Overton, the narrator (born 1802, friend of Alethea Pontifex but does not return her love; trustee of her estate; godfather to Ernest)

Ⅳ. Family tree of the Pontifexes

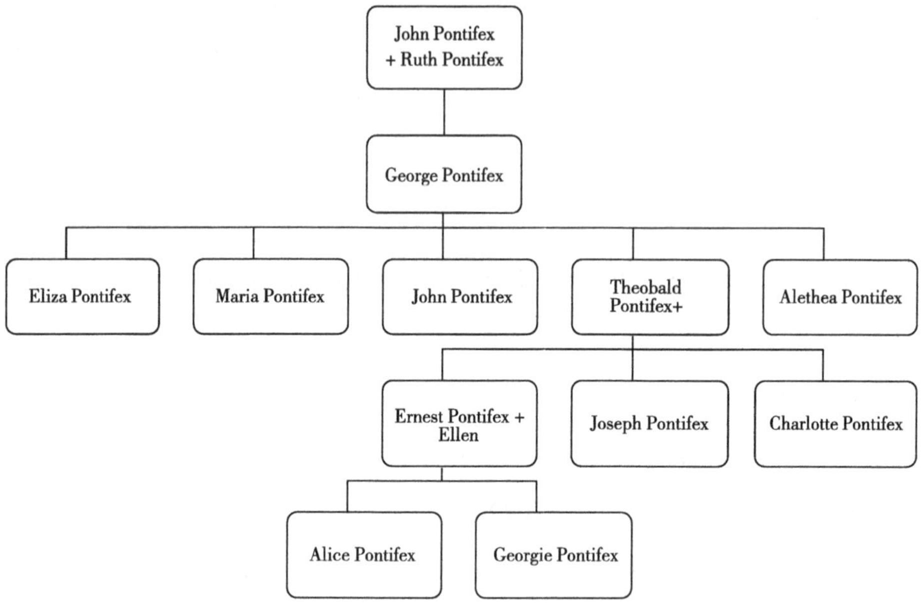

V. Places and locations in Samuel Butler's life and in *The Way of All Flesh* (1903)

Samuel Butler

Allesley

Where Samuel Butler went to school 1846 to 1848.

Clifford's Inn

Cliffords Inn Passage, City of London, Greater London.

Where Samuel Butler setled in 1864 when he returned from New Zealand.

Erewhon

In New Zealand, place named after Butler's 1872 novel. Where Butler was a sheep farmer from 1859 to 1864.

Langar

Where Samuel Butler grew up. Battersby, Crampsford, and Paleham are drawn from Langar.

Lichfield

At Staffordshire, where Samuel Butler's grandfather Samuel Butler was bishop from 1837 until his death in 1839.

Shrewsbury

Where Samuel Butler went to school from 1848 to 1853. His grandfather Samuel Butler was headmaster from 1798 to 1836. Many of the recollections of his school life at Shrewsbury are reproduced for the school life of Ernest Pontifex at

Roughborough.

St. Andrew Church

Where Samuel Butler's father was rector. Often called the 'Cathedral of the Vale' due to its large size for such a small village. This may be in part due to its importance as a place of pilgrimage in Saxon times.

St. James Church

Where Samuel Butler served as a lay assistant briefly in 1858.

St. John's College, Cambridge

Where Samuel Butler went to school from 1854 to 1858.

The Novel

Ashpit Place

Small working-class street in London near Drury Lane Theater. A more raffish, fictional version of Heddon Street, in which Butler actually lived during this time of his life, it is in a boardinghouse here, run by the colorful and eccentric Mrs. Jupp, that Ernest attempts to convert and minister to the poor. However, Ernest fails to do anyone in the area any good and instead undermines his own faith in his vocation. After mistaking a respectable boarder for a prostitute, Ernest is sentenced to six months in jail.

Battersby-on-the-Hill

Small English farming village that is based on Butler's own childhood home at Langar Rectory near Nottingham. Dominated by a large hilltop rectory, this clergyman's abode appears to be a cherished stronghold of Victorian family values, but it is here that Ernest is subjected to incidents in which his natural trust and affection is betrayed by his father, the rector Theobald Pontifex, and his slavishly devoted wife Christina. For Ernest, the rectory, which appears idyllic, is in reality the venue where his complacent, self-congratulatory parents subject him to relentless abuse. Battersby-on-the-Hill's name suggests the psychological and physical battering Ernest must endure at the hands of his parents.

Blackfriars Bridge Road

Street on the south side of the River Thames near the public house known as the " Elephant and Castle" , area where Ernest and his wife, the former Pontifex housemaid Ellen, had a shop for selling old clothes and books. It is here that his two children are born and where his wife reverts to her old, alcoholic ways.

Brighton

Where Ernest was taken to hear sermons for children by Mr. Vaughan.

Camberwell

Where Miss Maitland's father lived.

Coldbath Fields

Prison to which Ernest is sentenced to six months of hard labor. Here he loses his religion, realizes he is nothing but an insufferable prig, and begins to sense a great chasm opening up between his past and his future.

Debehams

Where Ernest took his stock when he went out of business.

Drury Lane Theatre

Near Ashpit Place where Ernest lived when he was trying to learn about poor people.

Emmanuel College

Where Ernest Pontifex went to school after Roughborough. Emmanuel College.

Fictionalized college of Cambridge University. Cambridge has an Emmanuel College, but Butler based this setting on St. John's College, Cambridge, which he attended himself. This setting is distinctive in that it is one of the few places in which Ernest finds himself truly happy. Cambridge University, located in the south of England and long renowned as one of the finest universities in England, is presented as a venue in which personal development and intellectual freedom are valued far more than in the rest of Victorian England. It is here, however, that Ernest comes under the baleful influence of his classmate Pryer, who persuades him to invest money unwisely in a venture called the College of Spiritual Pathology. It is at Cambridge that Ernest also becomes fervently religious and is ordained as a minister.

Gower Street

Street where Alethaea Pontifex had an apartment.

Gravesend

In Kent, where Ernest left his two children to be cared for by Mr. and Mrs. Rollings.

Laystall Street

Camden Town, Greater London, where Ernest lived after getting out of jail.

Newmarket

In Suffolk, where Theobald and Chrisina went for dinner at the inn following their marriage.

Paternoster Row

In city of London, Greater London, where George Pontifex worked with his uncle.

Regents Park Zoo

Camden, Greater London.

Where Ernest went to see the elephants. In 2001, the elephants were moved to Whipsnade after an elephant crushed a worker to death.

Roughborough Grammar School

School that Ernest attends. Typical of the exclusive British public schools of its day and based on the Shrewsbury School, which Butler attended as a child, this school is presided over by Dr. Skinner, a character modeled on the headmaster who succeeded Butler's own grandfather. Seemingly a figure of unassailable moral rectitude, Dr. Skinner is portrayed as foolish, pedantic, and self-deluding. At Roughborough, whose name, like that of Ernest's home, is apt, Ernest struggles against an impervious educational system that seems to exist solely to dog him with demerits. His only safe haven is his kind Aunt Alethea, who has moved to the area to make his life bearable.

The Temple

Overton lived in an area called The Temple, where set of courts and buildings in London by the Thames, with rooms originally intended for lawyers. Ernest moved here after he closed his shop in Blackfriars. Here Ernest finally lives as a contented bachelor and finds his true vocation writing iconoclastic books which question the conventional wisdom of the Victorian era.

Torquay

In Torbay, GB, where Ellen was from.

Woburn Square

Camden Town, Greater London.

Where the John Pontifex family lived.

Partly extract from the source online: see *The Way of All Flesh Map* created by Peter Biggins: http://www.communitywalk.com/the_way_of_all_flesh_map/map/496413

Ⅵ. Christina's letter to her children[①]

BATTERSBY, March 15th, 1841

My Two Dear Boys—When this is put into your hands will you try to bring to mind the mother whom you lost in your childhood, and whom, I fear, you will almost have forgotten? You, Ernest, will remember her best, for you are past five years old, and the many, many times that she has taught you your prayers and hymns and sums and told you stories, and our happy Sunday evenings will not quite have passed from your mind, and you, Joey, though only four, will perhaps recollect some of these things. My dear, dear boys, for the sake of that mother who loved you very dearly—and for the sake of your own happiness for ever and ever—attend to and try to remember, and from time to time read over again the last words she can ever speak to you. When I think about leaving you all, two things press heavily upon me: one, your father's sorrow (for you, my darlings, after missing me a little while, will soon forget your loss), the other, the everlasting welfare of my children. I know how long and deep the former will be, and I know that he will look to his children to be almost his only earthly comfort. You know (for I am certain that it will have been so), how he has devoted his life to you and taught you and laboured to lead you to all that is right and good. Oh, then, be sure that you *are* his comforts. Let him find you obedient, affectionate and attentive to his wishes, upright, self-denying and diligent; let him never blush for or grieve over the sins and follies of those who owe him such a debt of gratitude, and whose first duty it is to study his happiness. You have both of you a name which must not be disgraced, a father

① Samuel Butler. *The Way of All Flesh*. London: Grant Richards, 1903; published posthumously, as edited by R. A. Streatfield. London: A. C. Fifield, 1908. Edited with an introduction by V. S. Pritchett, London: Penguin English Library edition, 2012. Ch. 25, pp. 123-125.

and a grandfather of whom to show yourselves worthy; your respectability and well-doing in life rest mainly with yourselves, but far, far beyond earthly respectability and well-doing, and compared with which they are as nothing, your eternal happiness rests with yourselves. You know your duty, but snares and temptations from without beset you, and the nearer you approach to manhood the more strongly will you feel this. With God's help, with God's word, and with humble hearts you will stand in spite of everything, but should you leave off seeking in earnest for the first, and applying to the second, should you learn to trust in yourselves, or to the advice and example of too many around you, you will, you must fall. Oh, 'let God be true and every man a liar.' He says you cannot serve Him and Mammon. He says that strait is the gate that leads to eternal life. Many there are who seek to widen it; they will tell you that such and such self-indulgences are but venial offences—that this and that worldly compliance is excusable and even necessary. The thing *cannot be*; for in a hundred and a hundred places He tells you so—look to your Bibles and seek there whether such counsel is true—and if not, oh, 'halt not between two opinions,' if God is the Lord follow Him; only be strong and of a good courage, and He will never leave you nor forsake you. Remember, there is not in the Bible one law for the rich, and one for the poor—one for the educated and one for the ignorant. To *all* there is but one thing needful. *All* are to be living to God and their fellow-creatures, and not to themselves. *All* must seek first the Kingdom of God and His righteousness—must *deny themselves*, be pure and chaste and charitable in the fullest and widest sense—all, "forgetting those things that are behind," must "press forward towards the mark, for the prize of the high calling of God."

And now I will add but two things more. Be true through life to each other, love as only brothers should do, strengthen, warn, encourage one another, and let who will be against you, let each feel that in his brother he has a firm and faithful friend who will be so to the end; and, oh! be kind and watchful over your dear sister; without mother or sisters she will doubly need her brothers' love and tenderness and confidence. I am certain she will seek them, and will love you and try to make you happy; be sure then that you do not fail her, and remember, that were she to lose her father and remain unmarried, she would doubly need protectors. To you, then, I especially commend her. Oh! my three darling children, be true to each other, your Father, and your God. May He guide and bless you, and grant that in a better and happier world I and mine may meet again.

Your most affectionate mother, CHRISTINA PONTIFEX.

Acknowledgements

I would like to thank the staff and professors in the Department of EILA at Paris Diderot University Paris 7 for providing such a wonderfully supportive environment during my PhD years there. In particular, I must single out my PhD supervisor professor Michel Prum. I enjoyed my supervisions and academic career with his immensely. And to my husband, Dr. Qiang Zhou, an associate professor on political science who graciously has become expert on Samuel Butler, I want to say: you are at the centre of everything I do. Finally, I would like to thank my mother for her constant support.

Dr. Mingming Su

In Beijing

November, 2018